She wanted him to touch her, to kiss her . . .

She wanted to know if that would make the strange tightening she felt in her stomach every time he was near finally go away. She closed her eyes and pursed her lips, unconsciously arching her back toward him.

Genevieve was shocked at first by the roughness of his kiss, for it was unlike anything she'd ever experienced. The coarse dark stubble on his cheeks grated softly against the smooth, creamy skin of her breasts, sending a shiver of pleasure racing down her spine. Moving with practiced ease, he pushed her gown gently off her shoulders. He groaned, amazed at the raw passion she released. "My God, Genevieve . . ."

Genevieve heard the words as if from a great distance before they finally penetrated her foggy brain. Her senses slowly came back to her, and she gasped as she realized that any and all restraint she'd ever possessed had completely abandoned her. With the strength of pure panic, she pushed against his chest, breaking free from his embrace. "Captain," she cried, hastily tugging her gown back into place. *"Captain, let me go."*

The Captain

Vicki Joehnk

To Bertha,
Happy Reading!
Vicki Joehnk

J
JOVE BOOKS, NEW YORK

THE CAPTAIN

A Jove Book / published by arrangement with
the author

PRINTING HISTORY
Jove edition / January 1996

ISBN: 0-515-11750-1

A JOVE BOOK®
Jove Books are published by The Berkley Publishing Group,
200 Madison Avenue, New York, New York 10016.
JOVE and the "J" design are trademarks
belonging to Jove Publications, Inc.

PRINTED IN THE UNITED STATES OF AMERICA

10 9 8 7 6 5 4 3 2 1

CHAPTER ONE

❧

Charleston, 1856

"Darling, come back to bed," a sultry voice purred from across the room.

Jonathon Morgan turned, his deep amber gaze falling on the dark-haired beauty posing seductively amidst the rumpled sheets of the bed they'd just shared. She smiled mischievously as she stretched, allowing the sheet to fall to her waist as she thrust her full, heavy breasts in his direction.

Jonathon remained stationed at the window, his broad shoulders propped against the pane as he coolly studied her. "That's quite an invitation, Constance, but one I shall have to pass on." He returned his gaze to the activity taking place on the busy wharf outside.

"Really, Jonathon, you just don't appreciate me anymore." Constance affected what she considered to be her prettiest pout, throwing herself against the pillows with a dramatic sigh. From the corner of her eye she sneaked a glance at Jonathon to see if he was watching. He wasn't. Angered, she sat up straight, crossing her arms over her ample chest. "Fine. I suppose I should just leave now."

"If you like."

Constance glared at him in response, hating his indifference. With the mere flutter of an eyelash she could have any man in Charleston jump to do her bidding. Jonathon Morgan was the only one who eluded her. He was also the only man she wanted. She studied his tall, rugged frame,

1

clad at the moment only in buff-colored trousers, which clung to his powerful thighs. It was obvious that these had been pulled on carelessly, for they remained unfastened and hung loosely about his slim hips. His golden chest was bare, and she noted the ripple of muscles as he drew a hand through his thick mass of dark, wavy hair. Even now, in calm repose, he exerted a pure male force, a masculine energy so strong it made her mouth water. "What I would like," she answered, "is for you to show me a little attention. Otherwise, I don't know why we even bother."

"We 'bother' because you enjoy greeting me at the docks clad in only your cloak, wearing nothing but that tiny slip of lace underneath. It's a wonder my crew hasn't caught on yet."

Constance smiled triumphantly. "Darling, is that jealousy I hear?"

It wasn't. Truthfully, Jonathon didn't care if she chose to run around the docks naked. He knew she had other lovers and it didn't bother him in the slightest. She was a beautiful, spoiled woman, a pleasant diversion for him when he was in port, and nothing more. He avoided her question, crossing the room to retrieve a satchel he'd brought from his ship. "I've brought something for you."

Constance sat straight up, instantly alert, craning her neck to see what he held. Jonathon approached her slowly, holding in his hand a long, perfectly matched strand of pearls. Inclining his head slightly, he offered them to her. "Oooh," she breathed, her dark eyes shining. She grabbed them from his hand, holding them up to the light to better inspect their quality. Satisfied, she draped the long strand around her neck and leapt from the bed to admire herself in the tall mirror.

Jonathon watched her preen in front of the mirror, her ripe body naked save for the pearls. "Where did you get these?" she asked. "Did you bring me earrings to match? A bracelet?"

"No. You'll have to content yourself with just the necklace."

"Oh," she said flatly, disappointment clouding her face.

Jonathon wasn't bothered by her undisguised greed. She was selfish and pampered beyond belief, but so were most of the women he'd known. Constance's virtue, if it could be called that, lay in her absolute transparency. He watched her as she returned to the bed, knowing from the determined look in her eyes that she was about to embark on one of her favorite topics. "Jonathon," she began, her voice sugary sweet, "why don't you settle down now?"

"Settle down? With whom?" he teased, a small smile tugging at the corners of his mouth as he leaned back against the window frame.

"Why, with me, of course," Constance exclaimed as she slid forward, licking her lips. "After all, I do come from one of the best families in Charleston. I know all the right people, and you know what a striking couple we make. Why, after we're married—"

"Constance," Jonathon interrupted, "aren't you forgetting something?"

She blinked. "What?"

"You're already engaged."

"Hmmph." Constance dismissed that with a wave of her hand. "That isn't official. The announcement won't even be in the *Mercury* for another three weeks. Besides," she continued with a toss of her dark head, "it's out of the question now. Stewart told me last night that he loved me. Can you imagine?"

"You have my deepest sympathy," Jonathon replied dryly. "You'll keep the ring, I suppose?"

"Of course. But what do I need with a husband fawning all over me, wanting to know where I am night and day? How many married couples do you know that can even stand the sight of one another? Love isn't even a consideration." She leaned back, offering him a full view of her ample curves. "We're perfect for each other, Jonathon. We both know what we want and how to get it. And you know you'll never be bored in the bedroom," she finished with a tempting smile, her argument complete.

Jonathon frowned, considering her words. All of what she'd said was true. Marriage was just a matter of convenience, a task performed for propriety's sake in order to sire heirs. He studied the woman lying naked before him, trying to imagine her as his wife. Aside from being satisfactory in bed, she was beautiful, but something still held him back. "That's an interesting proposal, my dear. I thank you for not mucking it up with declarations of undying love and other sentimental rubbish. However, the institution of marriage holds little appeal for me."

Constance shrugged, then sat up and began to dress, obviously unaffected by his response. She stepped into a silk stocking and pulled it slowly up her leg, securing it at her thigh with a deep red ribbon. "I don't expect an answer today, darling. You take all the time to think about it that you need," she offered sweetly, having total confidence in her seductive abilities. "I'm sure you'll see that I'm right."

Jonathon said nothing, holding her cloak for her as she slipped it on over her skimpy undergarments. She brushed up against him at the door, and then she was gone, leaving nothing but the heavy scent of her perfume. He watched her walk away, then turned and finished dressing, leaving shortly thereafter for his next engagement.

A gentle breeze was blowing, but it did nothing to ease the smothering heat of the summer evening. Jonathon knew they would be more comfortable inside, but felt sure it was privacy, not comfort, that his host was after when he suggested they take their after-dinner whiskeys out onto the verandah. He eased himself slowly into a fragile-looking wicker chair, then, satisfied it would support his solid frame, leaned back, stretching out his long legs. He sipped his drink, waiting for his friend to speak.

"What is your opinion of the South?" Colonel Benjamin Haines asked at last. "As a Northerner, I mean."

Jonathon paused, weighing his words carefully. "It's a unique society, Ben. Vastly different from the North, both economically and socially."

Ben smiled. "That's a very diplomatic answer," he said as he leaned back against the porch rail. With his tall, lanky build and thick white-blond hair, he looked every inch the Southern gentleman. "But we've been friends far too long for you to offend me now. You know you can speak freely."

Jonathon nodded and set down his drink. "As a Northerner, I'd say your way of life can't last much longer. The abolitionist movement is growing stronger every day. Eventually the differences between the North and South will have to be reconciled."

"Reconciled?" Ben echoed bitterly. "Is that the polite term for it these days? It seems to me the North will not be satisfied until those differences are completely eliminated."

Jonathon shrugged, but the expression in his amber eyes was unyielding. "If we're talking about slavery, you're right. There can be no compromise there."

"I fear it's too late for compromise in any case. The problems that divide us have become too great."

"Such as?"

"Take those differences you mentioned—they've become points of honor. Questions about the Southern way of life have become moral questions; compromises of Southern lifestyle are now considered concessions of righteousness."

"That's taking Southern pride a bit far, wouldn't you say? Despite everything, we're all still Americans."

Ben sighed and shook his head. "My friends and neighbors think differently. They see themselves as more Southern than American. With each passing day, that becomes more deeply ingrained. Did you hear what happened in Congress last month?" he asked, knowing Jonathon had just returned from an extended voyage. "A Northern senator stood up to deliver a harsh antislavery speech. When he finished, the honorable representative from this proud state took it upon himself to avenge the insult. He took his cane and promptly began to beat the man senseless. Right there on the Senate floor."

He paused, his voice heavy as he continued. "He's now a hero to this state. My fellow South Carolinians have been sending him letters of praise, as well as whips, canes, and even pistols, with instructions to go back and 'finish the job.'"

Jonathon studied his friend, not liking what he was hearing. "I've heard talk that the South may secede from the Union. Are you suggesting those rumors may be true?"

Ben drew a deep breath, his expression pained. "Yes."

"That will mean war."

"I know."

Neither man spoke for several minutes. Jonathon rose and, crossing the verandah to stand beside the man who'd been his friend for so long, stared silently at the plantation grounds. A grove of ancient willow trees cast eerie shadows on the immaculately groomed lawns while flowers bloomed beneath them in neat, orderly rows. In the distance, lights twinkled faintly from the slaves' quarters as soft gray trails of smoke curled up into the sky, evidence that the night's meal preparation had begun.

Jonathon gazed at the familiar sight, then finally asked the question he wasn't sure he wanted to hear the answer to: "If it does come to war, where do you stand?"

"This is my home," Ben answered after a long pause. "This land has been in my family for generations; my children were born here. I'll do whatever I can to protect it."

"I see," Jonathon replied stiffly.

"No, I don't think you do." Ben turned to face him squarely. "If there is a war, all that I hold dear will be lost, no matter which side wins. The only way for the South to survive is by not fighting at all. I mean to do whatever I can to prevent this war from taking place." His soft blue eyes locked on Jonathon's. "I'll need your help," he stated plainly.

Surprise flashed across Jonathon's chiseled features. "I've no political influence—"

"This isn't about politics." Ben cut him off. He quickly scanned the verandah again, making certain they were alone, then continued, "There's a group operating here in Charleston. They've made arrangements with the French to purchase over one million dollars in arms—enough to outfit an entire army."

Jonathon nodded as he absorbed the impact of that statement. "Where are they getting that kind of money?"

"That's where you come in. They don't have it yet, and I'm asking you to see to it that they never do." He paused, his gaze intent. "I won't lie to you, Jonathon. These men are dangerous. If you choose to become involved, there'll be no turning back."

Jonathon drew himself up, resolve filling his amber eyes. "Tell me more."

The two men talked for hours, well into the night. Dawn was breaking softly over the harbor as Jonathon made his way back to his ship. "About time you got back," his younger brother, just coming on duty, greeted him from the bridge. "The crew's finished loading, and the repair to the foresail's almost complete. We'll be ready to sail in under an hour. Well?" he prompted at Jonathon's silence. "Where to?"

Jonathon thought for a moment, playing last night's conversation over in his mind. He nodded to his brother, his deep voice firm. "Martinique."

Paris, 1856

Having reached her destination, Genevieve DuPres glanced briefly at the richly carved doors of the exclusive dressmaker's shop, doors through which she and her father had once been welcomed effusively. Then she skirted around through the muddy alley to the servants' entrance.

"Well, if it isn't Miss High-and-Mighty. How nice of you to join us this morning."

Genevieve knew that it would be useless for her to point out that she was early. "Good morning, Madame Nirvi," she said as she tucked a stray lock of golden hair into the tight bun at the nape of her neck, the only style Madame felt was suitable for her charges.

"Well, get in already, the air's cold! And mind your boots, I'll not have you dragging mud all over my clean floors." Genevieve paused to wipe her feet on the coarse mat by the door. "Don't dally, girl! There's work to be done." With a look of grim satisfaction, Madame watched as Genevieve took her place among the other women, already busy at their toil. Candles illuminated the work space, for the sun had not yet risen.

Mme. Nirvi was a small, birdlike woman who always dressed in black. A serious bout of pox suffered in childhood had left her skin badly scarred, and the heavy white powder she wore only served to aggravate that condition. With her sleek black hair, dark piercing eyes, and beakish nose, she reminded Genevieve of a hawk stalking its prey. Unfortunately, Genevieve herself was usually that prey. "How the mighty have fallen," Mme. Nirvi would intone, taking great pleasure in reminding Genevieve of her reduced circumstances.

The morning passed in its usual drudgery. Minutes turned into countless hours as with backs aching, and vision blurring, the women plied their trade. Row after row of perfect stitches turned yards of silk and taffeta into beautiful gowns they would never again see. And all the while, Mme. Nirvi hovered in the background, issuing sharp reprimands of disapproval.

Genevieve's stomach growled. It was almost time for their midday break. She longed to stand, stretch, and breathe the fresh air outside their small, stuffy room. She felt the restless shifting of the women around her and knew the six hours they'd spent locked in the same position had taken its toll on them as well.

"Ah ha!" Mme. Nirvi cried triumphantly, shattering the silence. She raised her fist in the air, clutching the bodice of a green taffeta gown. "Who is responsible for this?" she demanded as her piercing eyes searched the faces of the women seated at the table.

Genevieve glanced quickly at Sylvie, whom she had seen working on the piece earlier that morning. Though not old, Sylvie looked as though she had never been young. She lowered her eyes and clutched her hands to her ragged clothing to keep them from shaking, but Genevieve could feel the fear emanating from her. Sylvie was terrified of Mme. Nirvi.

"I am responsible," Genevieve declared, rising slowly.

A ghost of a smile flickered across Madame's face. "The rest of you may leave now. I'll deal with this impertinent chit." The room emptied immediately. Genevieve caught Sylvie's look, her eyes flooded with gratitude and guilt, as she slipped out the door.

"So," Mme. Nirvi began, her dark eyes glowing against the deathly white powder of her skin, "you refuse to do good work for me, eh? I will not stand such disrespect! Look at those clumsy stitches." Wadding the garment into a tight ball, she threw it at Genevieve. "Do it again. Now. You will not get a single centime until it is perfect."

Genevieve let the fabric strike her chest then fall to the floor. "No."

Madame's head snapped up. "What did you say?" she asked menacingly, her shock quickly turning to anger.

"I am leaving your employ, madame. Today. I would thank you to give me the money due me—ten francs, to be exact."

Madame's thin lips twisted cruelly. "And where will you go, my precious one? You're nothing, common trash. I was the one who took pity on you when the rest of society had cast you out. It was I who gave you work when you came begging."

"I never begged, madame," Genevieve corrected her with quiet dignity. She lifted her slim shoulders, her deep blue gaze locked on her employer. "And you certainly never showed me any pity." With a long, fluid motion, she swept her arm around the room, the anger she had swallowed for so long finally surfacing. "The way you've treated me, treated all of us, is beneath contempt."

"Have you no shame? How dare you talk to me like that! Your father was a traitor, tried and convicted by his own men. You belong in the gutter, just like him," she hissed as she struck out, but Genevieve deflected the blow easily.

"You will not strike me, madame," she said, speaking with a force of will so strong that Mme. Nirvi quite froze. She hadn't expected this strength of spirit, this inner pride, in one who should have been downtrodden, broken. "You're wrong. My father was not a traitor. I intend to prove that."

"Ha!" Madame cackled. "Very well, go, my fine lady. But when you find out you're wrong, don't come crawling back to me, for I'll not have it. May the devil take you," she spat as she turned away, but Genevieve's voice stopped her.

"My francs?" she asked, gently extending her hand.

Mme. Nirvi stiffened, then crossed the room to unlock the heavy metal box that contained the shop's receipts. Swiftly counting out the francs, she slapped them onto the table. Genevieve scooped up the money and exited quickly, not looking back as Madame's dire warnings rang shrilly in the air around her: "You'll come to no good, I promise you! Blood will tell!"

Traveling alone and with tightly limited funds, it had taken Genevieve over two weeks to reach Marseilles. Walking now amidst the bustling crowds and noise of the wharf, she was barely able to contain her excitement. She'd made it! She no longer felt the bruises she'd sustained after long days spent being jostled in the back of bumpy wagons, nor did she feel the pangs of hunger that steadily assaulted her. She called out to a young sailor who was bent over his work, checking the rigging for his next long voyage. "Sir, I'm looking for Captain André Mercier. Can you tell me which ship is his?"

The sailor barely looked up, having noted right away the woman's ragged gown, the worn shawl thrown over her thin shoulders, and the dull scarf that covered her head. Another poor wretch who thought she could simply sail away to a better life. "Aye," he said, nodding absently, tilting his head to the left, "that be his ship there."

"Thank you," Genevieve replied, her face lit up by a dazzling smile.

The woman's glowing smile caught the young sailor off guard. As he watched her walk away, he couldn't help noticing her regal carriage, the way her slim form swayed gracefully under her drab gown. This wasn't just another poor wretch at all. He stood, cursing himself for the missed opportunity. "Where ye be bound for?" he yelled after her.

Genevieve turned, her face radiant as she called back over her shoulder, "Martinique."

CHAPTER TWO

St. George, Bermuda

"Captain, how long will we be in port?"

Captain Mercier turned, smiling at the young woman who stood beside him at the ship's rail. She had blossomed during their six weeks spent at sea. The sun had gently kissed her skin, chasing away the gray pallor and giving it a soft, rosy glow. Her hair, which had been pulled back into a severe bun when she boarded ship, now fell softly down her back in thick golden waves. Long nights of rest had erased the heavy lines of fatigue and brought a sparkle to her sapphire eyes. She had even gained a little weight. The drab gowns that had hung like limp sacks about her frail form at the beginning of the voyage now showed soft, womanly curves.

Many a sailor had felt the sharp lash of the captain's tongue when caught slacking from his duties to watch her stroll about the deck instead. The captain reached for her arm, tucking it protectively through his. "It shouldn't be too long, my dear. Perhaps a month, maybe two."

"Two months!" Genevieve gasped. "Why, we'll never make it to Martinique!"

He smiled at her youthful impatience. "It isn't so long. You'll find that time moves at a different pace here in the islands. Life is something to be enjoyed, not rushed through."

"But I have to get to Martinique at once," she pressed. "It's urgent family business."

"Your uncle will understand, my dear." The captain

12

patted her arm, his gruff voice oddly soothing. "I'll simply send him a note for you, explaining that we had to dock temporarily in Bermuda to make repairs and that your arrival has been delayed."

Genevieve winced at the small fib she'd been forced to tell the kindhearted captain. There was no one waiting for her in Martinique, certainly not the wealthy uncle she'd invented who had supposedly invited her to come visit his vast plantation. But as it was unheard of for a young woman to travel unescorted, the ruse had been necessary to secure passage.

She smiled fondly at Captain Mercier. Though not much taller than she, he carried himself with an unmistakable air of authority, having spent forty years commanding vessels at sea. In sharp contrast to the short white whiskers that covered his chin, his skin was brown and leathery from a lifetime spent in the sun. He reminded her of her father: all bluff and bluster on the outside, gentle as a newborn kitten inside. "No, thank you, Captain. I'll send the note myself." She thought for a moment, her quick mind seizing upon an idea. "Those ships that would carry my message, couldn't I board one as a passenger?"

"No, that wouldn't do at all. Those are merchant ships, captained by rough men with even rougher crews, interested only in profit." And pleasure, he added silently to himself. "No, that wouldn't do at all," he repeated, looking at the innocent young beauty beside him.

Genevieve sighed, her deep blue gaze focused on the dozens of ships in port, not one of which could take her to her destination. "Once the repairs are done, how long will it take us to reach Martinique?"

"Sailing directly, we could make it in about seven days time. But," he cautioned, seeing her face light up, "don't forget I've other business to attend. Passengers to pick up, goods to buy and sell along the way. Perhaps another month."

Genevieve's heart sank as she watched the captain walk

away. To have made it across the Atlantic in six weeks, only to be stranded—possibly for two months—with her goal so close at hand! She paced restlessly on deck, watching the activity on the busy pier below. The captain had promised to take Genevieve and her fellow passengers ashore that afternoon, but the wait seemed interminable. Finally, unable to bear the confinement of the ship's close quarters a second longer, she decided to sneak down the gangplank and explore a bit on her own. Her legs wavered beneath her for an instant as she touched the dock, the solid, motionless feel of land surprisingly foreign after the weeks at sea. She laughed at her own awkwardness, moving clumsily at first until she found her balance.

Genevieve strolled down the busy wharf, unmindful of the curious stares she drew. An unescorted woman was not an unusual sight on the docks at night, when sailors were hungry for rum and a little company, but it was unusual by day. Engrossed as she was in her own thoughts, Genevieve remained unaware of the attention she was receiving until two men suddenly fell into step beside her.

"'Ello, pretty one. 'Ave ye got a name?" The taller of the two spoke first. He leaned down, bringing his face mere inches from her own. His lips shone with the grease of a recent meal, the stench of it still lingering on his foul breath. The man's coarse accent was far different from the cultured English she'd been taught in school, but his intent was clear.

"Excuse me," she stammered, recoiling automatically. She took a step backward, her shawl clutched tightly to her throat, only to find herself pulled into the embrace of his swarthy companion.

"There now, missy," the shorter man croaked, "we ain't lookin' to hurt ye. We'll take good care of ye, and pay ye what's fair when we be done." His dark eyes followed the curves suggested underneath her threadworn dress as he licked his lips in anticipation.

"Please, there's been a mistake," Genevieve managed to say as she struggled to free herself from the man's painful grasp. "I'm sure you gentlemen are looking for someone else."

At the word "gentlemen" the two men paused for a moment, exchanging a silent smile. "So ye like to play games, do ye, missy?" A lewd smile played about the tall man's mouth as he reached out to finger the drab fabric of her gown and eyed her cheaply shod feet. "Ye want to play gentry, eh? All right, missy. Ye can call me Lord Roger and me mate Sir George whilst we're having away at ye." He turned to his smaller, thicker friend, delighted with his own humor. "Ain't that right, Sir George?"

The smaller man guffawed loudly, sending a blast of noxious fumes into Genevieve's face. Repressing a shudder of revulsion, she glanced quickly from the two coarse seamen to the surrounding dock. Taking advantage of the man's slack grip on her arm while he enjoyed his friend's joke, she raised her foot and brought her heel soundly down on her captor's instep. The man instantly released her arm, bringing his injured foot up to hold in his hands as he hopped about howling in pain.

Genevieve tore away, lifting her skirts as she raced for the refuge of a stack of crates she'd spied near a waiting schooner. She ran with a speed born of pure terror, not daring to slow down to look behind her. She might have eluded the smaller man, but she felt the heavy breathing of the larger, more threatening of the two directly at her back. It seemed the dock fairly shook under his heavy tread, his pace only a fraction slower than her own.

Reaching the stack of large wooden crates, she threw herself behind one, falling onto her hands and knees. Without pausing to catch her breath, she crawled between the first to the second to the third, scraping her hands and tearing her already ragged dress to shreds. Finally, feeling as though her lungs must surely burst, she stopped, huddling deep within the recesses of the dark crate. Struggling to catch her breath, she strained to hear but was aware of nothing save the feel of her heart as it slammed painfully against her ribs.

Then it came to her. Softly at first—no more than a slight creak. Followed by another. Slow, steady footsteps, the dock groaning beneath their weight. She felt the hair rise on the back of her neck as she realized he was steadily making his way toward her. "'Ere now, missy," he called out, his hoarse voice coming closer as he moved among the crates, "the game's over. Ye lost, and now ye're gonna pay."

Genevieve sat frozen as her mind whirled frantically: should she run or stay hidden? She clutched the folds of her gown, too terrified to move.

"Ay, Roger! Where is the bloody wench?" a voice demanded angrily.

She peeked out between the cracks to see George thumped heavily in approach, his face grimacing in pain as he favored his left foot. "I'll break her bloody foot when we're done, see how she likes it!"

That was all the incentive Genevieve needed. Taking a deep breath, she plunged from the crate, determined to make it to the schooner docked nearby. Surely there would be someone there who could help her. She thought fleetingly of Captain Mercier's warning not to leave the ship unless escorted, and she cursed herself for her willfulness. "There! I seen her!" As the hoarse cry reached her ears she abandoned all thought, concentrating only on speed. The ship was so close now.

Unfortunately, it was not close enough.

With a mighty lunge the larger seaman hurled himself through the air, landing squarely against Genevieve's back. The rough tackle brought her down instantly, slamming her slight form against the hard wooden dock as Roger fell heavily atop her. The air was immediately knocked from her lungs, leaving her gasping as she struggled to free herself from his horrid weight, desperate to ease the burning ache in her chest.

Roger finally drew himself up, roughly pulling her up

alongside him. "There. Ye led a fine chase, missy, but it'll cost ye." He shook her hard, his grip digging painfully into her upper arm. "Ye had no right to run like that, seein' as how we meant to pay ye fair 'n' square. Now we'll take what's due, and ye'll see no coin from us."

Genevieve's head hung limply, her shoulders heaving with exertion as ragged gulps of air filled her lungs. From the corner of her eye she saw the smaller man limping slowly toward them, his expression furious. "Please," she gasped, "this is a mistake, I'm not a—"

"Enough!" Roger cut her off roughly, shaking her again. "It's not talk we want from ye! Keep yer mouth shut and yer legs open and ye'll not be hurt too bad."

His words struck Genevieve like a pail of ice water. She stared hard at her captor, her lovely features frozen with rage. Moving with lightning speed she raised her free arm, sending a stinging slap across his coarse cheek.

Roger's eyes widened in amazement. "Why ye little—" This time Genevieve cut him off, bringing her knee up sharply into his groin. Denying herself the satisfaction of watching him double over in pain, she turned to run again, but this time she gained no more than a few steps. The dock was suddenly slick beneath her feet, sending her slipping and sliding into a pile she hadn't noticed before.

Fish guts. Fish heads, fish tails, and various fish remains had been dumped in the corner of the dock after the catch had been cleaned. This was obviously what she'd slipped on, and the hideous mess now covered and drenched her. Gagging, she clawed her way up through the pile, the stench and slime almost overpowering her. She stood unsteadily, her gown dripping as she wiped her matted hair off her face so she could see.

She almost didn't believe her eyes. Standing before her, holding their bellies as they roared with laughter, were the two seamen responsible for her predicament. As she stood silently fuming, a crowd began to gather. Men who had been nowhere to be seen when she was running for her life now materialized, crowding around her to jeer and point.

Stomping their feet and grabbing one another in an attempt to remain standing, they shouted uproariously, doubling over in their mirth. Having no other weapon at hand, Genevieve appeased her anger by digging into the pile at her sides and throwing handfuls of fish innards into the unruly crowd.

"What the bloody hell is going on here?" The deep voice lashed across the dock, as harsh and cutting as a whip. It had just the same effect.

The men froze. Those who had fallen to the ground in hysterics instantly came to their feet, suddenly solemn. Even Genevieve, her hand drawn back, ready to hurl more fish into the crowd, lowered her arm, letting the sticky mess drip from her fingers. The silence which had fallen over them all was thick, almost tangible after the previous melee.

Genevieve suddenly felt flushed, as though a wave of heat was slowly passing through her body. She gazed up at the man who had spoken, knowing his intense gaze was focused entirely on her. Unconsciously she squared her shoulders, lifting her chin to meet his eyes. But she couldn't.

The late afternoon sun shone directly at his back, casting his features in heavy shadow. Like a dark specter, he seemed to block out all light. She wasn't sure if the force emanating from him was real, or merely an optical illusion created by the way the bright sun danced off his figure, shrouding his form entirely in black. Though he stood only ten paces from her, Genevieve could make out nothing but the glowing outline of his body, his stance wide and aggressive.

With a flash of insight, she realized that she had been fleeing from the wrong men. This man was far more dangerous.

"Shefley!" he roared, causing the taller of the two men who had been pursuing her to visibly flinch, "I sent you and Jones out over an hour ago to secure two wagons. Where are they?"

"Well, ye see, sir, the missy here, she wanted us to, uh, that is—"

"Enough! You left your duties to go whoring with this creature," he finished simply, his voice thick with anger and disgust. "Of course you know what the punishment for desertion is. I could have you both hung from the yardarm." He stared long and hard at the two filthy seamen, finally coming to a decision. "Get out of my sight. Now. But if you ever cross my path again you'll wish I'd given you the yardarm." The two men didn't doubt him. With a speed that was almost comical, they scurried away.

"As for the rest of you," he continued, "shore leave is now revoked. I want the goods loaded tonight, all night if need be. We sail for Martinique at first light." His thick muscles tense, he held himself still, as if daring any man to protest. None did. The men immediately set about their tasks, relieved to be released with a mere tongue lashing. Satisfied, he watched for a moment, then turned to make his way back to his ship.

"How dare you?"

The man stopped, not really believing he'd heard anything—certainly not that low, angry feminine growl. He turned slowly back.

"How dare you call me a whore in front of your crew?"

He'd completely forgotten about her, the miserable wench covered from head to toe in fish slime. "What is it?" he demanded impatiently. "Did you not get your coin before they tossed you into that pile? Or did you perhaps overestimate your charms and demand too much, is that what got you tossed in?" His brutally sarcastic tone made it perfectly clear that he found her "charms" totally lacking.

"Nobody tossed me in."

"Ah, so you just decided to stroll in by yourself. How very clever."

Genevieve lifted her chin, her sapphire eyes blazing. "Your men assaulted me. I was running to escape them when I fell."

He eyed her coolly. "If you have such an aversion to being 'assaulted,' my dear, might I suggest you find another line of work?"

Genevieve sucked in her breath at the insult. With all the dignity she could muster, she waded carefully out of the pile of fish guts. Her shoes had somehow slipped off, but she did not allow herself to show the slightest discomfort as the horrid mess squished between her toes. She stood before him, her expression serene, and calmly picked a fish bone from her matted hair before she spoke. "That is the second time you have dared to insult me, sir. I demand satisfaction."

"You what?!" His deep voice rang with laughter.

Genevieve still could not make out the man's features, but she had little doubt she would find him as ugly as he was arrogant. "Perhaps you can make your men cower in fear, but that shall not work with me. You have slandered my reputation and I will see that avenged."

"And precisely how do you plan on avenging yourself?" he inquired in growing amazement.

"I believe that as I issued the challenge, the choice of weapons is yours," she answered calmly. "I am quite handy with a pistol, should you wish to test your skill. There are, of course, other options."

"Such as?"

"You are free at any time to withdraw your rude and unfounded allegations. I do not want to hurt you. I believe violence should be used only as a last resort."

"Hurt me?!" the man echoed, his deep voice booming across the docks. The girl was half his size. He eyed her for a moment as she stood proudly before him awaiting an answer. She was filthy and barefoot, her gown was tattered and torn, but she had spirit. Good for her. "A thousand pardons, madame." He stepped back a pace, making a deep, sweeping bow. "Had I known I was in the presence of such a magnificent lady, I'd surely have curbed my tongue. But as the damage has already been done, I can do naught but beg your forgiveness."

Genevieve knew he was mocking her, but chose to ignore it. With a regal nod of her head, she accepted his apology.

"And now, if Madame will excuse me—"

"Wait! You can't mean to leave me like this!" Genevieve gasped. At his haughty shrug, she pressed her case. Surely there was a gentleman lurking somewhere within his huge frame, and she could touch upon that to secure assistance in getting back to Captain Mercier's ship. "I can't walk back like this—look at me. And as it was your men who were responsible for the damage . . ."

So it was money she was after, the man thought, unaccountably disappointed. It was not pride or spirit he had seen in her, but mere greed. "Yes, I see. How remiss of me. Here," he said, tossing a gold coin in the air, his voice cutting with scorn. "That should take care of the cost of a new gown, as well as the money due for services rendered. While I will not be held responsible for the actions of my men, nor for their dubious taste in women, I can deduct the coin from the wages they were due. The debt is now paid. Good-day."

"Why you, you—" Genevieve began, stuttering with outrage.

"Captain Jonathon Morgan, madame. Though I trust this is the last encounter we shall ever have." With that he turned and strode brusquely away.

Genevieve stood motionless, silently fuming, as she watched his broad back recede. Throwing all caution to the wind, she bent to retrieve a glob of fish guts and hurled the sticky mess after him, narrowly missing. He stopped, standing ominously still, then shrugged and continued walking, obviously deciding that she wasn't worth the trouble.

Well! Of all the offensive, overbearing men she had ever met in her life, Genevieve concluded, that man was definitely the worst. No, not man, she corrected herself, beast. After all, she had not seen his face, but could easily imagine that it was as horrid as his temperament. That was probably the real reason his men cowered before him. She conjured up images of a huge man-beast, covered with coarse black hair, his face horribly scarred, with a protruding forehead and thick, sloppy lips. Captain Beast.

Genevieve allowed herself a small smile of satisfaction at the image, then turned her thoughts back to her own predicament. She gazed down at herself, amazed. She could never have believed that her situation could possibly get worse than it was in Paris, yet here she stood, penniless and alone, covered in fish guts. Well, not quite penniless, she amended wryly, noting the heavy gold coin at her feet. She chewed her lower lip thoughtfully, mulling over her most pressing concern: how to get to Martinique as quickly as possible.

Martinique. The word shot through her like a bolt of pure lightning. The beastly captain was leaving for Martinique at dawn! She had heard him say it quite clearly, but caught up as she had been in the heat of the moment, it had not registered. A radiant smile lit up her face, her deep sapphire eyes glowing with sheer devilry. So Captain Beast was going to escort her to Martinique. What sublime justice.

The only question now was how to get on board. She brushed off her gown as best she could, then moving cautiously over to where the schooner was docked, watched attentively from the shadows. It took a few minutes of study before she recognized a system in what at first glance looked to be utter pandemonium. One group of men transferred cargo from a steady stream of wagons into large crates, which were then passed to another group to be checked off and sealed, then passed to a third and final group to be loaded into the ship's hold. Screaming children, fighting dogs, and wobbly drunks added to the confusion.

Genevieve considered her options. She could not possibly try to sneak on board, for two strong men stood guard at the gangplank. Her only choice was to hide herself in one of the crates. Once they were safely at sea, she would announce her presence. Then it would be too late for the beastly captain to do anything about it, she decided smugly, approving her plan.

There was only one hindrance she could think of: Captain Mercier. She didn't want the kindly old man to worry over her disappearance. She didn't mind abandoning her possessions, for in truth, the only things she'd left aboard were two drab gowns that were almost as ragged as the one she wore now. The last letter she'd received from her father, as well as all the money she had in the world—fifty francs—was sewn neatly into the waistband of the gown she was wearing. She'd acquired that habit in Paris, after countless thieves had broken into her tiny apartment.

"Boy," she called softly, motioning to the eldest of a group of children playing nearby. The child approached her slowly, obviously taken aback by her smell and filthy appearance. "Come here," she whispered, not wanting their exchange to be noticed. The child appeared at her side reluctantly, fear and distrust written plainly on his face. Ragged clothes covered his too thin body, and a large purple bruise showed under his left eye. "It's all right, I'm not going to hurt you," she said softly. Then went on after a pause, "What's your name?"

"Tom," he answered warily.

"Tom. Now that's a fine name. How old are you, Tom?"

"Eight."

Eight! The child was so small and skinny, Genevieve had taken him to be no more than five or six. "Eight years old, why you're almost a grown man."

"Yes'm. Them's my brothers and sisters," he said, pointing to a group of hungry-looking children, their clothing as threadbare as his own. "I take care of 'em, on accounta my ma's not been feelin' too good lately. She says I been doing a real good job." His scrawny chest swelled with pride.

"Well, I should say so," Genevieve agreed. "Tom, how would you like to do a job for me?"

"What kinda job?"

"I need you to bring a message to someone for me:

Captain Andre Mercier. His ship just docked this morning;
do you know which it is?" At the boy's nod she continued,
"I need you to tell him that Mademoiselle DuPres has met
an old friend of her uncle's, and will be traveling to
Martinique under his escort. Tell him that he is not to worry,
and that Mademoiselle sends her sincere thanks and best
wishes. Can you remember all that, Tom?"

The child nodded slowly, his expression troubled. "That
ain't a lie, is it?"

Genevieve stared at the small boy, stunned by his acumen
and forthrightness. She bent down, bringing herself eye to
eye with him, and took his small hand gently into her own.
"It's not entirely the truth," she admitted, unwilling to
deceive the child. "I am leaving for Martinique tonight, but
I have no escort. Captain Mercier is a kind man, and I don't
want to give him cause to worry."

The boy nodded again, his wide eyes studying her. "Are
ye goin' to stow away?" he finally asked, gesturing to the
nearby schooner.

Genevieve's deep blue eyes flew open wide, her chin
dropping in surprise. "Am I that obvious?"

The child giggled, his head bobbing up and down. "Ye
said ye had no one to help ye, yer clothes is torn, and ye
smell bad. How else ye gonna go?"

Genevieve threw her head back to laugh. "You're right,
Tom, you're right." Impulsively, she reached out to hug the
impertinent child. "Will you help me?"

Tom nodded and smiled shyly, unsettled by the rare
gesture of affection. "Yes'm, I'll help ye."

They drew their heads together for a few minutes,
creating and discarding a variety of plans until they found
one they hoped would work. Dusk was falling softly as Tom
turned to leave. "Wait, Tom, this is for you." Genevieve
withdrew the large gold coin that had been so rudely tossed
at her feet and pressed it into the boy's palm. "Thank you,"
she said simply.

The boy's eyes widened at the size of the coin, enough to

feed his family for months to come. He stared up at her, his eyes shining not only with gratitude, but more importantly, with pride in himself for having earned the coin. "I'll do it right, Miz DuPres," he swore. "I won't forget nothin'." With that, he turned and ran away.

Five minutes later the child's blood-curdling scream filled the air.

The men instantly dropped their work, rushing to where the children had been playing. Genevieve would have panicked, too, had she not known that Tom was only pretending that one of the wagons bustling in and out to unload cargo had run him down. The ruse worked. In the deepening twilight it was difficult to see anything, and the boy's screams were terrifying.

Genevieve dashed directly to the open crates, praying the diversion would last. She leaned over and peered into the first, only to find kegs of rum and fine Madeira wine. She would be crushed if the waters were rough and the kegs or cases shifted. The second crate contained thick sacks of exotic spices: cinnamon, curry, paprika, and pepper. How could she breathe? There was one final crate left unsealed. She raced toward it, knowing it was her last hope.

Silks! Yards and yards of beautiful taffeta, rich velvets, soft wools, and shiny-smooth satins. She dove headfirst into the luxurious pile, pulling the fabrics over her head as she snuggled to the bottom. There, she curled into a tight ball, trying to occupy as little space as possible, and waited.

The men returned shortly and made quick work of sealing the crate. They lifted it easily, taking no notice of the additional weight. After much bumping and banging, the crate was hoisted on ropes, dangled in midair for what seemed to Genevieve to be an eternity, and then dumped unceremoniously into the ship's hold.

She listened as the men worked ceaselessly through the night. More crates were lowered into the hold, slamming into and on top of her own. Twice she heard the booming voice of the captain, issuing sharp commands, followed by much scurrying of feet as his crew leapt to obey. She wondered if he was actually helping with the work, but doubted it. He probably felt physical labor was beneath him, she decided contemptuously.

Finally the ship groaned and shuddered to life and she knew they were under way. She settled back, pleased with her success. Breathing a sigh of relief, she closed her eyes and eased her long, slender legs into a more comfortable position. Feeling safe in her little cocoon, wrapped in yards of brilliant silk, Genevieve fell asleep.

CHAPTER THREE

"There, Captain, that's the one."

"Yes, I see."

The deep voice jolted Genevieve awake. She shook her head, trying to focus. How long had she been asleep? And what was *he* doing down in the hold? She held her breath, praying whatever it was didn't concern her.

"What are the contents of the crate?"

"Silks, sir, traded off the coast of Madagascar," the crewman answered as Genevieve moaned softly, wondering what could have given her away so soon. Her body ached from her cramped position in the crate and she was itchy and sore, irritated by the fish slime, which had dried and now clung in thick, coarse flakes to her skin. Might as well get this over with, she thought resignedly, opening her mouth to announce her presence.

"Break it open and see what kind of damage the rats have done. Part of it might be salvageable," the captain ordered before she could speak.

Rats? Genevieve thought, panicking. There were rats inside? She curled up into a tight ball, staring in horror into the dark recesses of the crate. She wanted out now. A harsh blow cracked the lid, sending splinters of wood flying. She jerked up immediately, coming unsteadily to her feet.

"Holy mother!" the two sailors gasped as they backed away from her, their eyes wide.

"You!" the captain bellowed, turning that single word into the most dire condemnation.

Genevieve stood regally, refusing to be intimidated by the man this time. "Captain," she replied coolly, gracefully inclining her head. She could only imagine what she must look like. Her gown was torn and stiff, covered with a variety of repugnant fish remnants. Her hair, matted with the same sticky mess, stood straight up. Her skin was covered with gray, flaky scales. And to top it all off, she knew she smelled even worse than she looked.

As if reading her mind, the captain waved his hand at her offensive odor. "It would appear they are the only ones who appreciate your stench." Genevieve looked down at the dozen howling cats that were hovering around her crate. So that's what had given her away. She glared at them, silently cursing the mangy creatures. "It seems they've caught a rather large rat this time. Bring her above deck so we can all breathe," he commanded shortly.

Before she could protest, Genevieve was seized by both her arms and lifted out of the crate. The two burly sailors hauled her easily between them, following the captain's broad back through a maze of passages leading to the upper deck. Once there, they released her abruptly, so abruptly that she would have fallen had she not caught the ship's rail. She raised her head, shielding her eyes against the bright sun to study the man before her.

So this was the captain.

Solid. That was the first word that entered her mind. Genevieve was tall for a woman and could meet most men eye to eye. But now she stared directly into the captain's thick, powerful chest, her eyes drifting up past his wide shoulders and firmly sculpted arms. She tilted her head back so she could see his face. He was . . . not *bad* looking, she finally conceded, trying to reconcile the actual man with her image of Captain Beast. His features were square and chiseled, perhaps a bit too rugged for her taste. And his hair was too long, falling in thick, dark waves against the crisp white collar of his shirt. His eyes, amber she supposed they would be called, bored into her, burning as intensely as waves of molten gold.

"What are you doing on my ship?" he thundered, breaking the silence between them.

With a start, Genevieve pulled her attention back to the situation at hand. She drew herself up and answered calmly, "I was in need of passage to Martinique. As I knew you were leaving this morning, I took the liberty of arranging quarters for myself."

"Arranging quarters," he repeated in amazement. "Is that what you call stowing aboard and ruining a crate of my most valuable silks?"

"I knew you would refuse me, Captain, so I simply took matters into my own hands."

"You're damned right I would have refused you. I had every right to refuse you."

"You had no right," Genevieve stormed, her sapphire eyes blazing. "Your men were responsible for the condition of my clothing, for the fact that I could not make it back to my ship—"

"That debt was paid," he interrupted, his deep voice full of scorn.

"Once you have seen me safely to Martinique, you may consider the debt paid. I expect nothing less than full reparation for the attack made on my person. As a gentleman," she reminded him primly, "you should have seen to that."

"As a lady," he shot back, "you shouldn't engage in activities that get you thrown in fish piles."

Genevieve stiffened. "I have already corrected you twice on that count. I will not do so again."

Jonathon stared hard at her, wondering if she was quite sane. Certainly not judging by the looks of her. "What's your name?" he tested her.

"Genevieve DuPres," she answered calmly.

"And what is my name?"

Something in his tone made her stare at him quizzically

for a moment, then an amused expression showed on her grimy features. "You needn't worry, Captain Morgan, I'm quite sane."

He doubted it. "A sane person would realize the serious consequences of his actions. You're aware of how we deal with stowaways at sea?"

"Forty lashes? A flogging? Go ahead, Captain, I'm quite sure I can take it," she said baiting him recklessly.

"I don't want you here."

"Well, it's a little too late to do anything about that now, isn't it?"

Jonathon stared at her in silence, his rugged features becoming even harsher. His eyes were no longer blazing—that molten gold—but flat, cold, and dark, a dangerous signal for anyone who knew him well. When he finally spoke, his words were so soft that Genevieve didn't believe she'd heard him correctly. "Throw her overboard."

She'd completely forgotten the presence of the two other men, who immediately moved to follow their captain's order. They grabbed her upper arms and lifted her to the ship's rail, holding her over. "No!" she cried, her bravado forgotten as she stared into the deep waters of the Atlantic. "No, please! I'll pay for my passage!" The grip on her arms slackened, and as she felt the tangy salt water spray her face she closed her eyes to mutter a brief prayer.

Jonathon waited, watching her, expecting more tears and pleading. When none came, he nodded to his crewmen. "Set her down," he ordered coolly. He waited, noting that her shoulders shook and her breathing was ragged as she struggled to compose herself. Her tangled mass of hair hid most of her face, but he saw her bite hard on her lower lip to prevent it from trembling.

When she finally looked up, there were no tears. Her eyes blazed into his with an icy rage so intense he could almost feel it. She wasn't frightened. She was furious. "Very good, Captain. What little game are you planning next?"

"This is no game, Mademoiselle DuPres. This is my ship,

and I give the orders here. You would do well to remember that." Turning, he called out to the bridge, and a tall blond man quickly appeared at his side. "Tyler, escort this woman to my cabin. Have her bathe. Twice. With soap," he added, dismissing them all.

Jonathon strode swiftly away, tense and angry at the scene that had just taken place. And in truth, disgusted with himself. He had lost control, ordering the wench held over the ship's rail like that. He never would have thrown her overboard. He knew it, and his men knew it. It had been a stupid and childish maneuver.

And it hadn't worked.

The little fool had more courage than most men, he admitted with grudging respect. His stowaway had just spent twenty-four hours locked in a crate, in her disgusting condition, and yet she had stood before him defiantly, meeting his stare and challenging him. And she did it with more grace and dignity than most women could ever hope to attain, even at their richly gowned and bejeweled best. He shook his head, wondering what he would find under all that filth.

Tyler was wondering the same thing. He glanced at the ragged woman he was escorting, feeling the seething rage that emanated from her. She carried herself proudly, her chin up, her slight form swaying gracefully beneath the sodden mess of her gown. He shook his head, certain she'd been misjudged. This was no dockside whore.

Whoever or whatever she was, she had certainly stood up to Jonathon. He thought back to the scene on the deck, remembering the blazing fury in his brother's eyes. It had been a long time since anyone had gotten the normally stern and commanding captain so riled up. He decided he liked her already. "This is it, Miss, ah—"

"DuPres," Genevieve supplied coldly, sweeping past him and into the chamber. A rather large bed, obviously custom-made for the captain, dominated most of the room. There were also two chairs and a sturdy table, covered with maps and an assortment of nautical equipment. A small footlocker and chest of drawers completed the furnishings in the neat space. "I assume this is the best your captain can provide for bathing purposes," she said, motioning to the pitcher and basin atop the chest of drawers. She'd considered not bathing at all, just to spite his order, but she was far too uncomfortable.

"Actually, I believe the captain thought you might enjoy a more thorough soaking," Tyler answered smoothly, opening the door to admit four men carrying a large wooden tub and buckets of water. Genevieve's eyes lit up, thrilled. As there had been no facilities for bathing on Captain Mercier's passenger ship, she had certainly not expected to find such luxuries here. Reaching into the footlocker, Tyler retrieved a thick towel and a piece of soap and set them on a stool beside the tub.

"Is there anything else I can bring you?" he asked. Genevieve shook her head, impatient to immerse herself in the steaming water. "Very well then, I shall see that you're not disturbed." He bowed slightly and left, closing the door softly behind him.

Genevieve removed her clothing in record time, stepping quickly into the tub. A moan of pure pleasure escaped her lips as she leaned back, letting the water swirl around her body. She reached for the soap and took a delicate sniff. Lye, she thought, crinkling her nose in distaste. But even that was preferable to the way she smelled now. She sighed and set about thoroughly scrubbing herself with the harsh soap.

When she finally stood, the bath water was dark and murky. Needing a final rinse, she reached for the pitcher and poured its contents over her head. She shivered as the cold water ran down her body but welcomed the sensation nonetheless. She was wet and cold, but clean. It wasn't until she was drying herself that she realized what she had overlooked: she had no clothes. Her gown lay in a rancid pile at her feet, torn beyond repair. She gazed resolutely around the room, looking for an appropriate solution. Before she could resolve her dilemma, however, the door was thrown open behind her, sending a blast of cold air into the room. She whirled around, clutching the towel tightly to her.

Jonathon leaned against the frame of the door, his broad shoulders filling the space. So this was what was hiding under all that filth. He smiled appreciatively as he slowly took in the woman before him. Her damp towel clung provocatively to her curves, an enticing suggestion of what lay underneath. A wave of wet, golden curls cascaded down one shoulder, nearly reaching her waist. The other shoulder was bare, as were her slender arms and shapely calves. "Very nice," he commented dryly, his gaze resting on her smooth, creamy skin. "I shall insist that you bathe more often."

Genevieve hid her acute embarrassment beneath her anger. She brought her chin up, a gesture he was rapidly becoming familiar with. "Is it too much to ask that I be allowed a little privacy? Or should I be flattered that you stand there gawking at me like a lovesick schoolboy?"

Jonathon laughed, amused by her sharp tongue. "Do not flatter yourself overmuch, mademoiselle. I cannot be blamed for enjoying the sight offered me, as any man would. That's our nature, I'm afraid."

"Do you suppose you could find it within your 'nature' to be civil and help me find some clothes? I should like very much to relieve you of the burden of standing about gawking. I'm sure it must be as tiresome for you as it is for me."

Jonathon stared at her, amazed at her imperious tone, feeling himself reluctantly drawn to the half-naked beauty. He didn't like it. Doubtless he would find her as spoiled, selfish, and greedy as any other beautiful woman he'd known. She'd certainly been nothing but trouble so far. The sooner he was rid of her, the better.

He swiftly crossed the room to the small chest and pulled

open the bottom drawer, revealing a variety of lacy articles of clothing. "These were left by a friend of mine. You may find them a bit roomy in some areas"—Genevieve blushed furiously as his gaze fixed pointedly on her chest—"but I'm sure they will suffice." His demeanor was once again stern and commanding as he straightened himself and strode back to the door. "I will return in five minutes. I expect to find you dressed and prepared to give me a full accounting for your presence on my ship."

With that, he closed the door firmly behind him, leaving Genevieve little doubt that he would return in exactly five minutes, whether she was dressed or not. With an angry toss of her head she dismissed the rude captain from her mind and went to examine the contents of the drawer.

The clothing was ornate, elaborately decked out in lace and ruffles, ribbons and bows. There were two gowns and what she guessed was an undergarment. She frowned, picking up the smaller article first. A corset of some sort, but unlike any she had ever seen. She slipped into it, her fingers fumbling with the stays at the back. She looked down at herself and gasped in horror, realizing at once that pieces of it were missing.

Red satin cling to her torso then stopped right below her breasts, leaving them bare. She pulled at the shoulder straps to bring the fabric up to cover herself, but to no avail. The garment was designed in such a manner that her breasts were cupped snugly, lifted and thrust forward. The bottom half was no better. The fabric fit her slim waist, then fell in soft folds to her thighs, but it didn't close. She felt the air stirring softly between her thighs as she moved, a startling new sensation that made her quite uneasy. Genevieve considered taking the offensive garment off, but years of upbringing rebelled against the idea. A lady simply did not run around with *nothing* under her gown.

She quickly pulled one of the gowns over her head, glancing down in disgust as she rapidly secured the laces in back. Genevieve was glad there was no mirror in the cabin, for she had no desire to see how ridiculous she must look. The gown was dark green, heavily adorned with ruffles and bows, and streams of bright pink ribbons that tied around the waist. It was several inches too short, finishing at mid-calf, the sleeves barely reaching past her elbows.

And the bodice was too large, she noted, hating the captain even more for his crude perception. So the man liked short, buxom women with vulgar taste in clothing. Good. He would leave her alone.

She reached into the drawer once again and came up with a pair of slim leather slippers. They looked a little small, but they would do. She'd just slipped these on when a quick knock sounded at the door. She glanced up, surprised the captain had given her the courtesy of knocking. She straightened up, patted her hair, and made a final adjustment to her gown. "Come in," she called.

The courtesy demonstrated by knocking should have told her it wouldn't be Captain Beast. "The captain sent us to fetch your bath," a crewman mumbled as he and another man entered, keeping their eyes fixed firmly on the floor. They went directly to the large, wooden tub and without another word lifted it and carried it from the room. As soon as they'd left, two more men entered, setting down heavenly smelling trays on the table in the corner of the cabin. Genevieve suddenly realized how hungry she was, having gone for over twenty-four hours without eating anything.

She watched them set up, her eyes lingering over the platter of roasted chicken. The men silently finished their task, then turned and left without so much as a glance in her direction. She walked over to the table, studying the banquet laid out before her. Accompanying the chicken were fresh breads, glazed carrots and tiny new potatoes, a basket of exotic fruits she didn't recognize, and a sampling of cheeses. And best of all, chocolate cake for dessert. She reached out a finger, intending to sample the frosting.

"If you'd care to wait, mademoiselle, I'd be happy to join you," drawled an amused voice from the doorway.

"Of course, captain, though I'm not really hungry my-self." Stubborn pride made her stroll away from the table, feigning an air of indifference.

"That's too bad." Jonathon watched her move about the cabin, her back proudly erect. "I thought a little food might be in order. I don't want you fainting on me before I find out who you are and why you're on my ship."

"I don't faint," she replied tightly.

"Good. You're sure you're not hungry, then?" he asked, holding out a chair for her.

Genevieve hesitated, then glanced once again at the feast laid out on the table. "I believe I could manage a few bites," she answered regally. To her chagrin, her stomach chose that moment to growl loudly in response to the appetizing smells wafting across the room.

She could have sworn she saw the captain's firm lips twitch as he seated her, but he made no comment on the noise. He took a moment to light the lamps in the darkening room, then joined her at the table. His huge presence seemed to fill the space between them. She took a deep breath, bracing herself for the onslaught of questions she knew would be coming.

"Would you care for chicken, mademoiselle?"

Genevieve blinked in surprise, then nodded in mute acceptance. He served them both, filling their plates with a variety of the delicious foods, then poured a deep, golden wine, lifting his glass to hers in a small salute. "Enjoy," he said simply, and began his meal.

She lifted her fork, dumbfounded. So he meant to let her eat in peace, without harassing her with a barrage of questions. "Thank you," she replied quietly, taking a small bite of carrot.

Jonathon studied her discreetly as they ate their meal in silence. He was as surprised as she that he was allowing her to eat before questioning her. Normally, in dealing with stowaways, he would not have been so kind. But her face had been more than a little pale when he'd seen her after her bath, and he knew it must have been at least a day since she had last eaten, possibly more. He watched in satisfaction as she emptied her plate. She had quite an appetite for such a slim girl, he thought, unaccountably pleased.

"If you've finished, Mademoiselle DuPres, I've a few questions I'd like answered," he said, determined to find out more about this volatile creature.

"Certainly, Captain Morgan," Genevieve answered, her deep blue eyes as frosty as a winter's sky.

"Why did you stow aboard my ship?" he began bluntly.

"I needed immediate passage to Martinique. I will pay for my passage, of course, as well as for any inconvenience I've caused you," she added, sliding over the matter of the expensive silks she'd ruined.

"I see. And what is the nature of this journey that you could not wait for legitimate passage, and with a proper escort?"

"A family emergency. And that, Captain, is all you need to know," she answered defiantly, her beautiful features arranged in a haughty expression.

"What a shame, I had hoped you had a better memory. It appears you need another lesson as to who commands this vessel." Moving with lightning speed he reached out and grabbed her arm, pulling her roughly from her own chair and onto his lap. "Try again, mademoiselle. You insist you're not a whore, yet you stroll around the docks unescorted and sneak aboard strange ships. Why?"

Genevieve swallowed hard, her senses swimming. The man was intimidating at a distance, but up close, with her on top of him yet, his sheer male presence was overwhelming. She pushed against his broad chest in an effort to free herself, but the attempt was useless. Her stomach tightened as she felt his warm breath in her ear, driving her in her urgency to be free of him. She twisting, squirming in his lap as she struggled, then stopped, aghast as she realized the effect that was having on him. She felt the telltale bulge quite clearly through the fabric of her thin gown as her eyes widened in shock.

He smiled at her, not the least embarrassed by his condition. "You're quite certain you don't do this professionally, my dear? You're quite good, I might even have a use for you myself."

Fury flashed through Genevieve's sapphire eyes. "That is the last time you will ever call me a whore." She finally freed herself from his grasp and stood, grabbing a knife from among the scattered dinnerware. With a swift arc she brought it up, intending to send it flying into his smug face, but Jonathon caught her wrist and held it easily.

"I can see you need a lesson in etiquette as well. This," he said, lifting her wrist to indicate the broad, flat knife she held, "is to be used for cutting cake. If you want to carve meat, I suggest you try this." He held the knife he'd used to carve the chicken aloft. "Any questions?"

Genevieve glared at him murderously.

"No? Good." He gave her wrist a squeeze and the knife fell away from her fingers. "We have two choices now," he continued flatly as he rose, his huge frame towering above her. "The decision will be yours. I can take you below decks to the crew's quarters, where you can earn your passage on your back servicing my men, as any whore would be happy to do. Or, you can tell me who you are, and why you feel such a task to be beneath you."

Genevieve rubbed her wrist, glaring up at him. The loathsome man meant to carry out his threat, she was certain of it. "As you seem to show little reluctance to bully and threaten those weaker than you, it appears I have little choice," she said bitterly. She took a few steps away from him, needing a little distance and a chance to clear her thoughts. She briefly considered using the same ruse she'd used with Captain Mercier, about the wealthy, elderly uncle in failing health, but one look at Captain Morgan's stern features convinced her that it would not work on him.

She was trapped and they both knew it. She turned and

faced him squarely. "Very well, Captain, you shall have your answers. You know my name—Genevieve DuPres. You are probably also familiar with my father's name, Phillipe DuPres. He was murdered on Martinique eighteen months ago."

Jonathon stared hard at her, surprise and disbelief written clearly on his rugged features. "General DuPres was your father?"

She lifted her chin. "Yes."

"But the man was convicted of treason, not murdered."

"My father was innocent of all charges. I intend to prove it. He was wrongfully condemned, and that makes it murder as far as I'm concerned." Her deep blue eyes blazed righteously up into his, daring him to contradict her.

"I see," was Jonathon's only comment, his gaze moving in contemplative silence over the woman before him. She paced about the center of the room, her slim form moving gracefully under the absurd gown she wore. He recognized the same poise and style, the undefeatable spirit he'd only glimpsed when he'd encountered her on the docks. He also recognized something else: she wasn't lying. "So you decided to make the journey alone, without anyone to help you?"

Genevieve shrugged. "There was no one. But that's not at issue here; I can take care of myself. After all, I've made it this far, haven't I?"

"By the skin of your teeth, I would say. Do you have any idea what could have happened to you if you'd fallen into the hands of some low, degenerate—"

"I'm beginning to get the idea," she replied dryly, her gaze fixed pointedly on him. "I shall consider myself fortunate that we met at this late point in my journey, as we will be required to spend as little time together as possible."

"Believe me, mademoiselle, the idea of your companionship holds as little appeal for me as it does for you." Jonathon strode purposefully to the door, then turned and fixed her with his unyielding amber gaze. "I will escort you to Martinique, rather than putting you off my ship at the next port, not as a favor to you, but simply because my own schedule will not permit any delays."

He waited, expecting a response. When none came, he continued, "While aboard my ship, I will expect you to follow my orders to the letter, stay out of my way, and out of my crew's way. If that proves too difficult for you, I will simply lock you in the hold below until we reach Martinique. Do I make myself clear?"

Genevieve raised her chin. She made no answer, but her look of contempt spoke volumes.

"Good. We have an understanding," he finished curtly and left.

She went immediately to the table, then kicked it in frustration. Captain Beast had taken all the knives with him.

CHAPTER FOUR

Genevieve paced alone in the cabin, mulling over her situation. While far from perfect, things really hadn't gone as badly for her as they could have. She was still aboard and sailing directly for Martinique. The worst of it would be having to stomach the arrogant captain for a week, but that was a price she would gladly pay to see her father's good name restored.

A knock on the door interrupted her thoughts. After her call to enter, one of the crewmen who'd brought her bath came in to clear the evening's dishes. He finished his task quickly and silently, then left the room. Genevieve stared after him, wondering if all the men were as quiet as the ones she'd seen today. With the exception of the tall, blond man who'd brought her to the captain's quarters, the crew seemed uniformly silent, almost hostile toward her. The captain probably cracked a whip over their backs if they dallied for even a moment, she thought in disgust, adding yet another item to the growing list of reasons why she despised the man.

After the crewman left, she yawned and looked about the room, momentarily at a loss. The lamps that had been lit at supper were burning quite low, and she knew from the quiet of the ship that it was late. She looked with sleepy eyes at the large, comfortable-looking bed, wishing she could curl up under its linens. But that was the last place she would allow the captain to find her.

As the man had rudely neglected to make any sleeping

arrangements for her, and she had no idea when he would return, she decided to take the matter into her own hands. Marching resolutely to the bed she stripped the thick coverlet from the top, taking two soft pillows with it. She walked back to the thick chairs and pushed them together to form a small bed, then cushioned it with the pillows. She climbed in, pleased with her resourcefulness, and absolutely refusing to acknowledge how uncomfortable the chairs really were. She shifted restlessly, tossing and turning on the hard bed until sheer exhaustion overtook her and she drifted off to sleep.

By the time Jonathon returned, the candles had long since sputtered out and died. He waited a moment for his eyes to adjust to the darkness, scanning the room for the woman's form. His dark brows drew together as he checked his bed. Blankets and pillows were missing, but she was not there. He swore softly as he realized he would have to rouse his crew to search for the little fool. Lord knew where she'd decided to take herself off to, assuming that she hadn't already managed to fall overboard in the darkness.

A small sigh from the corner of the room caught his ear as he turned to leave. He followed the sound, smiling as he caught sight of his stowaway. She was huddled precariously across two chairs, her body cramped at an angle he was sure would leave her stiff in the morning. He watched as with every breath she took the chairs inched slowly apart, about ready to dump her on her rear. He stopped, torn between gallantly rescuing her from her predicament, and watching her take a well-deserved fall on her shapely behind.

He allowed gallantry to triumph, and swept her into his arms. He lifted her easily, expecting to meet with resistance from the moment he touched her, but she slept on, snuggling deeper into his arms. He felt her sweet breath blowing softly against his chest as a delicate, childlike fist curled about his neck. In that moment he felt something stir deep within him, making him glad he hadn't let her fall.

He laid her gently on the bed, her glorious golden hair

tumbling loosely about her. She's a haughty, stubborn troublemaker, he reminded himself as he studied her smooth creamy skin. The bodice of her borrowed gown shifted slightly as she breathed, allowing him an enticing glimpse of the softly rounded curves of her breasts. For a moment his resolve weakened. Maybe she wasn't *that* much trouble.

As if sensing his close scrutiny, Genevieve turned, presenting him with her back. Jonathon frowned, then decided it was just as well. He certainly wanted no messy entanglement with the wench lying in his bed. The sooner he reached Martinique and was rid of her, the better off he'd be. He undressed, hesitating briefly as he unfastened his pants. He'd never slept in his clothing before, but wondered if he ought to now. Then again, why inconvenience himself for her? That resolved, he slid under the sheets she'd already made warm. Within minutes he was as soundly asleep as she was.

Genevieve woke slowly the next morning, languidly stretching as she surveyed her surroundings. Then with a horrified gasp she sat up, instantly awake. She was in the captain's cabin, in the captain's bed. She threw the covers back, intending to scramble hastily out, then stopped in horror as she realized she would have to climb over the large, naked form of Captain Morgan, who was sleeping peacefully beside her.

Genevieve tore her shocked gaze away from his powerfully built body. She had never seen a naked man before, and the sight was both fascinating and disturbing. She chewed her lower lip, her face deeply flushed, then stole another glance. His body had a deep golden hue, and his muscles, even while he slept, were sculpted and defined. His broad chest narrowed at his firm, tight stomach, rich dark curls trailing down to—

"Good morning, mademoiselle."

Genevieve leapt from the bed as though it were on fire. She hit the floor and spun around defiantly, standing with her feet planted firmly apart, arms akimbo, ready to do battle.

"Well, you've certainly taken care of that problem," Jonathon drawled, propping himself up on one elbow, the sheet pulled up loosely to his waist, and looking at her with an expression that could only be defined as smug.

"What problem?"

"I usually have a much more difficult time persuading a woman to leave my bed."

"That's because I never wanted to be in your bed to begin with," Genevieve retorted, her eyes flashing in the morning sun like the sapphire jewels they resembled. "I was perfectly comfortable where I was."

"Very well," Jonathon replied, "next time I'll just let you fall on your bottom, as you were about to do. You can spend the night on the floor."

"That would be entirely preferable to spending the night with a, a—" She broke off, unwilling to admit out loud that she had just spent the night, the entire night, in bed with a naked man. "Where is your clothing?" she demanded angrily.

Jonathon shrugged. "I prefer to sleep like this."

"Did it occur to you at all that I might prefer that you didn't?"

He shook his head. "It still hasn't gotten through to you, has it? This is my ship, my cabin, my bed. What you prefer is of little importance." To demonstrate that, he stood up and crossed the room, flagrantly ignoring her shocked gasp. He hadn't really meant for this to happen. When he'd climbed into bed last night with her sound asleep, he had assumed he'd be long gone before she woke. The truth of it was, he'd simply overslept. But now he was determined to prove his point.

Genevieve squeezed her eyes shut and quickly turned away. "Would you please have the decency to cover yourself in my presence, Captain?" she choked out.

"How fickle you are, mademoiselle. Your gaze was quite

brazen when you thought I was asleep, yet now you claim I'm an affront to your delicate sensibilities. Which is it?"

Genevieve forced herself to turn back. He was deliberately trying to shame and embarrass her, but she refused to let him have the upper hand. Fortunately for her, he was already dressed, and was shaving himself at the washbasin. "You are an affront to decency, sir. My sensibilities are those of a lady, with whom you've obviously had very little contact."

Jonathon shrugged. "I've known many ladies. Most have impressed me as little as you."

"Wrong, Captain. Judging from your boorish manners and the vulgar clothing I'm forced to wear, you've known plenty of whores. Though I doubt you'll ever know the difference." She smiled in satisfaction as he nicked himself, a deep red spot appearing on his cheek.

Jonathon put down the razor and turned to face her squarely. "You do like to walk the fine line, don't you? Be careful, mademoiselle. I've been very patient with you so far, but if you push me any further, I shall not be responsible for the consequences." He sized her up, taking in the bright, awkwardly fitting gown she wore. "As to the clothing, I would think a little gratitude might be in order. You may not like the style, but it certainly isn't vulgar."

"Not vulgar!" Genevieve sputtered.

Jonathon puzzled over that for a moment, then remembered Constance's penchant for what she called "naughty" underthings. A knowing smile reached his lips as he recalled her latest creation. "Then again, perhaps I'm wrong. If you'd care to show me what you find offensive . . ."

"You can go straight to the devil!"

Jonathon threw back his head and laughed at that. "Mademoiselle, we have seven long days together before we reach Martinique. At least they will not be boring."

No, Genevieve fumed, staring after him as he left to attend his duties, *they won't be boring. I will probably end up killing the man.*

She was just finishing her morning toilette when a crewman rapped on the door and entered with her breakfast. He walked silently across the room, deposited the tray, then turned to leave. "Wait," she called, recognizing him as the same man who'd brought last night's dinner, "Mr.——"

The crewman glared at her for a moment before answering. "Wilkens. Henry Wilkens."

Genevieve nodded, offering him a small smile. "Thank you for my breakfast, Mr. Wilkens," she said cordially.

Wilkens stared hard at her, then with a brief nod turned and left the room. Genevieve shook her head in bewilderment. The crew seemed almost angry at her, and she couldn't understand why. She certainly wasn't the first person ever to stow aboard a ship, nor would she be the last.

She pushed those thoughts out of her mind and left the cabin for a walk, deciding the fresh air would do her good. She circled the deck a few times, immediately noticing the difference between Captain Mercier's ship and the one she was aboard now. The ship from France had been slow and sturdy, plodding steadily across the Atlantic. But Captain Morgan's ship moved swiftly, her sails booming, almost dancing with the water beneath her. The motion was as close to flying as Genevieve had ever come.

She stopped at the rail, lifting her face to enjoy the warm sunshine. A brisk trade wind tossed her skirts, pulling her thick hair free from the ribbons that had secured it and sending loose golden tendrils streaming about her face. She closed her eyes and leaned back, a smile of pure contentment on her face.

"Are you enjoying the voyage, mademoiselle?"

Genevieve opened her eyes and looked up into the face of the young blond man who'd showed her to the captain's cabin last night. "Yes, thank you."

"Good," he said approvingly. "My name's Tyler, by the way," he added as he settled in next to her at the ship's rail. "But everybody calls me Ty. Everybody but the captain, that is."

She smiled, instantly comfortable with him. She figured him to be about twenty, the same age as she, perhaps a year or two older. "My name's Genevieve," she replied.

"I know. It's a pleasure to be introduced, Genevieve, though I must say I've liked you from the moment I saw you."

Genevieve blushed, thinking of the embarrassing scene that had taken place yesterday, but Ty quickly rushed to reassure her.

"Don't take that the wrong way. You're the first person I've ever seen crack the captain's cool, collected exterior, and it was a pleasure to watch."

Her deep blue eyes sparkled mischievously. "I believe it would have given me greater satisfaction to crack his thick skull."

Ty laughed. "I believe you could, Genevieve. But don't be too hard on the man. He may be a bit rough at times, but he's the only brother I've got."

"Your brother," she gasped. "But you're so nice!"

He laughed again, enjoying her blunt honesty. "If you mean by that that he and I are very different, you're right. I don't think anyone would ever accuse Jonathon of being *nice*. He's stubborn, hardheaded, and arrogant. He's also loyal, brave, and fiercely protective of those he loves. I'd not choose another man for my brother."

Genevieve held her tongue, not wanting to disagree and shatter the fragile bonds of their newly formed friendship. She shifted instead to what she hoped was a safer topic of conversation. "You're the only one who's spoken to me besides the captain. Are the crew always so silent?"

Ty shrugged. "Don't take it personally. It's just that you're a woman."

"Don't tell me they actually believe that old nonsense about women on shipboard being bad luck."

"Not all women, just one in particular." At her puzzled expression, he continued, "Constance—I believe that's her gown you're wearing—kept the crew running ragged with her constant demands and complaints. Naturally, the men are now a little wary around the captain's new lady friends."

Genevieve bristled. "Then you may inform the crew that I am *not* one of the captain's new 'lady friends.'"

Ty smiled at the prim censure in her voice. "Constance isn't a bad sort, really. Spoiled, perhaps, and selfish as well, but undeniably beautiful."

"Beauty," Genevieve replied dismissively. "What fools men make of themselves for such an unimportant, transitory thing."

Tyler quietly appraised the woman at his side. "Those words are easily spoken by one so blessed with beauty as you are, Genevieve."

She turned to him in surprise. "Me? I'm—"

"Stunning," he finished simply, gazing at her in warm appreciation. It was not glib flattery, but an honest assessment. The moment passed, and Ty was quickly back to his natural, boyish self. "I can't wait to see the look on Constance's face when she sees you."

Shaking her head in dismay, Genevieve laughed. "I'm beginning to think that you're as much of a cad as your brother."

"Tyler," interrupted a deep voice, "if you're through flirting with Mlle. DuPres, I believe you have duties to attend."

Ty nodded and, after sending Genevieve a quick wink, moved away. Jonathon watched the younger man leave, then turned to Genevieve. "You do move quickly, mademoiselle. It seems you have my brother quite enamored."

Genevieve stared up into the stern, disapproving face of Captain Morgan, wishing she didn't always feel at such a disadvantage with the man. "Your brother is a gentleman," she replied coolly. "I enjoy his company."

"Unlike a cad such as myself?"

She lifted her shoulders lightly. "One who eavesdrops into another's private conversation has no right to object to what he hears."

A small smile tugged at the corners of Jonathon's mouth. "Well said," he replied. But instead of leaving, as she clearly wanted him to do, he moved to take his brother's place beside her at the ship's rail.

Genevieve watched him warily, not knowing what to expect.

Jonathon stared out to sea, a look of contentment softening his rugged features. He was clad in rich brown trousers, his ivory linen shirt open to show a broad expanse of his powerful chest. Deep gold streaks of sunshine had woven their way into his hair, bringing out the dazzling brilliance of his eyes. Even in this relaxed pose she could feel the power emanating from him. She wondered if that was what made her feel so decidedly ill at ease whenever he was near.

"What do you think of my ship?"

She started at the unexpected question. "I think she's wonderful," she answered honestly, somewhat taken aback that he would ask her opinion.

Jonathon nodded, apparently very much in agreement. "She's a tight ship, as is the crew that handles her." He paused, obviously uncomfortable with what he was about to say next. "I feel I owe you an apology for the misunderstanding on the docks. Those two men were not part of my regular crew. You needn't worry about anything like that happening here. My men will not bother you."

"Apology accepted, Captain. Though perhaps you should tell your men that I will not bother them either," she added, thinking of the last woman on board.

Jonathon did not attempt to interpret that remark. "That does not mean," he continued firmly, "that I condone your actions. You took a very foolish risk in stowing aboard, mademoiselle."

"I'm aware of that," Genevieve relied stiffly. "And it was well worth the risk, Captain. There is nothing that can stop me from seeing my father's good name returned and his murderer brought to justice."

"And you intend to accomplish this all by yourself?"

She lifted her chin. "Yes."

Jonathon sighed as he studied the woman before him, the wind whipping her golden hair, her small fists clenched tightly at her sides, her beautiful features set with determination. "Has it occurred to you at all that if you're right and your father was murdered, it might be exceedingly dangerous for you to go poking into it?"

Genevieve shrugged off the question as though it were of little import. "If someone hurt the one person you loved most in the world," she answered quietly, "would you worry about the risk to yourself in avenging that?"

Despite her soft voice, Jonathon felt his stomach tighten. *No*, he answered silently, *I wouldn't*. He knew that if he were in her position there wasn't a force in the world that could stop him. He said nothing, standing beside her in silence as they stared out at the deep sea.

"Look!" she cried suddenly, her solemn mood shattered as with a gasp of delight she tugged at his sleeve and pointed to the waters below. Jonathon leaned over the rail to see what she was pointing at. A school of six playful dolphins was trailing alongside the ship, frolicking in the waves that their wake created.

"Look!" she cried again, her whole face aglow as the dolphins leapt over one another and turned flips in the air, falling back with a splash into the bright turquoise water. "They're smiling! Do you think they know we're watching?" She turned to him, her blue eyes glistening, her face lit up with the most radiant smile Jonathon had ever beheld. It was a breathtaking transformation. She had turned from a defiant, avenging angel to a wild, exuberant child within the space of mere seconds.

"Perhaps they think they're entertaining a queen," he answered, his golden eyes giving nothing away.

"Now you're teasing me," she said, smiling. "Go ahead, make fun, but this is all so new to me. There's so much to see." She wrapped her arms around herself as she leaned against the rail, laughter and innocence shining from her face as she watched the dolphins swim away.

Jonathon watched her, his throat tightening as he thought of what would await her in Martinique if she was right about her father's murder. Or if she was wrong, and the man was actually guilty of treason. He wasn't sure which would be worse for her. "There's a whole world for you to see, mademoiselle," he stated gruffly. "Don't throw it all away, trying to change what's past."

Genevieve stiffened, lifting her eyes to meet his. "I believe that's my business, Captain," she replied. "You may command this ship, but you do not command me."

To her amazement, the captain smiled fleetingly before he responded. "We shall see about that, mademoiselle. We shall see." With those parting words he strode away, his long, aggressive strides carrying him swiftly to the ship's stern.

Genevieve made a face after him, her pleasant mood now thoroughly spoiled. Not knowing what else to do with herself, she headed back to his cabin. She paced restlessly about the small room, listening to the shouts and laughter of the men on deck above her. A feeling of intense loneliness swept over her and she longed to go and join them, but knew she would be unwelcome.

Now that she knew the reason why, she wasn't sure she blamed them. It was Captain Morgan's fault, she decided, for having such poor taste in women. Gazing down in disgust at the gaudy gown she wore, she abruptly decided to strip it of all its ribbons and bows. Feeling a little better, she retrieved the other gown from the chest of drawers and repeated the process on it.

That project complete, she was looking around the room for something else to occupy her time when the laughter from the deck reached her again. She glanced up and in that instant came to the conclusion that her situation with the crew was not going to get any better by itself. Taking a deep breath to bolster her confidence, she squared her shoulders and headed for the door. She had seven days left of the voyage; it was up to her to make the best of them.

She reached the deck and strolled casually past the men, pretending to inspect the ship's rigging. She felt their stares boring holes into her back as their voices instantly stopped. After a nerve-racking pause, the men's conversation was haltingly renewed. Genevieve continued her charade of being vastly interested in the many ropes, hoping to make her presence as little felt as possible.

The ship flew no colors, but she recognized the ropes that hung from the main mast on which a flag could be attached and hoisted up or down. That gave her just the inspiration she needed. She discreetly picked up the rope and began twisting and tying it into expert knots, a skill she'd learned after many voyages with her father.

That done, she listened intently to the men's conversation, her presence apparently now completely ignored. After a moment, she knew who her victim was going to be. "Always pick the strongest of a group to attack first," her father had always advised her. "If you can beat him, you've shown you can beat the others as well." This wasn't exactly an attack, but she figured it was the spirit of the advice that counted.

As she listened, a hoarse voice droned on, "The men were so worthless they couldn't even get up the mast to let out the sails. Wind ground us right into the sandbar. Ruined the hull . . ."

This was the moment. "But I suppose *you* could have gotten that mast up in a thrice?"

The crew was instantly silent as Ricco, the man who'd been speaking, stood and eyed her steadily. "That's right," he answered, his coarse, dark features showing nothing but contempt for the interruption.

"I see," Genevieve replied slowly, as if thoughtfully contemplating him. "Faster than a woman?" She was answered by his loud guffaw, which was echoed by the crew, but she held her ground, patiently waiting for their laughter to die down. "Care to make a wager on it?"

This time her question was met with silence, as the crew gazed expectantly at the big man. "Look, missy, I don't know what yer game is, but a fact's a fact. No woman could get up that mast."

"What a shame. You don't look like a man who'd be afraid to test himself against a woman."

She saw his face tighten with anger and knew she had won. He would never back down now. "How much are ye wantin' to lose?"

"Five francs will be the wager," she replied, then took a step back to point to the small, triangular strip of red cloth flying from the top of the main mast, where it was used to test the winds. "The first one to remove that flag will be the winner."

The men quickly made bets among themselves as Ricco took off his shirt and stood beside Genevieve at the bottom of the mast, his mammoth body dwarfing her. "I ain't one to be takin' money from a lady, but ye got yourself into it. See to it ye pay me when we're done."

"You haven't won yet, sir," Genevieve replied dismissively, her gaze scanning the crowd. As Ricco tested the ropes, taking them into his beefy fists, Genevieve bent down and fastened around her hips the seat that she had created earlier by knotting the rope.

A crewman counted off, "One, two, three . . . Go!"

Ricco leapt onto the ropes, his muscles straining as he heaved himself upward. Undeterred by his quick start, she turned calmly to the man who had been bringing her meals and handed him the other end of the rope she'd knotted. "I'll need your help, Mr. Wilkens," she said, praying she hadn't misjudged the man. Without his aid, she was lost.

Henry Wilkens frowned, but then a slow, comprehending smile broke on his face. "You ready?" he asked, taking the rope from her hand.

Genevieve nodded and with a sharp tug, she was lifted

up. Her slight weight was no problem for Wilkens. He hoisted her easily, using the rope's leverage to raise her smoothly to the top. She smiled as she sailed past Ricco, whose bulk was straining against the ropes. "Good-day, Mr. Ricco," she said, nodding to him politely as she flew by. No matter what happened next, she decided, it was all worth it just to see the stunned, dumbfounded look on the big man's face.

She reached the top of the mast almost immediately, it having taken as little time to raise her as it would to raise a flag. Setting her feet against the mast to gain her balance, she reached up and grabbed the small red flag, waving it triumphantly to the cheers and shouts of the men below. Smiling, she settled back into her seat and gave the rope a sharp tug, signaling to Mr. Wilkens to let her down.

Nothing happened.

She frowned, ignoring the sudden queasiness in her stomach as she looked down. But the distance was too great for her to make out anything but a mass of bodies. Her heart picked up its tempo as the winds blew her about in her little seat, and she now began to appreciate the true precariousness of her position. She tugged at the rope again, more frantically this time.

To her great relief, the rope let loose and she began her slow descent. But instead of the cheers and laughter she'd expected to hear, the crew was strangely silent. She frowned and looked down again and instantly saw the reason why. The crew had been completely dispersed, leaving only one man at the ropes to lower her.

Captain Morgan.

Genevieve immediately grabbed the robe, trying to slow her progress, but it was useless. She swallowed hard, cursing both her rotten luck and her impulsiveness. Her feet hit the deck and with great reluctance she let go of the rope, staring up into the furious face of the captain.

CHAPTER FIVE

Jonathon almost didn't believe his eyes. He had been standing at the ship's bridge with Ty, charting their course, when the roar and shouts of his crew caught his attention. Scanning the deck, his sharp eyes went immediately to the source: It appeared that a woman's skirts were being hoisted up the main mast. Unfortunately, it was all too apparent that Mlle. DuPres was still in those skirts. His long, angry strides carried him swiftly to the tight knot of sailors gathered at the base of the mast. Dismissing the crew, he lowered her himself, using every ounce of restraint he possessed to resist wrapping his hands around her smooth, creamy throat.

Genevieve looked up at the man towering above her, his face a mask of pure fury. Unconsciously, she took a step backward. "Captain, I can explain—"

"What," he choked out, his voice a low growl, "did you think you were doing?"

"I meant no harm—"

"No harm! You could have fallen and broken your neck!"

"Well, I didn't! Besides, it's my neck, and if I want to—"

"What you want doesn't matter here. I thought I'd made that perfectly clear. This is my ship, and I do not take my responsibilities lightly. Whether you like it or not, while you're aboard, your safety is my concern."

"How very touching, Captain. But you needn't bother, I can take care of myself. Now if you've finished . . . ," she responded coolly, picking up her long skirts as she turned to leave.

55

Jonathon's hand shot out, grabbing her upper arm in a grip of steel. "Finished?" he ground out. "Mademoiselle, I haven't even begun." He pulled her along with him, Genevieve almost running to keep up with his long, angry strides.

"Where are you taking me?"

Jonathon didn't bother to answer. When they reached the door to his cabin he flung it open, pushing her into the room. He slammed the door behind him and leaned against it, never taking his gaze from her. After a lengthy pause, he finally spoke. "You disappoint me, mademoiselle."

Genevieve stiffened her spine, standing proudly erect in the center of the room, her face as tightly set as his.

"I thought we had an understanding," he continued. "I give the orders, you follow them. Very simple, really, yet it is obviously beyond your limited capabilities."

Genevieve unleashed a look of icy rage that would have crippled a lesser man. "You are, without doubt, the most arrogant, callous beast I've ever had the misfortune to meet."

"And you, my dear, are nothing but a spoiled, impetuous child who has little thought or control over her own actions."

"I knew exactly what I was doing, Captain. I meant to prove a point."

"And what point would that be, mademoiselle? Proving to me and my crew that you are determined to disobey and defy my every word?"

"Actually, that was just a bonus," she replied flippantly. Then, seeing the dark flash of anger in his eyes, she continued in a rush, "What I was intending to prove, Captain, was that I am not like the other," she paused, searching for the right word, "*females* you are used to traveling with."

"What in blazes are you talking about? What I want to know is what provoked you into pulling that ridiculous stunt. You may leave my previous choice of traveling companions out of it."

Genevieve slammed her fist on top of the table. "That is exactly my point. If you hadn't been so blind as to the type of women you brought on board, the crew wouldn't have treated me the way they did, and I wouldn't have had to work so hard to prove myself."

Jonathon stopped, his eyes narrowing and his rugged features becoming even harsher as he tried to follow her line of thought. "What exactly are you implying, mademoiselle? If one of my men stepped out of line, you need only give me his name—"

"No, it wasn't like that." Genevieve stomped her foot in exasperation. It was pointless to try to explain to this thick-skulled man. "Captain, the crew expected me to behave like the last woman you brought on board, so they were cold to me. I didn't like it, and I thought my little trick would work to break through that," she said, finishing her explanation in one breath.

Jonathon eyed her incredulously. "That's it? My crew was 'cold' to you, so you decided to risk your neck to get them to like you?" He still wasn't sure how Constance fit into it, but he would get those details later. "What could it possibly matter to you what a group of men you don't know and likely will never see again think of you?"

With that unexpected question, they'd suddenly ventured into very dangerous territory. The captain's words had brought up thoughts and feelings she wasn't prepared to discuss with anybody, least of all with the arrogant, self-assured man standing before her. She clenched her fists at her sides, waves of anger and humiliation washing over her. How could she explain it to someone who hadn't been there, who hadn't lived through it?

The cold contempt she'd felt from the crew had brought back every painful memory of the year and a half she had spent alone in Paris after her father had died. In the beginning, nothing had been spoken, it was just the silent, horrible rejection from people on the street, eyeing her scornfully as she passed, or rudely turning their backs if she meant to stop and speak with them.

Eventually, even her lifelong friends no longer recognized her, turning Paris into a world of hostile strangers. Finally, her family's property and possessions were all confiscated. She'd been forced to move to a tenement on the Right Bank, near the shop where she'd gained employment. Life under Mme. Nirvi had been difficult, but at least no one recognized her there, and the months of rejection and scorn were at an end.

Now, Genevieve felt her stomach clenching into a tight knot. The crew's rude contempt of her had brought back all those feelings of shame. Like a child, she'd thought she could simply show them how wrong they were, and perhaps make everything all right. But it hadn't worked. And even if it had, she was far too late. "You're right, Captain," she said softly, backing down. "It was a foolish thing to do."

Those were the words Jonathon had wanted to hear, but it was a hollow victory. He had watched the play of emotions that crossed her face, and the naked pain he'd seen in her eyes drained him of all anger. Only minutes before, he'd been so furious he was afraid he might actually tear her limb from limb. Now he felt almost compelled to take her into his arms and soothe her hurt away.

And damned if he knew why.

He held himself back, fighting the impulse. "Very well, mademoiselle. I trust that it will not happen again." He crossed the room and retrieved a bottle of brandy from his chest, then poured two generous portions. He handed a glass to her, not sure which of them was more in need of a drink.

Genevieve took a small sip of the brandy. She choked as the fiery liquid burned down her throat, but the heat seemed to loosen the knot in her stomach. She swallowed the rest of it, unsure if the sudden stinging sensation in her eyes was caused by the potent liquid or the surfacing of emotions that had lain dormant for so long.

Jonathon studied her face as he removed the empty glass from her hand. She was once again unreadable, her expression cool and composed, leaving him at a complete loss as to what he should say or do next. A position that was not only uncomfortable, but entirely new to him. He set down their glasses and walked to the door. "You'll be staying in my cabin again tonight, mademoiselle," he finally said. "I'll send someone with your supper."

Genevieve watched the captain leave, then collapsed wearily on the bed. She closed her eyes and leaned back, intending to rest for only a minute but falling asleep almost immediately.

Jonathon returned to his cabin late, his body aching from the physical exertion he'd put himself through in the attempt to block out any thoughts of Mlle. Genevieve DuPres. Her image had lurked in the back of his mind despite all his efforts to clear it out. One moment she stood before him defiant and enraged, waving a knife in his face, the next she was laughing beside him at the ship's rail as they watched the dolphins play, her golden-honey hair lifted by the breeze and her brilliant blue eyes shining with joy. And finally there had been the raw emotion on her face as she withdrew from him, apparently lost in painful memories of other times.

He shook his head in yet another attempt to clear it and began to undress. She was nothing but a nuisance, he reminded himself. A disobedient, troublesome, unwanted stowaway. She had her own life, and whatever its problems were, they were none of his concern. He had enough to do trying to carry out Colonel Haines's plan without taking on any further complications from her.

Jonathon glanced at the table and frowned, seeing the heavily laden tray. She had obviously not touched the food that had been brought to her. He walked over to the table and picked at the dishes but found that he didn't have much of an appetite either, his attention captured instead by the woman who lay sleeping on his bed. He stood where he was, silently watching her sleep, then finally crossed to the bed, tucked her under the covers, and climbed in beside her.

When Genevieve woke the next morning, she found herself alone in bed. She sat up, her memory blurred. She vaguely remembered lying down on the bed to rest for a moment, but that was all. She had intended to pull the chairs together and spend the night there but obviously hadn't quite made it that far. She looked around, wondering if the captain had been to bed at all. Leaning back against the pillows, she inhaled the deep, masculine scent of the man, and had her answer. So he had joined her.

Refusing to dwell on the fact that she'd spent yet another night in bed with the captain, she turned her attention to the dreams that had plagued her all night. Dreams not only of Paris, but of Armand. Armand Berthot had been stationed with her father in Martinique, and as his first officer, had even testified at General DuPres's trial. Although she had received letters from him, it wasn't until the very day she was leaving Paris that she had actually seen him again. She closed her eyes and let her thoughts drift back to that afternoon.

"My God, Genevieve, I've been looking for you for days. I thought I'd never find you," Armand said as he released her from his tight embrace. "What are you doing here, in this hovel?"

"This is where I live now," Genevieve answered simply, indicating the small, squalid room. "Everything else is gone, confiscated by the government. Everything, Armand. They took our lands, property, rugs and furniture, even my personal clothing and jewelry."

"For God's sake, why? It was your father who was found guilty, not you."

She shrugged. "To compensate the state of France for the crimes committed by my father," she recited wearily, the phrase burned into her memory.

"Why didn't you write me? I would have come sooner. At the very least, I could have sent money. After all, I am still your fiancé." When she didn't respond, he slid a finger under her chin, gently lifting her eyes to his. "Don't tell me you were too proud to ask for help."

Genevieve stepped out of his embrace. "Armand, I can't marry you. Not now."

"I see," he said stiffly. "Have your feelings for me changed?"

"Oh, Armand, can't you see? Everything's changed. Everything except my feelings for you. You're still the dearest man I know." She laid a gentle hand on his arm, her eyes imploring him to understand. "Look at me, Armand, really look at me. I've changed. I've been working twelve hours a day sewing just to survive. This pitiful room is my home. I'm no longer welcome in polite society."

"I don't give a damn about any of that. Marry me, Genevieve, and we can leave all that behind."

"I can't. Not while whoever is responsible for my father's death goes free. I know I can't bring my father back, but I can restore our good name, our lands and properties, the things my father worked his lifetime to build. I won't see them destroyed now."

"It's time we built our own life. The trial's over, you've got to accept that."

She shook her head, her expressive face shining. "I'm leaving tonight, Armand. I've booked passage for the Caribbean," she said, her deep blue eyes filled with determination. "That's where my father was tried and hanged for treason, so that's where I must go to prove him innocent."

"No," Armand said, shaking his head firmly. "I won't allow it. It's far too dangerous."

Ignoring his protest, she took his hands into hers. "Tell me what happened at the trial."

Armand sighed and tugged his hand through his hair in frustration. He looked around the small room for a place to sit, but finding nothing except the straw pallet, which obviously served for her bed, he remained standing. "Very well," he began, "but only if you promise not to do anything rash."

"I promise," Genevieve swore quickly.

Armand hesitated, his handsome face troubled. "There's little I can tell you that you don't already know. I spoke in the general's defense, of course, but so many stood against him. They claimed your father stole the money we were sent to recover, nothing ever was found, but—"

"What proof did anyone have?" Genevieve demanded, angered at the injustice her father had suffered.

Armand shrugged, avoiding her question. "There were so many accusations, Genevieve, so much circumstantial evidence. Your father was so secretive back then, he didn't trust anybody."

"I have a theory," she said slowly, testing it out loud. "I think the real traitor must have been someone close to him, someone he trusted, but he couldn't speak until he had enough proof."

Lost as she was in her own conjecture, she was all the more shocked by Armand's sudden action. He grabbed her arm, pulling her to him roughly. "What proof are you talking about? What do you know?"

"Armand, you're hurting me!"

He immediately released her arm and stepped back, drawing a deep breath to compose himself. "I'm sorry, Genevieve, but I have to know. Did you receive anything from your father? A letter? A message of any kind?"

Shaken and upset by his reaction, Genevieve looked into the eyes of the man she'd known and trusted nearly all her life. "No," she lied.

Armand stared silently into her eyes, then turned and gestured at the room which had been her home for over a year. "Obviously we can't stay in this rat-infested hole. I'll go and secure suitable lodgings for us both. You can get your things together, I'll be back within the hour. We'll continue this conversation in the morning."

Genevieve had waited, listening to the sound of his

footsteps echoing down the hall. When the sound of his last step faded, she turned to collect her meager belongings. She left the room within twenty minutes, leaving no note. Two weeks later she was aboard Captain Mercier's ship, sailing for Martinique, alone.

Genevieve wondered if she'd done the right thing, leaving France as she had, not even having settled things with Armand. But he had been so changed when he returned, almost a different person. And, as she now realized, somewhat ashamed, she hadn't trusted him.

She forced her thoughts back to the present and climbed out of bed, relieved she didn't have to face the captain this morning. She'd just completed her morning toilette when a short knock sounded and Henry Wilkens entered, carrying her breakfast tray. She watched him uncertainly, wondering if he might be just a little less hostile toward her today. As usual, though, he entered without a word, walked straight to the table, and set down the tray. Then, still silent, he lifted the cover of one of the dishes.

Genevieve stared in dismay at the unappetizing dark brown mess. Apparently she hadn't broken through the crew's barrier at all, and now they intended to repay her for yesterday's prank by feeding her slops from the ship's galley for the remainder of the voyage. "What's that?" she asked, sighing resignedly.

"That's crow, miss. Ricco said he'd eat it if he were ever bested by a woman. I mean to serve it to him next and see that he does."

Genevieve's head snapped up. She stared into the seaman's face and saw his gray eyes twinkling with silent laughter. "Then you're not angry with me?"

"No, miss, we're the ones who done wrong, treating you like you were Miss Constance." He paused, eyeing her sternly. "But I'd like to see you behave yourself the rest of the journey. You know that weren't right, getting me to send you up the mast like we done."

Genevieve chewed her lip and looked away. "No, it

wasn't proper at all," she agreed, then looked back at the seaman with a playful smile. "Thank you for your help."

Wilkens nodded approvingly. "It was about time Ricco had a good setting down," he said. "Come now and eat your breakfast." He replaced the lid on the crow and pushed it to one side, presenting the other dishes: fresh fruits, breads with thick, sweet butter, and steaming coffee. At Genevieve's insistence he sat with her, keeping her company while she ate.

She learned that he had been with the captain for eight years. He evidently held him in high regard, for he had nothing but praise for the man. Once again, Genevieve found herself holding her tongue. The captain might be well liked by his brother and crew, but his treatment of women certainly left much to be desired.

When Wilkens left to attend to his duties, Genevieve went above to enjoy the warm sunshine of the day. To her further delight, she found that the hostility she'd been receiving from the crew had completely vanished. She was greeted with polite smiles and nods from all the men, even Ricco, who grudgingly stopped her to press five francs into her hand. Genevieve tried to refuse the money, but Ricco would have none of it. "I stand good by my wagers," he declared, staring down at her with reluctant admiration in his eyes. With her spirits greatly improved over yesterday, she scanned the decks for Ty, hoping for a little company.

"Looking for someone?"

Genevieve grimaced. The captain was the last person she wanted to see. "Actually, yes. I was looking for your brother."

Jonathon frowned. "Tyler? What do you need him for?"

"Nothing, really," she answered with a light shrug. "I guess I just wanted a little company. I was getting a trifle bored."

He nodded, moving to stand beside her at the ship's rail. "I can imagine," he said, his deep voice sympathetic. "No masts to climb today or sailors to wrestle? I half expected to see you throw yourself overboard and try to outdistance the ship."

Genevieve stared at him, incredulous. The man was actually teasing her. "Now there's an idea, Captain," she answered lightly. "But unfortunately, I can't swim."

He turned to her, surprised. "Your father never taught you?"

She bit her lip, stifling a giggle. "My father was afraid of the water," she admitted truthfully.

Jonathon stared at her in disbelief. "General Phillipe DuPres, commander of one of France's finest fleet of ships, was *afraid* of the water?"

"He used to tell me that was what made him such a good captain," she said with a soft laugh. "There wasn't anything he wouldn't do to keep his ship afloat."

Jonathon joined in her laughter, glad to see the sparkle in her eyes. "I trust the crew is no longer bothering you," he remarked, noting her good spirits.

"No, they've been wonder—" she began happily, then stopped. "What do you mean 'you trust'? You didn't say anything to them, did you?"

The captain shrugged. "Of course." In fact, that had been his first order of business that morning. He'd made it clear to every man aboard that henceforth Mlle. DuPres was to be treated as nothing less than a long-lost, beloved sister. And they damned well better do it, too, or he'd want to know the reason why.

"You ordered your men to be nice to me?" she shrieked, thoroughly humiliated. "How could you!"

"It's my responsibility to see that—"

"It had nothing to do with you."

"It happened on my ship, therefore it had everything to do with me. The men will now treat you with the courtesy and respect you wanted."

"Do you honestly believe you can order people's thoughts and feelings? Well, you can't. You've just made everything worse."

Jonathon met her angry stare, his jaw clenched firmly. He'd seen the pain in her deep blue eyes last night and been powerless to help her. Ordering his crew to treat her with respect and courtesy wasn't much, but at least he had tried to do something. Now she was throwing it back in his face. "Obviously I made a mistake," he said. He watched the triumph flare in her eyes, then went on coldly, "I never should have opened that crate."

"Why, you, you—"

Jonathon drew back from the rail, his expression once again stern and commanding. "As you seem to enjoy Tyler's company so much, I'll have him join us for dinner. Report to my cabin at dinnertime."

Genevieve glared at him in mute outrage as she watched him stride away. Report to his cabin, indeed. Who did she think he was talking to? She paced the deck the rest of the day, trying to bring her anger under control. The sun had long since vanished and the night stars were glimmering faintly on the horizon by the time she was finally, reluctantly, ready to join the loathsome captain and his brother.

"Genevieve, you look as lovely as I remembered you," Ty greeted her smoothly, coming forward to take her hand, as she entered the cabin.

Jonathon scowled, watching as his brother bowed to place a light kiss on the back of her hand. "That's enough, Tyler. You might let Mlle. DuPres through the door before you begin fawning all over her."

Ty reacted to that exactly as Genevieve knew he would. He lingered over her hand a moment longer than was really necessary, glancing up at her with a mischievous gleam in his soft brown eyes. He gave her a quick wink, then answered his brother. "I fear I can't help myself, Jonathon. I've never seen a woman of such grace and beauty."

"She would have looked even better two hours ago," Jonathon replied curtly. Then to her, "We've been waiting, mademoiselle."

Genevieve plucked her hand from Ty's light grasp and

sailed regally into the room. "Really, Captain. You mustn't waste all that charm on me."

Jonathon clenched his teeth as he held out a chair for her. "I thought we might try to be civil to one another this evening. The change might do us both good."

"That's very gracious of you, Captain," Genevieve replied coolly, "but please do not strain yourself on my account."

He shot her a dark look as he went to refill his glass. "May I offer you something to drink, mademoiselle? We seem to be fresh out of hemlock, but perhaps a shaker or two of vinegar would sweeten your disposition."

"Now just a minute, you—"

Ty cut her off, his face a mixture of laughter and amazement as he interposed himself between them. One minute he had been sitting having a peaceful evening with his calm, cool, and collected brother; the next minute Genevieve had entered the cabin, and the air had become so charged with tension he could almost see the sparks fly. "Is this some sort of ritual you two have? Or does one of you seriously intend to murder the other while I watch?"

Genevieve and Jonathon continued to glare at each other, their gazes locked in heated battle. Jonathon tore his eyes away first. "Tyler is right. We may not like one another, but that does not excuse our behaving this way."

"Very good, Jonathon," Ty began, but his brother sent him a look that let him know he'd had enough of his interfering remarks for the evening.

"I suggest we begin again. Truce?"

Genevieve nodded uneasily, for she doubted she would ever truly feel at peace with the man. Jonathon, correctly interpreting her expression, handed her a glass of wine. "Drink up," he said. "After a glass or two, you may even begin to like me."

She stared at the heady ruby red liquid in her glass. "There isn't that much wine in the world," she muttered under her breath.

"I heard that, mademoiselle. And I must say, it wasn't very sporting of you to attack so soon after our truce," he scolded, a small smile tugging at the corners of his mouth as he lifted one brow in disapproval. Genevieve arched a delicate brow of her own, perfectly mocking his sardonic expression. She made no further comment as she slowly sipped her wine.

Tyler leaned back against the wall, quietly watching the two of them, his expression of mirth uncontained. This scene was entirely new to him, and he thoroughly enjoyed watching it. Women usually threw themselves at his older brother, who generally couldn't care less. This woman wanted nothing to do with him, however, and Ty had never seen him so worked up.

The sparring continued throughout the meal, Ty baiting them both. "Jonathon stole the chef from one of the finest restaurants in New Orleans," he informed her when she commented on their dinner.

"Oh? And how did you manage that?" she inquired of the captain, imagining him using brute force on the poor man to persuade him to accept the position.

Jonathon, who was well aware of what his younger brother had been up to all evening, shot him a dark look before he answered her. "I don't think stole is the right word for it. I simply offered the man twice his salary to sail with me. The choice was his." He shrugged. "I travel too frequently to tolerate poor food on my ship."

Genevieve frowned, irritated by the reasonableness of his answer. "I suppose you always get what you want," she said, unable to stop herself.

"Always," Jonathon answered, his amber eyes focused entirely on her.

Until now, Genevieve thought, meeting his level gaze with her own haughty stare. She calmly brought her napkin to her lips, then placed it beside her plate. "I believe I've had enough," she stated, gazing pointedly at the captain.

Ty laughed, nodding warmly to Genevieve as he rose to

his feet. "Thank you, Genevieve, for an evening I won't soon forget. As much as I hate to leave your delightful company, I'm on duty at first light tomorrow."

"Oh, must you leave so soon?"

"Yes," Jonathon answered firmly, "he must." Ty laughed and headed for the door, knowing he had thoroughly tested the limits of his brother's patience tonight.

Genevieve watched him leave with a sinking feeling in her stomach, for she had no desire to be left alone with the captain. As she reached for her wineglass and quickly emptied it of its contents, her sudden nervousness was apparent. A slow, roguish grin crept over Jonathon's rugged face as he watched her. "So," he said, "here we are. Alone at last."

She jumped at the sound of his voice, answering with a shaky smile, "Yes."

"Anything wrong?"

"Wrong?" she said, forcing a false brightness into her voice. "What could be wrong?"

Jonathon's smile broadened at her transparency. "You're not nervous about tonight, are you?" he asked, stretching the question out suggestively.

Genevieve lifted her eyes to meet his, realizing with a start that he was enjoying her discomfort. She squared her shoulders, wanting more than anything to knock the silly grin off his face. "I should like to discuss the sleeping arrangements for tonight," she said bravely. Jonathon merely cocked an eyebrow, waiting for her to continue. "I thought perhaps you could arrange other quarters for yourself for the remainder of the voyage."

"You thought wrong," he answered flatly.

"I see," she replied, angered at his outright refusal. "Then I shall leave, if you would be so kind as to direct me to a cabin which is presently unoccupied."

"This is a cargo ship, mademoiselle, not a passenger ship. There are only two cabins: mine, and the one adjacent, which is occupied by Tyler and two senior crewmembers."

"Then you're not leaving?"

Jonathon shook his head. "I suggest the next time you decide to stow away you have the foresight to determine what type of ship it is."

Genevieve stood and walked swiftly away from the table. "I think first I should find out what sort of beast the captain is."

Jonathon watched her as she paced about the small room. "Why are you so worried about it now? You've already spent two nights in bed with me."

Genevieve sent him a look of scornful disdain. "Thank you for that gallant reminder, Captain. However, there is quite a difference between finding oneself in bed with a man—though that was quite horrible enough—and getting into bed with a man."

Jonathon laughed at her ladylike logic. "You trusted me before—what's happened to make you trust me less?"

"I never trusted you, sir. I was simply the victim of unfortunate circumstances."

"Yes, quite," he answered. "Circumstances entirely of your own making." He crossed the room and began to undress. "You may join me if you like. I give you my word as a gentleman that I will make no untoward advances."

"Your word as a gentleman," Genevieve scoffed. "You can imagine how that reassures me." She turned quickly away as he pulled off his shirt, flustered by the sight of his broad, muscular back.

"Suit yourself," he replied, settling into the soft bed.

Genevieve turned back, her ire rising at the sigh of contentment he gave as he snuggled beneath the blankets—a sigh she was sure he made particularly audible for her benefit. She stalked to the foot of his bed, and with a sharp tug, yanked the thick coverlet from the top. "I'll take that, thank you very much." She crossed the room, noisily banging the two chairs together to form her makeshift bed, then blew out the candles with a great huff.

Jonathon watched in the moonlight as she tossed and

turned on the hard, cramped seat. Such a stubborn little thing. He waited patiently as her breathing assumed a regular, soft sleeping pattern, then heard the telltale scruffing of wood against the floor. Within minutes the chairs separated, dumping Genevieve abruptly on the cold, hard floor. She woke with a start, banging the back of her head against the chair as she sat up.

"Are you sure you wouldn't be more comfortable over here?" he drawled.

Genevieve glared at him, nestled cozily in the soft linens, looking as tempting as the devil himself. His golden body was naked from the waist up, his dark head propped up as he leaned casually back, watching her struggle. "Thank you, no. I can manage perfectly."

She drew the chairs together again, this time locking her feet through the back slats as she stretched out. From across the room she could hear the captain's long, drawn-out sigh—she assumed of irritation—but she ignored it, pulling the thick coverlet over her head so she would neither see nor hear the man. As soon as she fell asleep, the scene played itself out again, the heavy chairs tumbling on top of her this time as she fell.

"That's it, I've had enough," Jonathon swore, bounding out of bed. His long strides carried him swiftly to the massive chairs, which he tossed aside as if they were mere kindling. Before she could open her mouth to protest, he pulled her into his arms and carried her across the room, dumping her unceremoniously into his bed. "I'm certain you're just obstinate enough to stay the night in those chairs, or at least until you're so black-and-blue you can't move, which is probably nothing less than you deserve. However, I have a ship to run, and I cannot sleep with that infernal racket. If you wish to torture yourself, you may do so in the morning when it won't disturb me."

"How very thoughtless of me," Genevieve shot back, her blue eyes blazing as she moved to climb out of bed. "I shall endeavor to fall more quietly next time."

"You will stay there and sleep, mademoiselle, if I have to tie you to the bed," he ordered, towering above her. But as he watched her weigh her options, a small smile threatened to break through his stern expression.

Genevieve glared at him, certain he would not only carry out his horrid threat but probably enjoy it as well. At least he was wearing his trousers tonight, she thought, greatly relieved that he wasn't completely naked. She grabbed the pillows, piling them down the center of the bed to form a barrier. "You will lose any part of you that crosses this divide. Understood?"

Jonathon laughed in earnest now. Bracing himself against the wall, he leaned over the bed until his face was only inches away from hers. "Any part?" he asked, assuming his most lewd expression.

"Try me," Genevieve answered, echoing his threat, her expression mutinous.

With a roguish grin the captain drew back, nodding gravely as he climbed into bed. "I shall respect your boundaries, mademoiselle. Good night."

Genevieve watched him warily, expecting a trick, but it soon became clear that he meant to keep his word. She fell asleep wondering why she was so disappointed.

CHAPTER SIX

Genevieve stood alone on the upper deck, enjoying the warm sunshine and the gentle breeze. She looked at the men below, watching them work, her eyes moving automatically to the captain. He was easy to spot. It wasn't just his size that made him stand out, but the way he carried himself, his air of absolute confidence and authority. It was easy to understand now how he'd earned the respect and dedication of his crew. In the few days they'd been traveling, she had watched him work right alongside them, seeing to even the most menial of tasks. He laughed easily with them, enjoying their company, yet never for a moment lost his power and position as commander.

She turned away from him, not liking how frequently she found herself seeking him out. The animosity she felt for the man had somehow softened during the past few days, and she actually found herself enjoying his company now that they'd achieved a sort of uneasy peace. But she could only truly relax with him at mealtimes, when Ty was present to act as a buffer between them.

She frowned, thinking of the way her stomach still tightened whenever he was near. She found herself nervous and strangely excited at the same time, as if all her senses were suddenly heightened in his presence. Food tasted richer, the wine became headier, a joke funnier, and the air warmer. Last night she had made the mistake of touching his sleeve while they talked, and the jolt of that slight physical contact had shocked her—and from the start he gave, she was quite sure he had felt the jolt as well.

Later, she had been careful to pile extra pillows between them on the bed, but she knew neither of them had been able to sleep. The bed seemed to shrink, and the pillows blocked out none of the overwhelming masculine presence of the man lying next to her. Jonathon had risen at dawn, bleary-eyed and moody, staring at her coldly before suggesting that she might find the chairs a more suitable bed after all. Genevieve grinned at that: just as *she* was deciding he might not be so despicable, *he* was developing an aversion to her.

She turned at the sound of footsteps behind her, covering her disappointment with a bright smile when she saw it was Ty.

"Hello, Genevieve. Expecting someone else, were you?"

"No, of course not."

He grinned at her attempted nonchalance, for he hadn't missed the way her expression had fallen when she turned. "You're sure you weren't hoping to see my brother?" he teased.

"Whatever would I want to see him for?" she replied, waving his question away. "You're much better company."

"I suppose that's true, especially today. He's been biting everybody's head off." He smiled down at her. "You two haven't been fighting again, have you?"

"If the captain is in a foul mood, it's of his own making. I had nothing to do with it."

"Really," Ty answered noncommittally as he looked at the beauty standing next to him. If he'd had to spend the past five nights in bed with her, as Jonathon had, without so much as touching her, he'd no doubt he'd be in as black a mood as his brother was.

Genevieve fell silent, surreptitiously studying the man beside her, wondering how two men so different could be brothers. The captain was stern and commanding, always in control, while Ty was easygoing and quick to laugh. They were even different physically, though both were big men, with chiseled, rugged features. The dark-haired captain with piercing amber eyes looked nothing like his golden-haired, brown-eyed brother.

Realizing with a start just how handsome Ty really was, she wondered why she'd never noticed it before. In fact, most women would probably have found Ty's good looks, charming manners, and smooth, roguish smile more appealing. But as she reluctantly admitted to herself, there was something about the captain that intrigued her, and she wasn't about to miss an opportunity to find out more about him.

"Was the captain always so difficult to get along with, even as a boy?" she asked, running her hand along the rail as she feigned an air of indifference.

Ty hid his smile at her transparency and answered as best he could. "I don't really know; I didn't know him as a boy."

"How can that be? You must have grown up together. Surely you remember something."

Ty shook his head. "Jonathon was sent away to school at the age of five, first to preparatory schools, and later military schools. I never even met him until after our parents had died."

"You never met him?" Genevieve interrupted, aghast.

"No. Not till I was eight and Jonathon was sixteen. He'd never even seen me, but he came back for me. I remember that morning clearly. He came home to Philadelphia, a stiff young boy in a dashing uniform, and introduced himself, telling me that he was my brother and that he was going to take care of me from then on." He smiled ruefully. "It was, of course, instant hero-worship on my part."

Genevieve smiled sadly, for she could well imagine the scene. "What made your parents send him away at such a young age?"

Ty shrugged. "Less trouble than having to raise him themselves, I suppose."

"But surely he came home at some point during the year. The holidays, a birthday, perhaps?" At the negative shake of

Ty's head, she pressed on without thinking. "Wasn't there money to send for him?"

For the first time in years, Ty found himself thinking of his boyhood home, of the endless corridors, the white-gloved staff, and the immaculately groomed grounds. The tense silence that echoed through the halls more loudly than any scream. "There was money," he answered tightly. "But I suppose they thought it was just too much bother."

It was an insight into the man that Genevieve had not been prepared for. Her heart ached as she thought of the captain as a young boy, stiff and proud, with parents who felt it was "too much bother" to send for him. And what must it have felt like for Ty, to be left behind? "I'm sorry," she said quietly, laying a gentle hand on his arm.

Ty looked down at her, genuinely surprised. "Sorry? Don't be. That was twelve years ago, and I wouldn't change any of it. I remember almost nothing about our parents, other than how distant they were, how cold and formal. It's a wonder Jonathon and I were ever produced." Genevieve blushed furiously at that remark, but Ty was too caught up in distant memories to notice. "Even the house was always cold," he continued. "They died of pneumonia that winter, within days of each other. That's when Jonathon came."

The estate and grounds had all been sold, and neither man had ever gone back, nor ever regretted it. Ty paused, running his hand along the ship's rail. "Perhaps that's why we both love the warmth and freedom of the Caribbean, and why Jonathon named this, his first ship, *Liberty*."

Genevieve smiled softly. "And how did a sixteen-year-old boy manage to take care of an eight-year-old child?" she asked, determined to move the conversation on to a lighter note.

Ty laughed. "Believe me, Genevieve, that sixteen-year-old boy 'managed' very well. Jonathon joined a crew sailing for Cape Horn, and convinced the captain to take me on as his cabin boy. I was in heaven—every one of my boyhood dreams coming true." He paused, shaking his head. "You can imagine my horror when Jonathon came aboard the day we were to depart, his arms loaded with schoolbooks."

She laughed. "He made you do lessons?"

"Not only did he make me do my lessons, he checked every night to make sure they were done properly." He shrugged. "He was strict, but he also looked out for me. Being so young, I was an easy mark for the rest of the crew to knock about. Jonathon had to lay flat nearly every man aboard before they decided not to bother me."

"I'm sure he enjoyed that," she remarked, ignoring Ty's frown.

"Jonathon isn't the kind of man who enjoys violence. I don't know what gave you that impression."

Genevieve's mouth flew open as she stared at him, stunned. "You don't know what gave me that impression? Haven't you listened to the way he talks, always ordering people about and issuing commands, even to me?"

"Tyler!" A deep voice boomed from across the deck, cutting off their conversation. "Tyler, you're needed aft. On the double."

"There, you see?" Genevieve said triumphantly. "He never talks, he bellows. And he never calls you Ty, like a normal person, always Tyler."

Ty grinned. "Noticed that, did you? It's a habit he acquired when he found his hands full trying to raise a wild eight-year-old boy. He thought it made him sound stricter, more authoritative." He winked at her and lowered his voice conspiratorially. "It never worked. I just haven't had the heart to break it to him after all these years."

Genevieve laughed and shook her head as she watched him walk away. She prowled restlessly around the ship the remainder of the afternoon, visiting briefly with the crew, but found herself unable to concentrate long enough for any real conversation. Back in the captain's cabin, she borrowed a book from his assortment of titles, but again found her attention wandering. After starting the same page for the fifth time, she gave up and laid the thick volume aside.

Finally resigning herself to her mood, she retreated to a relatively peaceful corner on the ship's lower deck to be alone with her thoughts. Tomorrow they were due to reach Martinique, she thought, chewing her lip. But now that she was so close to her destination, the revenge she'd been dreaming of seemed suddenly overwhelming, totally beyond her capability. She wasn't sure how long she'd been standing there when she felt the captain's presence behind her and noticed with a start that the sun had already set. "Good evening, Captain," she said quietly, not bothering to turn around.

Jonathon studied the woman before him and wondered what had given his silent approach away. She had been in his thoughts all day, his eyes constantly seeking her out as she moved about the ship. He had spent the past five days assigning the crew every strenuous activity he could think of, throwing himself into it alongside them, just for the sheer physical exertion of it, but none of it had helped.

He fell into bed each night exhausted but unable to sleep, his mind torturing him with visions of Genevieve as she stepped from the tub, her wet towel clinging provocatively to her body, her hair the color of raw honey, cascading in soft waves down her shoulder. Her touch on his arm last night had sent sparks shooting through his body, and he felt certain that if they actually made love they would create enough heat to set the bed on fire. With her lying there within inches of him, it took every ounce of his willpower not to pull her into his arms and test that theory.

"You're late again, mademoiselle. Tyler and I have been waiting over an hour for you to join us."

Genevieve shrugged, enjoying her solitude and needing a chance to sort out her thoughts. "I apologize, Captain, I'm afraid I lost track of the time. Please go ahead without me: I'm really not very hungry this evening."

"Is anything wrong?"

She sighed. "Nothing's wrong. I would just like to be alone, by myself, if you don't mind."

"Ah, I see," Jonathon answered with a lazy grin, settling in beside her. "I'll keep you company then."

Genevieve gave him a long, exasperated look, then turned her head to ignore him completely. It was impossible. She could feel his intense eyes focused on her, could sense the heat of his gaze almost burning her skin. "Don't you have somewhere to go?" she snapped.

"No," he answered easily. He leaned back, the gentle sea breeze ruffling the front of his crisp white shirt, showing a broad expanse of his bronzed chest. His long legs were encased in tight black trousers, tucked snugly into shiny black boots. His wavy hair was combed back, off his face, a style which served to emphasize his rugged features.

All he lacked, she thought after a quick but thorough glance, was a golden ring in one ear to perfectly complete the image of a swashbuckler from another age.

"What are you thinking about?" he asked after a few minutes, breaking into her reverie.

Genevieve, unable to come up with a suitable reply, answered honestly. "Pirates."

He gave a short bark of laughter. "Pirates? There haven't been pirates in these waters for over a hundred years."

"Perhaps not, but there were at one time. Up and down the entire Caribbean."

"I suppose that's true," Jonathon answered slowly, wondering why she'd brought up the strange topic. "This was one of the richest areas to traffic, the 'Golden Triangle,' it was called. Goods from Europe, slaves from Africa, and sugar from the islands."

Genevieve shuddered. "Those must have been horrible men."

"Pirates?" He shrugged. "Not necessarily. Most pirates were commissioned by their king to steal from his enemies. They were allowed to keep a share of the booty as payment for their services. Privateering was an almost noble profession, fully sanctioned by the state." He paused, then finished roughly, "Unless they were caught, of course."

"Any man who would resort to stealing deserves what he gets."

"How very like you, mademoiselle, to pass judgment without fully understanding the circumstances. Those men were pistol proof, the best of their time, and they deserved much better than they got. Better than being used as pawns for greedy rulers who turned their backs when it was time to acknowledge their involvement."

"Pistol proof?"

"Meaning a man who is an expert in ship handling, crew control, and the tactics of naval warfare."

"Someone such as yourself, no doubt."

"An excellent example," Jonathon replied smoothly, refusing to be baited. "But I worked to earn my ship. At that time, it wouldn't have been possible for them to do so. Because of their common background, only as pirates could those men attain the rank which suited their training, experience, and ability."

"If you were born a hundred years earlier, then, you'd have had no remorse at becoming a pirate?"

He shrugged. "A man does what he has to do. I let nothing stop me from getting what I want."

"How charming, Captain," Genevieve replied flatly, turning away from him. The night air was warm and damp, the glow of the moon softly illuminating the sea and the sky. She lifted her thick, golden hair, letting the breeze gently fan her neck.

Jonathon studied the smooth white column of her throat, his eyes automatically trailing down to the hollow between her breasts, slightly revealed within the bodice of her dress. Unable to stop himself, he reached out to draw a finger along the tender nape of her neck. "And what about you, mademoiselle," he murmured. "Do you always get what you want?"

Genevieve jumped, putting a hand to her neck as though she'd just been stung. "Apparently not, Captain. I wanted to be left alone."

Jonathon ignored her protest and took a step forward. "Is that really what you want?" he asked, his breath warm against her ear. He pulled her into his arms and lowered his head, bringing his mouth inches from her own. Genevieve's heart slammed against her ribs as she stared up into his chiseled features, but his expression was unfathomable, his eyes half-closed as he leaned in toward her.

"Yes," she whispered hoarsely.

"Yes," he echoed, tightening his hold.

Genevieve stiffened. She brought her hands up against his chest to push him back, but his body was rock-solid, her efforts feeble. "No, I don't mean yes," she stammered. "I mean, yes, I want to be left alone."

Jonathon abruptly dropped his arms and took a step backward as Genevieve slumped against the rail. The night air, which had seemed so warm only moments ago, was suddenly cool against her skin. "My apologies, mademoiselle. I'm usually not such a poor judge of these matters."

"What matters?"

"When a woman is interested. Surely you know you were giving me all the signals."

"Giving you . . . ," Genevieve began, outraged. "I did no such thing!"

"Really? Then what am I to make of all those heated glances? The way you manage to touch me while we talk?"

Her mouth fell open in disbelief. "Of all the arrogant, self-centered—"

"You mean to say that you're completely unaware of your behavior? Of the fact that you find me irresistible?" he drawled, grinning broadly as he watched her anger rise. She was protesting too much, definitely a good sign.

Genevieve stared at him, longing to knock the smug grin off his face. She pulled herself up, arranging her lovely features into a mask of haughty disdain. "The only thing I'm aware of, Captain, is that I find you completely contemptible," she declared hotly, turning to walk away.

Jonathon reached out and grabbed her arm, pulling her

roughly back into his embrace. "Then I suppose you never wanted me to do this," he whispered, crushing his lips against hers.

Genevieve struggled instinctively against him, then stopped, caught up in a flood of sensation as her body melted against his. Her lips gently parted, her soft mouth pressing for more. She locked her arms around his neck, her body completely betraying every word she had just said, but she no longer cared. A wave of desire washed over her, sweeping her good sense right out to sea. All that mattered now was the feel of the captain's strong arms as he locked her in his embrace, the burning, shocking heat of his kiss.

Jonathon withdrew slowly, a triumphant gleam in his eyes as he watched her struggle to regain her cool poise. "Then I shall withdraw, mademoiselle. Never let it be said that I would doubt the word of a lady," he uttered gravely, a mock bow accompanying his words. "You may have the cabin to yourself tonight. I'll sleep in Tyler's quarters."

Genevieve's eyes narrowed to dark slits. "You mean that's been possible all along? Instead of forcing me to share your bed, you could have moved into the other cabin days ago?"

The captain merely raised an eyebrow. "It's my ship, mademoiselle. I can do whatever I want."

Genevieve stood fuming, watching his broad back as he strode swiftly away. As angry as his words had made her, she was angrier still with herself. She had literally fallen right into his hands. Despite all her denials, everything he'd said was true. She was drawn to him, and had just made a fool of herself by letting it show. Never again, she resolved firmly.

Tomorrow they would reach Martinique, and she had no intention of letting the captain stand in her way. She had spent the day worrying, planning, doubting her abilities, and entertaining all sorts of misgivings. But this scene tonight with the captain had given her her spirit back. Even if she had nothing but stubborn pride to see her through, she would not stop now. She would return to France victorious, the proud daughter of General Phillipe DuPres, or she would not return at all. She walked back to the cabin and slept soundly, refusing to allow a single thought of the devious, golden-eyed captain to disturb her.

It was not so easy for Jonathon. He barged into the second cabin, summarily ordering everyone, including his brother, to sleep below with the rest of the crew. He paced about the small room, pausing from time to time to gulp from a glass of brandy that he didn't even taste as he played the scene with Mlle. DuPres over in his mind, furious with himself. That was not how he'd intended it to go.

He had wanted to be smooth and gentlemanly with her, as he was with other women. He'd wanted to coax tender kisses from her, until he discovered if she was as enthralling as he imagined her to be. Then he would have led her to his cabin and spent the night making love to her. That would have rid her from his mind, he'd decided, for it was only physical desire that kept her in his thoughts. Once his lust was quenched, he would be free of the images of her that haunted him night and day.

But it hadn't worked out that way.

She claimed she didn't want him, but her body had responded otherwise. He nearly crushed the glass in his hand as he thought of her ardent response to his kiss, her unrestrained passion as she pressed herself against him, the sweet hunger he'd tasted on her lips.

He had been completely wrong. He knew in that instant that if he had taken her, he would never have been able to let her go.

And his freedom was too high a price to pay for any woman. Once they reached Martinique, he fully intended to say good-bye to the lovely mademoiselle. His promise to Colonel Haines had to come first; there was just too much at stake for it to be any other way. He didn't sleep well that

night, for his rest was interrupted by dreams of a Southern
army marching to war, led by a blue-eyed, golden-haired
angel draped in a provocative towel.

Genevieve woke at first light and rushed through her
toilette, anxious to be on deck. She hurried to the ship's rail,
her breath catching in her throat as she had her first real look
at the island she'd dreamed of for so long. Martinique. It
was set like a deep green jewel in the bright turquoise
waters, gloriously encased by shimmering white sand. Steep
mountains loomed up in the distance, their craggy peaks
covered with thick, lush vegetation. From here the isle
looked exotic and wildly primitive, as though no man had
ever set foot on its shores.

"Good morning, mademoiselle."

Genevieve stiffened. "Good morning, Captain," she replied, equally formal. They stood together in silence,
watching as small parties of men lowered dinghies into the
water and slowly made their way toward shore. Genevieve
held her breath as the boats were tossed about in the
turbulent waters, lifted by the strong current, then sent
crashing down, coming perilously close to the sharp rocks
which jutted up throughout the bay. "When do we go
ashore?" she asked.

Jonathon frowned, waiting until the last of his men had
made it safely ashore before he turned to answer her. "We
don't, not here. This is La Trinité, we've only stopped to
deliver a cargo of food and medical supplies. We'll travel
south and make harbor in Fort-de-France this evening."

"This evening," she repeated, disappointment clear in her
voice.

"I believe you and I have some business yet to settle
before you depart."

She frowned, annoyed by the reminder. "You needn't
worry, Captain, I haven't forgotten. I told you I'll pay for

my passage and I will. Just tell me the amount you had in mind."

"I'm not talking about money, mademoiselle," he replied, equally irritated.

"I can't imagine anything else you could have to say that would concern me."

Jonathon took a deep breath, just managing to hold onto his temper. "As I told you before, once you put yourself on my ship, your safety became my responsibility, regardless of how unpleasant that may be for either of us. I don't intend to just dump you ashore like a package that's been delivered."

Genevieve bristled. "How fortunate for both of us, Captain, that I have more brains and self-reliance than the cargo you're dumping ashore. I'm fully able to take care of myself. In fact, I shall be much better off once I'm relieved of the burden of your company."

"Fine. We're in complete agreement. If you'll tell me whom you intend to stay with while you're in Martinique, I'll see you properly escorted there once we dock."

"My plans are my own, they needn't concern you."

"I'm waiting for an answer, mademoiselle." Jonathon towered above her, his expression unyielding. He was met with stony silence as Genevieve lifted her chin and stared stubbornly out to sea.

"Very well," he said, "if you do not choose to answer, I can only conclude that it's because you do not have a place to stay. Nor I imagine, do you know a soul on the island. That being the case, you will naturally stay with me, under my care, until I can put you on the first ship back to France."

"No!" Genevieve gasped, her heart jumping to her throat. It wasn't possible, it couldn't be possible—to have made it all this way just to be forced to turn around and go back. "No, you can't mean that!"

"I can and I do. I have important matters that await me, and I cannot be bothered to play nursemaid to—"

"Nursemaid! How dare you! I've every right to go ashore, and I will not be bullied or threatened by you. What I do and where I go is my business, Captain, not yours. You can go straight to—"

"Captain!" A voice called out urgently from behind them, cutting off her oath. "Captain, it's Jake. He was working on the foresail and took a fall. Think he busted his leg."

Jonathon swore under his breath. "I'll be right there. Call Clayton, and have him fetch a pair of splints and clean bandages. And bring some whiskey." He turned back to Genevieve, his eyes cool and commanding. "Stay right here," he ordered shortly. "You're not going anywhere until we settle this matter." He strode off, and after a moment she heard his deep voice in the distance, taking immediate charge of the men huddled around the injured sailor.

Genevieve wrung her hands, nearly frantic with worry. She had no idea what she could do to bend the iron will of the captain, but she was horribly certain he'd meant every word he'd said. She stared longingly at the rocky coastline, and wished desperately that she could swim.

The boats.

She didn't need to swim, she suddenly realized. She could make it ashore the same way the men had earlier. She glanced around she decided she couldn't waste another second. She had to get on that island. This was her only chance—while the crew was still focused on the fallen man. Once she made it ashore, she reasoned, the captain would forget all about her.

Not allowing herself time to question the wisdom of her impulsiveness, she climbed over the rail and into the small dinghy attached to the ship's hull. She quickly loosened the knots, and the boat tipped heavily forward as the front came undone first, then righted itself as it hit the water with a splash. She held her breath, waiting to see if the noise would rouse a call of alarm from the crew, but none came. Not wanting to press her luck any further, she grabbed the oars and began paddling furiously toward shore.

The island was much farther away than she'd judged it to be, and her arms soon began to ache. She was just slowing her pace to rest when the sound of fierce shouts from the ship reached her ears. Alarmed, she turned to see a boat being lowered into the water, and watched in dismay as the captain, along with Ty and four other men, set off in her direction. And judging from the black look on the captain's face, he was more than a little angry that she'd taken his boat.

Genevieve gulped, her palms suddenly sweaty as she grabbed her oars. With a great lunge, she began rowing toward shore, putting all her muscle into each stroke. She heard the distant clamor of voices as the men shouted something to her, but she blocked it out, focusing all her attention on rowing.

"I don't think she can hear us," Ty said, watching as she moved closer to shore.

"She wouldn't listen even if she could," Jonathon replied grimly. "That's why we have to reach her before she reaches those currents."

"Captain, it's too late, look!"

Jonathon paled and surged to his feet at the sailor's desperate cry. He watched in horror as Genevieve's boat was lifted by a huge wave, then thrown back down, missing a jagged outcropping of rocks by mere inches. "The little fool," he swore through gritted teeth. "I've seen these waters overturn boats with six strong men at the oars."

"If she does tip," Ty said, "let's hope she can swim well enough to stay afloat until we reach her."

Jonathon froze. She couldn't swim. "Row!" he roared, every muscle straining as he furiously pulled the oars through the choppy water.

Genevieve was terrified. She clung to the sides of the boat, the oars having been knocked from her grasp and swallowed by the turbulent sea. With a feeling of sinking dread, she realized what the captain had been shouting to her. He had been warning her to come back, not angered that she had taken the boat. But it was too late now.

Her stomach lurched as the small boat was tossed about on the violent waters. Powerless to control it, she held on with all her might, her body shaking as the boat tipped, nearly sending her over. A huge wave crashed down on top of her, leaving her drenched, gasping for air, and choking on the cold, salty water. She closed her eyes and muttered a brief prayer, certain the next wave would dump her into the angry sea.

"Genevieve! Genevieve, grab the oar, we'll pull you to us."

Her eyes flew open at the sound of the captain's voice, shouted above the din of the crashing water. Jonathon was perched precariously on the side of his boat, his long body stretched out, forming a human bridge as he extended his oar to her. He braced himself as best he could, his body beaten by the strong waves while the crew strained to control the boat.

With a cry of overwhelming relief, she lunged for the long paddle, feeling the slick, wet wood beneath her fingertips. At that same moment, a solid wall of water hit her boat. Half-standing, reaching unsteadily for the oar, she was not prepared for the violent impact. She was sent flying, her body instantly swallowed up by the churning water.

It was worse than any nightmare. She struggled, clawing frantically against the seething mass of water, but to no avail. Her mind whirled in panic as her body was pulled and twisted by the vicious currents and undercurrents. Her lungs burned for air, but even as she struggled against the pounding water she had no sense of direction, no idea which way she needed to go to bring herself to the surface.

Her body began to grow very heavy, her limbs incredibly weak. Her last thought was of the captain. Surely he had been knocked into the water, too, and was drowning, just as she was. The thought brought an overwhelming feeling of remorse. The captain was dead, and her father would remain guilty forever.

She felt a sudden, sharp pain in the back of her head, then the world turned a deep, misty red. She no longer thought of anything, nor did she fight the water as she sank slowly, almost peacefully, into its dark depths.

CHAPTER SEVEN

The room was softly swaying. Genevieve felt as if she had been floating and had just alit on a soft, warm cloud. She moved slightly, then gasped as a piercing pain shot through her temples. Jonathon, sitting in a chair at her side, moved forward immediately at her soft moan, gently taking her hand as he watched her eyes flutter open. "Welcome back," he said, his deep voice tender.

Genevieve blinked, trying to focus. Finally, the soft blur cleared and she recognized those features of his, his warm golden eyes full of concern. "Are we alive?" she asked, her voice a hoarse whisper.

Jonathon smiled at the look of sheer disbelief on her face. He squeezed her hand. "Yes."

She tore her puzzled gaze from him and looked around her, recognizing his cabin, and slowly realizing that she was lying in his bed. "How?"

"Fortunately for both of us, I can swim. You were knocked into the water and I jumped in after you. I was able to get us back into the boat," he explained simply, not wanting to frighten her with the details, or how close they had both come to losing their lives.

Once she'd been thrown from the boat he'd immediately jumped in after her, but she was lost in the turbulent sea. Panicking, he dove through wave after wave, his chest heaving with exertion as he called her name over and over. He received no response, nor could any of the other men locate her. But just as he had almost given up hope of finding her alive, he saw her.

Her limp form was carried up on a huge wave, then sent plummeting down against a rough grouping of rocks. He swam furiously, reaching her and grabbing her ankle before the current could pull her away from him again. He felt his heart slam against his ribs as he turned over her lifeless form, blood smearing his hand as he supported her head. He pulled them both onto the thick rock, where he somehow managed to stay put until the crew reached them with the boat.

Miraculously, she was alive. Her breathing was shallow, but she was breathing. Jonathon stripped Tyler of his comparatively dry shirt and ripped it to shreds, using it to bandage her head. He held her in his arms to keep her warm, cradling her against him until he could carry her back to his cabin. That had been six hours ago.

"How's your head?" he asked, thinking of the ugly gash at the base of her skull.

Genevieve's head was throbbing, every breath she took sending white-hot sparks through her temples. "I feel fine," she answered, jerking her hand from his grasp, irritated that he was feigning such concern.

Jonathon looked down into her deep blue eyes, eyes that were no longer clouded with pain but blazing with defiance. Not only was he immensely relieved, he found himself actually liking what he saw. He leaned back in his chair, quietly studying her. "Wasn't your escape attempt a bit drastic?" he finally drawled out.

"No," she snapped. "I thought—"

"Thought?" Jonathon cut her off, lifting an eyebrow. "You mean you actually thought before you decided to pull that careless stunt? I beg of you, mademoiselle, do not think anymore on my ship, or I fear neither of us will live much longer."

Genevieve glared at him, shifting angrily on the bed.

"How very like you, Captain, to blame the entire incident on me, when it was really all your fault."

"My fault?" His look of stunned disbelief would have made her laugh at any other time.

"Of course it was your fault. If you hadn't threatened to send me back to France, I never would have had to jump ship and try to make it ashore on my own."

Jonathon sourly digested that twisted piece of logic. He had already spent the past six hours sitting by her side and blaming himself for her injuries. And all he could do now was watch and wait helplessly for her to recover. Knowing how desperately she wanted to reach Martinique, he should have been watching her more closely. "I was trying to protect you. Surely you can appreciate how dangerous it is for a woman alone on these islands."

"It appears it's far more dangerous to try to keep me *off* that island," she retorted smartly. She was about to sit up and throw off the heavy bedding when she realized with a start that she was completely naked. "Where is my clothing?" she demanded, holding the blankets tightly at her throat.

Jonathon shrugged. "It was ruined, soaking wet. You couldn't very well remain in it all day."

"Yes, of course, Captain. And I suppose the odious chore of stripping me of it, piece by piece, fell to you. Did you enjoy yourself?" she asked scathingly.

Jonathon's golden eyes darkened with anger. Lust had been the furthest thing from his mind when he'd removed her garments. He'd been too busy praying she would live. Now he wanted to kill her himself. "Believe me, mademoiselle, it was a most unpleasant task," he answered stiffly, remembering the stark terror that had gripped him as he held her lifeless body in his arms.

Genevieve sucked in her breath at the insult, her pride wounded that he found her so unappealing. "If I was so offensive for you to look at, Captain, why didn't you put me back in my clothing?" she demanded, angered and embarrassed.

"You want me to dress you?" Jonathon strode across the room and threw open the chest, pulling out the remaining gown and flimsy undergarments. "Stand up," he ordered coldly.

Still clutching the blanket at her throat, Genevieve shrunk back against the wall. She looked at the revealing underthings, blushing furiously as she realized he had seen her in those horrible garments. Jonathon stared at the golden-haired beauty curled up in his bed. Her sapphire eyes were blazing in anger, but her cheeks were suffused with a soft pink glow. He glanced at the undergarments in his hand, correctly interpreting the reason for her embarrassment. Though he hadn't noticed it at the time, he remembered now how she'd looked in them.

He had seen Constance in the bright, garish satin and overexposed lace many times and thought nothing of it, but on Genevieve they looked cheap and tawdry. He thought of her smooth, gentle curves and ivory skin, imagining her in pale silks and soft, delicate laces. And perhaps tiny bows down the front, which he could untie one by one. . . .

"Don't worry, these don't suit you at all," he stated flatly, tossing the garments on the bed. "They look much better on the woman they were made for."

Genevieve lifted her small chin, not deigning to respond. The man obviously had as little taste as he had tact. She would not allow his insults to bother her.

Jonathon shook his head at the mutinous bundle on his bed, amazed that he could find her at the same time so infuriating and so damned appealing. "Get dressed," he commanded curtly. "I'll see about sending you something to eat."

Genevieve waited until the door had closed firmly behind him, then stood and hastily pulled on the offensive garments. She had disliked them before, and now they seemed even worse. She paced about the small room, her headache forgotten in her anger. To think she had let that arrogant man kiss her. She winced at the thought, cursing herself for being such a fool.

Much to her relief it was Ty, not the captain, who brought her meal. They talked for a while, keeping the conversation light, until she at last brought up the subject she'd been dreading. "Will he send me back now?"

Ty paused, considering. "I don't know, Genevieve. You gave us all one hell of a scare out there. If you had been badly hurt, or worse, Jonathon never would have forgiven himself."

"Hasn't anybody listened to a word I've said? I am not his responsibility. In fact, I'd like nothing better than for him to leave me alone."

"You obviously don't know my brother very well. He doesn't think anybody in the world can manage without his vast experience and knowledge." He took her hand, forcing her to face him. "He means well, Genevieve. If he didn't care for you, he wouldn't be so concerned about your safety."

"Care for me?" she scoffed. "The only thing he cares about is how I've inconvenienced him."

"That isn't true and you know it. Look how he took care of you when you were hurt."

Genevieve grimaced, thinking of the fight they'd had as soon as she'd regained consciousness. She remembered nothing else. There had been water, overwhelming, crushing water, then there had been waking in the captain's bed. That was all. She had no memory of Jonathon, who apparently hadn't left her side once, gently wiping her brow with a cool cloth, or taking her hand and murmuring soothing words to her as she tossed and turned.

She had been heedless, she admitted. She had tried to reach the shore without taking the money or letter still hidden in the waist of her fish-ruined gown. But she had to get to Martinique. It was her only hope for salvation.

She walked to the porthole and stood quietly, her back to

Ty as she gazed out. The island of Martinique was now just a dark silhouette, a deep purple shadow against the lavender evening sky. "Ty, I can't go back," she said softly. "Not now. There's nothing for me in France."

"What do you expect to find here, Genevieve?"

Everything she'd been dreaming of. Justice. Answers to the questions that had plagued her since her father's death. The proof she needed so she could put her life back together again. That was what she expected to find on Martinique.

Ty sighed at her stubborn silence. "Talk to Jonathon. Let him help you—he will if he can."

Genevieve made no comment as Ty left the room. Clenching her small fists she shook her head at the position she was in. What a choice: to have to discard her pride completely and ask the most arrogant man she'd ever met in her life for help, or to risk being sent back to France. She scowled, kicking the wall in frustration.

"If you're trying to destroy my ship, mademoiselle, you'll need to put a little more muscle into that kick."

Genevieve turned to see the captain, his broad shoulders filling the doorway as he leaned lazily against the frame. "I was just thinking," she replied tightly.

"I thought I'd warned you about that," he drawled, trying not to laugh at her childish display of temper. "What were you thinking about?"

"You."

He cocked an eyebrow, a small grin on his rugged features. "I didn't know thoughts of me could arouse such passion in you."

"What do you want?" she snapped, not in the mood for his teasing banter.

Jonathon shrugged, strolling casually into the room. He poured himself a drink, then sat down, propping his feet up on the table as he stretched out his long legs. He took a deep swallow of his drink. "First of all, let me remind you that this is my cabin, and I don't need a reason to be here," he stated with cool authority, pausing to let the words sink in. "Secondly, Tyler told me you wanted to speak with me."

Genevieve ground her teeth, silently vowing to give Ty a piece of her mind the next time she saw him. "As a matter of fact, I do," she stated in a prim voice as she drew herself up. "I insist you let me ashore in Martinique without further interference into my affairs. I can manage perfectly well on my own."

Jonathon studied her in silence, not moving a muscle. "Mademoiselle DuPres," he began as he slowly rose from his chair, "it appears we have come to an impasse. You are determined to carry out this scheme of yours, whatever that may be, and I am equally determined to send you back to France on the next ship."

Genevieve paled at his last words. "Captain, please," she choked out, unable to continue past the lump in her throat. She turned quickly away, embarrassed by the tears that suddenly filled her eyes.

Jonathon went to her and placed a sympathetic hand on her shoulder, sighing as she jerked away from his touch. "I'm not an ogre, despite what you're thinking. I simply have very pressing matters that await me in Martinique, and I don't have time to see to your safety."

"I never asked you to," she snapped, irritated that she had allowed him to see her so upset. She took a deep, shuddering breath to get control of herself, then continued, "I have a plan."

Jonathon looked down into her sapphire eyes, eyes that glistened with unshed tears, and knew that he had lost. Had she been angry, sulked, or yelled, he would have sent her back on the next ship as he'd resolved to do. But her quiet tears filled him with an ache he couldn't begin to explain or identify. "Tell me about it," he sighed.

Genevieve took a step back, amazed. The big brute was actually going to listen to her. There was only one problem: "I can't," she mumbled, her eyes on the floor.

"I beg your pardon?"

"Captain, I can't tell anybody," she explained in a rush, before he could change his mind. "You said yourself that whoever was responsible for my father's death would very likely kill again. Any information I give you would only put you at risk."

"Let me see if I understand you, mademoiselle. Now you're trying to protect me?"

Genevieve nodded earnestly, then smiled at his frustrated expression. "It's not much fun being protected, is it?" she couldn't resist asking.

Jonathon frowned at the barb, not in the least enjoying having his chivalrous instincts thrown back in his face. "Could it be that you simply don't trust me?"

She lifted her shoulders, her expression indifferent. "That too," she admitted.

Jonathon shook his head at the contrary bit of womanhood standing before him. "Your skills at flattery could stand improvement, mademoiselle."

"I've always preferred honesty, Captain."

"Good, so do I," he answered curtly, refusing to be sidetracked. "Now, about this plan of yours. Do you have a place to stay?"

"No."

"Anyone who will help you?"

"No."

"Money?"

"Yes."

"How much?"

"Fifty francs." She lifted her chin, daring him to ridicule that small amount. It had taken her six months of backbreaking labor at Mme. Nirvi's to earn it.

Jonathon let out a breath and went to seat himself at the table, pulling his chair around to face her. "It would appear this plan of yours needs work," he stated flatly, sipping his drink.

Genevieve followed him across the room, smiling triumphantly as she looked down upon him, enjoying a fleeting sense of superiority. "But I have something even more important than all that," she proclaimed.

"Such as?" he asked dryly.

"Information."

Jonathon set down his glass and stared at her, his muscles tense as everything suddenly clicked into place. From what he remembered of General DuPres's case, the man had been condemned and hanged for treason, found guilty of having stolen a fortune rumored to be worth millions. Up until that time, his reputation as an officer had been sterling. The money had never been found.

He thought back, replaying his conversation with Colonel Haines in his mind. At the time General DuPres had been hung, there had been a flurry of Southern activity on the isle of Martinique, the rumors just beginning to spread that the South was building up an arsenal of weapons to go to war. The most critical questions remained unanswered: who was ·involved, where were they suddenly getting the money to buy the weapons, and who were they buying them from?

Jonathon stroked his chin, deep in thought. It seemed incredible that the two events were linked, yet he knew that they were. He could feel it deep in his gut, and his instincts were never wrong. He grabbed Genevieve's arm and pulled her into the chair facing him. "Tell me what you know."

Genevieve jerked her arm away. "Why should I?"

"Because you need me, mademoiselle. And like it or not, you're going to get me."

Genevieve shot out of her chair, wondering why her heart had suddenly doubled its tempo. She paced about the small room, trying to organize her frantic thoughts. "If I say no, you'll send me back, won't you?" she asked, her stubborn pride forcing her to make one last attempt at independence. At the captain's cool nod she paced some more. "It's because I'm a woman, isn't it?" she asked bitterly, turning an accusing stare on him. "You don't think a woman is capable of taking care of herself. I'm almost the same age as Ty, yet you trust him completely."

Jonathon didn't bother to point out that Tyler was twice her size, and had been in and out of brawls since he was old enough to make a fist. He waited in silence for her anger to wear itself out while she mulled the matter over. She chewed unconsciously on her lower lip as she paced, making it even fuller, more deeply pink. "Well?" he demanded impatiently, tearing his gaze away from her inviting mouth.

"I'm thinking!" she shot back crossly. "Why are you suddenly so interested in helping me, Captain? I thought you had 'urgent' matters that awaited you."

Jonathon hesitated. If his suspicion was correct, General DuPres had been heavily involved in furnishing arms to the South, using both the fortune he'd stolen and his military connections to outfit their army. Once the South succeeded in splitting from the North, it could align itself directly with Europe, leaving the general, as the man who'd been responsible for producing that outcome, in a position of unequaled power and influence. Power so great that it would be tempting enough to sway almost any man. He knew, however, that if he tested his theory on Genevieve, she would be gone forever, for doubtless she was as loyal as she was stubborn.

Genevieve watched him, smirking contemptuously at his silence. "So much for trust, Captain," she said in a low, mocking voice. "You expect me to tell you everything I know, yet you won't give me a single answer as to why you're suddenly so willing to help me."

Jonathon racked his brain, searching for a plausible reason. Coming up blank, he leaned back in his chair, a smile of cool confidence on his face. "Why do you think?"

It worked. Genevieve took the bait, supplying him his motivation. "The money, of course," she responded with a wave of her hand, her lip curling with distaste.

He shrugged, not denying it. He suspected her father had been heavily influenced by greed, so perhaps it was only fitting that she accuse him of the same thing. "I think this would be a good time to discuss the particulars, mademoiselle."

"Such as?"

"How much money are we talking about? Where is it? Who else is involved?"

"I can assure you, Captain, you'll profit handsomely for the meager, unsolicited assistance you're forcing upon me."

"That's quite reassuring. However, that's not what I asked."

Genevieve widened her eyes, assuming an expression of complete innocence. "Of course, how silly of me. You'd like me to tell you everything I know of my father's activities, every last detail, wouldn't you?" At the captain's curt nod her expression hardened, sparks shooting from her magnificent eyes. "Then you'll put me on the next ship back to France. Well, you can forget it. You may be able to force me to accept your loathsome help, but you'll not get one word out of me."

Jonathon sighed as he rose slowly from his chair. "What a beautiful partnership. Such a shame it had to end so soon. Have a pleasant trip back, mademoiselle."

"Damn you!"

He turned, lifting a dark brow. "Such language," he said, shaking his head in mock despair, "and from a general's daughter."

Genevieve picked up the half-finished bottle from the table and hurled it at his head. Jonathon didn't blink as the bottle went sailing by, missing him by inches and shattering in the hall. Three men came running at the sound of shouting and breaking glass. "Leave us," he said, dismissing them curtly, his eyes never leaving Genevieve. "Mlle. DuPres and I are just having a little discussion."

Their eyes locked from across the room, her gaze hot and blistering, his eyes cool and commanding. "Correct me if I'm wrong, mademoiselle, but you seem a little upset."

Genevieve gritted her teeth at his patronizing tone of voice. "How very perceptive of you, Captain. Doubtless you've years of experience in dealing with angry women."

"No reason you should be," he said, ignoring her last comment. "The decision is entirely yours. Either you tell me what you know and let me help you, or I send you back to France."

"Isn't that convenient? Either way you win."

Jonathon shrugged. "I'm not in the habit of losing."

"Neither am I." She turned her back on him, hating the fact that he held the upper hand. But, as she suddenly realized, that was only while they were onboard ship. Once they reached the island . . . "Very well," she conceded, turning back to him, "you may help me."

Jonathon's eyes narrowed at her sudden change of heart. He was sure she was up to something, and just as sure that he would find out what it was. "Fine," he answered easily. "Where do we begin?"

Genevieve studied him silently as she slipped into the chair he held out, weighing her choices one last time. Seeing no alternative, she took a deep breath to summon her courage and plunged on, saying the words she had held inside for so long. "Bartholamew Roberts."

Jonathon drew back, anger and annoyance marring his rugged features. "Black Bart?" he asked. "That's what this is all about? Pirate's treasure?" His tone made it clear that he found the very idea ridiculous.

Genevieve stiffened. "What did you expect, Captain?"

"I thought you could do a little better than that, mademoiselle. Something more original, perhaps. Do you honestly expect me to partake in a treasure hunt?" He eyed her coldly, taking a long swallow of his drink before he continued. "Those are for greedy fools and gullible idiots, and I don't have time to waste on either one."

Genevieve bounded to her feet. "Then you're the fool, Captain, and I won't waste another second talking to you."

She stalked angrily to the door, but his long strides carried him there first. He grabbed her arm and spun her around, holding her there until she reluctantly tore her gaze from the solid wall of his chest and looked up into his face. He waited, his eyes questioning, searching for the truth. "Is that really what you came here for?"

She thought about not answering him, but knew he would continue to hold her until she did, and her senses were already swimming. "Yes," she spat, diving around him as he released her and took a step back. She glared at him from across the room. "If you intend on doubting my every word, Captain, then kindly say so now, then we may end this dreadful partnership at once. If you wish it to continue, then shut your blasted mouth."

"By all means, do let us continue, mademoiselle," Jonathon answered smoothly. "It was a natural mistake on my part; certainly you can see why I thought you were pulling my leg."

"No, Captain," she answered tightly, "I certainly do not understand."

"Then you've never sailed these waters, mademoiselle. If I had a coin for every story I've heard of buried treasure on deserted islands, sunken galleons, or pirate forts in lost caves, I'd be the richest man afloat. The isles are full of tales of treasure, each richer than the next." He leaned one hip against the table, bringing himself in his half-seated position eye to eye with Genevieve. "It's so bad it's become a joke, an initiation ritual for new sailors. They're told stories of the fabulous wealth that lies buried, waiting for discovery, then the crew has a good laugh waiting to see who's the first man to jump ship to try to claim it."

Genevieve stared at him, her face perfectly composed, her blue eyes colder than a winter's day. "And were the men who murdered my father laughing, Captain? Or did they perhaps believe the treasure was real?"

Jonathon sobered instantly, kicking himself for his thoughtless blunder. Buried treasure might be nothing but a joke to him, but to her it was obviously very real. "I'm sorry," he said softly, lifting a hand to gently stroke her cheek.

Genevieve pulled back instantly, hating the riotous response of her senses to his touch. It must be because she disliked him so much, she decided. "I don't need your sympathy," she snapped. "I don't need your help, either. But if I must have it, then let's get to work."

Jonathon tried not to grin at her imperious tone. She was a general's daughter, all right. He watched as she crossed to the chest of drawers and pulled out the torn gown she'd been wearing when stowed aboard. He wondered why she'd bothered to clean and keep it at all, for the garment was clearly not fit to be worn. He had his answer when she rolled the gown into a tight ball then brought it to her mouth, using her teeth to rip open the tightly stitched waistband. He nodded his head, feeling a new measure of respect for her as she withdrew a bundle of papers from the gown's lining. "Very ingenious, mademoiselle."

Genevieve did not bother to reply. She crossed to the table and sat down, smoothing the thick parchment out before her. Some of the pieces had slightly smeared, but for the most part they were still in good shape. She glanced up at the captain, all business. "May I assume you're familiar with this Bartholamew Roberts? Black Bart, as you call him?"

"You may. Black Bart was the most notorious pirate of his time. He ruled the Caribbean seas two hundred years ago, pillaging and plundering from every ship that had the misfortune to cross his wake."

"Correct. He was not only a ruthless man, Captain, but quite skilled. As his reputation grew, the ships he stalked would simply give up their cargoes without a fight, happy to be left with their lives. He amassed a king's fortune, but he made one final error."

"And what would that be?" Jonathon asked, keeping his voice neutral. He knew the outcome of her tale, of course, but wanted to hear her tell it.

"Greed," she stated succinctly. "Rather than retiring with his vast riches as he should have, he hid his fortune here on

Martinique, then went for one final raid along the Amazon coast. He never recovered his treasure."

"How can you be certain of that? After all, we're talking of events that took place over two hundred years ago."

"Look at what happened next, Captain. A French fleet arrived, determined to protect Martinique from the likes of Roberts. Roberts engaged them, but he was vastly outnumbered. He did, however, manage to capture the governor's ship, and offered to ransom him in exchange for safe passage on and off the island."

"As I recall, foreign governors weren't very popular back then."

"You and I may know that, but Roberts didn't. He became even more furious when the French navy openly laughed at his ransom demand, and he abruptly hung his poor hostage from the yardarm." She paused, passing him a rough sketch. It was a drawing of a man holding a cutlass high in one hand, while resting his foot on a skull. "Do you recognize that?" she asked.

Jonathon nodded. He had seen it before, and others like it. A pirate's flag. "Roberts."

"Yes. And look at the initials underneath: A. M. H. A Martiniquan's Head. As Roberts was unable to break through the blockade and recoup his treasure, he vowed to spend the rest of his life destroying any and all things Martiniquan. Fortunately, his was not a very long life."

Jonathon leaned back in his chair, rubbing the stiff muscles at the base of his neck. "That's very interesting, mademoiselle, but where does it leave us? One very angry, very dead pirate, and an incredible fortune that may or may not exist."

"It does exist."

He sighed, sorely fatigued and just about out of patience. "How do you know that? Have you seen it?"

Genevieve's next words were softly spoken, but they swept through the room with the force of a gale wind. "My grandfather has." She stood and began pacing the room, collecting her thoughts.

Jonathon's eyes followed her graceful form, noting the unconsciously provocative sway of her hips as she walked. He shook his head to clear his thoughts. "Explain yourself."

She scowled at his curt command, her blue eyes flashing angrily in his direction, but was too immersed in her own thoughts for his gruffness to truly annoy her. "Roberts died a year later. It was an easy task for the French fleet to capture what remained of his crew, who substantiated the existence of the treasure. None of them knew where the treasure was buried, though, for Roberts had murdered the men who'd brought it ashore with him."

Jonathon shrugged. "That was fairly routine. After all, 'dead men tell no tales.'"

Genevieve turned, smiling triumphantly. "Perhaps not, but they do leave clues. The officers came into possession of Roberts's captain's log, and within it a cryptic code which led to the treasure. But Roberts was a brilliant military strategist, and no one was able to break the code. For generations that book floated through the ranks of France's finest military men, with a lure as potent as King Arthur's sword Excalibur, stuck in stone, waiting for the right man to lift it out and claim his kingdom."

Jonathon could see where her story was leading. He stretched out, leaning back with his feet propped up on the table, his hands locked behind his head. He gave her a smugly confident smile, flattered by her confidence. "And you want me to crack the code for you," he surmised.

"You!" Genevieve whirled around, laughter bubbling from her beautiful lips. "You think I want you to try—but that's absurd," she gasped, pointing a slim finger at him as her shoulders shook with mirth.

Jonathon straightened instantly. "I fail to see the reason for such hilarity, mademoiselle," he gritted out, amazed to find himself, for the first time in his life, the butt of a joke.

"Yes, yes, of course," Genevieve gasped, trying to steady

herself. Her laughter subsided, but her sapphire eyes still twinkled mischievously. "I knew you were proud, Captain, but I didn't think you'd rank yourself with Napoleon."

"Napoleon," he repeated flatly, his ego still a little bruised.

"Certainly. The greatest military mind France has ever known," she stated matter-of-factly. "He alone was able to crack the code. He intended to use the fortune to build his empire, to man an army large enough to rule all Europe."

Jonathon clenched his fist, listening intently. He knew in that instant that he'd been right. This was the reason for the sudden flurry of Southern activity on Martinique. Only the name had changed: instead of Napoleon's European Empire, the dream was now of a Southern Empire. A dream that could tear his country apart. "What happened?" he asked.

"You may remember this, Captain, for it's recent history. In 1801 Napoleon sent twenty-two thousand men to the Caribbean, led by his brother-in-law, General LeClerk, under whom my grandfather served. Ostensibly, the objective was to retain Haiti under French rule, but there was another, even more important mission: to bring back Bartholamew Roberts's treasure. LeClerk traveled secretly to Martinique, where he discovered Napoleon had indeed been successful in cracking the code. They uncovered the treasure, which LeClerk promptly moved to another location for safekeeping."

Genevieve quit pacing now, crossing the room to join Jonathon at the table. He said nothing, waiting for her to continue. "Given the risk of attack at that time, LeClerk decided it would be best to journey back to Haiti and return with reinforcements before he loaded their precious cargo. Logical perhaps, but it didn't work. LeClerk never made it back. He died of yellow fever, as did the men who'd been ashore with him, this time leaving no clue as to the location of the treasure."

"How does your grandfather figure into this?"

"My grandfather was there when the treasure was uncovered, for he was in the party that went ashore with LeClerk. My family has a very distinguished military history, Captain," she couldn't resist proudly putting in.

"I'm sure," Jonathon agreed congenially, not wanting to get into an argument about her father's guilt or innocence.

"In any case," she continued, "my grandfather also became ill with the fever, but before he died he managed to compose a letter to my father, detailing as best he could the path LeClerk might have taken."

"He wasn't with him when the treasure was buried?"

"No. He was standing guard at their camp."

"But you have his letter."

Genevieve shook her head. She picked up a second piece of parchment and passed it to him. Jonathon recognized it as a crudely sketched map of Martinique, complete with a variety of illegible spots, swirls, and crosses. "Martinique," he said, studying the map. "What do these marks represent?"

"*My* code, Captain. My father sent me letters, dozens of them, during the year he was here in Martinique, each detailing various locations my grandfather had suggested would lead to the treasure. I made the map months ago, shortly before I burned all the letters."

Jonathon came instantly to his feet. "You burned them?" he shouted in disbelief.

"Of course," Genevieve replied coolly. "But don't worry, I've memorized them all. This way, you see, I'm the only link to the treasure, the only living soul who can possibly locate it."

"Do you have any idea what a dangerous position you've put yourself in?" he growled, wanting to shake her. It was insane—men would stop at nothing to acquire a fortune of that magnitude. They would certainly not hesitate to kill one lovely little French girl who thought she was invincible.

Genevieve came slowly to her feet, the challenge in her eyes unmistakable. "I'm well aware of that, Captain. I felt it was only fair that you be aware of it also. The treasure is great, but so is the risk. Should you not be further inclined to *protect* me, I shall understand."

Jonathon stared at her in disbelief. The little wench was actually giving him a chance to back down! For the second time within minutes, he found himself defending his manhood, and he didn't like it one bit. "That's very gracious of you, mademoiselle," he replied stiffly, "but I do believe I'm up to the chase." He strode across the room to the door, then turned back to her one last time, his amber gaze intense. "I suggest you get some rest tonight, for the hunt begins tomorrow." He left abruptly, slamming the thick door behind him.

Genevieve sighed and turned away, noting how very barren the room suddenly seemed without his powerful presence to fill it. She retreated to bed, exhausted after the day's events, but she tossed and turned for hours before she finally drifted off.

She felt as though she'd only been asleep for minutes when she woke, sitting straight up, her heart pounding wildly. She rubbed her eyes, disoriented, trying to figure out what had frightened her so, when she heard it again.

Cannon fire.

The ship was being attacked.

CHAPTER EIGHT

Genevieve threw herself out of bed. She had slept in her gown, and didn't waste a minute on her toilette as she rushed to the door, pausing only long enough to slip on her shoes. She flew up the gangway, her terror increasing with each boom of the cannons. She braced herself as she neared the upper deck, for she didn't want to be trampled by the men frantically rushing to their stations. She knew there would be utter pandemonium on deck, with men running to and fro, shouting, and readying their arms for battle. But surely there would be something the captain needed her for as well, some way she could help.

Taking a deep breath, she stepped out onto the deck, her mind whirling with fear, then came to a complete stop, staring about her in total disbelief.

The men were lounging about, working and talking casually among themselves as the cannons roared. The crew wasn't even attempting to defend themselves, she realized, her mouth agape. She looked across the bay at an English ship that was letting loose her guns and showing no likelihood of stopping. Her ship hadn't been struck yet, though, and she wasn't about to wait for them to take action. Though she'd never been near an actual battle in her life, she'd witnessed her father drill his men on many occasions, and was well versed with the commands. "You there—trim the sails! You—ready the guns!" she began, briskly and authoritatively assigning each man a task.

"What do you suppose she's doing?" Ty wondered aloud

as he and Jonathon watched her stride through the crew, giving orders and leaving each man staring after her in complete bafflement.

Jonathon shrugged. Seven days ago he would not have believed he would ever see a woman rushing around among his crew, calling his men to arms. But seven days ago he had not met Mlle. Genevieve DuPres. He leaned back, propping his elbows on the rail behind him as he watched her, his expression a mixture of amusement and curiosity.

Genevieve finally spied him. The captain actually had his back to the ship which was firing at them! Did the man value his ship and crew so little he was unwilling to defend them? She lifted her skirts and rushed to him, unmindful of the lovely expanse of slim ankle and calf she was displaying. "Do something!" she cried, horrified.

Tearing his gaze away from the shapely legs he had glimpsed as she ran across the deck, Jonathon let his eyes travel slowly upward. In fascination he watched the lifting and falling of her breasts, slightly revealed by the bodice of her gown, which she had left partially unfastened in her haste. Her hair was loose and disheveled, a soft golden cloud that framed her face and fell down her back in thick waves.

"Well?" Genevieve demanded impatiently. His ship was being attacked and the dense man didn't seem to notice!

"Yes, mademoiselle. Is there something I can do for you?" he inquired politely, resisting the urge to pull the wild beauty into his arms.

"Do for me?" she squealed, amazed. "Captain, your ship is being attacked," she yelled over the roar of the cannons. "Don't you intend to defend yourself?"

"Attacked? Really?" Jonathon repeated, his firm lips twitching as if he were trying to bite back a smile. Ty bowed his head to cough, emitting a noise which sounded suspiciously like choked laughter. Apparently convinced they were both quite mad, Genevieve stared from the captain to his brother. She looked so earnest and upset, Jonathon couldn't help teasing her a little bit. "Since I was so remiss in my duties, that must be what all the running around was for. You intended to single-handedly rally my men to arms."

"Of course. They're getting ready for battle, while we stand here. . . ." Her voice trailed off as she gestured behind her to emphasize her point and realized that the men had ignored her completely. Instead, they were now all standing and staring at her, as if she were crazy. Moreover, the cannons had quit, and the air was deathly still. She looked up at the captain, her face a study in confusion.

Jonathon couldn't hold back his smile any longer. "I appreciate your concern, mademoiselle. However, we are not under attack." He paused, shaking his head in disbelief. "I've been commanding ships for eight years, and I sincerely hope that if we ever are under attack, I'll be astute enough to figure that out all by myself."

Genevieve felt the heat rise to her cheeks. She'd just made a complete fool of herself in front of the captain, his brother, and the entire crew. She looked at the man standing before her, his feet firmly planted on the deck, his strong arms crossed over his broad chest, the wind whipping through his hair. This was a man in complete control, she realized, wondering how she could ever have doubted him. "My apologies, Captain," she mumbled as she turned away, anxious to extract herself from her embarrassing position.

"Mademoiselle," Jonathon called out, stopping her, "that was very brave of you." He meant it. Most women would have run screaming to hide below at the first sound of gunfire. He knew of no other women, and very few men, who would have shown enough courage and brains to take command of a ship under fire.

She turned slowly back, a rueful smile on her lips. "That was very stupid of me, Captain. But as there was no other vessel in harbor, I naturally assumed the English ship was firing at us."

"That's where you're wrong, then. There is another ship in harbor. Come, I'll show it to you."

Genevieve frowned, and scanned the horizon once again. "I see no other ship," she stated flatly, reluctantly joining him at the rail. She didn't notice that Ty quietly slipped away.

"Look again, it's right there. His Majesty's Ship, *Diamond Rock*."

She leaned against him, the top of her head tucking neatly against his shoulder, as she followed the line of his arm to where he was pointing. "All I see is a large rock," she said as she turned to study his face, sure he was deliberately teasing her.

The scent of her hair drifted up and around him, making it more than a little difficult for him to concentrate. "That's a warship, not a rock," he stated flatly, then, at her puzzled expression, continued, "As you know, fifty years ago the ownership of this island was greatly contested by both the French and the English. During the course of the battles that followed, the English succeeded in landing a party of two hundred sailors on that rock, complete with cannons and other arms, and declared that the rock was now a warship, the H.M.S. *Diamond Rock*. The position, as you can see, was ideal. From that point they were able to bombard any French vessel that tried to gain entrance to the harbor. The English held the rock for seventeen months, doing quite a bit of damage to the French fleet."

"What did the French do?" Genevieve asked, confident they were able to roust the English.

"For seventeen months, all attacks were repelled, until finally the French decided to embark on a different stratagem. Learning that the English were growing weary of their isolation, they caused a boat laden with rum to run aground on *Diamond Rock*. That had the expected effect: the British forces made short work of the rum, and thereafter the French had no difficulty in taking the rock."

Genevieve smiled approvingly, proud of her countrymen's ingenuity. Jonathon smiled, too, noting her obvious pleasure in the story. "To this day, British vessels still give the rock a twenty-one-gun salute. That's what you heard this morning," he finished.

She opened her mouth to make a disparaging comment about her overreaction, but the remark died on her lips as they rounded the southern corner of the island and entered Martinique's main harbor, Fort-de-France. There she saw, for the first time in months, the *tricolore*, the flag of France, waving boldly in the wind. Her throat tightened as she realized what lay at stake, for if she failed to prove her father's innocence, she would lose everything. Not only her lands and property, but her country as well.

Jonathon felt her stiffen at his side and followed her gaze to the harbor, but saw nothing unusual there. Aware, however, that the moment of easy companionship they'd shared had passed, he decided to press her for more information about the treasure. "You never did answer my question last night," he said. "Exactly how much money are we talking about?"

Genevieve tensed. "Do you mean, how much are you going to be able to extort from me in return for your miserable assistance?"

"I don't recall asking you to translate every word I utter, mademoiselle," he replied, biting back a grin. "Nor do I recall ever asking for a single penny from you. If and when we do find this treasure of yours, however, I expect to receive half," he stated, hoping to firmly fix greed in her mind as his only reason for searching for the treasure. The less she knew about his real motivation, the better.

"Half!" she cried, her sapphire eyes widening in shock.

"Of course."

"I hate to disappoint you, Captain, but the treasure is not mine to barter with. It belongs to the state of France. All of it."

"Ah, I see. Doubtless you feel that I should just be noble and assist you. Well, I hate to disappoint you, mademoiselle, but if you're looking for a knight in shining armor—"

"Ha! You, a knight in shining armor. Believe me, Captain, I have no illusions about that whatsoever."

"Come now, mademoiselle, I don't think you're being entirely honest," he teased, watching the sparks of anger that lit her magnificent eyes. "You'd love to see me in that suit of armor. Just think how quickly I'd sink once you pushed me overboard."

Genevieve bit her lip and turned away, refusing to let him see her smile. "The point is, Captain," she continued stubbornly, "once we've recovered the treasure, I expect that my father's properties will be returned to me, and I'll pay you for your time and efforts myself. You need only name your fee; I can assure you I'll be able to meet it."

"Most women," he reminded her, noting the distaste in her voice, "would be more than a little grateful for the assistance I'm offering."

"Most women," she retorted, "do not find themselves at the mercy of a complete rogue they neither trust nor like."

Jonathon clutched his heart, feigning a mortal wound. "Not like me!" he said. "Now that pains me, it truly does." He flashed a wicked pirate's grin, his even, white teeth glistening against his bronzed skin. She noted how his eyes glowed, the amber perfectly matching the deep, golden streaks the sun had woven into his hair.

"I notice you don't object to my not trusting you," she said doggedly, refusing to be swayed by the pull of his rugged charm.

His expression softened and grew solemn as he looked into her eyes. "Your trust is something I intend to earn, Genevieve."

She caught her breath. Though he hadn't moved, she felt as though her skin had just been lightly stroked. "I don't recall giving you permission to use my Christian name," she said tightly, forcing herself to protest.

"You did, Genevieve, when we agreed to work together. How else could I introduce you to Martinique, but as a dear friend who's come to visit Tyler and me? We shall be the best of friends for the next few weeks, or at least appear to be."

Genevieve frowned as she mulled that over. He was right, a friendly front would attract less attention than obvious sparring, and the last thing she wanted was curious eyes prying into her business. She sighed. "Very well, Captain."

"Say it," he ordered.

"I don't see what difference it—"

"Say it."

Genevieve set her mouth tightly, but was unable to escape the warm eyes that bored into her. Finally, she relented. "Jonathon."

He leaned back, a triumphant glow in his eyes and a small smile tugging at the corners of his mouth. "Very good. Perhaps one day, with a little practice, you may even be able to say it without looking as though you've just bitten into a lemon."

Genevieve gave him one last, exasperated look, then lifted her skirts and moved smartly away, heading back to the cabin to complete her toilette in time to disembark. The captain watched her walk away, then went back to his duties, guiding the *Liberty* into her tight berth and setting the crew to unloading her cargo. Ty found him at the rail, watching as the crate containing thousands of dollars worth of ruined silks was lifted and stacked on the dock. "Those silks were quite a heavy loss," he commented.

Jonathon shrugged noncommittally. "We've had worse."

"Hmmm," Ty drawled. He wasn't ready to let it go. "Then again, maybe you came out ahead. A crate of silks in return for Genevieve. I'd say you—"

"Was there something you wanted, Brother?" Jonathon cut him off, drawing himself up to his full height and assuming his most commanding expression.

Ty grinned, knowing Jonathon well enough to recognize just how far he could push him. He was sure Genevieve had found a place in his brother's heart, but wisely decided to refrain from sharing that piece of knowledge with Jonathon.

Let the two of them fight that one out, he decided. It would be much more amusing, and safer, to simply watch from a distance. "Actually," he answered, "I thought we should finish our conversation from this morning. The cannons have quit, so I assume we won't be interrupted again."

Jonathon nodded, his expression serious. He'd confided completely in Ty, and they'd spent the morning discussing and discarding various strategies for finding the treasure and entrapping whoever was responsible for the arms stockpile. "There is one more thing. If anything should happen to me, I'm depending on you to see Mlle. DuPres safely back to France, or wherever she wants to go. See that she has money and is properly taken care of."

"Of course," Ty responded automatically. The request was disturbing, however, for it was unlike Jonathon to speak so grimly. He frowned, asking, "Is there something you haven't told me?"

Jonathon shook his head, watching the activity on the busy dock below, his eyes scanning the carriages which passed through the busy streets.

"If there is a connection between General DuPres and the arms collectors," Tyler said with a searching look at Jonathon, "then we've charted a course directly into a hurricane. I have a feeling that whoever we're up against is deadly serious."

Jonathon drew a hand through his thick hair, agitation written clearly on his face. "Don't you think I've thought of that? What would you have me do, lock Genevieve in chains until we've resolved this?" he asked. "You've seen how stubborn she is: no matter what I do, she'll get to Martinique one way or another. At least this way I'll be with her every step of the way. If things get too rough, I'll put her back in that damned crate myself, and ship her back to France."

"Why don't you just try to reason with her? Genevieve's intelligent, surely she'll see how foolhardy it is for her to continue."

Jonathon turned, giving his younger, less experienced

brother a pitying glance before responding. "Try to reason with a woman? That's like trying to drown a fish. It can't be done, it goes against nature."

Ty grinned at the sardonic comment, then watched his brother's eyes light up as Genevieve approached, looking fresh and beautiful, glowing with an inner radiance as she rushed toward them. "Ah, but some of them are certainly lovely, aren't they?" he commented softly.

Jonathon caught the remark and nodded, a look of silent understanding passing between them before he turned to Genevieve. "Ready?" he asked briskly.

Genevieve nodded quickly, stopping herself just short of childishly grabbing the captain's hand in her excitement and pulling him down the gangplank. After what seemed to her to be an eternity of last-minute details, they left the ship and were strolling along the docks of Fort-de-France. Tucked safely between her two tall, handsome escorts, Genevieve was too busy taking in the sights around her to be aware of the admiring looks they drew.

Martinique was a wild swirl of color, scent, and sound, with people of every shade mingling easily, voices in every dialect imaginable shouting and laughing. Trade winds blew gently, carrying with them echoes of distant melodies and the soft beating of island drums. Genevieve drank it all in, deciding almost instantly that it was the most exciting, exotic place she'd ever seen.

Before she knew it, Jonathon was handing her into an open carriage and they were leaving the busy harbor, heading up the rocky coast for the bustling city of St. Pierre. The carriage swung up the steep incline, offering Genevieve a magnificent view of Fort-de-France, the ships in the harbor becoming little more than tiny specks as they climbed swiftly up. She jostled around, craning her neck for one last look.

The journey passed quickly, with Jonathon and Ty both pointing out sights of interest and relating stories of the island's colorful history. Lulled by the soft sway of the carriage and the sun resting like a warm, friendly arm on her shoulders, she closed her eyes and leaned back, smiling as she listened to the two men talk. They were brothers, all right, shooting stinging barbs at each other one minute, the next laughing in easy camaraderie at references made deliberately vague because of her presence.

She must have dozed off, for when she opened her eyes again the road had widened and was considerably smoother. It took a moment for her dulled senses to realize that the rich, masculine scent she was inhaling was the captain. She had snuggled up against him as she slept, using his broad shoulder as a pillow and pressing her face against his upper arm. She jerked away, her cheeks flushing with embarrassment. Jonathon said nothing, but she received a groan from Ty as she elbowed him in the ribs in her haste to back away from the captain.

In an attempt to escape the sudden awkwardness she felt, she directed her attention outside the carriage. The land had changed considerably from the rugged beauty she had seen earlier. It was now cultivated, a waving green sea of sugarcane stalks which flowed down gently sloping hills and into the blue waters of the Caribbean. Traffic on the road had increased also, and she looked on in fascination as ornate carriages bore ladies along, while finely dressed gentlemen reined in their prancing horses to exchange greetings.

"This doesn't seem real," she breathed, and was even more awestruck as they entered the city of St. Pierre. Jonathon directed their carriage down wide boulevards, past spectacular architecture and classic public buildings. She gazed in wonder as they passed a theater marquis announcing the arrival of a performing company whose name she recognized from its huge success in France. She strained her ear, listening. Though the public signs were all in French, what she heard was slightly altered, spiced with rhythms, words, and intonations that were distinctly foreign to her. "It's so like France, and yet not like it at all."

Jonathon smiled, watching her face glow like an exuberant child's on Christmas morning. "That's why St. Pierre is
often referred to as the Paris of the Caribbean," he said.
"Just imagine Paris if it were lifted up and placed on a
warm, exotic island."

"Yes," she agreed immediately, "that's it exactly. But how
can that be?"

"Martinique was largely settled by French aristocrats
fleeing from the Terror," he explained. "They've re-created
that society, blending it with the dark, tribal customs of
Africa, and the plantation lifestyle of the Southern states."
He drew the horses in, stopping at what looked to be the
city's most exclusive district. "I have some business to
attend. Tyler, why don't you show Mlle. DuPres around? I
shouldn't be too long."

Ty agreed immediately, jumping out of the carriage to
assist Genevieve, but Jonathon was there before him. He
ignored the hand she offered and clasped her firmly by her
slender waist instead, lifting her easily.

"Thank you, Captain, I believe I can manage from here,"
she said as soon as her toes touched the ground.

He slowly dropped his hands and took a step back, his
eyes locked into hers. "It's Jonathon," he reminded her
quietly, then turned and strode away.

Genevieve suddenly realized she'd been holding her
breath. She let it out as she turned to Ty and offered him a
shaky smile. "Shall we go?" she asked. She wasn't sure
what she'd read on the captain's face in that instant when
he'd held her, but whatever it was had left her decidedly
unsteady.

Ty offered her his arm as they strolled together, both of
them glad for the opportunity to stretch their legs after the
long carriage ride. The city was rich in parks, and they
meandered slowly about, pausing to enjoy the profusion of
lush, native flowers and cascading water gardens. They also
walked through St. Pierre's busy shopping district, Genev-

ieve pausing to look into the windows of the rich shop fronts as they passed.

But after a while she began to feel distinctly but unaccountably uncomfortable. She glanced at Ty to see if he felt it, too, but he only appeared slightly bored by all the shops. At that moment two fashionable women passed opposite them, and Genevieve realized the reason for her discomfort. Because she had been aboard ship for so long, and before that had been working night and day in Paris, she no longer paid any heed to her appearance. That was all too obvious, she realized now with a sudden feeling of shame as she saw the women's admiring glances at Ty, then heard their high-pitched giggles as they looked at her.

Genevieve blushed, looking down at herself. The gown she wore was ridiculously short, baring her ankles scandalously. She had pulled off all the fussy ribbons and bows, trying to make it simpler and more dignified, but had only succeeded in leaving it plain and ugly. The fit was horrible, too, hanging loosely at the bodice and waist. She had pulled her hair back into a neat chignon at the nape of her neck, but she had no hat, nor even a parasol to shield her from the midday sun.

"Ty," she said, now painfully self-conscious. "I'm a little tired. Do you suppose we could go back to the carriage?"

"Of course," Ty answered immediately. "You must be hot and thirsty, too. I know a place we can rest for a bit and have a cool drink."

"No, really. Thank you, but I think I'd rather just wait in the carriage," she insisted, tugging at his sleeve.

"In the hot sun?" He frowned, not moving.

Genevieve let out an exasperated breath, realizing that standing still in the middle of the busy walkway, they were only calling more attention to themselves. She whirled around to leave, hoping he would follow, and slammed into the solid wall of Jonathon's chest. "Going somewhere?" he drawled, reaching out to steady her.

"Genevieve was just saying she's a little tired," Ty answered for her.

Jonathon frowned, holding her at arm's length as he studied her beautiful face, wondering what had upset her so. He felt her stiffen as a group of finely dressed women walked by and had his answer. "Not *too* tired, I hope, for we've still some business to attend."

"If you don't mind, Captain, I'd just as soon wait for you in the carriage——"

"I said *we've* some business to attend, Genevieve," he said firmly, silently reprimanding her for not using his name as he took her arm and led her away.

"I'll meet you at home," Ty called after them, suddenly taking off in the opposite direction. If he wasn't mistaken, the auburn-haired beauty that had just passed, swirling her bright yellow skirts as she walked, was Clayton Moore's younger sister. And from the looks of her, little Amy had definitely grown up. He hurried off, anxious to catch up with her.

Jonathon led Genevieve to one of the fine apparel shops she'd noted earlier, then ushered her in. "Captain Morgan, it is always a pleasure," a warm voice called from across the room. Genevieve looked up and saw a large woman, with deep brown skin and even darker eyes. Despite her massive girth she moved smoothly, her bright, multicolored skirts floating around her as she approached. Like the other women of color whom Genevieve had been noticing, she wore a madras turban wrapped around her head, leaving one colorful end sticking straight up like a great plume.

Jonathon greeted her fondly, then turned to present Genevieve. "It is a pleasure to meet any friend of Captain Morgan's," Mme. Latourre said. Her smile was large and genuine, and Genevieve could feel some of the tension begin to melt away.

"Mlle. DuPres's trunks were lost on our journey, she'll need some new things immediately. I trust you'll be able to help us."

Before Genevieve could remark on that, Mme. Latourre took her hand and pulled her toward the back of the shop, then began piling fabrics on the counter in jolly abandon, overwhelming her with the luxury of choice. "I don't need that much, really," she protested. "Perhaps one or two simple day dresses"—she glanced behind her to make sure the captain was not within earshot, then lowered her voice—"and some undergarments."

"*Chérie*, we will find you beautiful things." Madame smiled reassuringly and patted her hand, then continued to make a small mountain of fabrics on the counter before her. "Now, there is so much, and it is all so beautiful, *non*? Where do we begin?"

Genevieve looked back at the captain for help, but he simply sent her a devilish grin, settling himself into one of the large, sturdy chairs that had been brought into the shop expressly for the comfort of husbands who chose to accompany their wives. She sighed and turned back to the fabrics before her, chewing her lip. She ran her hand hesitantly over the fabrics, finally lifting a soft blue crepe, her eyes full of uncertainty as she looked to Mme. Latourre for approval.

"Ah, *oui*. This will make your eyes sparkle like the sea." Madame praised her choice, lifting the fabric and setting it aside. The second choice was harder to make. She was torn between a deep rose brocade and a soft, buttery-gold cotton. Watching her, Mme. Latourre smiled again, spreading out both fabrics. "Mademoiselle has excellent taste. The rose will make your skin glow like the dawn, the yellow will make your hair shine like the sun."

Genevieve laughed at her effusive flattery. "You have a lovely way with words, madame, but I do not need so much. Just the yellow, if you please."

Mme. Latourre frowned, looking past Genevieve to the captain, but he didn't appear to be listening. It was strange, this beautiful young woman's reluctance. Captain Morgan had brought other women into the shop over the years, but they had not been satisfied until they'd bought nearly everything in the shop, whether it suited them or not. "Surely mademoiselle will need more than two gowns."

Genevieve stubbornly shook her head, her pride not allowing her to accept more than what was absolutely necessary. She conferred with Mme. Latourre briefly over the sketches she had available, selecting two simple styles, then stepped into the dressing room to allow Madame's assistant to get the measurements she required. She heard Mme. Latourre and the captain speaking in the outer room, but could not make out their muffled voices. When she reappeared, however, Madame was definitely happier than when she'd left her. As they prepared to leave her eyes swept around the room, taking in the elegant furnishings of the shop. "Have you forgotten something?" Jonathon asked, noting her frown.

Genevieve hesitated. Mme. Latourre seemed so nice, so warm, but so had Mme. Nirvi. She faced her squarely, hoping the woman would not be offended. "I should like to see your workroom."

"My workroom?" Madame repeated. Young ladies did not care where their gowns came from, or who had to make them, as long as they were delivered in perfect condition and on time. She looked at Captain Morgan, wondering if he could make any sense of the strange request, but he looked as puzzled by it as she did. "Very well," she replied. "It is this way."

Genevieve followed her through a side door opening to a small garden courtyard. As they followed a smooth stone path to a separate building, they could hear the sound of upraised voices and soft, feminine laughter. As Madame reached for the door it flew open, two small children darting around her in play in the garden. Mme. Latourre gently stroked their heads as they ran by, then looked over her shoulder at Genevieve and smiled. "Louisa's children," she explained simply.

When they stepped into the workroom the laughter quieted, but Genevieve could tell it was due to the presence of a stranger, rather than fear of Mme. Latourre. Fabrics and notions were spread over large tables where the women were seated, working comfortably. The room was bright, sunshine and cool breezes flooding in from the large windows. A pot of soup bubbled in the small kitchen in back, sending a delicious, spicy aroma wafting across the room. Madame approached one of the women and draped a loving arm across her shoulders. "My girls, you see how hard they work? They will make you beautiful things, *n'est-ce pas?*"

Genevieve smiled and nodded. "I'm sure the gowns will be lovely," she agreed. She returned to Jonathon with a satisfied smile on her lips. "Everything is just fine. You may purchase the gowns here."

Jonathon held the door for her, then fell into step beside her as they walked back to the carriage. "So that's what that was all about. You wanted to make sure the quality of workmanship met your high standards," he teased, a little surprised to find her so fussy.

Genevieve stopped, staring up at the captain with innocent blue eyes. "No, that wasn't it at all," she said automatically, then hesitated, not sure how to explain her actions without revealing too much about herself. "I wanted to make sure the women who worked there were treated properly, that's all. Sometimes the conditions in those shops, even the nicest ones, can be quite horrible."

Jonathon frowned, something in her tone making him grow uneasy. "How is it that you know so much about the conditions in workshops?"

"They have shops in Paris, too, Captain," she answered evasively.

Jonathon studied her, the truth painfully obvious despite her proud posture. "I see," he said grimly. He, too, was aware of the brutal conditions that were so common in workshops throughout Europe.

Genevieve, aware that he'd deduced far more than she'd wanted him to, lifted her chin. "I was given nothing but the best when my father was alive, Captain. After he was gone, it became necessary for me to seek employment. There is nothing shameful in working to support oneself."

"You're right," he said softly, his eyes full of compassion. "Did they treat you well?"

She lifted her slim shoulders. "I was treated like all the others," she answered fairly.

He felt his stomach tighten at her awful, but honest answer. "You won't ever have to go through that again," he swore.

"I know that, Captain," she answered brightly. "Because you and I are going to succeed."

Something she couldn't define passed through those golden eyes, then he smiled at her slowly, a wide, roguish grin that made her heart flip. "Yes, Genevieve, we are," he agreed huskily. He took a step forward and she forgot all about the people walking by, who had to dodge to get around them. She held her breath as he extended his hand to lightly cup her chin, raising her eyes to meet his. "And my name," he whispered in a voice that sent chills down her spine, "is Jonathon."

CHAPTER NINE

The open-air market of Martinique was even more bustling, more exciting to Genevieve than the city itself had been. She strolled slowly with the captain, feasting her eyes on all the new sights and sounds. All around them upended boxes and rough trestle tables had been set up for vendors to exhibit their wares: mounds of breadfruit, mangoes, pigeon peas, and fish so fresh their scales shimmered in the sunlight, as if they were still trying to swim away. Children ran and played underfoot, dogs barked, and chickens pecked at fallen scraps.

A dark hand reached out, extending three perfect oranges. "Here de best, m'sieur," said a voice in the softly slurred accent of the islands.

"De mon want bananas," interposed another vendor. "Look here, sah."

"Look, sah" became a chorus and Jonathon laughed, shaking his head as he took Genevieve's hand to pull her through the thick crowd.

"Fry fish and *bammy*!" called a woman who was moving gracefully among the jostling vendors while miraculously managing to keep her wares balanced on her head. Jonathon motioned her over and she lowered her tray. After Genevieve declined the fish, he purchased two pieces of *bammy*, handing one to her.

Genevieve nibbled on the sweet, crunchy cake while they walked on. Glancing from time to time at the captain as he guided her through the market, she couldn't help noticing how ruggedly handsome he looked. He also seemed to be in utter control, standing head and shoulders above the rest of the men there, radiating an aura of complete confidence and authority. He held her arm as they meandered about, and she found that that slight contact, as well as her own sheer physical awareness of him, left her almost dizzy.

Desperate for a chance to calm her racing pulse, she pulled away, pausing at a table to admire a display of hand-stitched laces. Jonathon immediately pulled a coin from his pocket. "Which do you like?" Genevieve shook her head and tried to back away, but he wouldn't allow it. "It might be cool later, on the ride home," he explained. Knowing he would not let her refuse, she selected a delicate pattern and he placed it on her shoulders, brushing his fingers along the base of her neck as he settled the shawl.

Genevieve shivered, his gentle touch stirring every nerve in her body. "I suppose you're right"—she laughed unsteadily in an attempt to cover her reaction—"it is getting a little chilly." Jonathon made no comment, nor did he need to, for the bright sunlight overhead and the thin film of perspiration on her brow were enough to belie her excuse.

He led her out of the market, stopping for a moment at a large display of coconuts. He pointed to his choice from atop the pile, which the vendor then quickly procured. There was a flash of silver as he swung his razor-sharp cutlass, slicing the top neatly off the nut before he handed it to Jonathon.

They left the noisy market behind, stopping at a small, secluded clearing overlooking the white sand and turquoise sea below. Genevieve leaned back against a tall palm, sighing softly as she took in the beauty of the island. Wild orchids clung to swaying vines, and the sweet fragrance of lilies and jasmine filled the air. Large butterflies floated by, moving from lush, overgrown ferns to sturdy mangroves. "It's like one large garden," she breathed.

Jonathon nodded and joined her under the shade of the tall palm, stretching a muscular arm overhead to support himself as he leaned in toward her. "I thought you might like something to drink," he said, offering her the coconut.

Genevieve nodded weakly, accepting the coconut with both hands. She knew it wasn't thirst that was making her tremble, but was unable to define exactly what she needed. Uncertain of what else to do, she lifted the large brown nut and brought it slowly to her lips. Tipping back her head, she opened her mouth, allowing the sweet milk to trickle slowly down her throat. It was delicious, cool, and light, not at all heavy and thick, as she had thought it might be. Smiling, she lowered it, and noting his hungry expression, offered a sip to the captain.

Jonathon's eyes never left her face as he took the nut from her hand and dropped it carelessly on the smooth green grass beneath their feet. Moving with hypnotic grace, he brought a finger to her mouth and gently wiped a drop of the white juice from her bottom lip. With his golden eyes languid and his lips slightly parted, he lowered his face toward hers and Genevieve felt her heart slam against her ribs. He paused for an instant, and she knew he was giving her the chance to pull away.

She didn't.

She wanted him to touch her, to kiss her. She wanted to know if that would make the strange tightening she felt in her stomach every time he was near finally go away. She closed her eyes and pursed her lips, unconsciously arching her back toward him.

Jonathon nearly groaned, overwhelmed by the innocence and beauty of her reaction. Wrapping a strong arm around her, he pulled her to him, his mouth slanting firmly over her own. Genevieve was shocked at first by the roughness of his kiss, for it was unlike anything she'd ever experienced. Soon, however, her shock eased, and she leaned into him, suddenly needing more. Jonathon felt her soft curves press against him, and he reacted instinctively, using the gentle, insistent pressure of his jaw to part her lips, then slipped his tongue inside her mouth.

Genevieve stiffened, jolted by such intimate contact, then slowly relaxed, melting into a sea of sensation. She drew her hands up and over his broad chest, loving the rock-solid, hard masculinity of his body. She let her hands rove, exploring the muscles of his powerful shoulders and thick arms, while her tongue explored his mouth. She felt him shifting, pulling her down with him onto the damp grass, but was too weak to protest, and too swept away to care. She lay atop him in a blissful, tangled embrace, their bodies locked, moving in an instinctive, primitive rhythm of desire.

Jonathon could taste the sweet milk on her tongue; it drove him wild, and he probed her mouth as if he meant to devour her. He drew a hand slowly, caressingly up her thigh, cupping her shapely bottom as he pulled her tightly to him. He finally tore his mouth away from hers, his firm, sensuous lips nibbling gently on her earlobe, then leaving a trail of burning kisses down her neck. The coarse, dark stubble on his cheeks grated softly against the smooth, creamy skin of her breasts, sending a shiver of pleasure racing down her spine. Moving with practiced ease, he pushed her gown gently off her shoulders.

He drew back, a fire lighting his eyes as his hungry gaze swept over her, taking in the glorious mass of thick, honey-colored hair that tumbled over her shoulders, the soft, rosy-tipped perfection of her breasts, her slender body, and the delicate arms that reached out to hold him. He pulled her fiercely to him, his mouth reverently covering the sweet, tight bud of her nipple. He felt her body tense, trembling against him in response to his touch, her nails raking slowly down his back.

He groaned, amazed at the raw passion she'd unleashed. "My God, Genevieve," he said, his voice deep and husky in her ear, "if I'd known it was going to be like this, we never would have left my cabin."

Genevieve heard the words as if from a great distance before they finally penetrated her foggy brain. Her senses came slowly back to her, and she gasped as she realized that any and all restraint she'd ever possessed had completely abandoned her. With a strength born of pure panic, she pushed against his chest, breaking free from his embrace, and sat up. "Captain," she cried, tugging her gown hastily back into place, "Captain, let me go."

Jonathon frowned. "Captain, is it? I would think after that little exchange you might finally be willing to call me by my given name."

Genevieve flushed deeply, lowering her head to concentrate exclusively on her clothing, which had been pulled into complete disarray. She was mortified that she had behaved so wantonly.

Jonathon ducked his head, trying to see her face, but it was hidden from him, veiled by her thick, golden hair. He sensed her discomfort and wanted to pull her back into his arms and assure her that there was no shame in what had passed between them, but knew she would not welcome his touch right now. He tried a lighter, teasing approach to break the silence between them instead. "Come now, Genevieve, don't tell me you've never been kissed before."

Genevieve thought back to Armand's chaste, dry pecks. They had been pleasant, of course, but had left her totally unmoved. How could the two be compared? How could a kiss be such a totally different thing? "No. Yes. I mean, not like that," she stammered in response to the captain's question.

She looked up at him, her confusion and embarrassment immediately vanishing as she noted the self-satisfied expression in his eyes, as if she'd just paid him a compliment. She clenched her small fists, wanting more than anything to knock the smug look off his face. "I was treated with respect," she clarified. "I was kissed properly, the way a gentleman is supposed to kiss a lady. Something you would never understand."

"Really," Jonathon said, a teasing lilt to his voice. "Why don't you show me?"

"That's hardly necessary, Captain. We've already established that you've had limited contact with ladies of any quality, so that lesson would simply be a waste of time."

"Ah, I see. Since I've no ladies of quality in my life, and no one has ever accused me of being a gentleman, a lesson in proper kissing would just go to waste."

"Exactly," she said primly, wishing to end the conversation.

But Jonathon would not let it go, fascinated by his discovery of her natural, instinctive passion, which she clearly struggled so hard to keep in check. Not to mention what the sight of her beautiful little body had done to him. "Perhaps you could at least satisfy my curiosity and tell me what it's like," he requested politely. At the tight set of her mouth he continued, "Chaste, modest, quick, is that what you want?" he asked, lifting a hand to her soft cheek.

Genevieve impatiently brushed his hand away. "Captain, you're trying to make a fool of me and—"

"Not at all. Forgive me for being confused, but I seem to recall that you kissed me back, and your response was quite—"

"Don't you understand?" she cried as she sprang to her feet. "That shouldn't have happened. That wasn't supposed to happen. I don't even like you!"

Jonathon was unable to squelch the shout of laughter that sprang to his lips. "You may not want to like me, Genevieve, but you do. Believe me, you do."

Genevieve drew herself up, glaring at him coldly. "You should have been born a spider, Captain. Think of all the fun you could have had seducing flies into your web." She swept haughtily past him, then stopped and turned back. "I, however, am not a fly. You would do well to remember that."

She did not miss the slight shaking of his broad shoulders as he struggled to hold back his amusement. "I'll try."

"Good. I trust we can put this whole episode behind us and proceed with what we came here to do," she finished in a brisk, businesslike tone.

Jonathon made a low, mocking bow. "By all means, do let us proceed," he agreed solemnly, but she would have had to be blind to miss the laughter that shone from his golden eyes as they turned to go back to the carriage.

When they got there, Genevieve moved to the far corner of the seat and stared silently ahead, trying to put as much distance between herself and the captain as she could. She tried to enjoy the lush scenery they passed, but was too upset to focus on anything other than her own body's betrayal. The captain had kissed her twice now, and both times she had behaved horribly, mindlessly, leaning into him as if his lips alone held the answer to all the questions she could feel but didn't know how to ask.

Genevieve sighed, trying to come to terms with what had happened. She had never felt so confused, so excited, so completely lost in her entire life. Even after her father had died, though she had suffered deeply, she'd had a plan of action, a course by which she could steer her life. Now she realized that such certainty was gone—if it had ever existed at all.

She let her thoughts wander, thinking of her life in Paris, and of Armand. They had become engaged four years before, when she was sixteen. The wedding had been set for her eighteenth birthday, though as events unfolded on Martinique, it became clear that would not happen. Earlier, however, her father had championed the match between them, his daughter and his first officer, for he had loved them both. And Genevieve had loved Armand. He was a dashing, gallant officer, ten years her senior—her protector when she was a young girl, and later, her suitor.

There had been no passionate declarations of love, nor did Genevieve remember quite clearly when and how their decision to marry had come about. It just seemed to always have been there, understood. The general had brought Armand into their family years ago, treating him like a son. In fact, the two of them were often mistaken for brother and sister, their physical resemblance was so striking. Both were tall and slim, with thick golden hair and deep blue eyes. Moreover, they suited one another, Genevieve's bright smile and sunny disposition a perfect match for Armand's carefree outlook on life. All in all, it had seemed the most natural thing in the world that they should marry.

Genevieve forced her thoughts back to the present and glanced at the enigmatic man seated beside her. He was nothing like Armand. Nor was he appealing to her in any way, she reminded herself. She had obviously been intoxicated by the beauty of the island, overexcited, and her natural good sense had run away. It was natural that she had misplaced her pent-up emotions on the captain, she decided, charitably forgiving herself for her lapse in judgment—so long as it did not happen again.

That resolved, she brightened considerably, and began to enjoy the countryside they were passing through. Soon they pulled off the main road and onto a long, smooth drive, shaded on both sides by magnificent swaying palms. The carriage reached a crest in the hill, then swung down and to the right, and she blinked, certain the sun and heat were playing tricks on her eyes.

Before them was an enormous, dazzling white structure, surrounded by lush lawns and spectacular gardens. It was nestled in the foothills, with dark, rugged mountains behind it and fronted by a green field of sugarcane which tumbled downhill into the turquoise sea. An ornate system of canals flowed throughout the property, cascading into waterfalls and fountains, filling the air with shimmering rainbows. It looked like something from a dream; it couldn't be real. "What is that?" she asked in awe.

"My home."

"Your home?" Genevieve gasped.

"Surprised?" he asked as they neared, seeing the look of stunned disbelief on her face.

"Yes," she answered honestly. "It's beautiful. It looks like something from a fairy tale, or a castle in France."

Jonathon smiled, pleased at her reaction to his home.

"You're close," he admitted as they pulled into the wide, circular drive. "For generations this belonged to a family living in the Loire Valley. When they decided to leave France and seek their fortune on a plantation in Louisiana, they couldn't bear to leave their ancestral home behind, so they took it apart stone by stone, with the intention of rebuilding it in the States."

"So how did it come to you?" she asked as he assisted her from the carriage.

"Their ship ran aground in the Bahamas, leaving them stranded without money for repairs. I happened to be in port, so we struck a deal." Using any time available between sea voyages; he and his men had spent three years of backbreaking labor rebuilding it, and he was justly proud of the results.

"Ay, M'sieur Jon, welcome back," called a friendly voice from across the yard. Genevieve turned to see a giant of a man lumbering toward them, his shirtsleeves rolled up and sweat glistening on his dark skin. He smiled broadly at Jonathon, shaking his hand as they exchanged a few words of greeting.

"Genevieve, my overseer, Luc. He runs the place for me while I'm away." She nodded politely and Jonathon continued, "Luc, this is Mlle. DuPres. She'll be my guest for the next few weeks."

"It's a pleasure, mam'selle," he replied in a rich baritone. "Please let me know if there's anything I can do for you while you're here." He led the horses away, promising to meet Jonathon back in his study to go over various business matters.

Jonathon led her under a white wooden trellis which framed the front door, the delicate arch nearly hidden under masses of brilliant bougainvillea, and ushered her into his home. Genevieve glanced around, finding the inside of the house as attractive as the outside. The captain had ignored the current trend of the day, which called for fussy, overstuffed furniture, dark wallpaper, and heavy drapery,

choosing instead to create his own style, one which she
found a vast improvement. The elegantly proportioned
rooms were simply furnished, and had a gracious, lived-in
look. Louvered windows filtered both light and air, and the
rich mahogany floors were polished to a high sheen. A
breeze circulated by overhead fans stirred the sheer white
curtains at the French windows, providing a glimpse of the
garden outside. "Marie will show you to your room,
Genevieve. I'm sure you'd like to rest after that long ride."

Genevieve looked up, startled by the sound of Jonathon's
voice, for she had been engrossed in admiring her surroundings. Her eyes traveled past him to the woman who stood
waiting, presumably for her, at the foot of the stairs. She was
incredibly lovely, straight and tall, with deep golden skin
that glowed like satin. She wore a long, flowing, green silk
robe, a yellow madras about her neck, and a green-and-
yellow handkerchief for her hair. Three large gold hoops
swung from each ear as she nodded at Genevieve, a serene
smile on her face. "If Mam'selle is ready, I will take you to
your room." Her voice flowed like honey. "Shall I send
someone for your trunks?"

Genevieve flushed. "Thank you, but I don't have—"

"Mlle. DuPres is having some things sent, Marie. Please
see that she finds everything she needs in the meantime,"
Jonathon interrupted her. Marie nodded graciously, apparently accepting that without question, and headed upstairs.

Genevieve paused, momentarily nonplussed by what the
captain had said. That was the second time he'd stepped in
to save her from the embarrassment of arriving without a
single possession or article of clothing. She was completely
unprepared for such a charitable gesture. She looked back at
him, trying to ascertain his motivation, but his expression
was completely unreadable. She turned and wordlessly
followed Marie upstairs.

The bedroom was surprisingly cool, with high ceilings
and fans that kept the tropical breezes moving. The furnishings were dark and simple, centered by a high four-poster

bed, draped with the same sheer white fabric that hung at the windows, giving the room a quiet, dreamlike quality. Genevieve walked to a table which held a delicate vase filled with freshly cut flowers, and she breathed in their sweet scent.

"Would Mam'selle care to rest before supper?" Marie inquired politely.

"Thank you, Marie, but I'm not at all tired. I think what I'd like most is to get the dust of the road off me."

"Certainly. I shall prepare a bath." Genevieve watched as Marie went to a window and called down to the women working below. In almost no time, buckets of steaming water were brought, by means of a sophisticated system of ropes and pulleys, right into the room. "M'sieur Jon says he got the idea from the rigging of his ship," Marie explained when Genevieve commented on the ingenuity of the system. "It does make bringing water in from the kitchens much easier. M'sieur Jon has a lot of ideas."

"I'm sure he does," Genevieve agreed cynically.

Marie made no comment, her back to Genevieve as she attended the bath water. "Mam'selle, the water is ready. May I help with your gown?" Genevieve welcomed her assistance, having spent the past week in almost contortionist positions trying to fasten and unfasten the stays of her gown by herself.

She sank gratefully into the oversized tub; it had been ages since she'd bathed properly. After the captain had rudely interrupted her bath that first night on board his ship, she'd warily taken no more than a quick sponge rinse each morning. The bathtub was large, allowing her enough room to fully stretch out. A soft, floral fragrance rose from the steam, and the water flowed over her skin like liquid silk. She closed her eyes and leaned back, a smile of pure pleasure on her lips. "Marie, this is heaven. Thank you."

"*Oui*, mam'selle. I've put herbs in the water to relax you and soothe your muscles."

"It's wonderful. How did you learn so much about herbs?"

"My grandmother was the *quimboisseur*, mam'selle," Marie informed her, her dark eyes shining with pride. "I do not have her gift for sight, but she taught me much about herbs and medicines."

Genevieve looked up at her curiously. *"Quimboisseur?"*

Marie nodded and went to a tall, mahogany armoire, pulling out a few delicate items of clothing as they talked. "*Oui*. The *quimboisseur* is a position of great honor. She is our seer, the one who will protect us from harm, as well as our doctor, who will heal us when we are ill. The gift is passed through generations, for it is my sister now who holds that power," she finished with a graceful shrug.

Genevieve rinsed the last of the fragrant soap from her hair, then wrapped a thick towel around herself and went to look at the garments Marie had laid out on the bed. She frowned, noting that they were remarkably similar to the ones she had worn while aboard ship. "Marie," she began, idly fingering the gown's frilly lace, "to whom do these belong?"

"Mam'selle Constance. She left them here long ago. I believe she has forgotten them."

Genevieve suspected otherwise. Doubtless the woman had planted a variety of personal articles around the captain's home, both to serve as a constant reminder of herself to Jonathon, as well as stake her territory against any other females. Her tactics were blatantly clear. Fortunately for Genevieve, she couldn't care less. Still . . . "Is she a close friend of the captain's?" She couldn't resist asking.

Marie shrugged noncommittally. "She has been a guest of M'sieur Jon's."

"A guest. I see," Genevieve replied, angrier than ever that she'd let the captain kiss her. The man was a complete rogue; he probably had hordes of women waiting for him in every port.

"Which gown does Mam'selle prefer?" Marie's calm voice broke into her thoughts.

None of them. Her angry blue eyes flashed back to the gowns arranged artfully on the bed, now more loath than ever to put one on. They were all excessively frilly, bedecked with a profusion of ribbons and bows. Genevieve shook her head in despair at the woman's lack of taste—in men as well as in gowns. "It doesn't matter," she finally answered. "They're all quite . . . feminine, aren't they?" She sighed resignedly as Marie helped her into a pale blue gown adorned with bright yellow lace and large pink silk roses.

Marie arranged her hair simply, sweeping the golden tresses up and away from her face, then securing it at the crown with a gold clasp and letting the magnificent curls tumble down her back. The style served to accent her high cheekbones and luminous sapphire eyes, but Genevieve saw none of that as she surveyed her appearance in the mirror. She grimaced, certain she looked like an absurd, overgrown doll. "Well," she said, injecting a false brightness into her voice, "I suppose I'm ready."

Jonathon and Ty stood as she joined them in the study. If they were amused at all by her attire, they mercifully did not show it. In fact, they had barely had time to exchange greetings when they heard the front door open, and a flurry of voices filled the entrance hall. "Never mind," a woman's voice scolded impatiently. "I know where the study is. I can announce myself. I'm sure the captain is quite anxious to see me." Jonathon and Ty exchanged a look of silent commiseration, bracing themselves for their visitor.

Genevieve jumped back as a small, dark-haired woman burst into the study. So intent was she on reaching the captain she probably would have run Genevieve down if she hadn't moved out of the way. "Jonathon, darling," she cried, her voice dripping sugar as she threw her arms around him. "It's so good to see you. I've missed you so." She leaned back, pouting as she realized that her embrace was not being returned. "Aren't you going to tell me how much you've missed me?"

Jonathon stepped neatly out of her embrace, holding her at arm's length. "Actually, Constance, I thought I might present you to our guest first."

Constance spun around, her eyes narrowing as she finally realized there was another woman in the room. "Your cousin, I presume, Jonathon," she said coldly, her dark eyes focused on Genevieve.

Ty gave a short bark of laughter. "I hate to disappoint you, Constance, but Jonathon and I haven't any cousins. And even if we did, I doubt we'd be fortunate enough to be graced with one as lovely as Mlle. DuPres."

Constance shot him a look of contempt. "How you do go on, Tyler," she said dismissively, moving toward Genevieve like a cat stalking its prey. "Allow me to present myself, mademoiselle. I am Miss Constance Prentiss. And this"— she paused to lift a finger to the sleeve of the gown Genevieve wore—"belongs to me."

Genevieve stiffened, amazed at the woman's rudeness. "I'm not at all surprised, Miss Prentiss," she replied, her gaze sweeping over the outlandish purple gown the woman was wearing. "Your sense of style is certainly unique. Marie offered it to me while I waited—"

"It was not Marie's gown to lend," Constance snapped, then caught herself as she saw Jonathon's dark brows draw together in a frown. "Of course, I don't mind your borrowing it," she interjected sweetly, "it's just a pity it doesn't fit properly. That waistband must bind you terribly."

The gown was loose and they both knew it. "Not at all," Genevieve answered with equal sweetness. "'Tis not the fit that's uncomfortable, but the design. Now that we've met, I can see how much more appropriate the gowns are for you, Miss Prentiss." She bit back a grin as she watched the wheels turn in Constance's head as she weighed that remark, trying to decide if she had been insulted or not.

"What are you doing in Martinique, Constance?" Jonathon asked abruptly.

Constance turned her back on Genevieve, abruptly dismissing her. "Darling," she purred, "that was so naughty of you, leaving Charleston like that. Daddy had some business down here with Uncle Douglas, and I just insisted he take me along."

"Daddy," Jonathon knew, was Franklin Prentiss, and her uncle was Douglas Phelps. They were two of South Carolina's most prominent spokesmen, especially as far as the issue of secession was concerned. "Here, on Martinique?" he asked, his tone casual. "What sort of business would bring them here?"

Constance shrugged. "Just business," she answered breezily. "Boring business if I know Daddy. Now aren't you going to be sociable and offer me something to drink?"

"Actually, we were just getting ready to dine—"

"Darling, of course," Constance purred as she locked her arm through his. "I know you don't like to be kept waiting for me," she said, looking up at him seductively.

Jonathon's golden eyes flashed irritation. "I take it I can convince you to join us."

"You can convince me to do anything," she replied in her huskiest voice, clinging to his arm like a drowning woman. Jonathon didn't answer, wanting more than anything to pry her fingers off his arm, but years of training in proper etiquette held him back.

Watching as they left the room, Genevieve did not fail to miss the triumphant smile on Constance's face. Her heart sank as she admitted to herself what a striking couple they made: Constance dark and petite, her luscious curves proudly displayed, her head nestled against the captain's broad shoulder as they walked. And Jonathon, so tall and ruggedly handsome . . .

"I would consider it an honor, Genevieve, if you would allow me to escort you in this evening." Her startled gaze flew to Ty, who offered her his arm and looked at her with warm brown eyes full of kindness. She flushed as she realized she had not moved since the others had left the room.

"Thank you, Ty." She lifted her chin, mustering up her brightest smile as she slipped her arm through his.

The dinner seemed endless. Constance took the seat next to Jonathon, taking every opportunity to touch his hand while they talked, whisper in his ear, or pour his wine. While the captain did not respond in kind, neither, Genevieve noted, did he pull away. Constance laughed and ate heartily, while Genevieve merely toyed with her food, finding it too difficult to swallow.

She listened to their light banter, and her stomach churned painfully with emotion. More than anything, she was angry with herself. Angry that she'd allowed herself to be attracted to the captain, who was so clearly an arrogant, self-centered womanizer, and worst of all, that her body had responded so traitorously. She could only look on as he responded to Constance's remarks—could only look on as the woman tossed back her head with shrill laughter, deliberately exposing a good deal of cleavage.

Constance fingered the necklace she wore, lifting the thin gold chain to reveal the small gold trinket nestled between her breasts. "Darling," she said, "I found this at a shop in Charleston. The woman assured me it was a good-luck charm, guaranteed to be the key to opening any man's heart." She thrust her bosom at the captain so he could better see the tiny key that hung from the chain, then turned to Genevieve to make sure she didn't miss the little scene she'd created. "Isn't this sweet, mademoiselle? It appears I've found the key to Jonathon's heart."

Genevieve looked up to see the captain, his eyes apparently locked on the other woman's breasts, and felt her spine stiffening with anger. She glanced at the tiny key, then returned Constance's overly sweet smile. "I do hope you didn't pay too much for that, Miss Prentiss. It would seem obvious that that key is far too large to open the captain's heart," she replied in her sincerest voice. "Perhaps they could find a smaller one for you," she suggested politely.

She heard an abrupt, choking sound from Ty, and watched as Constance's brows lifted in surprise and confusion, but it was the captain's response she was waiting for. To her amazement, he didn't scold her for her rudeness, or respond with a cutting remark of his own, as she'd expected of him. Instead, he leaned back in his chair, a lazy grin on his face as he studied her intently. "Was there any particular reason for that unjustified, unprovoked attack on my person, mademoiselle?" he drawled, his deep voice rich with amusement. "Or were you just bored with the conversation in general?"

Genevieve bravely met his stare, wishing she were anywhere else in the world, wishing the whole unpleasant evening would finally end, wishing she could control the erratic beat of her heart whenever she looked into his golden eyes. "My apologies, Captain," she said demurely. "How would I know if you even have a heart, let alone what size it is?"

Jonathon nodded, stretching a muscular arm across the back of the chair beside him. "Ah, yes, the size. Why is it that women are always interested in the size of a man's . . . attributes? Well, I can assure you, Genevieve, it's quite—"

"That's enough, Captain," Genevieve cut him off quickly, her cheeks burning as she conceded defeat. When it came to matters of a sexual nature, Genevieve knew very little. But she wasn't so sheltered that she didn't understand what he was referring to. "My remark was uncalled for, you may consider it withdrawn," she said, setting down her napkin as she gave up all pretense of trying to eat.

Jonathon, who'd been watching her throughout the meal, noticed instantly. "Is something wrong with the food? You haven't touched a bite."

She shook her head, avoiding his eyes. "The meal was wonderful, really—"

"How would you know that?" he teased. "You'd have to taste it to tell."

Genevieve looked up into his laughing, amber eyes, and his wicked grin once again made her heart flip, calling to mind how right his arms had felt about her that afternoon. She looked away. *You don't care*, she told herself, *it doesn't matter.*

But it did.

She saw Constance bring her hand to rest on Jonathon's thigh, and she knew she couldn't take it a second more. She leapt up from the table, hastily excusing herself, and dashed for the stairs to her room.

"Genevieve." Jonathon's voice from the foot of the stairs stopped her. She turned warily back, keeping her emotions tightly in check. "Genevieve, I'm sorry about tonight. This isn't the way I planned it—"

"No? And what did you have planned?" she asked harshly. "Let me see if I can guess. You wanted to seduce me before I met your mistress, is that it? Well, don't waste your time. Marie told me all about your 'guests,' and I've no intention of standing in line."

Jonathon's lips twitched despite himself. She was gorgeous. Her anger had brought a pink flush to her cheeks and fire to her sapphire eyes. His smile widened as he realized what her words revealed. "I do believe you're jealous."

"Jealous!"

"Certainly. And I can assure you, I find it most flattering."

"Ha!" she scoffed. "Your vanity is exceeded only by your imagination."

Jonathon sobered, his golden eyes glowing like twin flames. He answered softly, his deep voice like a gentle caress. "And I think you'll find, Genevieve, that there are absolutely no limits to my imagination."

Genevieve sucked in her breath. "I think," she said shakily, trying to put matters back in order, "that you and I have different goals. You've convinced me that I need your help in order to reach mine. Now let me convince you of something: all I want is to settle my father's affairs as quickly as possible so that I may return to France. I am not interested in your advances, Captain."

"Really." He took a step toward her.

"I mean it," she replied, backing away.

He kept advancing, moving in a single-minded pursuit of his one beautiful goal. Genevieve felt the wall come up against her back and she stopped, thrusting a hand against his solid chest to keep him at arm's length. "Your mistress is waiting for you."

"If you're referring to Constance, she's not my mistress, and I sent her home."

"How convenient. Do all your women follow your dictates so obediently?"

He stared down at her, running a finger along her delicate collarbone. "All but one. But I have faith that I can correct that."

"Captain—"

"Jonathon," he corrected firmly.

"Captain," she repeated stubbornly, brushing aside his fingers. "I am not one of your women, nor am I a toy for you to fondle at will. Ours is strictly a business relationship. If this is no longer satisfactory to you, please speak now and we will sever our arrangements."

Jonathon dropped his hand and stepped back a pace, a small smile playing about his lips at her prim little speech. "You're right, Genevieve, we do have important matters to see to. But no less important is the conclusion of what we began in the garden earlier today."

"That was a mistake. It's over."

"It's barely begun."

"Keep believing that, Captain," she retorted smartly, "and you'll set yourself up for a bitter disappointment."

Jonathon watched as she strode away from him, noting once again her seductive walk. "No, Genevieve," he answered softly, his eyes focused on her shapely bottom, "I won't be disappointed."

CHAPTER TEN

❧

Genevieve and Jonathon were riding through his estate in an open carriage. They'd breakfasted together peacefully enough, an unspoken truce between them, but still she'd been surprised when he'd invited her to accompany him as he toured his estate to view the progress that had been made in his absence. She'd accepted readily, anxious to acquaint herself with the island as quickly as possible. The morning sun beat down upon them as they rode along, making her glad for the oversized straw bonnet Marie had lent her, for it shielded her somewhat from the harsh rays. She glanced over at the captain, but unlike her, he seemed to be unaffected by the sun. He appeared as cool and collected as ever.

They had just gone north of his home, where coffee fields were planted in the relatively sheltered foothills. Now Jonathon directed the carriage due south, into a waving green sea of sugarcane. Genevieve was impressed by both the size and the scale of the operation, which appeared to run smoothly and efficiently. He stopped at a grouping of a dozen or more dwellings, all identical in shape and size, but each painted in a wild variety of color and patterns to reflect the owner's personality.

Genevieve frowned, staring at the cabins in puzzled fascination. "Didn't we just see those yesterday, on the eastern slopes?" she asked as they drew to a stop.

"Yes," Jonathon agreed. "Luc tells me they were just set up here this morning. The cabins have standardized dimensions to make them transportable, so the men can live near the field they're actually working," he explained as he assisted her from the carriage.

As at the other stops they'd made during the morning, Jonathon was greeted warmly and with obvious respect. This stop was unlike the others, however, for he stopped not only to visit the workers, but their families as well. Within minutes of their arrival he was surrounded by a boisterous group of native children. Genevieve watched as they shouted and laughed, tugging at his pants leg, the taller ones peering into the pockets of his linen jacket. Jonathon shook his head over and over, holding up empty hands with a solemn expression on his face, but the children weren't having it. They became louder and louder, laughing and pleading, until Jonathon finally picked up one little boy, placed him on his broad shoulder and walked back to the carriage, allowing the excited child to discover a hidden basket full of Marie's cookies and other home-baked treats. The little boy shrieked with joy, grabbed the basket, and went back to share his find with his friends.

Genevieve sighed, wondering how much longer she could continue to dislike the man.

Her thoughts were quickly diverted by the sound of a deep bell, which began suddenly and urgently to ring. She looked up, watching as the men who'd been working in the fields began to flee, and felt the sudden tension of the people gathered around her. "What is it?" she asked Jonathon, instinctively sliding up against him as she sensed danger.

"That bell was a warning," he answered, "meant to clear everyone immediately from the fields. Someone must have spotted a fer-de-lance in the stalks." He did a quick head count as he spoke, making sure all his men had made it out of the fields.

Genevieve recoiled in horror at the name of the poisonous snake. Its bite, she knew, was almost always deadly. "Is it gone?" she asked, automatically lifting her skirts as she nervously scanned the area around her feet.

Jonathon bit back a laugh as he watched her prancing on her toes, her skirts in one hand and a stick she'd grabbed in the other. "It's gone," he assured her as he swept her up into his arms, "though you needn't worry. I'm told snakes greatly prefer the taste of English or American flesh to the French. Too much garlic in your cuisine." Genevieve laughed self-consciously, knowing she had overreacted, but she was nonetheless relieved when the captain deposited her safely in the carriage.

They traveled in companionable silence the rest of the morning, returning to his home at midday. "There's a ball this evening to celebrate the beginning of Carnival," he said as they drew near. "I thought we should attend."

Genevieve frowned as she turned to study the captain. "Why?" she asked simply, wondering why he would want to waste their time at a ball when they should be out looking for the treasure.

"You mentioned several names at breakfast this morning, former acquaintances of your father's. They should all be in attendance this evening, should you want to meet them."

"I see," she replied quietly, then added, "Yes, I do." The chance she'd dreamed of for so long was finally here: someone on the island had betrayed her father, accusing him of stealing the treasure in order to protect himself, and tonight she would meet him. She wondered if she would be able to instinctively tell who it was.

"If you're worried about what you'll wear," Jonathon broke into her thoughts, misinterpreting her frown, "don't be. I've taken care of it."

Actually, she hadn't thought of that at all. She glanced up, surprised and amused, wondering if the captain's knowledge of women's fashions was as poor as most men's. "That must have been a little difficult. Surely Mme. Latourre hasn't had time to prepare anything."

"You're right—I'm afraid she hasn't. But I took the liberty last night of asking Constance to send you something suitable. It should have arrived by now."

Of course. Genevieve stiffened her spine, appalled at the thought of dressing up in his mistress's clothing. She held her tongue, biting back a scathing reply, for she knew she could not refuse. This was too important an occasion for her to miss, and she had nothing of her own to wear. Nothing at all, she realized as she looked down at the frilly gown she now wore, which also belonged to Constance. But that didn't make acceptance any easier. "Fine," she answered curtly, staring straight ahead as they swung into the wide, circular drive of his home.

"Genevieve, if I had anything else to offer you—"

"Thank you, Captain, but that won't be necessary. I'm sure whatever Miss Prentiss chose to send will suffice." She climbed down from the carriage stiffly, marching resolutely toward the house.

But she didn't quite make it in before his deep voice called out, stopping her. "There is one alternative, however."

She turned slowly around. "What alternative?"

"I happen to have a large supply of silks, you're welcome to use any of them—" Genevieve was eagerly taking in the idea, wondering if there was possibly enough time, when Jonathon abruptly brought his hand up, slapping it against his forehead as if suddenly remembering something. "What am I thinking of? That crate was ruined at sea. There was this rather large rat that stunk of fish, you see, and—"

Genevieve glared at him, sparks shooting from her sapphire eyes. "You, sir, are a menace," she said heatedly. "And you can spare me any further reminders, for I'm quite aware of my debt to you. I fully intend to make good the cost of the silks, as well as any other charges you've incurred on my behalf."

"I never asked you to," Jonathon answered quietly as he walked toward her. He placed his strong hands on her upper arms, silently forcing her to lift her gaze to meet his. "It's only a gown, Genevieve," he said after a long pause. "It doesn't matter."

She stared up at him, searching his eyes. He made her furious, then, within the space of seconds, subdued her with his touch. "Why are you doing this?" she asked. "Why are you helping me? It's obvious you don't need the money," she stated candidly, acknowledging what she had realized about the vast scale of his property.

Jonathon evaded her question. "Money is a powerful motivation for any man, regardless of the wealth he already holds."

"But not for you, I think," Genevieve replied slowly, studying his face. "You're like my father in that regard. He never would have sacrificed his honor for any amount of money."

He grinned at her unguarded words. "A compliment? Dare I hope I've been raised a notch in your esteem?"

Genevieve opened her mouth, then closed it, not sure what to say. "You still haven't answered my question, Captain," she stubbornly pointed out. "Why are you helping me?"

"Let's just say I believe in causes," Jonathon answered smoothly, taking her arm as he escorted her into his home.

The gown had arrived. Genevieve went directly upstairs, anxious to see what the captain's mistress had selected for her to wear. Her trepidation was well-founded. She stopped short, aghast at the sight of the hideous creation lying across her bed. It wasn't a gown, it was a punishment. But she couldn't for the life of her think of the crime she'd committed that was heinous enough to warrant it.

Aware that Marie was watching her, she put on a bright smile. "Well! I suppose I should try this on and see to the fit," she announced bravely, her voice unnaturally high. She slipped into the gown and turned. "There, it's not so bad, really," she lied, but her hope died completely when she saw the expression in Marie's eyes.

Giving up all pretense of cheerful optimism, she crossed to the mirror and studied her reflection. She was dressed in an absurd costume, she realized, not a gown. It was deep

red, with rows of black and yellow ruffles stitched to the
bodice, and blue lace hanging limply from the sleeves and
hem. It gathered thickly at her waist, then fell in heavy,
straight lines that stopped just above her ankles. "Oh,
Marie," she cried weakly, plucking at the long red feathers
which extended from the shoulders, "what am I going to
do?"

Marie crossed to her, moving with the smooth, easy grace
that seemed to be characteristic of the women of the island.
"Mam'selle, I am sorry, but that gown is truly horrible." She
circled Genevieve, her face thoughtful. "There is not much
time, but perhaps . . ."

"What?" Genevieve turned to her anxiously, ready to
agree to almost anything.

"Mam'selle, do you know how to sew?"

Genevieve thought of the countless hours spent at Mme.
Nirvi's. "Yes, Marie. I know how to sew."

"Good." Marie nodded approvingly. She turned Genevieve
back to the mirror and within minutes they had devised a plan
for major alterations. They worked well together, rapidly
tearing the gown apart and stitching it back together.

The afternoon flew by, but it wasn't until they had
finished completely that they stopped to share a light supper.
"Marie, I don't think I can ever thank you enough,"
Genevieve began, but Marie waved her words away.

"No, do not thank me. It is time M'sieur Jon had a good
woman. He is a good man, you two will be very happy
together."

Genevieve put down the bread she'd been eating. "Marie,
I don't think you understand. The captain and I have a
business arrangement, that's all. Once we've settled matters,
I shall return to France."

Marie shrugged, then continued as if she hadn't heard a
word as she went to the window and drew water for
Genevieve's bath. "My *quimboisseur* told me all of this
many weeks ago. She said that you were coming, and that
you would bring great treasures to this house."

"Treasures?" Genevieve echoed in alarm. The fewer people who were aware of her true purpose in coming to Martinique, the better.

"Yes," Marie answered, her dark eyes glowing with pleasure. "She said you would bring the greatest of treasures. Love, laughter, and later, many children. Girls with yellow hair like yours, and boys like their father. It will be very good, *n'est-ce pas?*"

Genevieve swallowed hard. Having seen the captain playing with the native children this morning, she had to admit that the thought of staying on this lovely island was appealing. To have children of their own one day, and share his life . . . With great effort, she reined in her thoughts, turning back to Marie. "That's quite out of the question," she replied stiffly. "In any case, the captain already has a—somebody."

Marie smiled knowingly. "You speak of Mam'selle Constance, *oui?* She wants M'sieur Jon, yes, but she does not love him. No, that is not good. She does not love anyone but herself."

Striving to keep her spirits from absurdly soaring at Marie's assurances, Genevieve continued, keeping her voice as neutral as possible, "Perhaps the captain is already in love with her." She stepped from the large tub, which Marie had once again sprinkled liberally with fragrant herbs, and wrapped herself in a bright robe. She seated herself at the dressing table, and Marie began brushing the tangles from her thick, wet hair.

Her touch was soothing, at once strong and gentle. "Have I told you of my man, Luc?"

"I met him yesterday. Captain Morgan didn't tell me he was your husband."

"He isn't. I do not think he is aware yet of how much he loves me. Soon I shall have to tell him." Their eyes met in the mirror, and the two women shared a knowing smile, their friendship firmly cemented. "Perhaps you must work a little bit on M'sieur Jon, *non?*"

Marie's hand rested softly on her shoulder, and Genevieve placed her own on top of it. "I don't think so, Marie," she answered firmly, "but I wish you all the best with Luc."

Marie clucked her tongue as she went to retrieve the gown from the bed. "My *quimboisseur* warned me you would be stubborn."

Genevieve finished dressing. While she wouldn't have selected the color herself, the deep red silk was indeed flattering, heightening the radiant glow of her skin. Devoid now of all excess ornamentation, the gown swirled gently around her as she moved. It had been recut and restyled, molded into the perfect picture of classic elegance. Marie had swept her golden hair up, piling it in luxurious waves at the crown, allowing a few wispy tendrils to escape and curl softly about the nape of her neck. A long red feather which had been removed from the gown now adorned her hair, giving her just the right dramatic touch.

She paused before going down, feeling as nervous as a debutante about to attend her first ball. "Go, *chérie*," Marie coaxed, seeing her hesitation. "M'sieur Jon will be waiting for you."

That thought did nothing to soothe Genevieve's nerves. Lifting her chin, she scolded herself for her foolishness. She had attended hundreds of balls in Paris, this was no different. Giving Marie a fleeting smile, she left the room.

Jonathon and Ty were waiting for her at the landing. Despite her resolve that this was an evening like any other, she felt her heart swell at the sight of her two handsome escorts. Ty was dressed in keeping with the day's fashion, his deep green jacket and rich brown trousers complementing his youthful blond good looks. Genevieve returned his warm smile, then turned to the captain.

Jonathon did not say a word as he moved toward her, his golden eyes locked on her as she slowly descended the staircase. He wore a black coat and trousers, both pieces expertly cut to emphasize his tall, muscular physique. His shirt was snow-white, the ruby that twinkled from within the folds of his cravat his only accessory. *Grace and power*, she thought as she watched him approach. "You look exquisite, Genevieve," he said as he took her hand.

"Thank you, Captain." She stopped two steps from the bottom, the extra height enabling her to meet his eyes without craning her neck back as she usually had to do. She had spent the entire morning in his company, but it felt as if it had been days, not merely one afternoon, since she had seen him last. She'd missed him, she realized with a start.

"I'd like it very much if you'd call me Jonathon." The request was softly put, not an order as before, and she couldn't help but acquiesce.

"Jonathon," she said softly.

He let out his breath, not realizing until that moment that he'd been holding it as he awaited her response. Their eyes held, and he felt an undeniable shift in their relationship, as if a crooked painting had just been righted. He silently searched her sapphire eyes, wondering if she felt it, too.

"Well, now that we have the business of names straight," Ty drawled, breaking into their private reverie, "I would think we're ready to depart." He studied Genevieve with admiring eyes as Jonathon placed the lace wrap she'd selected yesterday around her shoulders. "Did you say that gown is one of Constance's?"

"Hmmm," she replied absently, too distracted by the touch of Jonathon's fingers on her skin to pay attention to what Ty was saying.

"Strange, that's not really Constance's style. Far too demure, wouldn't you say, Jonathon?"

The captain agreed, thinking of Constance's gaudy creations and outlandish lingerie. What Genevieve was wearing was feminine and innocent, and a thousand times more provocative. He watched the way the red silk clung to her body, flowing into deep, graceful folds all about her as she moved. She was more enticing than anyone he'd ever seen in his life. He assisted her into the waiting carriage quickly, before he could give way to temptation and bring her back upstairs, strip the gown away, and explore the glorious curves that lay underneath.

Genevieve leaned back in the open carriage, letting her thoughts drift. She smiled as a soft breeze brushed her skin, carrying with it the sweet scent of the tropical flowers that bloomed all around them. The horses made their way steadily, their hooves beating out a gentle rhythm as they pranced along a familiar path illuminated by the moon.

They pulled up before a large, Southern-style mansion. Both the wide drive and the exterior of the house were covered with a deep black, shiny stone which gave off a beautiful, but almost unearthly pink glow. Genevieve had noticed it from a distance and assumed it came from the torches that were lit to welcome guests, but now saw that it was the stone itself that glowed. "That's lava rock," Jonathon explained in answer to her query. "Phelps had it brought down from Mount Pelée when he began construction five years ago."

"Phelps?" she asked, noting the distaste in his voice as he said the name.

"Yes, Colonel Douglas Phelps. He's the one hosting the ball this evening. I believe he and your father were rather close, Genevieve."

"But you don't like him."

Jonathon shrugged. "That's not important. We came so you could meet some of the people who knew your father. Colonel Phelps is a very prominent man; I'll let you judge for yourself."

Genevieve simply nodded as she glanced from Jonathon to Ty, noticing how closed off they'd both become. She didn't have time to pursue this observation, however, for a liveried servant appeared at that moment to assist her from the carriage.

She moved toward the house, but Jonathon was at her side at once, holding her elbow firmly as he nodded to Ty. "You go on ahead, Tyler. I need to speak with Genevieve for a moment." She glanced up at him, puzzled, but he didn't say another word as he led her away from the house and to a small, private alcove formed by an orchid-covered trellis. "Genevieve," he began softly, thinking of how sensitive she'd been when his crew was "cold" to her, "if this becomes too difficult for you, given your father's reputation, you need only ask me and we'll leave immediately."

To Genevieve, however, the two situations were entirely different. She lifted her chin. "You needn't be concerned. I'm well aware of the reception I'm likely to receive tonight. I intend to stay regardless of what anyone may think." She drew herself up, a glorious mixture of pride and courage emanating from her stance. "I'm not ashamed to be my father's daughter."

Jonathon looked into her deep blue eyes, noting the spirit and beauty that shone from her expressive face. "I'd say that if he's watching at this moment, he's damned proud of you, too."

Genevieve didn't know what to say to that. She waited, but the captain made no further comment, nor did he turn back to the house. "Was there something else you wanted to say?" she prompted.

Actually, there was. Jonathon had had serious misgivings all afternoon about bringing her to the ball. Although he was loathe to admit it, he knew he was using her, in effect, as bait to lure out whoever her father had been working with. And that thought did not rest easily on his conscience. He studied her now, her soft figure bathed in moonlight. She looked beautiful, feminine, and suddenly very fragile. "I don't want you to get hurt," he said at last.

So that was it. Again. He felt responsible for her welfare. "I can't say that I like the idea very much myself," she replied lightly, irritated that that was his only concern. "To that end, I shall endeavor to remain in one piece until we've finished our business. Now if you'll excuse me, I've a ball to attend."

Jonathon reached out and grabbed her arm, angered at her

flippancy. "You've obviously forgotten the danger you're in, just by being here."

"I've forgotten the danger," she repeated, her eyes wide. "My father died because of events that took place on this island. Do you think I could forget that?"

Jonathon drew a deep breath, summoning his patience. "I'm asking you to be careful, that's all. I don't want to see you hurt."

Genevieve shook her head, a rueful grin on her lips. "My goodness, Captain, concern for my welfare does seem to be a favorite theme of yours. I wonder how you'll occupy your time once I've gone."

Jonathon shook his head, her light humor washing away some of his tension. "I suppose I'll just have to find another golden-haired damsel in distress. Though I think next time I'll find one who listens to me."

"I was never in a moment's distress until two of *your* men chased me into a fish pile. Until that point, I was managing perfectly well on my own. And as for listening to you—"

"You needn't bother to finish that, Genevieve. You've already shown me quite well where we stand on that score."

The garden was quiet, except for the sound of the birds calling to one another from the low branches of the trees above them. Genevieve paused, studying him, but was unable to read his expression in the dim light. "What's this all about?" she asked straightforwardly. "Nothing's changed, after all. Our goal is still the same: find the man who implicated my father, and find the treasure."

Everything had changed. Jonathon looked at the golden beauty who stood before him, her sapphire eyes glowing with determination. He turned away from her, running his fingers through his dark hair in agitation. What he'd expected was to be able to remain a neutral observer, to stay by her side until it was clear whether the Southern rebels were at all connected to the vast fortune she claimed existed. What he had expected was not to care at all, not to get personally involved.

But it just hadn't worked out that way.

Genevieve almost smiled, seeing the frown that marred his handsome face. "Jonathon," she said gently, "you worry too much. Everything's going to be just fine. I'll be careful, I promise."

Jonathon was not yet used to hearing her say his name. It caught him off guard, making him feel fiercely protective. "You'll do more than that. I don't want you going anywhere without Tyler or me at your side. If anyone so much as mentions your father, I want to know about it immediately. If anyone frightens you, angers you, or even bores you, I want to know. In fact, if anyone talks to you at all, about anything, up to and including the weather, I want to know about it. Have I made myself clear?"

"Yes," Genevieve answered as a little spark was lit deep within her. Maybe, just maybe, he did care after all. "Speaking of talking, people will do just that, unless we make an appearance fairly soon."

Jonathon smiled, surprised at her easily won compliance with his demand. But he was in no hurry to leave. He reached out and stroked her cheek. "If that's the case, perhaps we should oblige them and give them something to talk about."

Genevieve felt herself tremble at his light touch, but managed to keep her tone level. "You do remind me of my father. He never retreated either."

Jonathon's eyes glowed as his hand moved down, lightly stroking the pulse point at the base of her throat. "Retreat? That's an odd word to use. Is that what you think, Genevieve, that we're in battle?"

"Sometimes it feels that way," she admitted breathlessly, thinking of her warring emotions. She knew she should turn and walk away, she wanted to turn and walk away, but something kept her firmly rooted where she stood.

His fingers now trailed softly across her shoulders, leaving her bare skin tingling along the path his hand took. "A battle is such an ugly thing. Is this really so unpleasant?"

he asked, his eyes locked on hers as his fingertips played lightly across the creamy skin exposed by the neckline of her gown.

Genevieve felt her breasts strain against the fabric of her gown, her body aching with the touch of his hands. The feeling was shocking, disturbing, filling her with a desperate longing for something she didn't know how to define. Even though they stood apart, she could feel the strength and power emanating from him, a magnetic force that seemed to reach out and touch her, pulling her to him. All resolve, all reason, left her. "No," she answered shakily, "this isn't unpleasant."

That was all the invitation Jonathon needed. He reacted instinctively, doing what he'd wanted to do since he'd first seen her that evening, seen her slowly descending the staircase, a vision of grace and beauty in a shimmering red ballgown. He pulled her tightly into his arms, his mouth fiercely claiming hers. Her body instantly molded against his, soft yet firm, a perfect complement to his hard masculinity.

He moved his hands over her back, pressing her even more tightly to him, exploring her gentle curves while his tongue probed her mouth. Genevieve returned his searing kiss, responding with an urgency and sweetness that was unlike anything he'd ever experienced in his life. Her tender caresses drove him wild, pushing him dangerously to the edge of self-control. He wanted more, needed more, but knew this was neither the time nor the place. He heard the dim strains of the orchestra as it began another waltz, and reluctantly he eased his hold on her.

Genevieve felt him draw back and tried to pull away, embarrassed by her reaction, but he wouldn't let her, keeping his strong arms locked firmly around her. "Before I let you go," he said, his breath falling softly against her ear, "I want you to understand something. Whatever else might happen, whether the treasure exists or doesn't, this, what we feel between us, is real." He gently cupped her chin, lifting her face to his. "Do you understand me?"

Genevieve searched his beautiful amber eyes. "No," she answered honestly, "I don't. Nothing makes sense to me anymore. My mind tells me to do one thing, then my body tells me to do something else."

It was only the look of sincere confusion on her face that kept Jonathon from shouting out his laughter. "I'll give you some advice then, Genevieve," he replied solemnly as he took her hand and led her back to the ball. "Listen to your heart."

They walked together toward the light and laughter of the ballroom, each engrossed in his own thoughts.

CHAPTER ELEVEN

❦

They were ushered through the house to a large, formal ballroom, as grand as any Genevieve had ever seen in Paris. The soft music of the orchestra floated out to greet them, competing mildly with the low hum of laughter and conversation. Huge crystal chandeliers hung from the ceiling, casting shadows on the beautifully attired guests who were swirling to the strains of the latest waltz.

"There you are, Captain Morgan. I saw that brother of yours not too long ago, and knew you couldn't be far behind."

Genevieve watched as Jonathon turned and greeted an older, distinguished-looking man. "Colonel Phelps, may I present Mlle. Genevieve DuPres."

The older man's eyes glowed as he took in the lovely young woman standing before him. "Mademoiselle DuPres, it is indeed an honor," he said as he bowed formally over her hand. "Your father was a good friend of mine, though obviously a bit negligent."

"Negligent?"

"But of course. How could he forget to tell me that his daughter was such a beauty?"

Genevieve smiled, then gently removed her hand from his grasp. "I knew you Southern gentlemen had a reputation for charm. Now I can see that it's well deserved."

Colonel Douglas Phelps drew himself up, stroking his thick white mustache in obvious satisfaction, then turned back to Jonathon. "How did you come to know one another? I wasn't aware you knew General DuPres."

"Actually," Jonathon lied smoothly, "the general and I were well acquainted." It wasn't much, but he hoped it would take some of the focus off Genevieve.

"I see," the colonel responded slowly, a slight frown on his face as he regarded Jonathon thoughtfully. He recovered himself quickly though, and turned back to Genevieve with a smile. "What do you think of our little island, my dear?"

"It's even lovelier than I imagined it would be. And I'm sure I'll enjoy it even more now that I've begun to meet a few of my father's friends," she answered graciously.

It was apparent, however, that the colonel had more on his mind. "Forgive an old man his tactlessness, my dear, but may I assume then that you don't blame the people of Martinique for what happened to your father?"

If Genevieve was at all taken back by the question, she didn't show it. "How could I? The dispute was between my father and the state of France, after all. Martinique was simply where he happened to be in service. It was my government that erred so grievously, sir, not the people of Martinique."

"Excellent, excellent. Such a sensible girl." The colonel said, and Jonathon couldn't help but admire how neatly she'd gotten around that issue.

"Unfortunately, your government is not alone in making mistakes," the colonel continued, warming himself to his favorite topic. "Just look at what's happening back in the States. The North has all but taken over the Senate and refuses to grant statehood to any new slave territories. The South still has some voice in the House, but by God, it's not enough anymore. What with the tariff structures the way they are—"

"Father," a deep voice broke in smoothly, cutting off the older man's tirade, "surely our guest came here to dance, not to talk politics. I'd hate for you to drive away such a rare beauty"—he paused, taking a step forward—"particularly before I've had the pleasure of meeting her."

Genevieve looked up at the man who had joined their small group. He resembled his father a great deal, being tall and handsome, but his coloring was quite striking. He had wavy auburn hair and a thick mustache, his cool gray eyes focused entirely on her.

"Don't worry, Harry, there's plenty of time for introductions. Mlle. DuPres and I aren't going anywhere," Jonathon stated flatly, placing a proprietary arm around Genevieve's slim waist as he drew her closer to his side.

"Ah, Morgan, you're back," the other man said slowly, his lips twisted in a half-smile. "How clumsy of me. I guess I didn't see you standing there."

Who could miss him? Genevieve wondered. Jonathon made no comment, but she could feel the tension that coursed between the two men. They sized each other up, the silence finally broken by the colonel. "Allow me to present my son Harry, Mademoiselle DuPres. These two young bucks have been after each other since the day they met, and it appears neither one's gotten any smarter with age. Perhaps this would be a good time to introduce you to a few of our other guests," he suggested smoothly, offering her his arm.

Genevieve glanced up at Jonathon, who gave her a curt nod and released his hold on her. "Tyler and I will both be right here if you need us," she heard him say as the colonel ushered her away.

Genevieve steeled herself for the cool rebuffs and silent hostility she had known in Paris, but she was not prepared for the reception she received. The colonel's guests actually seemed almost anxious to meet her, as though she held some special status, and they spoke nothing but words of praise for her father. Although she didn't understand it, she was glad her father had apparently made some true friends on the island.

And it certainly made her task easier, for she found herself greeted cordially by the men her father had mentioned in his letters. While she couldn't entirely rid herself of the suspicion that one of them might have betrayed her father, the possibility began to strike her as more unlikely. The men were prosperous and powerful, and far more interested in Southern politics than any other issue. Any connection her father might have had to any of them, other than social, seemed remote at best.

The colonel presented her to a Charles Winston, one of a succession of wealthy plantation owners she had met that evening, then excused himself to see to another guest. They talked lightly for a few minutes, but Genevieve soon became uncomfortably aware that his attention was not at all on their conversation, but rather on the portion of her anatomy revealed by the neckline of her gown.

"Was your wife able to attend this evening?" she asked, hoping to divert his attention away from her and back to the small woman across the room whose angry glare ought to have been boring holes into the back of the dense man's head.

"Hmmm? Oh, yes, certainly," he answered absently, his eyes locked on her breasts.

Genevieve felt herself blush furiously under his relentless stare, her anger beginning to rise. "Mr. Winston," she tried again, in a tone that clearly did not bode well for the man.

"Hmmm, my dear?" he mumbled, continuing single-mindedly to focus his attention on her neckline.

Genevieve had had enough of the insufferable man. "Have you injured your neck, sir?" she asked sweetly. At his muffled, negative response, "Then allow me to direct you," she stormed. "My face is up here!"

That finally got the man's attention. Winston's head snapped up. "Well!" he huffed, eyeing her coldly before stalking away.

Genevieve's lips twitched as she fought the urge to burst into giggles.

"Hmmm," a low voice drawled into her ear, "it appears you may have just lost a friend." She spun around, knocking into the solid wall of Jonathon's chest as she gazed up into his twinkling amber eyes. Grinning, he reached out to steady her, his gaze following the path Winston was blazing as he stormed across the room.

"I can't imagine why," she answered lightly, a satisfied smile on her lips.

"I don't suppose you'd care to tell me what that was all about?" She shook her head playfully and he let it go, knowing that Winston posed little threat. "I have another suggestion then," he countered. "Dance with me, Genevieve."

The solemnness of his request caught her off guard. He extended his hand to her, and she wordlessly placed her own in it, feeling a tremor of anticipation as he led her to the dance floor. She had already danced several times that evening, but as she had not seen him on the floor once, she'd assumed he either didn't like to dance or wasn't very good at it. But as he pulled her into his arms and began to guide her through the waltz, she realized she'd been wrong about him once again.

He moved with the grace of a natural athlete, his steps smooth and sure. They glided together effortlessly, moving as one to the gentle rhythm of the music. Genevieve was aware of nothing but the man who held her in his strong arms, his golden eyes locked on her as they softly swayed through the dance. "What are you thinking?" she asked, wondering what was behind those brilliant eyes.

Jonathon smiled. He'd been thinking about making love to her. "I was thinking about you," he answered simply.

"What about me?"

The way her body felt so right in his arms, how smoothly she moved, as if she could anticipate his every need. "How well you dance. You must have attended several balls in Paris."

Genevieve smiled softly and nodded, thinking back to the days when her father had been alive and her life had been nothing but an endless succession of balls and parties. Jonathon watched her, enthralled by the sweet, reminiscent expression on her face, her sapphire eyes glowing with pleasure at her memories. "Tell me about it," he coaxed.

She smiled and lifted her slim shoulders in a gentle shrug. "There's not much to tell, really. My father always encouraged me to dance. He said it was excellent training."

"Training?"

"Yes," Genevieve answered, a teasing lilt to her voice. "He said dancing was excellent training for young girls, for it teaches them how to guess what a man is about to do before he does it."

Jonathon laughed and tightened his arms about her. "What else did your father tell you about dancing?"

"Well, let me see. . . ." Genevieve let her mind wander back, surprised to find that her memories, for the first time in long months, weren't painful. There was a sense of security and well-being she felt when she was in Jonathon's arms that was unlike anything she'd ever felt in her life.

"When I was a little girl," she continued softly, immediately filling his head with visions of her as a child of five or six, her thick, honey-gold hair tumbling down her back, and her deep blue eyes shining with delight as she played with a puppy or a doll, "my father used to tell me that if I made a wish while I was dancing, it would come true by the end of the dance."

She looked up at him and smiled playfully, an irresistible combination of innocence and beauty. "What would you wish for?" she asked. "If you could have anything in the world right now?"

Jonathon stared at the woman he held in his arms. "I'd wish this dance would never end."

Genevieve's breath caught in her throat, but she managed a light laugh. "I'm afraid that's impossible."

"Why is that?" he asked, enjoying her little game.

"That's how it works: the dance must end in order for you to get your wish. You can't have it both ways." As if on cue, the music ended, and Genevieve stepped out of his arms.

"There, you see? You should have wished for something else."

"There wasn't anything else I wanted," Jonathon answered, his gaze intent.

They stood silently together on the dance floor, but the spell was soon broken by the intrusion of another couple. Genevieve was thankful for the interruption, for it gave her a chance to get her bearings once again. Jonathon, however, was not at all pleased, and even less so when he saw that it was Harry and Constance. "Darling, there you are," Constance gushed, interposing herself neatly between Genevieve and Jonathon. "You promised me a dance earlier this evening, and I intend to see that you keep your promise."

Jonathon frowned. "You have a very creative memory, Constance," he stated flatly, reaching for Genevieve. "If you'll excuse us—"

"Oh, be a sport, Morgan," Harry cut in. "What's one little dance between friends? Besides, it'll give me the chance to become better acquainted with Mlle. DuPres."

That was exactly what Jonathon didn't want. He realized, however, that short of pushing Constance out of his way, right in the middle of the dance floor, there was no way for him to refuse. And the smug smile on Harry Phelps's face told him that he was well aware of it, too.

Genevieve watched Jonathon's eyes darken from golden to deep brown, and thought for one heart-stopping moment that he meant to take a swing at the other man right then and there. "I think that's a wonderful idea," she interjected quickly. "I'd be delighted, Mr. Phelps," she said, but her eyes were locked on Jonathon, silently pleading with him to agree. She could feel the curious stares that other guests were turning on their little group, and the last thing she wanted to do was to create a scene on her first evening out in Martinique.

Feeling her stare, Jonathon finally turned from Phelps to her, and after a moment's deliberation, gave her a curt nod. "Really, darling," she heard Constance say as the captain took her by the arm and turned away, "don't you think you're carrying this a bit too far? After all, just because you've been saddled with looking after that little French—"

Whatever she intended to say next was lost, for Genevieve watched as Jonathon said something sharply to her, after which Constance stiffened, her lips tightened, and she made no further comment.

The next waltz began, and Harry turned to Genevieve and bowed formally. When he lifted his head there was a small smile playing about his lips, and a teasing light in his cool gray eyes. "Mademoiselle, the honor is mine," he said, drawing her into his arms.

They moved silently together, and Genevieve noticed that although the man danced well, she had to pay attention to her steps to follow. She couldn't help but compare him to the partner she'd just had. Dancing with Jonathon had been as effortless as floating on air.

"Tell me, mademoiselle, have you ever visited Martinique before?"

"No," she answered absently, trying to discreetly observe the other couples on the dance floor.

"Now that you've graced us with your presence, dare I hope that it will be a long stay?"

"No," she answered again, shaking her head. She had located Jonathon, but his back was to her. She watched as he guided Constance smoothly through the dance. They looked as though they belonged together, she thought dismally, wondering why that thought should cause her chest to ache so peculiarly.

"Are there many women in Paris as lovely as you?"

"No," she repeated with a sad frown, lost in her own thoughts. It took her a minute to realize what Harry's question had been, then her eyes flew open wide. He silently stared at her, an expression of undeniable amusement on his face. "Oh, Mr. Phelps, I didn't mean to say no," she stammered, horrified at her faux pas. "I meant yes, several, everywhere," she finished clumsily, her cheeks burning.

"Ah, that's better."

"Better?"

"Yes, having you join the conversation. I happen to have this funny aversion to talking to myself." He gave a mock shudder of dismay. "Flirting with myself is even worse."

Genevieve smiled. "I'm sorry, I didn't mean to be rude, I was just—"

"Watching Morgan and Constance dance," he finished for her.

She nodded, appalled that she'd been so obvious, though Harry didn't appear at all slighted.

"They do make a striking couple," Harry said. "My cousin has been trying to drag Morgan to the altar for some time now, and I do believe she may finally succeed."

Genevieve stumbled, sending Harry a shaky, apologetic smile for her clumsy footwork as he tightened his arm about her. Then she looked blindly away, not seeing anything. "How nice for them," she said, amazed that her voice was able to get past the heavy lump in her throat. "I didn't realize Miss Prentiss was your cousin," she continued in a desperate attempt to steer their conversation to a topic that was less painful for her.

"Yes. We were both raised in Charleston, but since my father started this little plantation here, we find ourselves doing quite a bit of traveling between the islands and the States."

"What brought your father to Martinique?" she asked. She could well understand the French who had left their homeland during the Terror, but she didn't understand what drew so many Southerners to the Caribbean.

Harry paused, looking at her, then seeing that her interest was genuine, continued. "Are you at all aware of what's taking place back in the States?"

Genevieve reluctantly shook her head. She had once prided herself on being well-informed, but the past eighteen months had changed all that. She'd concentrated only on surviving, and redeeming her father's good name.

"Our country is being torn apart," he answered. "While it's growing at an amazing rate, the power is steadily being shifted to the pro-Northern territories. In effect, the South's voice in our government is slowly being choked out."

"But the root of the issue is slavery, is it not?" she asked straightforwardly. "How can you condone that?"

"I admire your candidness, mademoiselle," Harry replied, "but I fear you've been the victim of Northern propaganda. That is indeed the moral cry the North uses to defend its actions, but before you judge us, I wonder if you've ever seen the working conditions in the factories the North boasts so highly of. They have their own form of slavery: wage slaves. Men, women, and children toiling twenty hours a day, never seeing the light of day, living in shanty-towns of squalor that would never be permitted on any plantation. I would suggest the North clean up its own backyard before they point an accusing finger at us."

Genevieve chewed her lip, considering his words, as Harry pressed on. "The real issue at hand is one of power, economics, and control. I beg you not to be too swayed by the emotional lies the North spreads to cloak their true intentions."

"Then what is the purpose in coming to the Caribbean?" she persisted. "Surely leaving your country will not amend the wrongs you see taking place."

Harry smiled patiently. "I can assure you, I've no intention of leaving my country. It's simply a question now of balancing the power. While the North is expanding to the west, the Southern states have decided to expand south, starting with the lush islands of the Caribbean, which already have settled firmly into the plantation way of life, and later, perhaps, into Mexico."

"Is that possible?" Genevieve asked, trying to conceal her surprise at his words.

"Of course. Why, just last year President Pierce offered Spain one hundred million for the island of Cuba. Though that offer was rejected, we shall continue our efforts." He smiled broadly, twirling her to the music. "But I fear now I'm guilty of the same thing I accused my father of earlier: boring a beautiful young woman with talk of politics. Forgive me, mademoiselle."

"Not at all, Mr. Phelps, you've been most kind." He had, in fact, been nothing but a gentleman. She couldn't help but wonder what it was that caused Jonathon to dislike the man so. Hoping she wouldn't offend him, she decided to voice her thoughts. "Why is it that you and the captain are so at odds? I would think you would have much in common."

Harry laughed at that. "I would warn you not to repeat that remark around Morgan, for I can assure you he wouldn't find it much of a compliment."

"But it doesn't bother you?"

He shrugged easily. "I have no quarrel with the man. I fear it is his dislike of me you sensed, not the other way around." Seeing her puzzled expression, he continued. "Morgan and his brother lost a wager to me, you see. It wasn't anything important, a race, as I recall, but the sum they lost was quite large."

Genevieve could not imagine Jonathon or Ty holding a grudge against someone over a lost wager, but before she had a chance to continue that thought, the music ended and Harry released her. "Mademoiselle," he said, drawing his heels together and bowing formally, "it has truly been a pleasure." He lifted her hand and brushed the back of it lightly with his lips. "I do hope we shall have the opportunity to become better acquainted."

"Don't bet on it, Phelps," Jonathon growled, appearing at Genevieve's side.

Harry straightened and lifted his eyebrows, an expression akin to amusement on his face as he regarded Jonathon. He turned back to Genevieve, his point made. "Mademoiselle," he repeated smoothly, then departed without another word.

Genevieve turned immediately to Jonathon. "That was needlessly rude, Captain."

Jonathon wasn't sure which angered him more: the fact

that she appeared to be defending Phelps, or that she had reverted to calling him "Captain" once again. In truth, he wasn't pleased with either development. Taking her arm, he guided her off the dance floor and to a more secluded spot, away from the prying eyes of the other guests. "Rude, was I? I thought I was being remarkably tolerant, considering Phelps's character."

"His character? Personally, I found the man quite charming, Captain. I would thank you to leave me out of whatever petty quarrel might exist between you two," she replied coolly, lifting her skirts to walk away, but Jonathon caught her arm.

"'Petty quarrel'? Is that what he called it? What else did your good friend Phelps have to say?" he demanded, remembering ruefully that only minutes earlier she'd been laughing as he held her in his arms, a golden angel who was just beginning to trust him.

Genevieve lifted her chin, striving to hold onto her anger so he wouldn't hear the hurt in her voice. "Nothing of great importance, though I do understand congratulations are in order. I hope you and Miss Prentiss will be very happy together."

"What the hell is that supposed to mean?"

"You know perfectly well what it means. The only thing I can't figure out is why you were so determined to make a fool of me. 'This, what's between us, is real,'" she mimicked, her eyes bright with unshed tears.

Jonathon's first impulse was to find Phelps and tear the man apart. But more importantly, he needed to soothe the pain and anger he saw in Genevieve's deep blue eyes. "Genevieve," he began quietly, placing his strong hands on her shoulders and turning her to face him, "I've no intention of making a fool of you, or hurting you, ever. Nor will I lie to you. I don't know what Phelps said to you about Constance and me, but I'm sure it wasn't true. I was involved with her in the past, I can't change that, but it's over now."

Genevieve looked away, unable to meet his eyes. When he looked at her as he was doing now, his golden gaze washing over her and his voice gentle, she found herself wanting to believe every word he said. She shook off his hands, afraid she would succumb to his touch yet again. Not this time, she decided, resolve stiffening her spine. She'd made enough of an idiot of herself already. "Tell me, Captain, have you informed Miss Prentiss that your 'involvement' with her is now over? For it appears to me that she firmly believes otherwise. Or perhaps you're just waiting until it better suits your purposes."

That, in fact, was exactly what he was doing. But not for the reasons she'd concluded. Both Constance's father and her uncle, Colonel Phelps, were key political figures in the Southern party. If there was a plan to purchase and stockpile arms, it was highly likely both men would be involved. This was not the time to do anything that would push him outside that inner Southern circle.

And judging from the reception Genevieve had received tonight, a welcome deserving of a hero's daughter, it also seemed highly likely that her father had been involved. From what Jonathon had been able to piece together, General DuPres had been guilty of treason, but had been arrested before he could turn the treasure over to the South.

There was only one thing left for him to resolve: how to tell Genevieve this.

He looked at the proud beauty waiting for him to speak and realized he couldn't accuse her father, or even voice his thoughts, without the evidence he needed to back them up. And he wouldn't be able to collect that evidence, or get to the treasure before the South did, without her help. He swore under his breath, raking his fingers through his hair in agitation.

Genevieve watched the ripple of muscles in his arm, his fingers tangling in the waves of his thick hair, noting the now familiar gesture which signaled his frustration. "Well, Captain," she prompted, "I'm waiting."

"Don't call me captain," he snapped, turning sharply. He drew a deep breath, summoning his patience. "Genevieve," he began again, choosing his words carefully, "I gave you some advice earlier—I told you to listen to your heart. I'm asking you to do just that. I'm asking you to trust me."

"Those are pretty words, *Captain*, but they don't address the issue at hand, do they? I would like to know if you have any intention of ending your relationship with Miss Prentiss."

"There are factors at work here, Genevieve, things I can't explain to you now, but if you'll just have faith in me—"

"You're not going to stop seeing her, are you?"

Jonathon had had enough. He drew himself up, his face unyielding. "No," he said flatly, "I'm not."

Genevieve instinctively clenched her fists, holding them tightly at her sides, her entire body rigid with pain and anger. "Thank you for telling me the truth," she said tightly, the ice in her deep blue eyes showing anything but gratitude.

He nodded coolly. "You have your answer, mademoiselle. Are you satisfied now?"

Satisfied? She wanted to lunge at him and beat him with her fists. She wanted to curl up in a ball and sob her heart out. "Yes," she answered with a regal nod, "I'm satisfied."

"Then why don't you answer some of my questions now?—because I damned well can't," he growled out, his handsome features dark with anger. "You've known Phelps for just ten minutes, and yet you believe him over anything I say to you. Have you always shown such a remarkable lack of faith in those who try to help you? Or is it just me in particular that you distrust?"

"Don't you dare try to turn this around, Captain," Genevieve stormed, her color high. "You are not the injured party here. You make advances toward me, demand that I give you my unconditional trust, then accuse me of having no faith when you refuse to stop seeing your mistress." She laughed quiveringly, shaking her head in disbelief. "I thought I'd already explained that to you, Captain. You can't have it both ways."

Jonathon stared at her, his expression hard and closed off, an expression a thousand times more chilling than when he was angry. "I can see we're both wasting our time here. If you're determined to believe the worst of me, then so be it."

He looked away in disgust, glancing around the great hall. The crowd had started to thin, the orchestra long since retired. He turned back to Genevieve, his amber eyes hard. "I suggest we leave," he said flatly. "The party's over."

Chapter Twelve

The sugarcane waved gently in the breeze, an inviting field of shimmering green that flowed over soft hills to the turquoise waters of the sea below. Hummingbirds darted through the garden, drinking the sweet nectar offered by the rich abundance of bright pink blooms. A soft breeze carried the laughter of a small group of children, playing in a nearby stream.

But Jonathon saw and heard none of this as he gazed somberly westward, toward the city of St. Pierre. He placed one long leg on the verandah rail, leaning over his bent knee, his body tense. Ty sat in a chaise longue nearby, silently observing the dark, brooding stance of his older brother. "I take it," he commented dryly, "that things are not going well."

Jonathon turned slowly around. "No," he answered grimly, "they're not. I'm no closer now to finding the treasure and discovering who General DuPres was working with than I was in the beginning."

"It's only been two weeks."

"That's right," he agreed, folding his arms across his broad chest as he regarded Ty. "Two weeks of wild-goose chases and dead ends. Two weeks of social calls on men I detest, and two weeks of running around like a fool with a shovel tied to my saddle, digging for buried treasure."

"You don't believe Genevieve is purposely misleading you?" Ty asked, coming to her defense.

Jonathon shook his head. "She has no reason to. As far as

she knows, my only interest in finding the treasure is so I can claim part of it as a reward. She agreed to that in the beginning, and I doubt that's an issue now."

"Then what's wrong?"

"I'm not sure," he answered honestly. "But I can't understand why whoever was working with General DuPres hasn't come forward yet and approached Genevieve. There are only two ways to answer that: either they already have, and she hasn't spoken of it, or they're waiting and watching us, not certain yet that she can be trusted."

"Genevieve would have told you if anyone had come to her with information about her father, whether good or bad."

Jonathon shrugged his shoulders. "What Genevieve wants, more than the treasure itself, is to clear her father's name. I highly doubt she'd come to me with information that would implicate the man."

Ty knew his brother well enough to recognize that what was really bothering him was inherent in that last statement. With a voice of studied indifference, he broached the one topic they'd been deliberately avoiding. "How are things between you and Genevieve, anyway? Not still fighting like cats and dogs, I hope."

Jonathon turned away, but not before Ty glimpsed the expression of pure disgust on his face. "Quite the contrary," he answered tightly. "Mlle. DuPres has been nothing but polite."

In fact, that's all she had been, every day for the past two weeks. So damned polite he found himself grinding his teeth every time he had to speak to her. He found himself actually missing their arguments and stormy confrontations, for at least then he got some sort of reaction from her. Now she was cool and reserved, rarely speaking unless she had to, and then using the minimum number of words necessary to convey her thoughts.

She was determined to put up walls between them and was succeeding very well at it. The problem for him, however, was that despite her obvious lack of trust in him, despite her rebuff of every attempt he made to ease the strain of their relationship, he was still drawn to her. He wanted her more than he'd ever wanted a woman.

Yesterday afternoon he'd gone to her room to look for her. She hadn't been there, but he'd noticed one of her gowns lying haphazardly across her bed, as though she'd just taken it off. Unable to stop himself, he lifted the soft fabric, inhaling the sweet perfume of her dress, the soft scent of her skin. When Marie entered the room he threw the gown down, feeling as guilty as a schoolboy. "The gown's dirty. See that it's cleaned properly," he'd blustered as he swept from the room, but Marie's knowing smile told him she didn't believe a word of it.

Jonathon pushed his thoughts aside and turned back to Ty, his expression once again cool and unreadable. "There's obviously nothing I can do to convince Genevieve to trust me. That choice is hers alone to make." He paused, his firm jaw stubbornly set. "What I can do, however, is make it patently clear that we've become very interested in furthering the Southern cause."

"So that's the reason for this little party you're throwing? I believe I saw the name of every prominent Southerner on the island on the guest list."

Jonathon nodded. "I want to make it very easy for whoever Genevieve's father was working with to step forward."

"There's just one thing you're forgetting."

"What's that?"

Ty smiled, lifting his drink slowly to his lips. "You could be wrong."

Jonathon's eyes darkened as he took a threatening step forward. "If you're trying to provoke me, Tyler, this isn't the time."

"Not at all," Ty answered, not in the least threatened, though he did make an effort to hide his grin. "What I'm suggesting is that Genevieve could be right, and therefore this little setup of yours is pointless. She's maintained from the start that her father was innocent. Why won't you listen to her?"

"Because she's reacting emotionally, not rationally," he replied dismissively.

"And you're not?"

Jonathon straightened, looking every inch the stern, commanding officer that he was. "What's your point, Tyler?"

Ty looked at his brother, warm brown eyes locking on cool amber. "If you want Genevieve to trust you, you should begin by trusting her." He waited for a reaction but none came, other than the tightening of Jonathon's jaw. "Have you told her yet that you believe her father may have been working with the South?"

Jonathon's lips curled into an ugly imitation of a smile. "That's exactly what she'd expect me to say."

Ty shook his head bemusedly. "And here all this time I thought you two were working together."

Jonathon turned angrily, giving full vent to his frustration. "The girl has no reason not to trust me. I'll be damned if I'm going to explain my every move to her. There's too much at stake here to worry about what she believes or doesn't believe."

"Well, I guess that settles it then," Ty replied easily, rising from his chair. "Since you're both so at odds, I'll just run up and tell her about this evening."

That was as far as he got before Jonathon shoved him, none to gently, back into his chair. "Never mind, blast it. I can tell her myself."

Ty watched his brother storm off. This time he made no effort to hide his wide grin.

"Marie, look at this one," Genevieve exclaimed, lifting a pale blue gown accented with soft, cream-colored trimmings. The packages from Mme. Latourre's had just arrived, and with the rich profusion of silk and lace that covered every surface, the room looked like the result of an explosion at a dress shop. "Oh, look, there's a hat to match!"

She picked up a large straw bonnet, one of several that had been made to match the gowns, and placed it cockily on her head, holding the ribbons under her chin while she executed a laughing twirl.

It was at that moment that she noticed Jonathon, his large form filling the doorway as, leaning one broad shoulder against the frame, he silently watched her. She stopped awkwardly, letting go of the ribbons as she gestured around the room. "Look, Jonathon, the gowns have arrived," she explained needlessly as Marie quietly slipped away.

"So I see. Do you like them?"

Genevieve's eyes lit up. "They're beautiful!" she gushed. "But I'm certain there's been a mistake. I only ordered two, and there must be at least twenty here."

"Twenty!" Jonathon raised his brows in mock horror. "I distinctly told Mme. Latourre that one gown would suffice."

Genevieve laughed, knowing he was teasing her. "You're a poor liar, Jonathon. You told Mme. Latourre to completely ignore everything I said."

"Absolutely."

"Thank you," she said simply, her gratitude sincere. It had been years since she'd had one new gown, let alone several.

Jonathon stared at her, enjoying the radiant smile she was now bestowing upon him. Her bonnet was cocked deliciously askew, framing her beautiful face with trails of soft blue ribbons that set off the sparkle in her sapphire eyes. Her cheeks were bright and rosy, giving her smooth ivory skin a warm glow. His eyes moved down to her full, sensuous mouth, and he nearly groaned out loud as her small, pink tongue darted out to moisten her lips.

Genevieve felt his amber eyes burning into her with an intensity that made her feel warm all over. She licked her lips again, suddenly nervous under his intense scrutiny. Then, remembering her bonnet, she pulled it off, taking advantage of the opportunity to turn away from him and return it, with the utmost precision and care, to the box it had come in. "Was there something you wanted, Captain?" she finally asked.

"Yes."

"What?" she asked with a shaky smile, trying desperately not to show how much his presence, the mere sound of his deep, masculine voice, affected her.

Jonathon ignored her question, walking slowly, silently, toward her. Genevieve had a sudden, wild impulse to flee, feeling as defenseless as a rabbit being stalked by a greater, stronger creature. She didn't move though, save to stubbornly lift her small chin. He stopped before her, a slight, almost triumphant smile on his lips. "You're slipping, Genevieve."

"Slipping?"

"Yes. Several times in the past few days you've called me Jonathon, rather than captain."

"That's ridiculous, Captain, I—"

"As a matter of fact, it seems to take an almost deliberate effort on your part to remember to call me captain."

Genevieve clenched her teeth in frustration. Was there anything the man didn't notice?

"I'd almost believe," he continued, "that you're afraid to call me Jonathon. And do you know why?"

"I'm not afraid of any—"

"You're afraid of letting me get too close, Genevieve. You need to put every barrier between us that you can think of, and calling me Jonathon leaves you with one less defense."

Genevieve could have argued the point, of course, but the fact that he was absolutely correct dampened her enthusiasm for debate. "Defense? Barrier?" she countered instead. "You make it sound as if I'm a fortress under siege."

Jonathon bit back a grin. He lifted his hand to her arm, drawing his fingers lightly from her wrist to her shoulder in a slow, gentle caress. "I told you before, Genevieve, this isn't a battle."

Genevieve felt her heart lurch to her throat, and unconsciously clutched the bedpost for support. He had to know what he did to her, how her senses rioted every time he came near. "No? Then call off the attack, *Jonathon*," she replied, meeting his challenge.

This time Jonathon couldn't hide his smile. He reluctantly shifted his gaze from her to one of the many gowns that lay in a pile on her bed. "Will you wear this tonight? I've invited some guests to join us for dinner."

Genevieve glanced at the gown. It was a deep emerald green, trimmed in black, and she could tell by looking at it that the fit would be exquisite. It would be perfect for this evening. "No, I don't think so."

To her surprise, he smiled again, his low, easy grin, the one that made her think of pirates and long, hot summer nights. "You seem to take particular delight in defying me, Genevieve. I wonder why that is."

"Not at all, Cap—Jonathon," she said, ignoring the tremors that raced down her spine at his disarming smile. "In fact, I don't consider you at all—either to defy you or to please you."

"Now there's an interesting thought. And quite a challenge for you as well. You've shown you can defy me, now let's see if the reverse is true." A soft light filled his golden eyes as he lifted her small hand and placed it against his chest. "Please me, Genevieve."

His chest was a solid mass of muscles, as firm and sculpted as she remembered it to be. His heart beat steadily beneath her hand, matching the mysterious rhythm she felt surging within herself. She tore her hand away and took a step back, amazed that her wobbly legs still functioned. "Please me," she repeated, shaking her head. "That's rather primitive isn't it? Even for you. What do I have to look forward to next—your clubbing me over the head and dragging me by my hair to a dark cave?"

Jonathon shrugged. "If I thought it would work, yes."

"Well, it won't, so you can spare me the headache."

He bit back a laugh at her indignant reply. "Tell me, then,

Genevieve, what will work?" he asked, pleased to have finally broken through her icy coolness. He stepped forward, lightly stroking her hair, capturing a golden curl in his palm. "What do you like? What do you dream of? What are the words you long to hear?" His voice was deep and smooth, inviting her innermost thoughts and confessions.

It took all the will she possessed not to be drawn in by the irresistible pull he seemed to have on her. "Nothing from you, Cap—Jonathon," she answered shakily, trying to convince herself that it was true.

"Nothing? Not even this?" he asked as he bent his dark head, leaning in toward her, his arm wrapped around her slim waist as he pulled her gently to him. The thought of resisting didn't even enter her mind. Her body reacted instinctively, pressing eagerly against his, her mouth parting as his lips met hers.

She kissed him fiercely, hungrily, unconsciously releasing her pent-up frustration of the past two weeks. Her hands slid along his broad shoulders, then traced the deep muscles that ran down his back, amazed at his strength. He pulled her tighter to him in response, his solid thigh shifting between her legs, rocking her against him as his hands roved expertly over her gentle curves.

She stifled a moan of pleasure as his mouth moved lower, covering her throat and neck with a trail of burning kisses, then moved lower still, his tongue playing lightly across the tops of her breasts, his gentle kisses sending shivers down her spine and leaving her yearning for more. "Now tell me that you don't want me, Genevieve," he murmured, his breath warm against the delicate column of her throat.

Genevieve knew that he was daring her, forcing her to admit that she knew what she was doing and worse, that she wanted him to do what he was doing. No. "I don't want you, Jonathon," she answered, the words coming out much more breathless than she'd intended.

Jonathon stopped. He stepped back from her, his hand gently cupping her chin as he lifted her eyes to his. He cocked an eyebrow, his teasing grin back in place. "It appears I'm not the only one who's a poor liar." He waited a beat, searching her delicate features for something, then shrugged, continuing before she had a chance to reply. "Our guests are due to arrive at eight. The attire is formal," he said briskly, handing her the emerald gown. "This would be a lovely choice."

Genevieve accepted the gown mindlessly, too shocked by his abrupt change in mood to react. When she finally came to her senses, he'd already left the room, but that didn't prevent her from storming to the door and slamming it in his wake. She threw the gown down, fuming. How dare he doubt her words. She did not want him.

Well, she didn't want to want him.

And the beastly man was determined to prove otherwise. She wrapped her arms around herself, but the comfort was meager compared to the feeling of his holding her, of his strong arms locked around her. She paced about her room, trying to bring her emotions back under control. She had worked so hard for two weeks to be cold and distant to him, to focus on nothing but their search for the treasure. A defense she'd thought was foolproof, absolute.

A defense he'd been able to dissolve completely with one touch and a few softly spoken words, leaving her vulnerable to him once again.

She swore softly under her breath, cursing the captain for being a good-for-nothing rake, a rogue, a complete philanderer, then cursing herself for falling for him anyway. She had tried so hard to convince herself that she couldn't possibly feel anything for him, that it was too absurd to even consider.

So why did she miss him when he wasn't with her? And why were her eyes constantly drawn to him when she thought he wasn't looking? He even seemed to do something to the air, for she found it difficult to breath whenever he got too close. She grimaced, thinking what a fool she'd made of herself to Marie, making up flimsy excuses to ask the most personal questions about Jonathon, questions which Marie had rightly shrugged off, leaving Genevieve with nothing but that knowing smile of hers.

And most of all, why was it so important to the captain that she admit she wanted him? Why couldn't he just take her, whatever that meant? she thought wantonly, a wry grin on her face.

Jonathon was asking himself the same thing as he headed toward his chambers, in need of a long, cold bath. He frowned, realizing that it had never mattered to him before what a woman felt about him, as long as she wanted him the way he wanted her. The sticky business of emotions had never been considered. It had always been a simple matter of mutual lust to be quenched, and he usually gave the matter no more thought than quenching the thirst.

Not that he hadn't always been a considerate lover, attending to his lady's needs before his own, then bestowing her with a gift or sweet words when it was over. Everything had always been straightforward and efficient.

But not with Mlle. Genevieve DuPres. For some absurd reason, despite the fact that her body was telling him that she wanted him, he needed to hear the words from her. He wanted her trust. He wanted her complete surrender, and nothing less. "Yes, Jonathon, I want you." Those were the words he longed to hear, in that sweet, silky voice of hers that made him mad with desire. Anything less would be an empty victory.

It wasn't enough that she offered him her delectable little body. For the first time in his life, he wanted more than that from a woman. From one stubborn, beautiful, independent, troublemaking woman in particular. He kicked open the door to his room. She wanted him, too, he decided for her. She just damned well better admit it, and soon.

He went to the washbasin and poured a pitcher of cold water over his head.

CHAPTER THIRTEEN

Standing amidst Jonathon's guests, Genevieve assumed the role of hostess with natural grace and ease. She had not spoken to him since that afternoon, having waited until she heard the arrival of the company to make her appearance downstairs. She sipped absently from the glass of sparkling wine she held in her hand and glanced around the room for a certain pair of broad, masculine shoulders.

As usual he was not hard to find. The captain seemed to draw admirers as easily as most men drew breath. Older men sought his opinion on topics ranging from planting to politics, while younger men tried without success to emulate his smooth, urbane style. She watched as an aggressive older woman pushed eagerly forward to present her daughter, a large, plain girl who looked embarrassed enough to sink through the floor. Jonathon gave the woman a brief scowl for her rudeness, then turned the full force of his smile on the young girl, charming her until she looked ready to fly away in sheer happiness.

Genevieve, feeling an unreasonable surge of jealousy at the tender scene, quickly averted her eyes. She glanced at Ty, standing in a secluded corner with a beautiful brunette in a yellow evening gown so low cut it was almost scandalous. Ty didn't seem to mind. In fact, from what she could tell, he appeared intent on divesting the girl of her garment. Feeling her eyes upon him, Ty looked up, whereupon Genevieve assumed a stern expression and shook her finger at him, warning him to behave. Ty grinned and winked at her in response, then went back to his serious business of flirting with the beauty beside him.

"It's useless, you know. The Morgan men are unreformable rakes."

Genevieve turned around, doing her best to hide the smile of pure pleasure his voice brought her. "Thank you for that edifying piece of information, but I believe I was able to figure that out on my own."

Jonathon shrugged. "I just thought I should warn you, should you have any foolish notion of trying to change me. I happen to be very content with my life just the way it is."

"I'm so happy for you."

Jonathon ignored her sarcasm. "Good. Then you understand that despite what happened between us this afternoon, our relationship shall remain strictly business," he said, continuing to bait her, saying the words he expected to hear from her and waiting for her heated response.

Genevieve just looked blank. "This afternoon?" she asked, her deep blue eyes wide and full of innocence.

Jonathon stared at her. She had forgotten their embrace? How was that possible, when it had taken him two cold baths and all the willpower he possessed not to storm back to her room and finish what they had begun? Genevieve had to bite her tongue to keep from smiling, seeing the expression on his face, a hilarious blend of anger and amazement. Her lips twitched and she knew she had given herself away, for his amber eyes immediately changed, flashing annoyance for a second, then gaining that strange, hungry light, as if he meant to devour her.

"Teasing me, are you, sweetheart?" he whispered. Genevieve's stomach did the most unusual flip at the endearment. "Or was that an invitation for me to remind you?"

"Neither one," she replied, lifting her shoulders in a dainty shrug. But she ruined the effect of studied indifference by looking up at him with a jaunty smile and adding, "Besides, you started it."

Jonathon shook his head, wondering if he'd ever be able

to keep up with her. He'd actually expected a cold reception from her tonight, her usual reaction after anything intimate had passed between them, and was greeted instead by her light, teasing banter. That was the last thing he'd expected, particularly after she'd kept him on pins and needles while he waited to see if she was planning to come down at all. He'd very nearly gone blazing upstairs to demand that she present herself, but seconds after he'd resolved to do just that, he saw her coming slowly down the staircase, looking as regal as a young queen. She had fairly taken his breath away.

As she did now.

A radiant smile lit up her face, and her creamy skin looked as smooth and soft as satin. Her luscious curves were draped in a rich, deep teal, setting off the sparkle in her eyes. The fabric was interwoven with a shimmering gold thread, enhancing the glorious highlights in her hair and casting a soft glow about her as she moved. "You look beautiful," he told her frankly, resisting the urge to pull her into his arms. "But I notice you're not wearing the gown I asked you to."

"No, I'm not."

"May I ask why?"

Genevieve tossed her head defiantly, her thick golden curls spilling over her shoulder. "You may not have noticed, Jonathon, but I do have a mind of my own."

Jonathon let out a short bark of laughter at that statement. "Believe me, Genevieve, you've made that abundantly clear."

Genevieve stared at him, wishing he would smile more often, for he was incredibly handsome when he did. He was incredibly handsome even when he didn't, she admitted to herself. She let her eyes wander, wondering if he was aware how the dark brown jacket he wore set off the deep gold streaks in his hair and emphasized his broad, muscular shoulders. He'd tucked his pale ivory shirt into matching dark trousers, which clung to his powerful thighs. Her eyes trailed up to his chest, remembering the strength and power she'd felt there.

"You look very nice tonight, too," she offered softly, the words coming out before she could stop them. She blushed and looked down, wanting to kick herself. Of all the things she could have said to fill in the gap of their conversation, why did those have to be the words that came tumbling out?

"Thank you," Jonathon replied automatically. There was silence for a moment as she felt his amber gaze study her, then amazement in his voice. "Are you flirting with me, Genevieve?"

She nodded miserably, her cheeks on fire. "Apparently doing a very poor job of it, too, since you have to ask."

"You want to flirt with me?" he asked in growing amazement.

Genevieve lifted her eyes in exasperation. "No, I don't want to flirt with you, exactly, I just want. . . ." Her voice trailed off, uncertain of the words she needed and wishing she hadn't started the whole thing.

"What exactly is it you want?" Jonathon persisted, not about to let the matter drop.

"I want things to be normal between us. I don't want to always fight."

"We don't always fight."

"We do every time you kiss me."

"I see." Jonathon straightened, a dark scowl on his face. "I take it, then, you're asking me not to kiss you again," he concluded harshly.

"No," Genevieve answered immediately, nearly as frustrated and confused now as she'd been when he'd left her earlier that afternoon. "I just don't want to fight about it anymore if you do. Kiss me, I mean. Not that I'm asking you to or anything," she interjected hastily, "but if you were to decide, one day perhaps, to kiss me again, I thought it would be nice not to have to fight about it afterwards." Her face was open, thoughtful. "That is the normal way to conclude a kiss, is it not?"

Jonathon was too astonished by her words to think about instructing her as to the "normal" way to end a kiss. "You want me to kiss you?"

"I didn't say that, did I?" she shot back, her sapphire eyes shining. She squared her shoulders primly, delicately cleared her throat, then continued. "I simply stated that I don't want to fight about it afterwards if you do."

Jonathon just stared at her, stunned. "What exactly is it you suggest we do afterwards?"

Genevieve shrugged. "Whatever a man and woman normally do after a kiss, I suppose." She thought for a moment, then looked up at him hopefully. "Smile and be friends?" she suggested uncertainly, thinking back to the chaste pecks she'd shared with Armand. But somehow that didn't seem quite the right solution as far as the captain was concerned.

"I don't think so," he answered flatly, confirming her suspicion.

She thought about it some more, but was unable to come up with another suggestion. "Very well, you're the great romantic, you tell me. What do people do after a kiss?"

Jonathon nearly groaned out loud, torn between pulling her into his arms and sweeping her off to his chambers to demonstrate exactly what followed a kiss, and wanting to strangle her for having brought up the highly charged subject while surrounded by a room full of guests. "A kiss is a prelude to making love, Genevieve."

"Oh." She blinked, then licked her lips, staring off blindly at some distant point.

He waited, but there were no more words forthcoming. "Is that what you're suggesting?" he prompted.

"Certainly not," she answered automatically, wondering why the room had suddenly become so warm. Perhaps if she could just get away from Jonathon long enough to go open a window . . .

"Good."

Genevieve's attention snapped back at that remark.

"Good? You mean you don't want to . . ." Her voice trailed off, her whole body aching with embarrassment. Perhaps if she could get to the window, open it, and throw herself out . . .

Jonathon cupped his fingers under her chin, forcing her eyes to meet his. "You've no idea, Genevieve, how much I want you. How long I've been waiting to make love to you."

"Then why—"

"I'm waiting for something," he replied shortly before she had a chance to finish her question.

Comprehension slowly dawned in her eyes. "The treasure? You're waiting until we've found the treasure?"

That remark drew a frown from him. "I'm waiting for you, Genevieve," he told her, unconsciously drawing his hand along her arm in a soft caress.

"For me? But I just told you—"

"What did you tell me? That you won't object too loudly if I force myself upon you?"

Genevieve had the grace to blush. "I didn't mean it like that."

Jonathon smiled gently. "I know you didn't, sweetheart. But it's still a long way from telling me that you want me, too."

"You want me to say the words?" she objected, trying to salvage what was left of her pride. "Isn't it enough that I've come this far?"

"No, it isn't. Not from you, Genevieve. I need to hear you say that you want me. I need you to tell me what pleases you, and how my touch feels against your skin. I need to hear my name fall from your lips when I hold you in my arms and show you the deepest part of the night. Then, maybe, it'll be enough."

Genevieve forgot to breathe. The rest of the world dropped away, leaving just the two of them. "Why?" she asked, her voice a hoarse whisper.

Jonathon couldn't answer her question, so he ignored it. He wasn't sure why it was so important to him that she admit she wanted him, he only knew that it was. "Just say the words, Genevieve."

"What about you?"

"What about me? I've just told you—freely and without hesitation—that I want you. What more can I say?"

So much more, she realized sadly. She needed to hear so much more than that. That Jonathon wanted her was obvious, but as what? Another mistress to add to his collection? She shook her head. "It appears to me that I've a great deal to lose, and very little to gain."

Jonathon frowned. "What are you afraid of losing?"

My heart, Genevieve answered silently. If she gave herself to him, body and soul, as he wanted her to, there would be no turning back. That was it. If she gave herself to him that completely, there'd be nothing left of her.

Jonathon studied her, wondering at her sudden silence and worried frown, then finally understood. A soft light filled his golden eyes as he turned her to face him, his voice low and gentle. "You've nothing to be frightened of, Genevieve. It will hurt a little, at first, but the pain won't last long, I promise."

It took Genevieve a full minute to figure out what he was referring to, then every ounce of her self-restraint to keep from knocking the tender expression off his smug face. Of course that was all he had on his mind. "How very selfless of you to be so concerned, Jonathon. However, that was not what I was thinking of!"

"It wasn't?" he queried, his lips twitching.

"It most certainly was not!" she flared. Watching him struggle to control his laughter did little to soothe her temper. "This whole conversation is absurd," she finished hotly, lifting her skirts to walk away. She must have been insane to think she could ever understand the man.

He stopped her, placing his hand gently on her arm. "Wait a minute." She turned, glaring up at him in response. "We've come this far, Genevieve," he said soothingly. "Tell me, what is it you're afraid of losing if you become involved with me?"

She stared at him coolly. "My mind. Now if you'll excuse me," she said, pulling her arm away.

"Is this a private conversation, or can anyone join in?" a sugary voice purred, interrupting them. Constance slid up, looking darkly exotic in a deep purple gown as she smiled seductively at Jonathon.

Genevieve glanced briefly at the other woman. "Frankly, Miss Prentiss, I was beginning to wonder what had kept you away for so long," she replied, then with a toss of her golden head she moved smartly away, not caring to stay and watch the captain flirt with his mistress.

To her surprise, she found her irritation faded quickly. For other than lying to her about Constance no longer being his mistress—for it was quite obvious to her that she was— Jonathon had been entirely honest. He hadn't tried to sweep her off her feet with declarations of undying love, nor taken advantage of her willingness to return his embrace to seduce her completely. He'd made it perfectly clear that he was determined to wait instead, until she admitted that she wanted him, too. She didn't know what to think of that.

She frowned, feeling rather like a mouse about to enter a trap. But at least the mouse wasn't forced to admit the folly of his own weakness, or how badly he wanted the cheese.

"I can't imagine what could cause a frown on such a beautiful night as this."

Genevieve smiled wistfully at Harry Phelps, who had walked up silently to stand beside her. "I was thinking of the advantages of being a mouse," she admitted.

Harry raised his eyebrows at her remark, his thick mustache lifted by his smile. "How fortunate for myself, and every other man in this room, that that is not the case. There is absolutely nothing mouselike about you, my dear."

Genevieve smiled absently. Phelps was smooth and suave, his manner charming, but his flattery left little impression. Amazing, when compared to the impact Jonathon had on her just uttering her name. "So, has Morgan been a good host?" he asked.

"Yes, quite."

"I'm happy to hear it," he said, his cool gray eyes taking her in appreciatively. "Perhaps you'll allow me the honor of escorting you around the island, mademoiselle. There are several places I'm familiar with that I doubt Morgan has thought to show you."

"Thank you, Mr. Phelps, perhaps we can arrange that one day," she answered noncommittally, knowing Jonathon would never allow it, and wondering why she cared whether he did or not.

"Morgan wouldn't begrudge you a simple outing with a friend, would he?" he pressed, correctly guessing the reason for her hesitation. "After all, he appears quite busy with his own endeavors." He glanced significantly at Jonathon and Constance, who appeared to be engrossed in an intimate conversation across the room.

Genevieve followed his glance, feeling her anger rise, then turned back, her eyes full of determination. "As it happens, Mr. Phelps, I find I'm free tomorrow morning."

He smiled. "Call me Harry."

Their conversation was ended by the announcement that dinner was being served, and Genevieve graciously allowed Harry Phelps to escort her into the dining room. She took great satisfaction in the dark scowl on Jonathon's face upon seeing them together. What did he expect? she thought crossly. After all, there he was, with Constance clinging to his arm as though she expected a flood to sweep through the room at any minute. If he could flirt with her and then move on to his next paramour as if nothing had taken place, then so could she.

Genevieve thought the meal was never going to end. It wasn't that she minded a lively political discussion, but the group gathered tonight talked of nothing but the unjust plight of the Southern states. She sighed and glanced discreetly around the table, taking in the heated faces of their guests, working themselves up over the volatile subject. All except Jonathon and Ty, who both remained rather reserved, and Constance, of course, who just looked bored and pouty. Probably because she no longer had the captain's complete attention, Genevieve surmised.

"What is your opinion on the matter, Mademoiselle DuPres?"

Genevieve jumped, caught completely unawares. She turned to the man who had spoken, racking her brain for his name, and smiled hesitantly. "I fear I'm not much of an expert in matters pertaining to American politics, Mr., ah, Porter," she finished, the name coming to her at last. Mr. Porter, of Virginia.

The man beamed at her scattered statement, patting her hand as if she were a precocious child. "Women never are, my dear. Don't you worry your pretty little head about it," he cooed. "But as your father was a man of some influence, I thought you might have some insight on the position France would take in the matter."

Genevieve's eyes narrowed at his condescending tone. "Doubtless you're well aware, sir, that France abolished slavery, both at home and in her colonies, years ago. I should think that that indicates quite clearly the position France would take in the matter."

Mr. Porter's patronizing smile vanished. That was obviously not the answer he'd been expecting. "What a shame you weren't able to see your father before his untimely demise," he said coldly, "for it appears he neglected to make his views on the subject clear to you."

Genevieve frowned. "What are you saying?"

"General DuPres was a firm believer in the Southern cause. I only regret that he will not be here to see the glory we shall achieve in the years to come."

Genevieve shook her head. Obviously the man had her father confused with someone else. "My father would never support a system that survives only by the complete subjugation of others."

Porter's fist came crashing down on the table, sending fine china crashing to the floor. Genevieve gasped, jumping back instinctively, while the rest of the table swung around toward them in stunned silence. "Slavery is not the issue here!" he bellowed, his face purple with rage. "It's the Southerners who are oppressed, trapped by Northern domination. I will not have it!" he finished, pounding his fist atop the table in time to his words.

Jonathon was out of his seat and around the table within seconds. Before Genevieve had even caught her breath, he stepped forward, clamping his hand over Porter's fist and holding it down steadily, with apparently as little effort as it took to restrain a child. "That's enough, Porter."

Genevieve watched a muscle twitch furiously in Jonathon's jaw and knew he was fighting to get hold of himself. She wondered what it was that had angered him so, Porter's awful table manners or the broken china. She was not prepared for what she heard next.

"You frightened Mlle. DuPres," he said softly. Porter flushed an even deeper shade of purple and tried to raise his fist, but the effort was useless, embarrassing. Jonathon waited a beat, staring at him intently, the threat implicit in his golden eyes. "Don't ever do it again."

Genevieve felt her mouth drop open in shock. The man had startled her, yes, but she hadn't been truly frightened. At least not enough to merit such a strong reaction from the captain. She considered explaining that to him, but it was obvious that he was not in the mood to listen to her explanations. Instead, she lowered her eyes, feeling unreasonably guilty for having caused such a scene.

Jonathon turned back to the table, inwardly cursing himself for what had been an instinctive reaction. He'd been in a foul mood to begin with, finding himself forced at his own dinner table to listen to the self-righteous talk of his "guests" all night. When he saw Genevieve jump back from Porter with an unmistakable glimmer of fear in her beautiful eyes, he'd reacted without thinking, wanting to pound the man into a bloody pulp for daring to frighten her for even the briefest second.

That, however, did little to endear him to his other guests, who were now silently staring at him. Damn, he'd gone through the whole blasted evening, only to ruin everything now. He ran his hand through his hair in pure frustration, uncertain of what he could say to smooth things over.

To his amazement, it was Genevieve who spoke next. Keeping her eyes deliberately averted from his, she stood, her voice brisk. "Well, ladies, it appears we had best leave the gentlemen alone for a bit to work off some steam, or there'll be nothing left of this room." There was a smattering of high, feminine giggles, then the ladies swept out, more than a few casting admiring glances at Jonathon before leaving. These were followed, of course, by sighs of dismay as they shook their heads over their own, unromantic husbands.

Porter stood up, working his way cautiously around Jonathon to take a seat on the other side of the table. "Really, Morgan," he started, trying to force a gruffness into his voice and steadiness into his hand as he poured himself a generous shot of whiskey, "I'd no idea you'd suddenly become so damned chivalrous."

Jonathon just growled in response as he returned to his seat, but it was too good an opportunity for Ty to let by. "Bad luck, Porter. Chivalry seems to be a quality my brother didn't develop until after he met the lovely Mlle. DuPres."

Porter grunted in response and downed his shot, the burning liquid wonderfully comforting. Jonathon simply glared at him. Ty ignored them both as he glanced around the table, looking delighted by the recent turn of events. He lifted his glass of brandy. "Gentlemen, I propose a toast. To Jonathon Morgan, our illustrious host this evening: may he finally get exactly what he wants," he paused, a wicked grin on his face as he ignored his brother's look of dire warning, "rather than what he so richly deserves." His comment was met by low, masculine guffaws. Even if Jonathon did kill him tomorrow—and judging from the dark scowl on his face he had every intention of doing just that—it was worth it.

The men followed the women into the main salon shortly thereafter, remaining there for the rest of the evening. The party wore on for several more hours, during which Genevieve tried to sort out her tangled emotions. By late evening, at the sound of Constance's high, tinkling laughter, Genevieve knew that if she had to maintain her serene smile for one second longer her face would surely crack. As most of their guests had already departed, she gave up all pretense of being a graceful, worldly hostess, and retreated to the dining room to see if Marie needed any help.

Unfortunately, she wasn't the only one who'd thought to return to the dining room. She recognized Porter instantly, though his back was to her as he pressed up against Marie, pinning her to the wall. His hands roved clumsily over her body while his weight kept her pinned beneath him. His thick lips crushed her mouth, silencing Marie's protests.

A surge of revulsion coursed through Genevieve, followed immediately by a white-hot anger that was unlike anything she'd ever experienced before. Grabbing the first thing she could get her hands on, a bottle of brandy from the table, she brought it crashing down on Porter's head, then jumped back so he wouldn't fall on her when he collapsed.

Porter, however, failed to collapse. He staggered back, simply staring at her, then blinked twice. Frowning, he brought his hand to his head, feeling the wetness there, and, Genevieve hoped, a throbbing ache. His eyes traveled back to the shattered bottle she held in her hand and he finally made the connection. "What in God's name did you do that for?" he bellowed, temporarily forgetting Marie.

Genevieve could smell the noxious whiskey fumes on his breath from where she stood. She ignored him, turning instead to Marie. "Are you all right?" Marie drew herself up and nodded regally, her dark eyes full of gratitude and a sadness that made Genevieve's heart ache. "He didn't hurt you, then?" she pressed, reaching for her friend.

"It's none of your damned business what I do with her!" Porter bellowed, enraged. He reached for Marie, but Genevieve quickly put herself between them.

"Go home, Mr. Porter."

Porter frowned, wanting to knock Genevieve out of his way, though what was left of his good sense warned him of the retribution that such an action would surely bring if the little bitch went crying back to Morgan. His face flushed an even deeper shade of purple as he remembered that it was all her fault that he'd been embarrassed earlier that evening. When he'd come back looking for more whiskey and seen Marie, it had seemed perfectly reasonable that he release some of his frustration on the servant. Morgan owed him that much, after all.

"You listen here, Miz DuPres," he slurred, the smooth, cultured tones Genevieve had heard earlier now completely gone, "I don't know what you let your darkies get away with in France, but things don't work that way here. That girl's just gonna get herself in more trouble if she don't do what I tell her to."

Genevieve's eyes flashed fire. "Get out of here. Now."

Porter smiled. This time he reached for Genevieve. "I can see you're not gonna be reasonable about this, are you?"

Genevieve lifted her hand, brandishing the shattered bottle as she slowly backed up.

"I'm beginning to believe you're too stupid to live, Porter," a deep voice rang across the room. Jonathon stood in the doorway, his stance wide and threatening, looking larger and more menacing than any man Genevieve had ever seen. She wondered briefly how he could possibly be the same man who touched her so softly, whose voice was so gentle when he spoke to her.

Jonathon scowled, seeing that Porter had not yet lowered his arm. "Touch her, man, and you'll be making the biggest mistake of your life," he warned softly.

Porter's arm came down hastily to his side. "Really, Morgan, this is all—"

"What happened?" Jonathon cut him off, turning to the women.

"He was hurting Marie!" Genevieve cried, angered and outraged on her friend's behalf.

"I'm all right, M'sieur Jon," Marie interposed, placing a restraining hand on Genevieve's arm. "Mam'selle DuPres thought to discourage him with that bottle of brandy." All eyes went to Genevieve's hand, and she realized she was still tightly gripping the neck of the shattered bottle, as if she meant to do battle.

"I see," Jonathon replied darkly, stepping toward Porter with unmistakable menace in his golden eyes.

"M'sieur Jon," Marie said softly, shaking her head, "you know it won't do any good. You can't beat everyone who thinks the way he does."

"No, but it's a fine start, isn't it?"

"No, m'sieur. That is not the way."

Jonathon stopped reluctantly, turning to her. "What would you have me do?"

"Just make him go away, that's all."

Jonathon didn't move as he studied Marie, reading the certainty in her eyes, then he finally nodded. He strode across the room and flung open the back door, calling out to the stables. He conferred briefly with a shadowed figure who retreated back to the stables, then focused once again on Porter, disgust written clearly on his chiseled features. "It must be your lucky night, Porter. I'll do as Marie asks me to—this time. But if I ever see you near her, or Mlle. DuPres again, you won't live long enough to regret it."

Porter gulped almost audibly, his fear and relief evident. Then, remembering himself, he threw back his shoulders and looked around the room in haughty disdain before marching out the door.

"Thank you, m'sieur." Marie nodded good night to them both as she swept from the room with quiet dignity.

Genevieve turned to Jonathon, her eyes wide. "How could you just let him go like that?"

"I think it's safe for you to put down your weapon now, Genevieve."

Genevieve followed his gaze to her hand, then set the shattered bottle down absently. "How could you just let him go?" she repeated.

Jonathon shrugged. "That was what Marie wanted me to do." He smiled as he watched her eyes grow even larger, and forestalled her next question. "That was Luc I called to the door to get Porter's horse. Though after I explained to him what happened, I doubt very much that Porter will be in any condition to ride anywhere."

Genevieve nodded approvingly, satisfied that justice would indeed be done. "Well, then, I suppose we should get back to our other guests."

"They've all left. Porter was the last to go."

"Oh." Genevieve stopped, feeling guilty. "We weren't very good hosts tonight, were we?"

"They all had their fill to eat and drink. I suppose everyone left happy enough," he replied coolly as he escorted her to her room.

As Genevieve glanced at him curiously, a question that had been forming in the back of her mind finally took shape. "Those people who were here tonight, they're not your friends, are they?"

Jonathon frowned, but he didn't deny it. "It's late, Genevieve. Can't this wait until tomorrow?"

"Why did you invite them here?"

He sighed, not wanting to get into the weighty subject right then, but he knew she was too stubborn to let it go. "There's talk of war in my country, Genevieve. The men who were here tonight were powerful, important both on Martinique and back in the Southern states. If it does come to war, I want to know what they've planned."

"All that talk about building a Southern empire, of taking

over the Caribbean and expanding into Mexico, do you think it's possible?"

Jonathon shook his head. "If it does come to war, the dream of a Caribbean empire will be its first casualty. You can't expand a nation and fight a war at the same time."

Genevieve thought of the Terror that had swept through France, leaving a bloody legacy and thousands of her countrymen dead. "This war of yours, will it be like the one which fell upon France?"

Jonathon considered her question. The result would be the same, the bloody, needless killing of thousands, tearing his country apart. "Yes," he answered grimly, "the war will be the same, it's only the cause that's changed. It's not about who will control the government, but the division of my country into separate nations. The South will be fighting for her independence from the North."

"Is it really worth going to war for?"

"I've simplified it, Genevieve, for there are many other issues involved. Whether a man has the right to own another human being, for instance," he continued, his expression of disgust showing clearly where he stood on that issue.

They'd reached the door to her bedroom and Genevieve stopped, considering his words carefully. "Do you think this is somehow connected to what happened to my father, and the treasure?"

"I'm not positive," he admitted, "but it is possible, isn't it?"

He studied her so intently that Genevieve had the strange sensation that he was waiting for some sort of confession from her. She must be imagining it, she decided as she looked up at him, her deep blue eyes soft and sleepy as she stifled a yawn. "We shall have to find out, won't we?"

He searched her eyes a second longer, then reached out to stroke her velvety cheek. Genevieve didn't pull away. She leaned against the door, tired as the events of the long day finally caught up with her. She looked up into his eyes, feeling a sudden coyness rising within her. "Jonathon, you didn't really mean what you said earlier, to Mr. Porter, I mean. You wouldn't actually hurt him just because he came near me again."

Jonathon was tired, too. He answered without thinking, dropping his hand. "No, I wouldn't."

Genevieve straightened instantly. "Good," she choked out. "Violence, after all, is so—"

"I'd kill him," he said quietly. He stared into her eyes, leaving her little doubt he meant every word, then turned and strode silently away.

She watched him leave, then entered her room, pressing her back against the door as she closed it, her lips slowly curving into a soft smile of pure feminine delight.

CHAPTER FOURTEEN

The morning broke bright and beautiful, and Genevieve felt a momentary twinge of conscience at having agreed to meet Harry Phelps. She was not one for deception, and knew that Jonathon would be furious if he ever found out. She chewed her lip, debating whether she should go, then caught herself, amazed and irritated that she was wasting her time considering his feelings.

Why should she care what the blasted man thought? She was here to clear her father's name, that was all. Besides, he'd already informed her that he had some business to see to in town, so it made perfect sense for her to continue their search without him. Genevieve lifted her chin and marched resolutely out of her room. This was ridiculous. She was a grown woman. She had every right to go where she pleased, when she pleased, and with whom she pleased. That resolved, her stubborn pride firmly in place, she sneaked quietly out the back door.

Harry was waiting for her a short distance away from the main house, as she'd asked him to be. Much to her relief, he didn't question why she hadn't wanted him to call for her at the house. "You look beautiful, mademoiselle," he greeted her as he assisted her into his carriage. "A ray of sunshine on an otherwise dreary day."

Genevieve smiled, knowing he was referring to her cheery yellow gown and matching bonnet. She looked up at the cloudless blue sky as a warm breeze gently brushed her skin. "If this is a dreary day, Mr. Phelps, I cannot imagine what you could consider perfect."

Harry smiled as he seated himself next to her. "You, mademoiselle, are almost perfect."

"Only almost?" she teased, enjoying his light, easy charm. He was so relaxing to be with—especially when compared to the nervous, heated tension Jonathon always evoked within her.

"Yes, almost. Though I confess I would find you absolutely perfect if you would just change one thing."

"What's that?" she asked, her curiosity piqued.

"Call me Harry."

She laughed. "Only if you'll agree to call me Genevieve."

"Genevieve, I'd be honored."

Harry soon proved himself to be a wonderful companion. The morning passed quickly as Genevieve enjoyed both his company and the breathtaking scenery they passed. After rolling smoothly through fertile jungles, the trees so thick and heavy that not a ray of light filtered past their limbs, the carriage crept steadily upward, onto roads which hugged sheer, jagged cliffs above the beach, the sun so dazzling Genevieve had to shield her eyes from its white intensity.

"Where are we?" she asked as the terrain became gentle, the landscape populated by small farms and quaint houses.

"This is Les Trois-Ilets. Many people believe it's one of the prettiest villages on Martinique."

Genevieve looked around her, taking in the small shops with their wares displayed prominently on carts and tables before the doors, enticing would-be customers to come in and explore what else might be offered within. As in St. Pierre, there was an abundance of graceful public squares and flower-filled parks. People bustled cheerfully along the narrow streets, the women walking proudly, their hair tucked neatly into the bright madras scarves Genevieve had seen everywhere.

Harry guided them through town, then off the main road and onto a rough dirt path. He stopped their carriage in front of a large, dilapidated farmhouse which looked to be perhaps a century old. "Hungry, Genevieve? I had a light lunch prepared for us, and thought we might stop here."

Genevieve glanced at him curiously. The house appeared to have been completely abandoned. Behind it were fields, which had presumably yielded bountiful harvests of sugar-cane in the past but were now overrun by thick vegetation as though years had passed since any field hand fought to keep it back. The mill which had once processed the sugar stood in ruins, too, the walls crumbling down and leaving gaping pockets of mortar.

A small wooden church stood opposite, but it was obvious no one entered it any longer. The steps leading up to the front door had all collapsed, and the cross which hung above it had been knocked about by either a storm or strong winds, leaving it hanging strangely askew. Genevieve wrapped her arms around herself, a feeling of deep dread suddenly filling her stomach as she stared at the abandoned church.

"What's the matter, Genevieve? Don't you like it here?" Harry stepped in front of her, his gray eyes as cold as his voice.

She looked up at him, quelling the shiver of apprehension that ran through her. "Actually, it does seem a rather bleak spot for a picnic, doesn't it?"

Harry shrugged and turned away from her, his deep auburn hair glowing an almost fiery red in the bright sunlight. "I'm so used to the look of the place, I didn't consider that at all," he answered, his voice faraway, "but I guess to anyone else it would appear rather run-down." He took her arm. "Come, then, Genevieve. I know another spot I'm sure you'll enjoy."

Genevieve didn't move. "Why did we come here?" she asked.

Harry smiled, looking almost embarrassed. "I guess I'm guilty of trying to impress you," he admitted as he gestured to the property behind him. "I know it seems rather ignoble now, but you happen to be standing at the birthplace and childhood home of Marie-Rose Josephine Tascher de la Pagerie."

Genevieve's eyes widened. "Empress Josephine? Napoleon's wife?"

"The very same. Her parents were married in that church, and later, held her christening there."

"That's the reason we're here?"

Harry frowned, a puzzled look in his eyes. "Of course. I thought you might enjoy seeing her family home. As it appears I was wrong, however, we needn't stay."

"No, you weren't wrong, Harry," Genevieve answered slowly, wondering what had made her so uneasy earlier. She had probably allowed Jonathon's dislike of the man to cloud her judgment, and she vowed not to let that happen again. "It was very sweet of you to bring me out here." She looked again at the grounds. The old buildings were bathed in bright sunshine as birds sang from nearby trees. There was nothing at all sinister about the place, she thought, chastising herself for her foolishness. She pointed to a grassy bank above a cool, bubbling stream. "In fact, that would be a lovely spot for us to enjoy our lunch."

Harry didn't comment on her sudden change of heart, but simply went to retrieve the basket from the carriage, then silently spread a thick blanket at the spot she'd indicated. They resumed their friendly banter easily as they shared their meal. "Harry," Genevieve ventured cautiously after they'd finished, "I was thinking about last night."

Harry leaned back on the blanket, propping himself up on his elbows. "What about last night?"

"Well, all that talk about Southern independence, it was rather frightening. The South doesn't really want to go to war, does it?"

He smiled at her reassuringly. "Of course not, Genevieve. No one wants war. That does not mean, however, that the South will meekly allow itself to be ruled by an unjust government. Our freedoms and beliefs are too precious to be handed over without a fight."

"That will mean raising an army."

"Yes, it will."

Genevieve's heart beat furiously in her chest as her mind focused on one simple question: Was there a connection between the South's rise to power and the treasure? She tore her eyes away from his, feigning a casual indifference as she framed her next remark. "That's quite an expensive undertaking, isn't it?"

Harry lifted his shoulders philosophically. "I believe it was your Napoleon who said: 'If a people don't want to feed their own army, they'll only end up feeding someone else's.'"

Genevieve nodded, keeping her eyes deliberately lowered as she played with the folds of her skirt. "What else do you know about Napoleon?" she asked offhandedly.

"Napoleon?" He frowned, shaking his head. "Very little, I'm afraid. Unlike your Captain Morgan, I was never much of a military man."

Genevieve frowned, too, disconcerted by this last comment. "I didn't know Jonathon had been in the military," she mused, speaking almost to herself. "Military schools, yes, when he was younger, but—"

"Not today, Genevieve," Harry cut in, reaching over to give her hand a light squeeze. "Let's not talk about Morgan. Let's talk about us. Tell me what it was like to live in Paris."

Genevieve could resist neither his gentle entreaty nor the soft smile that accompanied it, and she soon found herself sharing her memories, particularly of the years when her father had been alive and life had been an endless succession of balls and parties. As she spoke, she realized she didn't miss any of the busy social whirl, and in fact, couldn't remember ever being as happy as she was now. There was a sense of purpose to her life today, a richness and completeness she'd never missed before but now couldn't imagine living without. "What about you?" she asked at last. "Tell me about Charleston, and what it was like to grow up on a plantation."

Harry smiled. "Wonderful. Have you ever seen the South, Genevieve?" She shook her head and he continued, "I'd love to show it to you one day, then. It's not like any other place in the world. There's a special beauty to it, born of strength and pride in the land, and a sense of duty and honor that's been lost in the North. And the Southern nights, well, I don't even know how to tell you about those, with the sky so warm and dark it seems to reach down and wrap itself around you."

"It sounds like you miss it."

"Very much. The South is in me, Genevieve, it's what I am. The same is true for every Southerner I know. That's why we won't sit idly by and watch it be destroyed by the North."

Genevieve sighed. "Now we're right back to where we began, aren't we? Talking of armies and war."

"I suppose we are. And all I should really be telling you is how lovely you look this afternoon, and how much I've enjoyed your company."

Genevieve tried to return his smile, but it didn't quite reach her eyes. "It's getting late," she said as she began to pack up what remained of their lunch. "Perhaps we should head back."

Harry studied her silently for a moment, then nodded his assent. "If you like," he finally replied, then turned to see to the horses. It was nearly dark by the time they reached Jonathon's home, and despite her fervent, silent prayers that he hadn't yet returned, the door flew open as soon as their carriage swung up the drive.

Jonathon stood silently watching them, his golden eyes dark with anger. "Get inside, Genevieve," he ordered curtly.

Genevieve stiffened, embarrassed by his sharp tone, while Harry simply returned his fierce look with a small, almost triumphant smile. "Hello, Morgan. Nice night, isn't it?"

Jonathon walked slowly toward the carriage, his angry

eyes focused intently on Harry. "I'm only going to tell you this once, Phelps," he said, his voice a deep growl, "so I suggest you remember it. Mlle. DuPres is here as my guest. She doesn't go anywhere, with anybody, without my permission."

"Really?" Harry replied, looking almost amused.

Genevieve started to protest, but Jonathon cut her off, pulling her from the carriage and, with a steel grip on her arm, leading her into the house. He slammed the door behind them, releasing her abruptly as she turned the full force of his heated glare on her. "If you ever, ever, pull a stunt like that again, I guarantee you won't be able to sit down for an entire week."

Genevieve drew herself up, her sapphire eyes blazing. "How dare you embarrass me like that!"

"Embarrass you? You're damned lucky I don't put you over my knee."

Genevieve's eyes widened. "You wouldn't dare," she said, backing up nonetheless.

Jonathon seriously contemplated it. It would have been a small price for her to pay after what she'd put him through. He and Tyler had left at dawn and spent the entire day down at the docks, chasing what had proven to be a false lead concerning a shipment of arms that was due to be delivered by a private vessel. He'd arrived home a few hours ago, weary and frustrated, only to discover that Genevieve had disappeared earlier that morning, leaving no word as to her whereabouts. "Where the hell were you?" he demanded.

"I was continuing our search, that's where I was. Mr. Phelps was kind enough to take me on a tour of the island, and afterwards we stopped for a picnic at—"

"You did what?"

Genevieve took a step backwards, hastily rethinking her words. "It was a short tour, really, and—"

"How could you do that?" he thundered. "Don't you realize the danger you put yourself in?"

"Danger? We weren't in any danger. Harry and I were simply—"

"HARRY?!"

"At least *Harry* doesn't yell at me, and lets me finish my sentences!" she yelled back.

"You don't need to say anything further, Genevieve. I'm going to finish this for you right now. I forbid you to ever see Harry Phelps again."

Genevieve stared at him in amazement, but saw no sign of compromise in his harsh, unyielding features. "Oh, really, this is too much," she said, shaking her head in disbelief. "All this rancor over a senseless wager that was made years ago?"

"Is that what Phelps told you?"

"Yes, and you lost, didn't you? I would have thought you could be a better sport about it."

"Did he tell you why I lost?"

"Your horse was slower?" she drawled.

Jonathon said nothing for a long moment, staring at her coolly. "I wasn't riding that day," he finally answered, "Tyler was. He was thrown halfway through the race, as the horses rounded the Straights." Genevieve paled as she remembered the narrow, rocky terrain she'd seen there. "Though I suppose 'thrown' is the wrong word for it, considering that the cinch on his saddle had been deliberately severed, the leather cut through almost completely, just enough to hold together until they'd reached the roughest part of the race, where it came apart. Tyler was damned lucky he didn't break his neck, or wasn't trampled by the other horses," he finished grimly.

"Jonathon," Genevieve countered softly. "I understand you were upset by what happened, but I don't think Harry is capable of doing something like that. You don't know it was he, do you? It could have been anybody."

"Harry was the last person anyone saw near the horses. He also needed the prize money the most urgently, for it was well known he had heavy gambling debts to pay off. Tyler was his only real competition."

Genevieve sighed, knowing it was useless to try and change his mind. "Very well," she conceded. "I'll be careful the next time I see Harry—"

"Obviously you didn't hear me," Jonathon interrupted coldly. "I am not asking you to be careful. I am telling you you're not going to see Phelps again. Period."

Genevieve's eyes narrowed as she placed one small, clenched fist on each hip. "You're telling me?"

"That's right."

"Very well, Jonathon, then let me tell you something. You have absolutely no right to tell me anything. You want the treasure as badly as I do, only I haven't figured out why. Except that the money isn't your only motivation, is it?" She raised one delicate brow, a cool imitation of an expression she'd seen so often on him.

"Genevieve," Jonathon began softly, speaking in a low, menacing voice, "this is not the time to play games. Give me just one reason not to trust you, and I'll put you on a ship back to France faster than you can say *au revoir*."

"You do that, and you've lost your only lead. Don't forget that I'm the only one who's seen my father's letters, who has the clues to where the treasure may be hidden, or even knows of its existence," she boasted.

"That's very impressive. Now why don't you tell that to everyone else who's been hunting that same treasure for the past year." With that parting comment, obviously a rhetorical question, he strode rigidly from the room.

Genevieve stared after him in stunned silence, then lifted her skirts, running to match his long, angry strides, unable to prevent herself from slamming into his broad back when he stopped abruptly. He turned around, an expression of cool disdain on his face. "I take it there's something else you wish to say to me?"

She was too overwrought to be bothered by his condescending tone. "Who else knows about the treasure? No one else can know. That's not possible," she stammered, shaking her head in wild disbelief. As far as she knew, no one, with the exception of Armand—her father's first officer—her father, and a few very select, high-ranking French officers, knew that her father had actually been sent to Martinique to recover the treasure. She sank slowly into the chair beside her as the dull suspicion she'd harbored earlier grew even stronger. Could Armand possibly have betrayed her father and herself?

Jonathon watched her face pale as she collapsed weakly into the chair. But it was the expression in her eyes, the shock and sorrow he read in their deep blue depths, that caught his attention and left him with little choice but to continue. "Obviously someone else knows about it. And I think you know who it is."

Genevieve took one look at Jonathon, noting his unyielding stance and the harsh, determined clenching of his jaw, and she knew that to even mention Armand's name would condemn him. He wasn't even on the island now, it couldn't be him, her mind screamed hopelessly. *Please, not Armand.* She took a deep breath and shook her head. "I don't know," she whispered, her voice barely audible past the dry ache in her throat.

Jonathon stared at her. "You're a poor liar, Genevieve. But then, we've already established that, haven't we?"

He spoke so softly it took her a minute to fully grasp what he'd just said. Once she had, she was out of her chair in an instant. "How dare you, of all people, accuse me of deceit!" She laughed bitterly, her eyes bright with unshed tears.

"Whoever it is you're protecting doesn't deserve it," he replied simply, ignoring her insult.

"I know that!"

Jonathon let out an exasperated breath. "Then tell me who it is, damn it."

Genevieve stood and walked to the window, taking a deep breath as she tried to get her emotions back under control. She waited a moment, then turned back to him, her tone once again measured and cool. "You want complete honesty, Jonathon? Very well. Let's start with you, shall we? Why don't you begin by telling me what it is you know that you've been keeping from me."

Jonathon considered his options. He could answer her evasively, as he had in the past, or voice his suspicions straightforwardly. He opted for the latter with some hesitation, not because he didn't trust her, but because he didn't want to hurt her, for he could see she was perilously close to tears already. But his conviction that it was time they both heard the truth outweighed his caution.

"Genevieve, this won't be pleasant for you to hear," he began, watching as she physically braced herself, stiffening her spine and arranging her beautiful features into a mask of taut composure. "I believe your father may have been working with Southern agents, using the treasure as leverage to stockpile an arsenal of arms." He had expected any number of reactions from her, ranging from outrage to heartbreak, but was not prepared for what she actually did next.

She smiled.

Her smile turned into light, bubbling laughter. "You've no idea how that relieves me," she gasped as she struggled to catch her breath.

Jonathon drew himself up, frowning darkly. "I don't believe you quite understand what I've just told you."

"Oh, but I do," she assured him hastily. "You see, I've been beside myself with worry these past few weeks, knowing there was some information you were withholding from me, but I couldn't quite put it together." She shook her head, her tone of voice now brisk. "I only wish you'd come to me sooner with that suspicion, for we could have put it to rest immediately and moved on."

"That's it?" Jonathan asked, incredulous. "You're just going to laugh it off?"

"Well, you certainly can't expect me to take that ridiculous accusation seriously."

"Genevieve," he replied, his tone grave, "I happen to be very serious. If you have any information that would vindicate your father, now would be a good time to say so."

Genevieve lifted her chin, her posture that of a young, imperious queen. "How very gracious of you, Jonathon, to allow my father a defense. I realize what an inconvenience that must cause you, when it's so much easier to simply condemn someone who can no longer defend himself."

Jonathon's golden eyes narrowed. "Are you quite finished?" She inclined her head regally, giving silent assent. "Good." He grabbed her arm and thrust her roughly back into her chair, then leaned in, his expression fierce, his blazing eyes only inches from her own. "You believe your father was innocent?"

Genevieve nodded mutinously but otherwise sat still. She didn't dare try to force her way past the solid wall of his chest.

"Then convince me," Jonathon commanded.

"Why should I?"

"Because I want you to," he stated flatly. "Unless, of course, you prefer to remain locked in this cozy position all night."

Genevieve blushed, wondering if he'd made that remark because he could hear the wild pounding of her heart or feel the heat that seemed to suddenly rise within her. She turned her head away to escape him, only to have her cheek brush against the fabric of his smooth linen shirt, which filled her nostrils with the heady, masculine scent of him. Every nerve within her was aware of him, screamed that awareness, as his firm body was poised inches above her own, almost on top of her, his breath warm against her neck. She swallowed, trying to moisten her mouth, which had inexplicably gone dry. "Very well, you want proof?" she managed to ask.

"Yes."

"Then let me up. I can't breathe when you're so close to me."

Jonathon stood slowly, a roguish grin on his face at her

tacit admission of his effect on her. That, combined with her reluctant admission that she liked his kisses, was quite encouraging. Genevieve, however, was nothing if not stubborn. He smiled as she leapt up from her chair and scrambled across the room, determined to put as much distance as she could between the two of them. Her breasts rose and fell as she struggled to catch her breath, while fiery indignation shot from her sapphire eyes. He'd never seen her more beautiful. "Let's hear your proof, Genevieve."

Her small, proud chin came up once again. "I haven't got any." She watched his expression immediately darken as he took a step toward her. "Wait," she cried, holding out an arm in a weak attempt to keep him at bay. "I haven't any proof now, but I will, as soon as we find the treasure. I know it."

"How can you be so certain?"

Genevieve stared at him, her eyes shining with the love and loyalty that formed her conviction. "He was my father. That's why."

Despite everything he knew, Jonathon wasn't immune to the unwavering faith in her deep blue eyes. He found himself hoping, for her sake, that she was right. "Very well," he agreed tersely, "you've made your point, Genevieve."

She nodded graciously, pleased with her victory as she moved to leave the room, but he quickly stepped in front of her. "Not quite yet. Now it's your turn. Tell me who you were protecting."

Genevieve gasped—she'd forgotten about that. She chewed her lip, then lied softly, "Henri Rabine."

"Rabine? Who is he?" Jonathon demanded, experiencing for the first time in his life the new and altogether unpleasant sensation of jealousy.

"He was my father's first officer. He was like an uncle to me. But that was before . . ." She broke off and looked away. Before Armand. Henri, her father's trusted friend, had died, and Armand had taken his place.

"Before?" Jonathon prompted her, seeing the pain which suddenly clouded her eyes.

"Before what happened here on Martinique. Henri Rabine died, though—I remember now—so he couldn't have had anything to do with it."

"Who replaced him?"

Genevieve looked away, pretending to search her memory. Lying to Jonathon was harder than she could ever have imagined, but loyalty to Armand kept her from speaking his name. She couldn't accuse him, not without proof. "Ummm," she murmured, feigning concentration, "he was a member of my father's crew. . . . I met him once, just before they sailed, but so much happened afterwards, I'm afraid I just don't. . . ." She finished shakily, hating the lie.

Jonathon put a soothing hand on her shoulder. "It's all right, Genevieve. Just promise me you'll let me know if you do remember."

She nodded mutely, feeling guilty and ashamed of her ploy, and completely undeserving of his sympathy. "About tomorrow," she said, wanting to change the subject as quickly as possible, "I'd like to visit Mount Pelée. It's the only place on my map we haven't explored yet."

Jonathon nodded. "It's a long trip. We'll need to start early."

"Fine," she answered, anxious to leave before he asked her any more questions that would force her to choose between lying to him and protecting Armand. Escape, however, was not that easy.

Jonathon reached out, his hand wrapping firmly around her upper arm as he turned her to him. "Wait a minute, we haven't finished. I want you to give me your word."

Genevieve looked up nervously. "My word?"

"Yes. I want you to swear to me that you won't see Phelps again. Not unless Tyler or I are with you."

Harry? Genevieve had completely forgotten about him. Her relief that he wasn't going to ask her anything more about Armand quickly turned to irritation. "Very well, you have my word," she agreed reluctantly. "But I want you to know you're completely wrong here. Harry has been nothing but a perfect gentleman and companion."

"Don't you understand?" Jonathon growled, anger flashing in his eyes as he tightened his grip on her arm. "What if something had happened to you?"

Genevieve jerked away, tired of trying to reason with him, tired of being the recipient of his anger and brutish manners. She gave him a good glare for his rudeness, then shrugged her shoulders carelessly. "You would have lost your treasure."

Jonathon stared at her for a never-ending moment, a meaning she couldn't identify hidden in his golden eyes. He stepped back a pace, his rugged features once again unreadable. "You're right," was all he said.

CHAPTER FIFTEEN

Marie was submerging the long branches of the hyacinth in a pail of cool water while she trimmed the stems. She passed the beautiful lavender blossoms to Genevieve, who arranged them in a sturdy blue vase. The two women had spent the morning working together in the gardens, collecting the flowers that now covered the immense dining room table, and were finishing their task of clipping the varied blossoms and arranging them in vases to be distributed throughout the house.

A change in the weather had postponed Genevieve and Jonathon's trip to Mount Pelée. The air was hot and sticky, the sky heavy with thick, gray, low-hanging clouds which trapped the heat. A sure sign, she'd been informed, of an approaching tropical storm. Jonathon and Ty had worked with Luc to board up the house to protect it from the harsh, battering winds and driving rain they expected, but three days had passed, and not a drop of rain had fallen. Genevieve glanced irritably outside at the dark clouds, angry at the inclement weather for conspiring against her to delay her trip.

She reached up to wipe the wetness from her forehead, the mugginess in the air making her feel damp and warm all over, then looked at Marie, wondering at her ability to always remain so poised. "Marie, how do you do it?" she asked, giving voice to her thoughts. Not only did she feel sticky and uncomfortable on the outside, she was a bundle of nerves on the inside. "How do you stay so cool and calm all the time?"

Marie lifted her shoulders in a graceful shrug as she placed a vase of roses on the sideboard. "I suppose that is just my nature, mam'selle. It is the way of the islands. We do not see life the same way the Europeans do."

That was certainly true. Outwardly, Martinique reminded Genevieve of France, the city of St. Pierre, Paris. A remote, fascinating version of Paris, one that had been flavored with exotic spices, caressed by gentle trade winds, and enlivened with the brilliant colors of the turquoise sea, lush jungles, and dazzling villages. But it was the people that set it apart the most, their melodious rhythm of speech, friendly smiles, and warm, easy charm giving it a special character that she thought must surely be unique in the world.

Genevieve smiled at Marie, wanting to know more about the island and its customs. "Tell me about the headdresses I see all the native women wearing," she said, referring to the large madras handkerchiefs which were folded about the women's heads like turbans, with one or several bright ends left sticking up like plumes. She wore one now herself, having gratefully accepted Marie's offer to tie her hair up and out of the way while they gardened. "I've seen them tied several ways, almost as if the women were sending out some sort of signal, but I haven't been able to figure out what it is."

Marie smiled. "You're very observant, mam'selle. Very well, I shall tell you. One point left sticking up signifies 'my heart is free, I am looking for a friend.' Look and you will see all the pretty young girls in the city wear their scarves tied just so." She nodded approvingly, then continued, "Three points—'don't bother me, I'm happily married.'"

"What about you, Marie? What does your scarf mean?"

Marie's scarf was artfully tied, with four bright points sticking up. She smiled mischievously. "It means, 'I am not exactly free, but there is room in my life for one more.'" Genevieve's eyes flew open as Marie casually shrugged. "I am thinking this might encourage Luc to let his intentions to me be known. Also, it is good for the wives whose husbands take them for granted."

Genevieve laughed and reached up to touch the scarf which covered her thick, golden hair. "What about mine? What do two points indicate?"

Marie's eyes softened. "Two points mean, 'I am promised, you are wasting your time.'"

"Marie! You know that isn't true," Genevieve protested.

"Of course it is true," Marie countered smoothly. "You belong to M'sieur Jon, just as he belongs to you. You have been given a very rare gift, *chérie*, a wonderful gift. A love that will last a lifetime and beyond."

Genevieve felt her eyes well up inexplicably with tears. "That's a lovely sentiment, Marie, but I'm afraid you're quite mistaken. There's nothing between Jonathon and me. Nothing."

"Why do you struggle so, *chérie*?"

"Struggle?"

Marie nodded, her dark eyes shining and wise, as if they held all the wisdom in the world. "My grandmother was a great woman, mam'selle, and she taught me many things when I was a little girl. She taught me that a smile on the face does not mean that the heart is smiling, too." She paused, looking intently at Genevieve, then continued. "Life is good, *chérie*. All things will pass as they are meant to pass. When we fight against this, we are only fighting ourselves."

Genevieve swallowed hard. As much as she didn't want to admit it, Marie was right. Somehow, somewhere, between the weeks they'd spent at sea and the time together on his plantation, she'd fallen more than a little bit in love with Jonathon. And *that* realization scared her to death. She shook her head ruefully, wondering how she'd come to find herself in such a vulnerable position.

"You are a good woman, mam'selle," Marie said, breaking into her thoughts. "Life has brought you here, to this island, to these people. You must trust. Do not be afraid to reach for what you want."

"I don't know if I can, Marie," she whispered.

Marie's eyes shone with conviction. "You can, *chérie*. You are afraid your heart will break, but that is not so. It may crack just a little, but that is necessary to let someone in. Then your heart will be full, and it, too, will be smiling."

Genevieve stayed and talked with Marie for a little longer, then left the dining room, looking for a diversion from her tumultuous thoughts. She went to her bedroom and picked up a shirt that needed mending, but she was too restless to focus on her task. What she needed, she decided, was to get away from the house, for Jonathon's presence was everywhere. How could she possibly think clearly here? She changed quickly from her morning frock into a riding habit, tugging the scarf from her head and letting her hair tumble freely in riotous honey waves down her back. She felt better already.

She headed downstairs and walked past Jonathon's study, hearing his deep voice as he talked with Ty. She heard the sudden boom of rich, masculine laughter, the first she'd heard in days. Jonathon barely talked to her anymore, preferring to remain locked away in his study, attending to other business. When they did run into one another, he was coolly polite and distant, as if it were a strain just to see her.

Ignoring the dull ache in her chest, she headed determinedly for the stables. They'd been waiting for this stupid storm for days—surely the weather would hold for another hour or so. She glanced up at the dark, blustery sky, then mounted the gentle mare she'd ridden last week, sending her into an easy canter toward the beach.

"Tell me again. Where was the *last* place you saw her?" Jonathon demanded. The rain drove down in heavy torrents, pounding ceaselessly against the shuttered windows. A fierce wind roared outside, whipping the tall palms and drenching the rough grass lawns.

The groom gulped. "By the stables, riding the chestnut mare. I tried to warn her that the storm was likely to start at any time, but I don't think she heard me."

"So you just let her go?" Jonathon bellowed.

The groom hastily shook his head, wiping the sweat from his brow. "She took off so fast I—" The deep, rolling boom of thunder filled the room, silencing him. Jagged streaks of lightning filled the sky, briefly illuminating the tense faces of the occupants of the room.

Jonathon realized at once there was no way Genevieve would be able to control the skittish mare in a storm like this. He grabbed the innocent groom by the shoulders. "Where?" he demanded, his voice harsh with fear. "Where did she go?"

"The beach," he stammered. "She took the path to the beach."

"Wait, I'll go with you," Ty called as Jonathon bolted for the door.

"No," Jonathon yelled over his shoulder, not breaking his stride. "Take Luc and cover the grounds near the house. She may have tried to make it back and need help."

His horse was saddled and waiting for him. He leapt into the saddle with one broad jump, jerking the stallion's reins around as he drove his heels into its flanks, sending the horse racing down the path Genevieve had taken. Though it was midday, the sky was as black as midnight, the driving rain blinding. But Jonathon knew the trail well, and his mount, sensing his urgency, did not hold back, galloping bravely down the narrow path. Jonathon tensed his knees against the stallion's sides and leaned forward, his thoughts racing as wildly as his mount.

His heart twisted painfully as images of Genevieve, thrown and badly hurt, screamed through his brain. He should have known she would try something like this, he raged inwardly; he shouldn't have assumed she was still with Marie when he couldn't find her earlier that afternoon. Another bolt of lightning lit up the sky, startling his mount and causing it to rear suddenly, kicking his forelegs angrily against the summer sky.

Jonathon clenched his jaw, pausing to get control of both himself and the animal. He took a deep breath, then drove on, fighting his inner panic. If he arrived home and found Genevieve sitting by a cozy fire, chatting about the weather, he was going to quite cheerfully break her lovely neck.

Genevieve, however, was having no such luck. The same lightning that moments ago had almost unseated Jonathon proved to be very successful in separating her from her horse. She landed in a thick puddle of mud, then tumbled partway down a grassy bank before she was able to stop her fall. She lay there stunned for a few moments—more shaken than hurt—then rose shakily and climbed up the bank.

Tears of sheer misery streamed down her face and mingled with the rain which drenched her cheeks. "Please," she cried weakly, whether to herself or the skittish mare who regarded her distrustfully from a few paces down the path, she wasn't sure. "Please, I just want to go home."

The mare shook her head in response, tossing her dark mane nervously as she pawed the ground, prancing sideways and back in agitation. Genevieve choked back a sob, then forced a deep, painful gulp of air into her chest. She walked slowly toward the mare, speaking to the animal in a low, soothing tone. "Everything's fine now. We're going back." The mare nervously tossed her mane again, but remained still.

Genevieve reached for the reins.

A deafening boom of thunder filled the air at the same time that a blinding bolt of lightning streaked through the sky. The horse reared instantly, her sharp hooves slashing through the air. Genevieve threw her arms in front of her head to protect herself, but she wasn't fast enough. She felt a piercing pain in her left temple as her legs gave way beneath her. Fortunately, the blow had not been strong enough to seriously injure her. She lay sprawled out on the muddy path, lifting her aching head just in time to watch the horse bolt away without her. Perfect, she thought dismally as the rain beat down upon her, just perfect.

Jonathon raced along the trail, pulling his reins in sharply at the sound of an approaching horse. His heart lurched to his throat as he recognized Genevieve's mare, riderless. Afraid that his worst fears were about to be confirmed, he grabbed the mare's lead and tied it to the back of his saddle. Then, urging his mount slowly forward, he scanned the thick terrain beside the trail for any sign of Genevieve. He called her name over and over, the pouring rain making it difficult for him to see further than a few feet.

Genevieve thought at first that it must be her own mind playing tricks on her, that she couldn't possibly have heard her name. Then she heard it again. Very faintly, almost blocked out by the roar of the wind. She knew instantly who it was. "Jonathon! Jonathon, I'm here!" she called desperately, lifting her sodden skirts and running blindly toward the sound of his voice. She nearly collapsed with relief as his huge stallion appeared before her. "Jonathon," she choked out softly, a shaky smile on her lips as her eyes brimmed with tears of relief that he had come looking for her.

Jonathon leapt from his saddle and raced to Genevieve, pulling her against his chest in a bone-crushing embrace she wished would never end. Never mind the rain, the wind, the skittish horses. She just wanted to stand there and hold him forever.

That thought wasn't very practical, though, a point that was driven home as a bolt of lightning struck a nearby palm, the explosion electrifying the air around them and sending the huge tree crashing down a mere ten feet away. "Are you hurt?" he asked, shouting to make himself heard above the din of the storm.

Genevieve shook her head wordlessly as Jonathon lifted her onto his saddle, then seated himself behind her, his strong arms wrapped around her as he urged his mount steadily forward. They left the trail, moving into the jungle. The deeper they went, the thicker and more densely spaced were the trees, protecting them from the brutal forces of the storm. Jonathon stopped at a small, grassy clearing, dismounted and removed a blanket from his saddle, tying it high in the branches of the trees above them to provide even greater shelter.

Genevieve dismounted after him, watching silently. He hadn't said another word to her after he'd asked if she was hurt. She noted unhappily his tense, rigid movements, the muscle ticking furiously in his jaw a clear indication of his mood. She sighed resignedly. Might as well get this over with. "Jonathon," she began, "I know how angry you must be—"

Jonathon turned abruptly, his golden eyes dark with rage. "No, Genevieve," he answered through clenched teeth, "you have no idea how angry I am. What the hell did you think you were doing, riding off in a storm like this? Do you realize Tyler and Luc are out there looking for you right now?"

A wave of guilt washed over her. "I'm sorry. I had no idea how quickly the storm would open up. But I was on my way back to the house when you found me," she added, defending herself.

"And just how far do you think you would have made it without a horse?"

Genevieve's chin came up. "As far as I needed to go."

"You wouldn't have made it more than two feet if I hadn't found you."

"Is that so? And I suppose you expect my undying gratitude for your heroic rescue? Well, I hate to disappoint you, but I was managing perfectly well without your help."

"Yes, of course. That's why you were stumbling blindly down the path when I found you, shaking so badly you could barely stand up."

Maybe that was true, but it didn't mean she had to like his mocking, superior tone. Her sapphire eyes narrowed as she closed the distance between them. "I'm beginning to wish you hadn't found me! I don't need your help, Jonathon, I never did. If you hadn't forced yourself upon me in the first place—"

Jonathon grew absolutely still. "I never forced myself—"

"Of course you did!" Genevieve insisted, not understanding that he'd misinterpreted her remark. "If you hadn't forced your help on me, threatening to send me back to Paris if I didn't agree, we wouldn't be in this whole mess right now."

Jonathon was somewhat mollified once she clarified her remark, but not by much. "The only reason we are in this 'mess,' as you call it, is because you, Genevieve, seem to delight in doing anything and everything you can think of simply to provoke my temper."

"Well, I certainly wouldn't need to risk riding out in a storm to do that. Lately even my saying 'hello' to you seems to be enough to put you in a bad humor."

Jonathon ignored that. "What were you doing out riding then, when you'd been warned there was a severe storm approaching?"

"I needed to think."

Jonathon looked incredulous, then shook his head. "Thinking seems to be a very dangerous occupation for you, Genevieve."

Genevieve snorted inelegantly, having no trouble figuring out he was referring to the incident with the rowboat. "Ah, yes, another of your heroic rescues. My, you are humble today, aren't you?" She tossed her head, reaching up to brush a few damp strands of hair off her forehead.

"What I am is sick of your—" he broke off abruptly, staring at her. "I thought you said you weren't hurt," he said, his voice almost accusing. He pulled her to him, his fingers gently supporting her chin as he examined her bruised temple. "What happened?"

Genevieve barely heard the question. He was standing too close to her. Her eyes met his shoulders, taking in their broad, muscular width, then moved on to his neck, fascinated by the rough texture of his skin, the way his dark hair curled up where it met the collar of his shirt. He smelled wonderful, masculine, fresh from the rain. Her gaze traveled up past his sensuous lips, firm nose, and clearly defined, almost harsh cheekbones to lock on his beautiful eyes. She'd never noticed before how long and dark his eyelashes were.

"What happened?" he repeated softly, searching her face.

"Nothing, really. The horse shied and I wasn't quite able to avoid her hooves," she answered absently. She longed to reach out and touch him, wanting that more than she'd ever wanted anything in her life.

"Does it hurt?" he asked, concern written on his face.

She shook her head. *Do not be afraid to reach for what you want.* Marie's words echoed through her head. Summoning all her courage, Genevieve laid her small hand gently on his chest, amazed at the feelings that flooded through her at that slight contact. She raised her eyes slowly to his. "I'm glad you came to look for me, Jonathon."

In that single moment, everything changed. The anger that had been between them was gone, replaced by an altogether different emotion, one which smoldered with white-hot intensity. The air was suddenly charged, sparked with an electricity not unlike the lightning which streaked through the sky. Jonathon traced his finger from her temple to her cheek, then ran it slowly over her soft, parted lips. "What happens now that I've found you?"

"I'm not sure," she answered in breathless, nervous honesty. "I want you to show me." She heard Jonathon's quick intake of breath, and watched a fire light in his golden eyes.

"Do you know what you're saying?" he asked hoarsely.

"Yes," she whispered, her sapphire eyes deeper and bluer than any sea he'd ever seen. "I want you, Jonathon."

Jonathon emitted a low groan, not wasting another second as he pulled her tightly into his arms, his lips crushing down on hers, needing her with a hunger so fierce he could barely control it. He wanted to touch every part of her at once. His hands roved over her slim back, then down to cup her shapely bottom, and further still to caress her soft thighs. Then back up to start all over again. He wrapped his strong arms even tighter around her, and with their bodies locked together, he still felt as if he couldn't get close enough to her. He finally lifted her into his arms, loving the feeling of having every ounce of her pressed against his body.

He ran his tongue across her mouth, softly insisting she part her lips. She did. She tasted better, sweeter, wilder than he remembered. He went down on one knee, cradling her in his arms as he balanced her on his thigh. Brushing her thick, golden hair aside, he lifted his mouth from hers and began nuzzling her smooth, creamy throat, while his fingers brushed lightly along her soft breasts.

Genevieve threw back her head, a low moan escaping her lips, then nearly jumped at the jolt of hot pleasure that streaked through her when he traced his tongue along her ear. Her entire body was trembling, her stomach felt as if it had been turned upside down, and a strange, burning sensation filled the lower half of her. She clung to Jonathon, unconsciously pressing herself against him, aching for something she still couldn't define, overcome by a desire she couldn't begin to understand.

Jonathon groaned softly, tearing his mouth away from her body long enough to ask, "Your head—are you sure you're not hurt?"

Genevieve stared at him in complete bewilderment, wondering dazedly why he'd stopped kissing her. Her eyes were glazed with passion, her full lips deep rose. He couldn't tear his eyes away from her mouth as he watched her form the words to answer his question. "Do you mean, am I quite sure I wasn't knocked senseless, and that's why I decided I wanted you?"

Jonathon's lips twitched. "No. I was only asking if you were in any pain."

"Oh." She shook her head. "I don't feel a thing," she assured him.

Jonathon's lips curved into a wicked smile. "You will," he promised, his golden eyes glistening as he gently lowered her onto the damp grass.

Genevieve had the distinct impression he wasn't referring to her head anymore.

He stretched out on top of her, careful to brace himself up on his elbows so his weight wouldn't crush her, then slipped one hand through her hair, tangling his fingers in the glorious mass of honey-colored silk while his lips once again found hers. Genevieve arched her back, her hips pressing against his, instinctively matching the rhythm set by his probing tongue. She heard Jonathon's low moan of pleasure as if it were from a great distance, then felt a stab of dismay and abandonment as he lifted himself off her.

His hands were back within seconds, though, pulling her up against him as he worked the fastenings on her gown. "Let me see you, Genevieve," he murmured huskily, gently removing her clothing with an expertise she didn't want to think about. He lowered her back down to the grass and swallowed hard, his eyes roving over her like a starving man at a banquet. "My God, you're so beautiful," he said, his deep voice full of reverence. Her curves were full and lush, her waist tiny, her legs long and shapely. Her pale ivory skin seemed to glow in the dim light of the sheltered trees.

He reached for her, but Genevieve stopped him, wrapping her arms lovingly around his neck as she drew herself up. "Now let me see you, Jonathon," she answered courageously. She leaned into him, her long hair falling softly against his neck, her breath warm against his chest as she slowly undid the buttons of his shirt. Jonathon clenched his jaw, his hands locked firmly at his sides in an attempt to restrain himself from moving too fast, forcing himself to yield to the sweet torture of her tender ministrations. He was amazed at the effect she had on him, the power of her innocence and beauty. His desire for her made him shake.

Genevieve ran her hands lightly across his powerful shoulders as she slowly removed his shirt, following the shape of his broad chest and the rippling muscles of his flat stomach, then stopping at his narrow waist, where her fingers rested on the cold metal of his belt buckle. Her courage deserted her. She looked up at him, her eyes hesitant and unsure. Jonathon placed his own hands gently on top of hers. "Genevieve," he said, looking into her deep blue eyes, "you've nothing to be frightened of. Trust me. I'll never hurt you."

Genevieve nodded, her throat dry. His assurances were a far cry from the words *I love you* that she was foolishly aching to hear, but they helped nonetheless. Her fingers stiffly worked the buckle free, but she couldn't quite manage the buttons to his pants. There was a distinct bulge there, and the more her hands nervously struggled against it, the larger it became. She heard a low, almost pained groan from Jonathon as he brushed her fingers roughly away. "I'm sorry," she stammered awkwardly, "but the buttons seem to be stuck—"

The rest of her words were cut off as Jonathon's lips crushed down hungrily over her own. He rolled her back onto the damp grass, himself on top of her. Evidently he'd had no trouble with the buttons, for she realized immediately that he was as naked as she. She felt neither guilt nor embarrassment, but simply wonder. She was awed by the intensity of emotions that filled her, by the absolute glory and beauty of the moment. With his magnificent body pressed along the length of hers, the sensation of skin on skin was more thrilling than anything she'd ever imagined.

Although she truly hadn't thought much about it, Genevieve had always assumed that a man's body would feel fairly similar to her own, only larger. How completely wrong she'd been. Jonathon's body felt nothing like her own. She ran her fingers across his thick chest, his broad shoulders, then along the thickly corded muscles of his arms. He was rock solid everywhere, like steel encased in rough velvet, except that his skin seemed to burn at her touch. His hard thighs pressed against hers, sending pulsating waves through her body. She didn't recognize the low moans she heard as her own as she strained against him, their bodies gently rocking to a primitive, ageless rhythm.

Jonathon's hands roamed wildly over her body, exploring every lush curve and gentle valley. Emboldened by his touch, she lifted her mouth to explore the roughness of his skin, then trailed her tongue along the firm column of his neck, feeling the muscles in his back tense in response.

Jonathon lifted himself from her, his eyes staring at her in amazement. He'd imagined making love to Genevieve a thousand times, but he'd never expected such passion from her, such innate power and intensity. Nor had he expected the feelings she would arouse within him. Tenderness and desire surged through his veins, his heart pounding as furiously as the storm which raged on around them.

"Genny," he murmured hoarsely, pressing her tightly to him. He lowered his dark head to her breast, his tongue capturing the tight, pink bud of her nipple, sucking until it stood hard and proud, then flicking his tongue against it yet again, teasingly, while she shivered with delight. She wove her hands through his dark, wavy hair, her breath coming in short, hot gasps. Satisfied, he turned his head and gave her other breast the same loving attention.

Reluctantly lifting his mouth from her beautiful breasts, he worked his way down, placing gentle kisses on her slender ribs, resting his rough cheek on her flat, smooth belly while his fingers stroked the golden curls which covered the lush, enticing area between her soft thighs. His hands moved on, tracing the smooth curve of her hips, then gently cupping her firm bottom.

Genevieve moaned softly and drew Jonathon back up, feeling as if she would surely explode if she had to take another second of such intense pleasure, and wishing at the same time that it would never end. His strong arms were locked around her, but it wasn't enough anymore. He was still too far away. It didn't make sense, she didn't understand it, but with a longing so intense that it was almost painful, she wanted him closer. "Jonathon," she whispered, her breath hot against his ear. "Jonathon."

Jonathon understood. He raised himself above her, bracing himself on his elbows, gently, slowly, seeking entrance. He stopped at her threshold, his brilliant amber gaze locked on deep sapphire, then slowly entered her.

Genevieve's eyes widened in astonishment. So this was what it was all about. This touch, this intimate connection with another human being. It felt wonderful. Beautiful. She felt Jonathon trembling above her, absolutely still, an expression on his face which looked almost like pain. Instinctively sensing that he was waiting for something from her, she reached up to stroke the rigid muscles of his shoulders. "Yes," she whispered against his lips.

Jonathon let out his breath in a rush of relief, knowing he couldn't have borne the waiting a second longer. He'd entered her slowly, her walls as smooth as velvet, wet and tight. So tight it had taken every ounce of self-control he possessed to keep him from driving on. Even after she gave her assent, he still hesitated, knowing his next movement would cause her pain. "Genny, I'm sorry," he said. He pulled back slightly, then pushed his hips forward, breaking through her fragile barrier and filling her completely.

Genevieve cried out in surprise at the sharp pain that tore through her, the hazy, impassioned daze she'd been in suddenly clearing. "Wait," she gasped, clutching Jonathon's shoulders tightly. "Wait, that hurts. I don't think we're doing this right."

She heard a muffled sound from Jonathon in response, part laughter and part groan, then he brushed a light kiss atop her forehead. "Trust me, sweetheart. We're doing it right."

Genevieve shook her head, firmly unconvinced. "Maybe

we should start over," she suggested. Hoping Jonathon wouldn't take too great an offense at her suggestion that he'd made some sort of error—men could be so touchy about that, after all—she decided a compliment was in order: "I liked everything else, but that last part hurt."

Jonathon sighed.

"You promised you wouldn't hurt me," she reminded him.

He groaned. This was the most exquisite torture he'd ever endured. It was all he could do not to move deeper into Genevieve right now, as tightly sheathed as he was within her. Sweat stood out on his brow, his muscles taut with the strain of holding back. "Genevieve, that was your virgin's pain," he explained as patiently and as rationally as he could under the circumstances. "It will only happen once, and that can't be helped."

She looked at him as if he were selling snake oil. Jonathon sighed again. "Does it hurt now?"

Genevieve thought for a moment, then her eyes widened in surprise. It didn't hurt at all. In fact, it felt rather wonderful. Her face lit up in a slow, radiant smile as she reached for him, hugging him tightly. She was about to tell him how nice it *did* feel when his mouth slanted over hers, swallowing her words. He kissed her deeply, hungrily, then began to move his lean hips.

That felt even better.

The slow, burning sensation returned, stretching her every nerve as it built steadily within her. She instinctively arched her back, lifting her hips to meet his, the rhythm and sensation of their union blocking out any thoughts she'd had. She clung to his broad back and felt the muscles and power there as she dug her nails into his broad shoulders, and tasted the saltiness of his skin. She felt as if she were being slowly lifted, riding the crest of a giant wave, and clung even tighter to Jonathon, her hips pushing against his as the wave rose higher and higher, lifting her faster and faster. She caught her breath. The tempo built and she strained against Jonathon, reaching. . . .

The wave peaked. Genevieve felt as if a thousand sparks had been set off within her body. Jolts of pure pleasure raced down her spine as every nerve and muscle from her fingertips to her toes seemed to expand and explode. She gasped, calling out Jonathon's name in a husky voice she didn't recognize as her own.

Jonathon clung to her as her release came, her breath coming in short gasps, then watched her face as an expression of pure joy and amazement overcame her. Her face and body were so open to him now, so trusting. When she called out his name he could wait no longer. He drove into her harder and faster, shuddering as his seed poured into her, his climax more powerful than anything he'd ever known in his life.

He collapsed weakly on top of her, his strength entirely depleted. Then he rolled over, his arm wrapped around her slim waist to take her with him. They were still joined intimately and he moved carefully, not wanting to disturb their union. Genevieve lay on top of him, her thick golden hair spilling over his chest, listening to the wild hammering of his heart. His skin was slick with perspiration, as was hers, and she ran her hand lightly over his chest, matting the damp hair beneath her fingers. A sigh of pure contentment escaped her lips as she propped her small chin on his chest, gazing up at him with wonder and love in her deep blue eyes.

She didn't know what to say.

He didn't say anything.

Jonathon was overwhelmed by the emotions racing through him, stunned by the intensity of their union. She'd opened herself to him fully, giving him not only her body, but her trust, her heart. Touching his very soul. And leaving him without a damned clue as to what he should do next.

The storm, which had thundered all around them while they made love, had passed. The air was now warm and calm, and around them the wet foliage seemed to steam, almost purr, in luxurious relief. Jonathon lifted Genevieve from him and stood, passing her clothes to her. "The rain's stopped," he said. "We should go back." They dressed in silence and made their way back to the house.

CHAPTER SIXTEEN

"Tell me again why you think LeClerk might have moved the treasure to Mount Pelée."

Genevieve sighed and glanced at Jonathon, who walked up the steep, rocky terrain beside her. They'd left for Mount Pelée early that morning, tying up the horses where the terrain became too rough and progressing from there on foot. Nothing had been said about what had passed between them yesterday afternoon.

Genevieve chewed her lip, her stomach aching as she considered the possibility that what happened yesterday had been nothing more but a minor dalliance on his part. After all, there had been no promises made between them, either before their lovemaking or after. But even as she steeled herself for that possibility, her stubborn heart wouldn't believe it. There had been a promise made, even if unspoken. She'd felt it as she rode back to the house cradled within the safety of Jonathon's arms, leaning back against the solid expanse of his chest and feeling his breath warm against the top of her head.

She didn't know much about making love, but surely a man didn't hold a woman like that, kiss her so tenderly, be joined so intimately, without feeling *something*.

Pushing that weighty issue out of her mind now, she turned her attention back to the question Jonathon had just posed. "My father wrote to me about visiting the 'Ruler of the People.' I mentioned that to Marie, and she told me the natives sometimes refer to the volcano that way." She paused to disentangle her skirt from a thorny bush, then continued. "He also mentioned that he'd journeyed there three times, though I haven't yet figured out what that might mean to our search."

Probably nothing, Jonathon thought to himself, wondering why Genevieve had insisted they not delay in making this trip. Not only was he certain it would be a waste of time, it also drew him away from observing any Southern activity that might be taking place in town. They reached a stream that was normally calm and gentle but had become swollen by yesterday's storm. Jonathon studied the rushing water, judging it to be about thigh-high, then turned to Genevieve. "I'd better carry you across."

"I'm sure I can manage," Genevieve objected quickly, stepping back. Maybe he could act as if nothing had happened, but unfortunately she wasn't as immune to his touch. The more distance she kept between them, the better. "It really doesn't look that deep."

"Genevieve—"

She hurried to the bank of the river but he was right behind her, lifting her into his arms before she had so much as a single toe in the water. "You'd make it a lot easier if you didn't struggle. I'm having a hard enough time trying to keep my balance as it is."

Genevieve instantly stopped trying to squirm out of his arms. "Why don't you just put me down, then?"

"Because I don't want to."

Well, good for him. Why did the man always seem to get whatever he wanted? *Including herself*, she thought, her cheeks blushing furiously. She felt angrier still because she couldn't blame him for her seduction. She'd fallen into his arms eagerly, willingly, just as he'd wanted her to all along.

Jonathon treaded slowly across the rapidly moving stream. The stones beneath his feet were covered with moss, making them slick and damp—as wet and smooth as Genevieve's thighs when they'd made love, he thought achingly. A light mist from the water dampened her skin, giving it the same radiant glow he'd seen yesterday. Honey-colored wisps of hair curled about the nape of her neck, the delicate, feminine scent of her body driving him wild.

"You can put me down now," Genevieve prompted when they reached the opposite side and he showed no sign of releasing his hold on her.

"I'm thinking about it," he replied.

"I realize what a strain that must be for you."

"It's no strain at all, Genevieve. You don't weigh more than—"

"I was referring to the process of you thinking, not to my weight," she corrected him irritably.

Jonathon just grinned in response and set her down. "Testy, are we? And what grave error did I make to warrant such an attack?"

If only his golden eyes didn't twinkle so when he smiled, she thought, it would be so much easier for her to hold on to her anger. "I was perfectly capable of making it across that river on my own. I don't appreciate being ignored and manhandled."

"Manhandled, is it? You seemed to have a very different reaction to my touch yesterday."

Now he wanted to bring yesterday up. Genevieve looked away from him, busily brushing imaginary dirt off her skirts in an attempt to hide the color which flared in her cheeks. "That was different. I was merely frightened by the storm and needed comfort."

"Comfort?" Jonathon scoffed. "I think you needed quite a bit more than just comfort. We both did."

She gritted her teeth. "Must we talk about this now?"

He shrugged. "Why not? What's wrong with now?"

Genevieve fixed her icy blue gaze on him as the doubts and anxieties, which she'd been trying so hard to bury, quickly resurfaced. "What's wrong with now is that you're twenty-four hours too late. What happened to your tongue yesterday? Didn't I merit something then? Couldn't you have thought to tell me what you were feeling, what I meant to you, if things were to change between us? Don't you think I wondered?"

Jonathon just stared at her, amazed. Couldn't she tell what he was feeling? That he never wanted to let her go, that making love to her had been sweeter and wilder than anything he'd ever experienced in his life? That just looking at her, listening to her voice, watching her breathe, for God's sake, filled his loins with an insatiable yearning to have her again and again? "Genevieve," he began, reaching for her.

She drew herself up haughtily, an expression of pure disdain on her lovely features. "As it happens, I am not in the mood to discuss this further at present."

He took a deep breath as he summoned his patience, then tried again. "Genevieve, I had no idea you were feeling—"

"That's because you didn't ask me, isn't it?" she interrupted. He opened his mouth to reply, but she rushed on. "Don't bother. It's too late now for your sweet words of love."

Jonathon's lips twitched as he fought back a grin, the laughter unmistakable in his eyes. She was so very transparent, such a joy to tease, that he just couldn't resist. "What makes you so certain that's what you were going to hear?"

Genevieve's mouth dropped open. The idiot man—he wasn't going to beg her forgiveness, to whisper tender words in her ear! "Well!" she huffed in stunned amazement as her anger caught up with her. "You can go straight to the devil!" she yelled, turning from him in a fit of feminine pique and marching resolutely away.

Jonathon caught up with her easily, matching her angry strides with little effort. He whistled cheerfully as they walked, his apparent good humor grating on her nerves, just as she knew it was meant to. She willed herself to ignore him, but that was impossible. "Do you mind?" she finally snapped, her patience at an end.

He quit whistling, giving her a look of complete innocence, a look so out of place on his rugged features it would have made her laugh at any other time, and asked simply, "Where are we going?"

"We are not going anywhere," she informed him curtly. "I am going to that village up ahead to enlist a guide to take me to Mount Pelée. I believe I've already told you where you can go."

"I see," Jonathon replied simply, nodding his head as if in deep thought. He pointed ahead. "That village there?"

Genevieve clenched her fists. It was the only village within miles, probably on the entire side of the mountain. "Yes," she said through gritted teeth, "that village."

"Hmmm."

She glanced at him contemptuously. "Let me guess. I suppose now you're going to tell me that I won't be able to find a guide, that I'll be stranded without you, and that I'll be turned away by the villagers."

Jonathon shook his head, his tone casual. "Actually, I doubt very much you'll be turned away. It is near noonday meal, after all."

"Oh." Genevieve hesitated uncertainly, knowing it would be impolite to barge in on them just as they were preparing to eat.

"Well," Jonathon said, coming to a stop. He took her hand, giving it a firm shake. "Good luck to you, Genevieve, it was nice knowing you." He turned and started to walk away.

"Wait," she called immediately, running after him. "Are you just going to leave me here? I can't walk in now."

"Of course you can. As I told you, it's nearly time for their meal and I'm sure they're most hungry. They'll be delighted to see you." He paused, letting his words sink in, then took a step back. "Well, this is as far as I go. I've been told by those who come back that the villagers' sense of smell is extraordinary." He frowned. "But then again, so very few actually do come back. Good-bye, Genevieve."

What?! Genevieve ran after him, grabbing his arm as she searched his face for any sign that he was just trying to frighten her. She found none. "Are you trying to tell me that those villagers actually *eat* people?" she asked, her voice a frantic whisper.

"Of course. I thought you already knew that."

"You thought I already knew that! You thought I would simply march into a village full of man-eating cannibals to ask for directions and a guide?"

Jonathon shrugged. "Frankly, Genevieve, nothing you do would surprise me anymore."

Well! She lifted her chin, matching his long, steady gait as they walked away from the village, skirting it widely. She mulled his words over in her mind, eyeing him suspiciously. "I seem to recall being told how peaceful the natives were, and how friendly."

He nodded. "That's true. The original natives were very friendly, known for their quiet, gentle way of life. They were no match for the tribes that came out of the jungles of South America."

"What tribes?"

"The Caribes. The Caribbean is named after that fierce band, you know. They attacked, killing and eating all the men and male children. The women were kept as prizes of war."

Genevieve shuddered, aghast that such a thing could happen in so beautiful and tranquil a setting. "How horrible," she said softly, chewing her lip.

Jonathon didn't miss the solemn, worried look on her face. "This happened several hundred years ago, Genevieve. There are no war parties scouting through the jungle at present." He took her arm firmly, however, and added for good measure, "Still, you'd best stay at my side."

Genevieve had no intention of doing otherwise. "What did the women do?" she asked, automatically imagining herself in that position. "Did they fight back? Did they let their captors know how low and despicable they were?"

"Perhaps," he answered, "but that may have been difficult for them to do. You're forgetting, the men and women came from different nations, different worlds in a way. Everything about their lives was different, their customs, rituals—they even spoke separate languages."

Genevieve's eyes widened. "You mean the men and women lived together, in the same village, but couldn't even speak to one another?" She shook her head. "Can you imagine what our lives today would be like if men and women couldn't talk to one another?"

Jonathon thought about it. No more petty quarrels, no more regrets and recriminations. No more agonizing hours spent trying to figure out how the female mind worked. Just eat, sleep, and make love. What would that be like? "Bliss," he answered her.

"Thank you very much."

He bit back his laughter at her thoroughly disgruntled tone. "It must not have been too bad, for they lived that way for generations. The men spoke one language, the women another."

"Yes, but they must have eventually resolved their differences. After all those years there must have been enough to draw them together: births, deaths, marriages, celebrations. Men and women needn't always be on opposite, warring sides."

The point she was making referred to more than what had occurred within the ancient tribes, and Jonathon knew it. He stopped, drawing her to face him. "You're right," he said simply.

Genevieve smiled softly. "And in the end, which language did they speak?"

"The women's, of course," he answered, allowing her a moment of victory. "Talking seems to have always been held in high regard by you ladies."

She didn't miss the teasing gibe in his voice. "There, you see," she replied, her sapphire eyes sparkling, "that's why you men always muck things up with your silly wars and greed. You haven't yet learned the value of a few well-chosen words."

Jonathon leaned toward her, his firm, sensuous lips slightly parted. "You're right, Genevieve. We men tend to be much more direct with our needs."

She waited until his arms had nearly closed in around her, until his lips were softly brushing hers, then deftly pulled away, slipping from his grasp. She laughed, her face lit up with a mischievous smile. "But that doesn't get you very far, does it? Not when it's soft words we ladies want to hear." He reached for her again but she danced away, looking like a young, beautiful elf, her golden hair streaming all around her, shining in the afternoon sun.

He frowned. "Men are judged by their actions, not by their words."

Genevieve merely lifted her shoulders, unimpressed. She strolled around the quiet glade where they'd stopped, noticing for the first time its lush, almost unreal beauty. Huge overgrown ferns formed a natural border, and the steam from volcanic vents added to the dank, sweet, exotic aroma. Birds trilled to one another from the trees overhead, while brilliant, iridescent hummingbirds darted into the delicate lips of wild orchids. Butterflies of a hundred hues and sizes floated through the air, landing gracefully on rich stems of oleander and bouganvillea. A small stream cascaded over moss-strewn boulders, providing the scene with the music of trickling water.

Their previous exchange forgotten, Genevieve turned to Jonathon, wonder and delight shining in her eyes. "I feel as if I've just discovered the Garden of Eden."

"Not quite," Jonathon replied, smiling as his eyes followed her as she moved about in her soft, rosy-pink gown. If it were the Garden of Eden, she would be as naked as Eve, and he would be as bare as Adam. Then they would be in paradise.

She smiled self-consciously, aware how silly and romantic her words must sound to him. "Well," she said softly, "it's almost Eden."

Motivated by hunger, and entirely unaware of Jonathon's

thoughts, she reached up to pluck a small green apple from the branches of the tree above her. She raised it to her mouth, then, remembering her manners, offered it to him first.

He declined with a shake of his head, a wry smile curving his lips. "If Eve looked anything like you, Genevieve, I'm beginning to understand why we were cast out of the Garden. It would take more than a mere man to resist that kind of temptation."

She laughed shakily, determined this time to resist the pull he seemed to have on her. "I beg you not to read too much into it. The only thing I'm offering you is an apple."

"Is it?" Jonathon asked, slowly approaching her. He took the apple from her hand, staring into her deep blue eyes. "And if I were to eat this, the results would surely be as disastrous for me as they were for Adam."

Genevieve's pulse rocketed at his nearness. "Why is that?" she managed to ask.

"That's a machineel tree. Its fruit is poisonous," he informed her. He lifted her hand, turning it over to examine her palm. "You didn't touch the bark, did you? The sap can burn your skin, especially after a rain."

She shook her head, her eyes locked on his. "What about you? I thought I saw you touching that very tree."

"No. But it wouldn't matter even if I did. Your touch is the only thing that burns my skin."

Genevieve sucked in her breath, almost dizzy from the longing and desire surging within her. The urge to collapse into Jonathon's arms, to feel the firm, hard planes of his body pressing against hers, was almost overwhelming. She closed her eyes as he reached for her, shivers running down her spine as he drew his hands gently up her arms, then clasped them at the small of her back, slowly pulling her to him. "Touch me, Genevieve," he whispered. "Feel how your touch can set me on fire."

The thought of refusing him didn't even enter her mind. She did as he asked, wordlessly lifting her hands to his broad, muscular shoulders, letting her fingers once again follow the lines of his strong arms and play lightly over his thick, corded muscles. She reached for his chest, working her hands underneath the cool white linen of his shirt to feel the heat of his skin. She heard his sharp intake of breath and felt his heart pounding beneath her palm. Still, part of her held back, searching his eyes, longing for the words he hadn't spoken.

Jonathon felt her hesitation. He placed his hand over hers, capturing it against his chest. "You've been living so long for tomorrow, Genevieve, have you forgotten how to live for today?"

Promise me tomorrow, Genevieve thought achingly, *and I won't be afraid to give myself to you today.* But she didn't say it. She wasn't that brave. Or foolhardy. "Is that all you believe in? Just living for the moment, with no thought of what's to come?"

"Is that what you think?"

"I don't know what to think."

"Then don't think at all. Just feel." He pulled her tightly to him, his lips crushing down on hers. His touch worked its magic once again as she felt her body sigh into his, molding against him in a perfect fit, as if they were two halves made complete only when together. At his gentle pressure she opened her lips, allowing his tongue entrance to her mouth. She dug her fingers into his shoulders, holding him tightly, feeling as if the world had spun away beneath her feet and he was the only anchor that could keep her from floating away.

She felt him bend down and wrap one strong arm behind her knees, then she was lifted effortlessly into his arms. Jonathon tore his mouth away from hers as he carried her to a sunbathed spot within the glade. "Do you feel what I feel?" he asked. Her head moved in mute agreement against his chest. "Then you know that what's between us is real, Genevieve, and rare. Not something you'll find growing on trees like apples in Eden."

He set her down, his hands moving automatically toward the fastenings of her gown. Genevieve stopped him, placing her hands gently on top of his. "Eden, is it? Are you sure we should be doing this, then? Original sin and all that?"

Jonathon looked up sharply, alarmed at her reluctance until he saw the teasing light in her eyes. He grinned wickedly in response, meeting her challenge. "Let me assure you, sweetheart," he replied, "the sin I have in mind is no longer very original." Genevieve sighed contentedly, happy just to be back in his arms. They moved together as one, locked in a tight embrace.

The noise was sudden, soft, and froze them both with its deadly intent.

Genevieve's head snapped to the left, her heart lurching to her throat as her worst fears were confirmed. There, curled up in the grass, unmistakable because of its light brown color and the black-and-white diamond pattern that ran down its back, was the island's most feared enemy, the fer-de-lance. The snake hissed as it raised its ugly head, opening its jaw to reveal large, deadly fangs. She watched in mute horror as the snake swayed softly back and forth, as if locked in an evil debate as to which of them it would strike first.

"Shhh." She heard Jonathon's deep voice in her ear, breaking through the fog of fear that held her. His strong hands came up slowly, very slowly, to clasp her shoulders. He gripped her tightly, then threw her roughly away from the deadly snake.

The snake moved in the same instant, hurtling itself through the air. Jonathon felt a flash of white-hot pain as its razor-sharp fangs dug into his ankle. He reached down, prying the vicious jaws free of his skin, then held the snake in both hands, holding its jaw shut, squeezing until he heard the snap of its spine and the fer-de-lance went limp in his hands. He threw the dead snake into the bushes.

Genevieve got to her feet shakily, her heart hammering wildly as she rushed to his side. Jonathon was kneeling on the grass, his jaw clenched tightly. She dropped to her knees beside him, seeing that his ankle was already red and beginning to swell. *Oh God. Oh God. Oh God.* The phrase echoed inanely through her brain, her body nearly paralyzed with fear.

"Here," Jonathon said, his voice hoarse as he pulled a knife from his belt and passed it to her. "Cut it open. Draw out the poison." The planes of his face were rigid but controlled, showing little reaction to the pain he must be in.

Genevieve nodded and took the knife from him as she eased him back onto the grass. She knew what she had to do. She lifted his ankle up, then pulled back the cloth of his pants leg. Taking a deep breath to fight back the nausea, she held the knife against his skin, then plunged it in, carving a deep *X* over the marks left by the snake's fangs. She felt Jonathon's body tense in response, but he made no sound. She quickly brought her lips to the wound, drawing his blood into her mouth and spitting it out, repeating that again and again, trying to drain as much poison out of his body as she could.

She glanced at Jonathon, who lay immobile now, a fine sheen of perspiration on his brow. Panicked, she wiped the blood from her mouth, then yanked off her petticoat, using the knife to tear it into rough strips to bind his ankle. She bunched the remainder of the petticoat under his foot to elevate the wound and slow the flow of blood.

Not knowing what else to do, she turned away from his ankle, her hands gently brushing his dark hair away from his face. "Jonathon, can you hear me?" she asked softly. "Jonathon?" she repeated, barely keeping her panic under control. She searched his face, noting the pallor of his normally deep-golden skin and his shallow, labored breathing. She reached frantically for his wrist. His pulse was there, but thready and erratic.

A choked sob escaped her lips as tears sprang to her eyes and coursed down her cheeks. She grabbed his shoulders, shaking him roughly. "Don't you dare leave me, Jonathon

Morgan," she swore. "Don't you dare." She found his hand and squeezed it, willing her strength into him.

There was no response. She threw back her head, lifting her eyes heavenward in a mute appeal for help. Help—she had to go get help. She took a deep breath and squeezed Jonathon's hand once again, bending low to whisper in his ear. "Wait for me, Jonathon. Wait for me. I'm going to get help." She gazed at him for one loving second longer, hoping he heard and understood, then rose and ran into the jungle.

She stumbled blindly along, trying to remember the course they had taken earlier. Twilight turned quickly into night, throwing her into a maze of eerie black shapes and twisting shadows. She tripped over rocks and tree roots, falling to her knees, then pulling herself back up. Branches reached out to grab her, tearing her gown and cutting her skin, but she didn't slow down. She didn't know how long she'd been running, hours or minutes. If she could just get to where they'd left the horses. . . .

She stopped, a low sound suddenly capturing her attention. She filled her lungs with deep, painful gulps of air, straining to hear over the furious rush of her blood. Then it came to her. The steady pounding of a drum, the rhythm as low and pulsing as a heartbeat. The sound seemed to echo all around her, filling the air with its haunting melody. She swung around, trying to identify the direction from which it came.

A glowing light in the distance caught her eye, revealing a string of brightly lit torches. She knew instantly where she was, and what she was looking at. Her heart lurched to her throat and her breathing stopped.

The cannibals.

She automatically turned away, then, just as automatically, turned back, chewing her lip. She had to get help. Who knew how long it would take her to get down the mountain, and if she'd even be able to find the horses in the darkness. Jonathon needed help now. Terrified, Genevieve lifted her skirts and ran.

Straight toward the village.

Chapter Seventeen

The village consisted of a group of thatched huts, arranged around a central courtyard which was the gathering place for meals and social events. It was nestled against Mount Pelée's southern side and was therefore shielded from the destructive forces of the island's storms. A nearby stream carried fresh water to the village's inhabitants, and a small garden located behind the huts provided the bulk of their food.

Genevieve sat quietly in one of the huts, watching as the local doctor changed the dressing on Jonathon's ankle. She held her nose as the old woman peeled off the pack of spongy herbs, now brown and foul, and applied a new, fresh balm. As before, the woman's movements were accompanied by the low murmur of incantations as she softly swayed over Jonathon's body. She stopped abruptly, smiling as she surveyed her patient, then turned and silently left the hut.

Genevieve watched the ancient *quimboisseur* leave, wishing she knew the words to express both her gratitude and apprehension. Gratitude for the fact that his ankle seemed to be healing rapidly since the old woman had taken him into her care three days ago: the swelling was now nonexistent, the jagged purple streaks that had shot up from his ankle to knee had vanished, and the bleeding had stopped completely. And apprehension because even though his fever had receded and his breathing was once again normal, Jonathon had yet to regain consciousness.

She moved to sit beside him on the low mat of palm

fronds and took his large hand gently into her own. She leaned over him, using her free hand to gently brush back his thick, dark hair, memorizing the handsome contours of his face. His skin was back to its normal deep golden shade, and three days worth of dark stubble shadowed his cheeks. Genevieve had always found beards attractive, but she couldn't help but feel what a shame it was to cover any part of Jonathon's rugged, gorgeous face. *Captain Beast*, she thought to herself, smiling softly.

A noise at the door caught her attention, and she turned to see a young girl motioning for her to follow. She sighed, hating to leave Jonathon for even a minute, but she knew from past experience that the girl would not leave until she did as she was bid. She let go of Jonathon's hand and rose reluctantly, following the girl out of the hut.

At least she wasn't frightened anymore. Not as she had been that first night when she'd raced into the village, terrified that she would be set upon and eaten before she'd had a chance to explain that Jonathon had been injured and needed help. At the time, she hadn't much cared what happened to her after she conveyed that message.

As it was, she'd had little to fear. Though she couldn't make the villagers understand her words, her silent urgent gestures—culminating in her hissing like a snake, howling in pain as she grabbed her ankle, falling to the floor in a dead faint, then leaping up and grabbing the hand of the nearest stunned villager as she pulled him along with her—finally got her point across. And though it had looked to her that for one moment the dumbfounded villagers were more inclined to applaud her antics than to take action, a cot was finally produced and a team of four sturdy men followed her up the mountain to where Jonathon lay.

The *quimboisseur* had treated his wound that night, returning regularly to change the dressing. She'd also taken care of Genevieve, rubbing a soothing, minty ointment onto her cuts and scratches. Other than that, the villagers had basically left her alone.

Except for meals. When she first smelled cooking in the air, a wave of terror had washed over her. This was not eased when a man and woman appeared at the door to the hut, holding large knives in their hands as they beckoned her forward. Realizing she had nowhere to flee, Genevieve nodded and rose. Her legs were trembling, but she was determined to go to her death bravely.

Her heroic impulse was short-lived, however, once her hosts seated her at the place of honor in the village circle, ceremoniously handing her the knives to carve the food for that day's meal. Seeing that the fare consisted of no more than fish, fruit, and vegetables, and that neither she or Jonathon was to be included on the menu, she was so relieved that she made a mess of everything, her shaky hands spilling and smashing food everywhere. She was not given that honor again.

As she followed the girl to the village circle, she realized that tonight was some sort of celebration. The low, steady pulsing of drums once again filled the air, and torches lit up the perimeter. The women danced as they brought in the various trays of food. The last dish, served on a huge, black platter, was carried by the village's most stunningly beautiful girl. Her hips moved sensuously, and her dark eyes were gleaming as she set down the platter. Genevieve glanced nervously around her, hearing the villager's low murmurs of hungry approval, then looked at the dish.

Meat.

The platter was piled high with a strange white meat. She swallowed hard, noting that it had been stripped clean of any bones that would indicate the type of animal from which it had come. *I won't panic,* Genevieve thought, her mind racing, *I just won't eat any. No one will notice.*

The dish was lifted and passed directly to her.

Feeling the eyes of the entire village upon her, she smiled and shook her head, attempting to politely decline. There was a moment of tense silence, followed by the low rumbling of angry disapproval from around the circle. "Take," urged the young girl who had seated her.

Genevieve looked at her warily. Communication had improved since her arrival in the village. She'd remembered a few of the native words Marie had taught her, and the villagers seemed to grasp a little French. She sensed a warning beneath the girl's urging, as if she were committing a grave blunder in refusing the food. With great reluctance, she reached for the meat and placed a portion in the rough wooden bowl she'd been given. "What is it?" she whispered to the girl.

The girl merely smiled, happy to have secured Genevieve's cooperation, and passed the meat around until everyone had a portion. They lifted their bowls in unison while the *quimboisseur* chanted a lengthy and emotionally charged blessing. The ritual complete, the villagers started their meal. "Eat," urged the girl.

Genevieve's stomach felt as if it were full of lead. "What is it?" she whispered back, dreading the answer.

"Eat," was the girl's only reply.

She realized the other villagers had stopped eating and were watching her, glowering with displeasure. She lifted her bowl, staring in horror at its contents, then finally selected a piece of the strange white meat and placed it in her mouth. Low grunts of approval were heard from around the circle as the villagers resumed their own meals. Genevieve chewed slowly, praying she would be able to force it past the tight lump in her throat. Suddenly her eyes widened in astonishment as she turned back to the girl. "Chicken?!"

She repeated herself until the girl's cloudy expression lifted and understanding dawned. "Mountain chicken," she agreed.

Mountain chicken? Genevieve thought, puzzled. She hadn't seen any chickens in the village, and didn't remember hearing of wild chickens in Martinique. She shrugged it off, too relieved by what she *wasn't* eating to care how the village raised its fowl. She finished her dish and was rewarded with beaming smiles from all around the circle.

The last part of the meal she'd grown accustomed to, so she let her mind wander as the women cleared the empty platters away and returned with fresh, untouched samples of what they'd consumed, in order that the village might give thanks for what it had received. Genevieve paid no attention until the last platter was brought out. It took two women to carry it. They held it aloft between them, then set it proudly in the center of the circle.

There, staring directly at Genevieve, sat the most hideously ugly creature she had ever seen in her life. It was a huge, green, wart-ridden bullfrog, with bulging eyes. The young girl she'd been sitting next to tugged urgently at her sleeve and pointed, but Genevieve didn't need a translation now. She nodded grimly, placing a hand over her stomach. "Don't tell me," she whispered hoarsely, "that's mountain chicken."

The girl nodded happily.

Genevieve just moaned.

She wasted no time in getting away from the gruesome sight and back to the hut where Jonathon lay. He still hadn't moved. She sighed, going silently forward to sit beside him on the low bed. Though she knew he was unaware of her presence, the rhythm of running her hand through his hair, of just touching him, brought her some solace. She leaned forward, reaching out her hand.

Jonathon's hand shot up, locking her wrist in a steel grip. Genevieve gasped, shocked by both the lightning speed with which he'd moved and his viselike grip; his strength after three days illness was amazing. He stared hard at her, his golden eyes blazing, then just as suddenly his eyes softened and he let go of her wrist, the tension leaving his body. He leaned back, an easy grin on his face. "Well, Eve, I believe I've met the serpent."

He was back. Overwhelmed with relief, Genevieve didn't know whether to laugh or cry. She smiled instead. "You certainly did," she answered, then shrugged lightly. "It was only a matter of time before we were cast out of Eden in any case."

"Why is that?" he asked. She didn't respond, but the delicate pink blush that crept up her cheeks was answer enough. "Ah, yes. We weren't exactly resisting temptation, were we?"

Genevieve automatically defended herself. "I was not at fault. I merely offered you an apple."

"Funny how history repeats itself, isn't it? I believe that's exactly what Eve said."

She smiled despite herself, realizing just how much she'd missed him. "How do you feel?" she asked softly.

"Fine," he answered. His ankle was a little stiff, that was all. His eyes flicked from her to their surroundings, taking in the dark interior of the primitive thatched hut. "Where are we?"

Genevieve's eyes immediately darkened. "That reminds me. I have a bone to pick with you," she said, drawing herself up stiffly. "And it's not a human one," she added darkly.

Jonathon frowned. "What do you mean?"

"You know exactly what I'm talking about. These villagers aren't cannibals. You just said that to deliberately frighten me."

"Ah, yes, my little story," he said with a grin as he leaned back, propping his hands behind his head, looking not the least bit repentant.

"You're not even sorry! You lied to me and you're not even sorry."

"It wasn't a lie. Everything I told you did happen— hundreds of years ago." He studied her, remorse dawning on him as he realized how frightened she must have been when the villagers found them in the jungle, how defenseless she must have felt when she thought she was being taken captive. "What happened, Genevieve? Did the villagers find us in the jungle?" He wondered absently if she'd stayed by his side or tried to hide. Not that he'd really blame her for trying to save her own skin, he decided charitably. He had, after all, told her the villagers would just as soon eat her as look at her.

"Ha!" she scoffed, her deep blue eyes stormy. "Nobody just 'found' us. I ran to get help, heard the drums from the village, and came here to get aid."

Jonathon's eyes widened. "You actually walked into a village, thinking it was full of cannibals, to save me?"

"Yes," she admitted sourly. "But I wouldn't do it again. Not to save *your* worthless, lying hide."

He just stared at her, amazed at her bravery, then smiled smugly. "Genevieve, I'm flattered. I had no idea you cared for me so."

She was in no mood for his teasing. "Don't start with me, Jonathon," she warned. "Here I've been making a complete fool of myself for the past three days, cringing every time a villager walked by with a bowl or spoon in his hand, and all because of you."

He couldn't help smiling. "Are you very angry?"

"Yes," she answered, but there was no heat behind it. She tried to muster up an angry frown, but to her horrified embarrassment, felt her lower lip begin to tremble instead as hot tears sprang to her eyes and streamed down her cheeks. "I was so frightened," she choked out.

Jonathon instantly pulled her into his arms, ashamed and thoroughly disgusted with himself for having told her that ridiculous story. "Genny," he soothed, softly stroking her back, "Genny, you were never in any real danger. The villagers never would have hurt you."

She struck her fist weakly against his strong shoulder. "I wasn't frightened about that," she mumbled against his chest, trying to get control of herself.

"Then what were you so frightened of?"

She pulled back, staring up into his face, her sapphire eyes glistening with tears. "I was afraid you were going to die," she admitted with a soft sob.

Jonathon felt something twist inside him, like a band being pulled tightly around his heart. He crushed her against his chest, humbled by her soft admission. It took him a minute to find his voice. "You're not getting rid of me that easily, sweetheart. I'm staying right here with you. It's going to take more than a snake to chase me out of Eden."

Genevieve breathed a sigh of relief, his recovery lifting a great weight off her shoulders. She snuggled against his chest, lulled by the strong pounding of his heart beneath her cheek. She closed her eyes, the worry and sleepless nights of the past days catching up to her. "Are you hungry?" she suddenly thought to ask. "Shall I bring you something to eat?"

"No." He didn't want her to move. Not when she was lying so cozily in his arms, without any protest or resistance. He wrapped his arm around her shoulder, pressing her soft curves gently against him.

"I'm still angry at you," she mumbled drowsily, her breath warm as her lips brushed softly against his neck.

"Are you?"

"Yes. Very." She fell asleep in his arms.

When Jonathon woke up she was gone. He found her not very far away, playing with a group of native children. She looked almost childlike herself, her skirts hiked up in a fetching display of shapely calves and slim ankles. Jonathon watched as she gracefully dodged a ball thrown at her, her laughter mixing with the excited shouts of the children. Genevieve must have seen him watching, for she left the circle of children, walking directly to where he stood and joining him under the shade of the tall palm. "Hello," she said, a little breathless after the exertion of the game.

A fine sheen of perspiration clung to her skin like a gentle mist, giving it a glorious golden glow in the early morning light. Her cheeks were radiant and rosy, her blue eyes sparkling. "Hello," he returned, drinking her beauty in, savoring it like a fine wine. "So this is how you spent your time while I was lying on my deathbed—playing games with children," he teased.

Genevieve shrugged, embarrassed to admit that in fact she'd done nothing but sit at his side, worrying over him like a mother hen for three days. She told him instead about the one afternoon she'd been briefly coaxed away from the hut. "I'll have you know I did more than just play games while you lounged abed," she informed him. "One of us had to continue our search. Those three boys there led me up to the rim of Mount Pelée."

Jonathon immediately darkened. "That was a foolish thing to do. What will it take to convince you how dangerous the jungle can be?"

"We were perfectly safe. You'll notice we managed to make it back without falling into any pits, getting lost, or"—she paused, smiling mischievously—"getting bitten by snakes."

He sighed and shook his head, taking her elbow as he guided her down a path away from the village. "You have absolutely no respect for a man's ego, sweetheart. That remark stung almost as much as the snake's bite."

Genevieve glanced down at his ankle, seeing that he wasn't limping or even favoring it at all as he walked. "It doesn't hurt now? Has it healed completely?"

"Completely."

"Do you think it was magic?"

Jonathon looked at her, raising an eyebrow at her wild conjecture, but she rushed on, "Surely you've heard the talk—about the magic practiced by the natives." She glanced around, then whispered, "Obeah."

He frowned. "Who told you about that?"

She shrugged. "Nobody in particular. I've just heard rumors about it." Rumors about its dark power, a combination of magic and sorcery, deep secrets and ancient medicinal cures.

Jonathon frowned again, his reaction not unlike that of her three young guides when she'd ventured to ask them about the treatment the *quimboisseur* was using on Jonathon's ankle. Up until that point, she'd been pleased with the open friendliness of the boys. When she asked about Obeah, however, their smiles vanished as they looked uneasily at one another and said nothing. "It's not something that's talked about," Jonathon said.

"But people do believe, don't they?" she pressed.

"They do. It accounts for much of the strange behavior you'll see on the island: maids who walk to the table backward when carrying salt, and grown men who hop ten paces if a black bird flies across their path."

"It doesn't sound as if you believe."

He shrugged. "I've also seen perfectly healthy people die within hours of a heated exchange with a *quimboisseur*, and brand-new, sturdy ships sink when they left harbor without a blessing."

"And don't forget about your ankle," she put in. "The wound was deep, I saw it. A wound like that should have killed an ordinary man."

"Maybe I'm not an ordinary man."

She laughed, immediately opening her mouth to reply, but Jonathon cut her off by placing his finger against her lips. "Have a care, sweet. My ankle may be cured, but my self-esteem is sorely bruised."

Genevieve looked up, meeting the teasing gleam in his golden eyes. "Really? Bothered by the fact that you were rescued by a woman?"

"Not at all," he assured her with a wicked smile. "But it disturbs me greatly that that same woman spent the night in my bed, fell asleep in my very arms, before I could properly demonstrate my appreciation."

"And just what sort of demonstration did you have in mind?" she asked as she moved out of his reach, suddenly shy. Stalling for time, she reached for a piece of fruit from the low branches of a nearby tree. Her entire concentration focused on her task, she peeled the thick green skin from the fruit to reveal the soft, golden-orange flesh within. "I don't know what these are, but they're delicious. Have you tried one?"

"They're mangoes. And yes, I've tried them."

"Would you like some?" she offered politely, hoping to divert him. For a moment it seemed to work. Jonathon nodded, moving slowly toward her, as Genevieve wordlessly lifted her arm. But instead of taking the fruit from her hand, he lightly grasped her wrist, licking the sticky ripe fruit from her palm, his tongue twirling between her fingers as he sucked the sweet juice from her skin.

Genevieve felt her knees go weak beneath her and was sure she would have sunk to the ground if she hadn't been gripping his shoulder for support. "I see I shall have to stop offering you fruit, Jonathon," she murmured shakily, "for it seems only to awaken other appetites within you."

Jonathon lifted his head, his sensuous lips curved into a small smile. "You're right. And you taste delicious, Genevieve." He brought his mouth to the smooth, ivory column of her throat, nuzzling the sensitive area beneath her ear.

Genevieve wrapped her arms around him, giving herself up to the sensations flooding through her. *I won't think about tomorrow*, she silently resolved. The only thing that mattered now was that she was in the arms of the man she loved, the man she had almost lost. No matter what happened between them, she knew she would always have this moment: the smell of his skin, the taste of his tongue, the sound of his husky voice as he murmured her name. The way his amber eyes looked as they burned into her, melting her with their loving intensity. This moment would always be hers. And it was enough.

She sought his mouth with hers, pressing herself against him with an urgency born of wild desire and complete surrender. She held nothing back, hungrily opening her mouth to receive his tongue, then felt his shoulders tighten beneath her hands as her own tongue entered his mouth, fervently tasting and exploring. A familiar ache filled her belly, an exquisite longing she knew could only be satisfied by Jonathon's touch.

Her soft curves were molded against the firm, hard planes of his body, locked in a tight embrace, but she still needed more. She needed to feel his skin. Her hands moved almost frantically, tearing open his shirt and pulling it off, roving over the thick muscles of his arms and chest. Her tongue trailed down his throat. She heard his quick intake of breath as she flicked it against his hard, brown nipples, bringing them into her mouth. She moved lower, pressing soft kisses against the flat planes of his stomach while her hands worked free the buckle to his belt, lowering his trousers past the rock-solid firmness of his thighs.

Jonathon had meanwhile succeeded in removing her gown. He lowered them both onto the damp grass, amazed at the passion of Genevieve's response. She kneeled above him, naked, her eyes roving over his glorious masculine body. He was hard and ready for her, and she watched him grow harder still under her direct and unembarrassed gaze. She placed her hands on his body, gently massaging his skin, feeling his corded muscles ripple beneath her fingers in response to her touch. Emboldened, she moved her hands lower, down his firm stomach to his upper thighs, where Jonathon caught them before she proceeded to her goal.

He gazed at her in wonder, aware that he had somehow gone from being the seducer to the seduced. "God, Genny, do you know what you do to me?"

"Don't you want me to touch you?" Her golden hair softly framed her beautiful face, cascading past her shoulders to the small of her back in thick, honey-colored waves.

"Yes," he whispered hoarsely, "but I can't hold back now, and if you touch me like that . . ."

"Don't hold back, Jonathon. Show me what you feel."

That was all the urging he needed. He pulled her down roughly against him, his lips crushing hers in a kiss of insatiable hunger. He drew his hands along the silky-soft curves of her lush hips. He lifted her up, placing her atop his rigid shaft, his burning gaze locked on hers as he lowered her slowly, filling her with his male hardness. He watched as her deep blue eyes widened, then closed, her soft pink lips parting to emit a low sigh.

She moved instinctively, torturously slow at first, then faster, finding her rhythm, lifting and lowering herself to meet each powerful thrust of Jonathon's hips. They found their release together, a deep, shuddering climax that left her collapsed on top of him, filled with a sense of peace and contentment that was unlike anything she'd ever known.

After a moment, she rolled over and snuggled against his chest, his arm wrapped tightly around her shoulders. She gazed up at him, her sapphire eyes shining. "I'm trembling."

Jonathon looked down at her, his expression full of pride and satisfaction. "Me, too. It was incredible, wasn't it, Genevieve?" he murmured softly against her ear.

"No, not that. I mean the earth is shaking—it must be from the volcano. Can't you feel it?"

He laughed, his lips curving into a wry smile as he ruefully shook his head. "One day, Genevieve, you're going to actually pay me a compliment, and I believe I shall surely sink to the floor in shock."

"Really?" she asked, thrilled and amazed that such a strong, self-sufficient man as Jonathon actually yearned for bits of praise from her. "Tell me what you want to hear," she said quite seriously.

Jonathon obliged her immediately. "Tell me I'm the best lover you've ever had."

She raised an eyebrow, an unconscious imitation of an expression she'd seen so often on him. "You're the only lover I've ever had."

A thrill of pleasure ran through him at her frank admission. He was also the only lover she was ever going to have, he amended silently. He rolled over, bracing himself up on his elbows above her. "Doesn't matter. Surely you're a woman who recognizes quality when you see it."

Genevieve laughed, running her hands through his wavy hair. "Very well. You're the best lover I've ever had."

He nodded approvingly, rewarding her for her agreement by pressing soft kisses on her belly. "You're wise beyond your years, sweetheart."

"Then again . . ."

Jonathon's head immediately came up.

Her sapphire eyes twinkled as she tried to hold back her teasing grin. "Perhaps I was too hasty in my judgment. I am, after all, somewhat of a novice in these matters."

His dark brows drew together. "What exactly are you saying?" he demanded. If she was even considering taking another lover . . .

"Well, how am I to know if your talk is nothing but a vain boast?"

"Genevieve—" he began warningly.

"I do know of a way to settle the matter, however."

He would kill any man that tried to lay a hand on her.

"I will consent to letting you prove your boast, sir," she continued in mock solemnity as she wrapped her slender arms around his neck and pulled him down. "It's only fair, after all."

The tension instantly left Jonathon's body, and his lips curved into a roguish grin. "And just what sort of proof did you have in mind?"

A glorious rosy blush tinged her cheeks. "Well, I thought perhaps another demonstration of your . . . skill might be in order."

"I see," he returned, amazed at how quickly and how desperately he needed her again. He reached down to brush the thick golden hair off her forehead, and his eyes burned into hers. "And would this be a good time for such a demonstration?"

Genevieve felt her breath quicken as he lowered himself onto her, the heat in her belly spreading like fire through her veins as he settled himself between her thighs. "As it happens," she answered breathlessly, "I find that I'm entirely at your disposal."

"Well now, I like the sound of that. I truly do."

The remainder of the day was spent in the worthy pursuit of fairness as Jonathon provided proof of his boast. Again, and again, and again . . .

Chapter Eighteen

Genevieve hated to leave the village. Her time there, once Jonathon was well, was the happiest she'd ever spent in her life. As if by unspoken agreement, neither of them mentioned the treasure or what would happen once it was found. Their time was spent instead in taking long walks together, exploring the village, or simply talking, sharing memories of old friends and favorite places.

And, of course, making love.

Late one afternoon, Jonathon discovered a shallow, secluded lagoon and offered Genevieve a swimming lesson. But it was one that was short-lived once he was treated to the tantalizing display of her bare, round cheeks as she floated on her stomach, splashing and kicking in his arms. "What about my lesson?" she cried in mild protest as he carried her from the water to the soft, grassy bank of the lagoon.

Jonathon dropped her gently on the grass, then kneeled beside her, their wet bodies warmed by the sunshine. "The swimming lesson's over, Genny," he informed her huskily. His mouth and hands moved urgently over her body, across her flat belly, then lower still, Genevieve gasping as his tongue found her most private, inner places. He lifted his head briefly, his golden eyes shining, and made a promise. "Now I'm going to teach you how to fly."

And so he did.

When she remembered that particular afternoon and others like it, a small, contented sigh escaped Genevieve's lips. Hearing it, Jonathon glanced at her, seeing the soft regret which shaded her eyes as they drew their horses to a stop in front of his home. "I would have liked to stay longer, too, sweetheart," he offered consolingly. "But perhaps it's just as well we're returning when we are. It's generally this time of year that the natives perform their annual celebration of the tides." At her curious look, he continued, "There's not a great deal to the ceremony, really. Just music, dancing, and the like."

"I think it sounds charming. We should have stayed."

"Staying would mean having to partake in the meal which follows: bullfrog. The natives are very offended if a guest refuses." He was about to shrug it off, then glanced at her face. "You didn't . . ."

Genevieve lifted her chin, the stormy ire in her deep blue eyes rising at the sound of his shocked laughter. "I don't wish to discuss it."

"You ate it? You actually ate it?"

"I'm warning you, if you say another word—"

Jonathon's shouts of laughter filled the entry. "I've heard it tastes like chicken," he managed to choke out.

"I'm going to kill you, Jonathon Morgan, I swear I am." Genevieve swept past him through the entry and up the stairs to her room, her dire pronouncement eliciting nothing more than a soft smile from Jonathon.

Such a volatile little thing, he mused, amazed at her red-hot flashes of temper and how entirely unschooled she was at hiding her emotions. In the past week he'd seen the whole range cross her face: anger and fear, tenderness and wonder, and everything in between. She was more than just beautiful. She was alive. Her every look, every gesture, held him captivated. She was everything he'd ever wanted to find in a woman but had never let himself believe really existed.

"Welcome back, brother," Jonathon reluctantly turned from Genevieve to Ty, who stood regarding him from the doorway to his study. "Well, appears nothing's changed between you two," he drawled, referring to Genevieve's comment before she took herself upstairs.

Jonathon didn't bother to correct him. "If you'll excuse me, Tyler," he said absently, heading toward the stairs to follow Genevieve to her room.

"Jonathon, wait. I need to speak with you."

Something in Ty's voice made him pause. "Now?"

"Now."

He met his brother's eyes, then nodded, following him into the study. "Be quick about it, will you?" he said curtly as his long strides carried him swiftly across the room to his desk. Too impatient to take his customary seat behind it, he propped one hip up against its sturdy mahogany length, rocking his leg absently as he waited for Tyler to begin.

"I intercepted a package a few days ago, one that arrived on a ship just in from the States."

Jonathon nodded for him to continue, but his mind was on other matters. Genevieve. She loved him, too, he was certain of it. He would ask her to marry him tonight, after dinner, he resolved, his mind darting off in a thousand different directions. He couldn't just blurt it out, though, it had to be perfect. It should be romantic, and private, with maybe some roses and wine. Genevieve would like that. Then there was the ring to buy, of course. He wondered if he would be able to find a diamond large enough for her on Martinique. . . .

"You haven't heard a word I've said, have you?"

"Not a one," Jonathon admitted cheerfully, too happy to care. "Tyler, I'm afraid this is going to have to wait," he said as he stood, heading for the door.

"Damn it, Jonathon, you were right. DuPres was guilty."

That finally got his attention. He came to a dead stop, then turned slowly around. "What did you say?"

Ty ran his hand through his thick, golden hair, a gesture of frustration he'd picked up from his older brother. "I know. I'm having a hard time believing it myself."

Jonathon regarded him intently, then walked slowly back to his desk, seating himself behind it. "What happened?"

Ty sunk into the chair facing him, his usually laughing brown eyes somber as he started over. "I was down at the docks, checking to see how repairs were progressing on the *Liberty*, when I noticed one of Phelps's men rush off a ship just in from Charleston, carrying a small, thick package. I sent Wilkens and Ricco to follow him."

"What was in the package?" Jonathon didn't bother to ask how it was procured. Knowing Ricco, the carrier was probably still moaning.

Ty pulled a thick envelope from his coat pocket and set it wordlessly on the desk in front of him. Jonathon hesitated, the instincts he'd relied on all his life warning him he didn't want to know what was in that envelope. He slowly reached for it and drew the papers out. He scanned them quickly, frowning as he went through the thick wad of documents. Pages and pages of invoices, in French, for military weaponry, ranging from rifles and ammunition to cannons and exploding shells. Enough arms to outfit an army. He set the pages down. "This proves that Phelps is in fact negotiating with France to purchase arms, but I see nothing here that specifically incriminates DuPres."

"The man was also carrying this."

Jonathon took the thick parchment from Ty's hand. A letter of credit, signed and guaranteed by General Phillipe DuPres, in the amount of one million American dollars, to be given in exchange for the invoiced weapons.

Damn. *Damn.* He set the letter on top of the invoices then stood up and crossed to the window, his body rigid as he stared blindly out, his worst suspicions now confirmed. Not only was the South negotiating to buy arms, pushing his country toward civil war, but Genevieve's father had been instrumental in putting the whole scheme together.

"Obviously DuPres was supplying the money, but the weapons were coming from another source," Ty remarked.

"I've gone through those pages several times. There's no clue as to who that source might be."

Jonathon nodded, his dark brows drawn together in a frown. "You say the carrier rushed off the ship with these documents? Why the rush? General DuPres has been dead for over a year now."

"Look beneath DuPres's signature. Another name has been added."

Jonathon glanced again at the document, then back at Ty. "Armand Berthot?"

"He arrived on Martinique four days ago."

"Who—"

"He was General DuPres's first officer. He now commands a vessel of his own, as well as an impressive rank. I've had him watched, he's met with Phelps twice since his arrival."

Jonathon nodded. He'd suspected from the start that even if DuPres wasn't guilty, one of his officers had to be. It came as no surprise, then, to learn that they'd been working together. But how was he going to tell Genevieve that? She had never quit believing in her father, and now he was going to destroy that belief. He let out a low, weary breath. "I've got to speak with Genevieve."

"Before you do, there's something else you should know." Ty hesitated, obviously uncomfortable, then finished brusquely, "Berthot's been asking for her. He claims to be her fiancé."

Jonathon's eyes immediately darkened with anger. "That's a lie," he said tightly.

"I thought so, too, so I did some checking. Apparently the general treated Berthot like the son he never had, not only making him his first officer, but arranging the engagement between him and Genevieve. They've been engaged for almost four years now." He paused, torn between telling Jonathon everything he knew and exonerating Genevieve at the same time. "There must be some explanation. Have you ever asked Genevieve about Berthot?"

"As a matter of fact, I did ask her about her father's first officer," Jonathon answered. He held himself stiffly, his only sign of emotion the rapid tick of a muscle along the hard, flat planes of his jaw. "She told me she couldn't remember his name."

A heavy silence filled the space between them as their eyes met across the room. Jonathon finally turned away, again staring, unseeing, out the window as everything suddenly, horribly, clicked into place. That had to be the reason for their urgent trip to Mount Pelée: to get him out of the way when her fiancé arrived. "She lied," he said flatly. "She's been lying all along."

"No one's that good a liar. I think she really believes her father was innocent."

Jonathon turned sharply, bringing his fist crashing down on the damning evidence stacked on his desk. "The man was obviously guilty," he stormed, his golden eyes blazing. "She must have known that from the start. Why else would she lie about her relationship with Berthot?"

Ty had no answer to that, nor any words to take away the pain and anger he saw in his brother's eyes. He waited, and asked instead, "What do we do now—have Phelps arrested? We've enough here to see him hung for treason."

Jonathon shook his head, forcing himself to concentrate on the problem at hand, willing himself to ignore the pain that was slowly tearing at his gut. "No. Not yet. Arresting Phelps gives us only one corner of this triangle. Berthot and"—he stopped, forcing his voice past the sudden tightening in his throat—"Genevieve," he bit out, "form the second corner. But we still don't know who they're buying arms from. Until we have that, there's too great a risk they may yet succeed."

Ty nodded in mute agreement, his handsome face deep in thought. "So we just go on as before. As though nothing happened."

As though nothing happened, Jonathon's mind echoed. As if he hadn't met the one woman he could love above all others in the world. Whose every glance, every touch, every word, made his heart soar. Whose beautiful face danced like a vision before him every time he closed his eyes. Whose luscious curves and gentle passion stirred a fierce lust within him, making him ache with tenderness and animal longing. Made him ache with wanting her. Needing her.

And she'd betrayed him from the start.

"Right," he said to Ty, his face rigid with the effort of holding his emotions tightly in check, "like nothing happened."

Ty studied his brother silently for a moment then crossed to the door, hesitating before he left. "Jonathon, I'm sorry—"

"Don't."

The single word shot across the room, stunning Ty with the rage it conveyed. "Very well," he answered tightly. "Constance came by two days ago to see you. She left invitations for a dinner party she's having this evening."

Jonathon nodded. "We'll both go. I highly doubt Phelps has been orchestrating this by himself. Tonight may be our last chance to discover who else he's been working with."

After watching Tyler leave, he stared at the door in impotent fury long after it had closed behind him. A thousand images poured through his mind: Genevieve, racing across his ship's deck, bravely calling his men to arms, Genevieve, laughing as they danced, her sapphire eyes shining with joy, and finally, Genevieve, wrapping her soft arms around him in complete, tender surrender as they made love.

He began to feel a dull ache in his jaw, and was only then aware how tightly he'd been clenching his teeth. He forced himself to relax his jaw, then looked at his hands, noting that they, too, were clenched, balled into tight fists. These he didn't unclench. Not until after he'd sent them flying through the paneled mahogany wall.

Genevieve woke with a start, not sure what it was that had disturbed her. She sat up with a frown, looked around her room, then shrugged it off and lay back again. She lifted her arms above her head, indulging in a long, languid stretch, a warm smile curving her lips as she remembered her dream. She'd been dreaming about making love to Jonathon. She let out a soft sigh and slowly stroked the empty space on the bed beside her, imagining he was there. She giggled at her silliness, then bounded up, anxious to dress and go down to see him.

"Hello, Marie," she called cheerily when the door opened after a soft knock. Genevieve smiled, meeting her friend's eyes in the mirror as she sat before the dressing table brushing her hair. She'd bathed and changed earlier, slipping into a soft, ivory gown with blue ribbons that encircled its capped sleeves and bodice, accentuating her smooth, delicate arms and tiny waist. She chatted absently as she wove a matching ribbon through her thick golden hair. "We saw the most beautiful things on our trip, Marie. Waterfalls, wild orchids, swarms of butterflies larger than my fist. And a native village," she continued, smiling as she shook her head. "Jonathon told me it was full of cannibals. Can you imagine?"

She noticed Marie had not said a word in response, and laughed self-consciously. "Listen to me go on! I'm sorry, Marie, I just can't help it. I'm so happy," she exclaimed, wrapping her arms around her friend in a tight hug. "But I want to hear everything that's been happening with you, now. Tell me how things are with Luc."

"Everything is very well here, mam'selle."

Genevieve laughed, grabbing Marie's hand and giving it a gentle shake. "That's it? That's all you're going to tell me? Very well, I shall just have to pry it out of you later." She stood up, executing a graceful twirl. "But first, tell me how I look. I'm going down to have supper with Jonathon." Her sapphire eyes sparkled as she said his name. She looked beautiful, radiant, glowing with happiness.

Marie hesitated, then spoke softly. "I thought perhaps you

might like me to fix you a tray this evening, mam'selle. You must be tired after your trip."

Genevieve smiled. "Thank you, Marie, but that won't be necessary. I'm not a bit tired." She glanced in the mirror to give her hair one last pat, then turned for the door. "Tell me, has Jonathon come down yet?"

"No, *chérie*. He said he wouldn't be having supper this evening."

Genevieve turned back to Marie, her head tilted to one side in silent question. "Not having supper," she repeated, then her eyes flew open wide. His ankle—he had seemed completely well! "Oh, Marie, he's not ill, is he?" she asked in panic.

"No, mam'selle, he's fine," Marie rushed to reassure her.

"Then why—"

"I believe he said he has other plans for this evening. He will be dining elsewhere. Now," she continued briskly, "what shall I bring for you? I have prepared a beautiful fish. . . ."

Genevieve walked slowly back into the room, a frown marring her delicate features as she sat down. It didn't make sense. Surely Jonathon was as anxious to see her as she was to see him. "I don't understand, Marie," she interrupted. "Has he left already? He didn't say a word to me. Where did he go?"

Marie sighed as she looked into Genevieve's innocent blue eyes. She would not lie to her friend. "He is dining with Mam'selle Prentiss this evening," she said softly.

For a moment Genevieve just stared at her, certain she hadn't heard her correctly. "Oh," she finally managed, sinking onto her bed in stunned disbelief. Once, when she was a little girl, she'd experienced a sensation similar to what she was feeling now. She'd been pushed out of a high swing by a child she'd considered her closest friend. She'd plummeted through the air for one dizzying moment, landing hard on her backside, hard enough to knock the breath from her. It wasn't just the physical pain she remembered, or the helpless feeling as she struggled to fill her burning lungs, so much as the sheer misery caused by her friend's sudden and inexplicable betrayal.

She'd never considered that Jonathon might return to his mistress once they got back. It had just not occurred to her. How could she have been so stupid? So naive? Of course he'd just been passing time with her until he could get back to Constance. He'd made it clear from the start that he wasn't giving his mistress up. What had she thought? That he would fall so in love with her that everything would change?

She heard Marie's soft voice as if from a great distance and turned toward her, shamed and embarrassed by the sympathy she saw in her beautiful dark eyes. She bit her lower lip to keep it from trembling, then shook her head in response to Marie's question. "I find I'm not very hungry after all," she answered in a hollow voice, anxious to get Marie out of her room before the tears she felt building behind her eyes broke free.

Marie hesitated, then went to place her hand gently on Genevieve's shoulder before she left. "I'll be here, *chérie*, if you need anything." The door closed softly behind her. She walked slowly down the hall, her heart heavy with the pain she'd seen in Genevieve's eyes. She couldn't understand it. She'd seen the way Jonathon's eyes had glowed as he lifted her from her horse when they'd arrived earlier, the way he'd held her against him in a brief lover's embrace. She'd smiled at the tender scene, knowing they'd at last opened themselves to each other. One hour later, Jonathon had stormed out in a rage, bound for Mam'selle Prentiss's. Marie shook her head, wishing she'd been blessed with her grandmother's gift of sight.

Genevieve wasn't wishing for anything. She had no wishes left. Every one of them had been granted when she was in Jonathon's arms. When she thought he loved her as deeply and as endlessly as she loved him. Obviously she'd been wrong. She'd given him everything she had to give, heart and soul, but it hadn't been enough. That knowledge, that devastating rejection—both burned through her body like a fever, leaving her weak and empty.

She lay back on her bed, staring up at the sheer netting that formed a soft canopy above her. She was only vaguely aware of the salty tears that spilled from her eyes and rolled across her cheeks, forming damp pools on the linen bedding. Sleep must have come to her at some point, for she woke slowly the next morning, the sharp pain of the night before now just a dull, heavy ache. She rose and moved listlessly about the room, washing and dressing, barely recognizing the hollow eyes which stared back at her from the mirror as her own.

"It's over," whispered an ugly voice inside her head. She closed her eyes and took a deep breath, urging the voice away. She'd come to the island with only one purpose in mind: to find the treasure. Forcing herself to think only of that, she headed downstairs.

"Good morning, Genevieve." Ty rose politely as she entered, but there was a coolness to his tone she would have recognized if she hadn't been so miserable herself. Jonathon was nowhere to be seen. Doubtless he was still with Constance, she decided, her stomach aching anew at the thought.

"Ty," she answered, her lips lifting in a quivering imitation of a smile. She shook her head in response to the breakfast fare a servant offered, the bile rising in her throat at the mere aroma of food, and helped herself to a cup of tea instead.

Ty frowned as he watched her pour the tea, noting how her hands shook. Her face was pale and drawn, the violet smudges under her eyes testimony to her lack of sleep. "Is everything all right?" he asked carefully, wondering if perhaps she'd overheard his conversation with Jonathon last night.

Genevieve caught it this time. The warmth she'd always

heard in his voice was gone. She lifted her eyes to his, noting that the kindness she'd always seen there was gone, too, leaving nothing but cool politeness. "Everything's fine," she answered shakily.

He searched her face. "Are you certain?"

What could she say? *I'm in love with Jonathon, Ty. I became his lover, and now he doesn't want me anymore. He doesn't want me.* To her horror, tears suddenly filled her eyes, spilling down her cheeks before she could stop them. "Y—y—yes," she choked out, "I'm certain."

She heard the scuff of a chair being pushed back, and immediately felt Ty's arms go around her. She fell into his embrace, desperately needing a friend. He waited patiently, softly stroking her back until her muffled sobs turned into gentle gasps of breath as she fought to bring her emotions under control. She pushed out of his embrace, offering him a wet, embarrassed smile. "That was foolish of me. I don't know what brought that on."

"Why don't you tell me what's wrong, Genevieve? You know I'll help you if I can."

"Yes, Genevieve, tell us. That sentimental display was really quite moving."

She gasped and whirled around. Jonathon was standing in the doorway, one broad shoulder propped casually against the wall, the bored expression on his face perfectly matching his tone of voice. He was dressed in his evening clothes, his ruffled white shirt open at the throat, his cravat undone, hanging limply at his collar. He looked tired and a bit disheveled, as if he'd just come in from his night's pursuits.

In that instant an image flashed through her mind. She pictured Jonathon holding Constance in his arms, kissing her, whispering her name. All sadness and despair left her, replaced by an awful combination of burning rage and white-hot jealousy. Her eyes became narrow slits of sapphire as in a sharp, brittle voice she asked, "Just getting in, are you, Jonathon?"

He shrugged, moving slowly into the room. He and Tyler had returned shortly after midnight, but he'd passed the remainder of the evening in his den, not even bothering to try to sleep. Genevieve watched as he poured himself a cup of strong, black coffee, catching a whiff of Constance's cloying perfume as he passed. "You might consider telling your mistress to be a little less liberal with her perfume the next time you see her," she remarked bitingly. "Your clothing reeks of it."

Jonathon made no comment, simply arched one dark brow as he sipped his coffee. She watched him set the cup down slowly and seat himself across the table from her. The silence mounted in the room, stretching, pulling on her nerves until it became a force she could almost touch.

"Well?" he finally prompted.

"Well, what?"

"I'm waiting for an answer to my question. Why that maudlin outburst of tears? I presume you thought it might gain you Tyler's sympathy."

"Jonathon—" Ty objected, coming immediately to his feet.

"Leave us, Tyler. This doesn't concern you."

"Like hell it doesn't—"

"He's right," Genevieve put in quietly, her sapphire eyes never leaving Jonathon's. Ty drew himself up, looking angrily from one to the other, but their faces were set, locked in their own private battle. He walked stiffly out, leaving nothing but an awful stillness echoing through the silent room as he pulled the door closed behind him.

Genevieve spoke first. "I want to leave your house. I want to get off this island. Now."

"Just like that?"

"Yes."

"All that talk about your father—proving his innocence, restoring his rank and property"—he made a vague gesture with his hands, as if bored by the subject—"that no longer matters to you."

Genevieve said nothing, clenching her fists tightly in her lap. Jonathon waited, then leaned back, stretching one arm out along the back of the chair beside him. "I see," he remarked flatly. "And to what do you attribute this sudden change of heart?"

It hurt just to look at him. Even now, knowing he'd betrayed her, the longing was still there, the unquenchable yearning to run her fingers through his hair, to feel his strong arms crushing her against him, to submit to the pressure of his lips on hers. She lifted her chin, forcing into her voice a strength she didn't feel. "Nothing's changed, Jonathon," she answered coldly. "I'm going to leave this island as soon as I find the treasure just as I've always planned. I think there have been enough pointless delays." She watched his eyes darken in response, the expression on his sharply defined features grow harder still.

"Just as you've always planned," he repeated. "You've had everything neatly planned out from the start, haven't you?"

"Of course," she replied bravely, quickly, before the humiliating truth fell from her lips: *No. Nothing went as planned. I never planned to fall in love with you.* Her stubborn pride would never let him see that, would never let him know.

He lifted his hand, running his fingers through his thick hair, then turned to stare blindly out the window. "Was it worth it, Genevieve?" he asked, so softly she wasn't sure she heard the question at all. He turned back, staring at her for a long moment. "You'd do whatever it takes to insure you get that treasure, wouldn't you?" At her defiant nod, he asked again, "Tell me, sweetheart, was your sacrifice worth it?"

Genevieve frowned. "My sacrifice?"

"Your virginity, of course," Jonathon answered ruthlessly. "Given in exchange for my aid in helping to find the treasure. That wasn't part of our initial bargain, so the stakes must have been raised. Would you care to tell me why?"

Genevieve's eyes flew open wide as she shot out of her chair. "How dare you—" she began, lifting her hand.

Jonathon stopped her effortlessly, wrapping his strong hand around hers in a grip of steel. "But that puts me in a rather awkward position, doesn't it, seeing as we haven't found the treasure yet. I suppose I'll just have to find some other way to repay you."

"How dare you," Genevieve choked out, fighting to hold back her tears. "How dare *you* insult *me*. You've nothing to be angry about."

"Do I seem angry, Genevieve?" he asked mockingly, his amber stare unyielding as he tightened his grip on her hand. "Surely you haven't done anything to make me angry, have you?"

"Me?" she cried, frightened by his cold fury. "I don't know what you're talking about."

"No, of course you don't," he sneered, releasing her abruptly.

Genevieve drew a deep, shuddering breath as she stared up into the fierce, harsh planes of his face. Her defenses, her resolve, her pride, were now as broken as her dreams. "Why are you doing this, Jonathon?" she asked in a soft, trembling voice. "Why?"

Jonathon simply stared into her deep blue eyes. When he finally spoke, he answered her question with one of his own. "Tell me, Genevieve, have you been able to remember the name of your father's first officer?"

The question caught Genevieve completely off guard. She searched his eyes, reading nothing in their golden depths but anger and accusation. She turned away, shaking her head in utter defeat. "No," she answered miserably.

Jonathon clenched his fists against the flash of pain that ripped through his gut. There was no turning back now. It was too late for both of them. He'd fallen for Genevieve from the moment she'd entered his life, loving her, needing her, as he had needed no other woman. What he had shielded himself from, not believed in, she alone had broken through. Like Adam, he had given in to sweet temptation, and his world would never be the same.

He stared at her for one last, long moment, then quietly left the room.

CHAPTER NINETEEN

"Is everything set for tonight?"

Jonathon nodded grimly. "A meeting has been arranged between Colonel Phelps and Berthot. It'll take place this evening, during the ball." He turned away from Ty to pour two stout glasses of whiskey, passing one to his brother before he resumed his place by the window. Outside, night was falling over the island, darkness quickly replacing dusk. "They're to be joined by whoever it is that's supplying the arms."

"You're sure your source is correct?"

"He'd better be. I've been paying him enough." Jonathon frowned as he thought of Phelps's personal steward, a thin, greedy man who looked perpetually hungry. He'd been keeping Jonathon abreast of Phelps's activities for some weeks now, his cooperation easily secured by the large sums of money Jonathon had been doling out. But the fact that he'd been reduced to relying on the word of a man whose loyalties were so easily bought left a sour taste in his mouth, and he took a deep swallow of whiskey to clear it.

Ty shook his head in wonder. "I'm amazed that Phelps has the nerve to go through with this. He must know that the papers outlining the arms sale were taken from his carrier—he must realize that the risk of being discovered now is enormous."

Jonathon lifted his shoulders in a cool shrug. "He knows someone has the papers, but he doesn't know who. There's little he can do but proceed as planned. In any case, I doubt

Phelps could postpone this meeting even if he wanted to. I've a strong suspicion that our mysterious arms supplier will be in Martinique only a day, two at most." That was the man who posed the real danger, he sensed intuitively. A man who lurked in the shadows, moving evasively, and who yet had enough power and connections to orchestrate the sale of over a million dollars in weaponry.

But that man wasn't the one who caused the blood to surge through Jonathon's veins in a pounding rage. It was the Frenchman Berthot. He would meet him tonight: the man with whom Genevieve had conspired from the start, the man she was planning to leave him for when it was all done. The man who would be her husband, her lover. He felt his fists tighten in silent fury as he imagined his hands closing around Berthot's throat, only to look down in disgust as he realized he'd very nearly shattered the whiskey glass he was holding.

"We still don't know what DuPres's motivation was." Ty's voice broke through his murderous thoughts. "I can understand Phelps, and whoever it is that's selling the arms, but not DuPres. What reason could he have for getting involved in something like this? He had wealth, a brilliant reputation, a daughter who loved him—"

"It doesn't matter what his motivation was," Jonathon cut him off. "All that matters is that the man was guilty."

But Ty wasn't convinced. "Why he did what he did may very well be the key we need to unlock this. The Southern cause could not have meant anything to him, so why get involved? If he knew where to find the treasure, why not simply take the money?"

Jonathon frowned. Ty's questions were the same ones that had echoed through his mind, tormenting him for the past three days. He offered his brother the only conclusion he'd been able to reach. "It wasn't the money DuPres wanted. It's what the money will buy." He finished off his whiskey and set down the glass, his eyes hard and flat. "Power. If the South succeeds in this war, Phelps, DuPres, Berthot—they would all become leaders in the creation of a new nation. Think of it, Tyler, they'd be heroes. Who better to rule their new country?"

"What about Genevieve?"

Jonathon's jaw automatically tightened. "What about her?"

"You still believe she's involved?"

"I'm certain of it."

"There's no chance you could be wrong?"

"None."

"So she'll be arrested and hung with the rest of them."

"Damn it, Tyler," Jonathon exploded, the strain clear on his face, "don't you know there's nothing, *nothing* I wouldn't do if—" he stopped abruptly, taking a deep breath to get his emotions back in check. "Berthot is her fiancé," he continued flatly. "They've obviously been working together from the start. She and Berthot will supply the treasure, Phelps the connections, and someone else the arms. It's very simple, really."

Ty shook his head, unable to reconcile what Jonathon had just said with the lovely, brave girl that he knew. He thought back a few days, to the morning after their return. He'd seen the naked pain on her face, her tears had been real. "Did anything happen on your trip to Mount Pelée?" he asked on impulse. "Anything that might have upset her?"

Genevieve came around the corner just in time to hear Ty's question—and Jonathon's scathing reply. "Nothing happened. It was a complete waste of time."

She sucked in her breath, fighting back the tears that immediately surged to her eyes. She waited a moment to regain her composure, determined to show him that his words had no effect on her at all, then stepped into the room. Her golden hair was swept up into a sophisticated chignon for the ball; her brilliant sapphire gown was the exact shade of her eyes. She moved regally across the room, her small, stubborn chin lifted defiantly, then stopped before Jonathon, looking him directly in the eye. She waited a beat, then spoke. "You're wrong. It wasn't a complete waste of time. I did, after all, learn how to handle a snake."

Jonathon met her stormy gaze. Though he towered above her, she stood before him unwaveringly, challenging him, her preposterously aggressive stance only serving to underscore her delicate femininity. She was brave to the point of being foolhardy, beautiful beyond compare . . . and a selfish scheming woman. "If you're ready now, Genevieve," he answered calmly, "I suggest we leave. The ball began over an hour ago."

Genevieve's eyes flared for a moment, then she gave her consent with a terse nod of her head, turning abruptly from him. His cool indifference was not what she wanted, she admitted miserably, her emotions churning within her like the dark, ugly brew of a witch's cauldron. What she wanted was to start a fight, to rail at him for his heartless betrayal, to cry and to rant and to rave. And finally, worst of all, she wanted him to comfort her, to wrap his strong arms around her as he had in the past, and somehow make her believe that everything was going to be all right.

But that wasn't going to happen. Jonathon, acting, she knew, more out of perfunctory courtesy than any desire to actually touch her, handed her up into the carriage. He dropped her hand as quickly as possible, then followed her inside, taking the seat opposite her and leaving Ty to sit beside her. She bit her lip and looked quickly away, silently commanding herself to quit taking note of every slight, of every cold, silent rebuke, and yet knowing at the same time that she was unable to stop.

Forcing her attention away from the uneasy silence within the carriage, she focused her gaze on the activity outside. One month ago, she had attended her very first ball on Martinique, to celebrate the start of Carnival. This evening's ball represented the climax of that event, Mardi Gras. There was a curious tension in the streets as masked revelers in fantastic and macabre costumes began to assemble in loose groups. Torches were lit and raised, and the smell of strange, pungent herbs filled the air. A warm breeze carried the sound of a drum slowly, tonelessly beating. She shivered as a sudden, dark premonition sent a chill down her spine.

"Cold, Genevieve?"

She jerked her head around. The sound of Jonathon's voice, so cool and detached, as it had been since their confrontation days ago, was more painful to her than any heated words could have been. A bitter retort sprang to her lips but she silenced it, realizing it was useless to try to provoke a response from him now. He watched her with studied indifference, an expression on his face that could only be described as boredom. Nothing she said now could change the fact that he'd chosen Constance over her, that he held her in so little regard he hadn't even tried to deny it. "No," she answered simply, "I'm not cold."

Jonathon clenched his jaw in silent rage at her nonchalance, using every ounce of restraint he possessed to keep from reaching across the carriage and grabbing her by her smooth, lovely shoulders and shaking her until she admitted her deceit. His eyes focused on the creamy-white column of her throat, remembering her soft gasps as he'd placed gentle, loving kisses there, his stomach tightening as he imagined it burned by the pull of a rope. "We've arrived," he announced in grim finality as the carriage pulled to a stop.

He leapt out, ignoring the liveried servant who approached to assist Genevieve, and pulled her from the carriage himself. This time, however, he didn't let her go as rapidly, his hand like a steel grip on her elbow as he pulled her aside for a private word before they entered the ball. "It's time you and I came to an understanding, before we enter this farce of a ball."

"An understanding," she hissed as she jerked her elbow out of his grasp. "Exactly what sort of understanding did you have in mind?"

Jonathon drew himself up, his expression unyielding. "I

want you to think, Genevieve, one last time, about what you're doing. Only you can decide what you really want, and what the consequences will be."

There was a warning to his words she couldn't begin to decipher. For a moment Genevieve just stared up at him with angry, bewildered eyes. She cleared her throat and finally spoke. "All I want, all I've ever wanted, is to find the truth."

"The truth," he repeated, his face cynical and hard. "The truth doesn't frighten you?"

"Of course not," she replied automatically.

She thought she saw something flicker for a moment in his amber eyes, but it was gone too quickly for her to be certain. "It should," was all he said, taking her once more by the arm and leading her toward the ball.

They traveled a long hallway brilliantly lit by candlelight and arrived at last at the grand ballroom. But there was something different, something lewd and almost frightening about the spectacle before them. The guests were elaborately dressed, either in formal attire and carrying exquisitely jeweled and feathered masks, or outfitted in outrageous costumes of their own fantasy and design.

Visions from the exotic to the erotic paraded proudly by, evidently heedless of the customs dictated by etiquette and good taste. The great hall rang with a deafening roar as its occupants shouted to make themselves heard above the cries and laughter of their neighbors, while in the background the orchestra played bravely on. Alcohol flowed freely, distributed through the crowd by male and female servants even more shockingly clad than their guests.

Genevieve swallowed hard and, truly afraid to step into that mad crush, glanced at Jonathon. For a moment she thought she saw distaste on his face, but it vanished as soon as he felt her eyes on him. "Ready?" he asked impassively, gesturing her forward. They stepped into the crowd quietly, with no butler to announce them, Genevieve sensing quite correctly that anonymity was prized at this particular gathering.

Jonathon moved doggedly forward, checking his impulse to take Genevieve firmly by the arm and lead her safely away. This was not the type of event to which he would usually bring a woman, any woman. Mardi Gras was a night of pagan rituals, a night in which animal lusts surfaced and were satisfied. This party, he knew, catered to those very appetites.

He glanced at the beautiful woman at his side, hardening his heart against the fear and nervousness he saw written on her delicate features. She'd wanted to come to this, she'd asked him to bring her, providing further proof of her guilt. Not for a moment did Jonathon believe it was mere coincidence that Berthot and Phelps were meeting with their arms supplier at this very same event. "Well, Genevieve, here it is. The night you've been waiting for. I do hope you're not disappointed."

Genevieve's eyes flickered from Jonathon to the large, unruly crowd which surrounded her. She knew this was the last ball of the season, and therefore her last chance to unearth any information that might clear her father's name. But as she gazed at the great masked mob which filled the hall, she realized just how difficult that was going to be. She chewed her bottom lip nervously, feeling suddenly very vulnerable, and in completely over her head.

"Well?" Jonathon prompted tersely.

"It's very nice," she replied as firmly as she could, determined not to show how frightened she truly was.

"Very nice," he repeated, his deep voice filled with disgust. He turned from her, scanning the crowd for Tyler, who had entered before them. He found him across the room, deep in conversation with Roger Wilkens and James Pierce, two of several men from the *Liberty* he had stationed about the building.

"Before you go—"

"Oh? Am I going somewhere?"

"Well, I thought, perhaps . . ." Surely he'd been searching the crowd for Constance. But her words dwindled off as the cold hardness she'd become accustomed to returned to his eyes. "I thought perhaps you could introduce me to our host," she finished, her courage slowly returning.

"Our host? Good God, what do you think this is? You'll notice you were not given a dance card to guide you through this evening's activities, my lady."

Genevieve felt her stomach tighten at the obvious derision in his voice. "Fine, if I've made a mistake—"

"Not at all. If you're truly interested in meeting our illustrious host, you can begin your search for him in the upstairs chambers. Though I would suggest you knock before entering."

Color stained her cheeks, but she stiffened her spine, refusing to let him intimidate her any further. "Really," she commented, arching her brows in cool disdain. "In that case, why don't you find your mistress and join her? I certainly have no further use for your services." She watched his eyes darken to a deep, stormy amber, and she knew she had finally struck a nerve. But she felt no satisfaction whatsoever. Righteous pride deserted her, and her words, meant to be cutting and strong, left nothing but a thick, dull ache in her throat.

Jonathon simply took her arm and thrust her deeper into the frenzied crowd. "Business before pleasure," he ground out in reply.

They'd managed to move but a few feet when Genevieve's opposite arm was grasped firmly. A tall man, his face entirely concealed by an elaborate mask, lurched forward. "A dance with the beautiful lady," he slurred. He attempted a deep, formal bow, but failed miserably, swaying and pitching forward instead.

Jonathon caught him before he collapsed on top of Genevieve, hauling him up by his lapels. "Get your filthy hands off her," he hissed in the man's face, repelled by the strong, noxious odor of whiskey that emanated from him.

"Really, Morgan," the man answered, his voice full of drunken indignity. He tugged ineffectually at Jonathon's fists, trying to remove them from his clothing, then, having no luck at all, shrugged it off. "Someone ought to remind you that this is a"—he paused, burped, then finished—"party."

A high, feminine giggle escaped from the woman who'd been standing behind him. She stepped forward now, tottering unsteadily in red slippers with heels at least four inches high. Though her face was covered as well, Genevieve had no trouble figuring out it was Constance behind the red, sequined mask. Her lips were rouged the same brilliant shade, and her heavy perfume filled the air.

She moved forward now, her hips swaying outrageously beneath her scarlet gown, and planted herself between Genevieve and Jonathon, wrapping her arm through his. "You see, Harry?" she purred, her voice dripping satisfaction, "I told you Jonathon would come tonight." Her dark eyes gleamed from behind her mask as she gazed up at him possessively.

"So you did, my dear, so you did," Harry agreed amiably, staggering back a bit as Jonathon abruptly released him. He shook his head as though trying to focus. "I'm surprised at you, Morgan. I didn't think this type of affair appealed to you."

"It doesn't," Jonathon answered curtly. "I'm here only at the request of Mlle. DuPres. She expressed particular interest in the event." His biting tone left no doubt as to his own contempt for the commotion swirling around them.

Harry pulled off his mask, his cool gray eyes running over Genevieve as if seeing her in an altogether new and surprising light. "Really?" he said, leaning in to examine her more thoroughly, a lewd smile on his face. He straightened, attempting a sophisticated demeanor despite his obvious overindulgence. "In that case, mademoiselle, it shall be my honor to escort you through this evening's festivities."

The decision was not a hard one for Genevieve to make.

The sight of Constance curled up at Jonathon's side, gazing at her with unmistakable malice in her eyes and a triumphant smile on her lips, was more than she could bear. Harry might be foxed, he might reek of whiskey, and his words might be nearly unintelligible, but he was managing to stand up by himself now. "I'd be delighted," she answered firmly, stepping forward.

"Unfortunately, Mlle. DuPres will have to decline," Jonathon cut in, his hand landing heavily on Genevieve's shoulder.

Harry's eyes flashed irritation for just a moment, before a heavy, drunken dullness once again took over his features. He sent Genevieve another lewd smile and a clumsy wink, then reached for Constance's arm. "Come, my dear," he slurred, at the same time managing an arch tone, "it's obvious we're not wanted here."

Constance opened her mouth immediately, her objection plain, then shut it just as quickly. A mysterious smile lifted her lips as she allowed Harry to lead her away. She turned back briefly, calling out in a sugary-sweet voice, "See you soon, Mademoiselle DuPres." Then they were gone, swallowed by the crowd.

Genevieve didn't waste a second puzzling over Constance's parting remark. She jerked out from under Jonathon's grasp, her sapphire eyes shooting sparks. "Go! Go join your mistress. I told you, I don't need your help. I don't want your help."

"I'm well aware of that," Jonathon agreed darkly, knowing he should have let her go. Though Harry was too drunk to pose any real threat himself, he would undoubtedly have led Genevieve to his father. Berthot would be there as well, and the arms dealer, and the meeting would take place. Then they would all be arrested. Simple. Neat. Exactly as he'd planned it. Exactly what they all deserved.

But in that single, irrational moment, he couldn't let that happen. For despite everything he knew, despite Genevieve's obvious guilt and betrayal, the overwhelming urge to protect her, even from herself, was too strong to ignore.

"Then go!" she shrieked, her voice edged with hysteria. "Leave me alone."

"I will when I'm ready to," Jonathon answered implacably. He grabbed her wrist firmly, wrapping his other arm tightly around the small of her back, and pulled her to him. "Dance with me, Genevieve."

"What?!"

Jonathon said nothing, merely began propelling her through the boisterous crowd, smoothly avoiding the other couples gliding and weaving through the great hall.

Genevieve struggled against him, painful memories of the last ball they had attended suddenly flooding her mind. He'd uttered those same words to her and taken her into his arms. Her body, she remembered, had merely floated on air. Her heart had soared. And for a while, for a very brief and wonderful while, she'd actually believed he never meant to let her go.

But she knew better now.

She twisted in his arms, trying to break free of his steel grip, but it was useless. She was pressed firmly against him, the hard planes of his body molded to her soft curves, her cheek pressed against his thick, powerful chest, so that she was forced to inhale the rich, masculine scent of him. To her shame and horror, her body was betraying her even now, the heat of desire rising slowly within her. She pulled even harder to break free, hating her weakness, hating herself for wanting him. For loving him still.

"Why are you doing this?" she cried desperately.

Because this is the last time I'll ever be able to hold you in my arms, Jonathon answered silently, his teeth clenched in private agony. *Don't hurry me, Genevieve. Give me this one last chance to memorize how this feels, to know what it was like to hold you and to love you. I just need a little more time.*

A little more time.

As if forever would have been long enough.

"Please let me go," she pleaded.

"Not yet," he answered tightly.

"Please."

Jonathon glanced down at her, his body rigid as he saw the obvious distress on her face. He stopped, abruptly releasing her. "I was merely announcing our presence," he informed her coldly. "Even in a crush like this a tour or two around the dance floor should be enough to alert anyone who might be interested that we've arrived."

Genevieve barely heard his words, for she was too busy backing up, moving out of his reach. In fact, so intent was she on escaping Jonathon, she didn't even notice the woman standing behind her until she'd nearly knocked her over. The woman stumbled, reaching out to grab Genevieve's arm for support, and tearing the sleeve of her gown in the process. "Oh, dear," she gasped, "I'm so sorry. Do let me help you."

Genevieve shook her head, thoroughly embarrassed by her clumsiness. "No, that was my fault—"

"Nonsense, come with me," the woman insisted, pulling her along. "There's a maid waiting in the ladies' chamber who can sew that back so well you'll scarcely know it was ever torn."

When Jonathon moved to accompany them the woman shook her head, her giggle filling the air. "It's ladies only, sir," she said. "But don't worry. I'll have your pretty little friend back right away."

"This really isn't necessary," Genevieve protested, her gown the least of her concerns at that moment.

"No, dear, I insist," the woman answered, pulling Genevieve through the crowd. Her eyes darted about her as she reached a thick door. She pulled it open and with a quick, sudden shove, sent Genevieve stumbling headlong into the dark chamber. Genevieve caught herself from falling and whirled around, grabbing for the door, but it was slammed shut before she could reach it. She felt frantically in the darkness for a handle, realizing too late that it had been removed from the inside. She pounded her fists against the solid wood. If this was meant to be a joke, it had certainly gone too far.

"Let me out!" she called. "Can anyone hear me? Let me out!" She pressed her ear against the thick wood and heard nothing but the dull roar of the crowd outside, realizing at once how useless her cries were. With a heavy sigh she turned back, slumping wearily against the door as she slowly scanned the dark chamber for another way out.

Suddenly she stopped, feeling her heart jump to her throat and the hair rise on the back of her neck as she stared straight ahead in wordless terror.

She wasn't alone.

CHAPTER TWENTY

The room was too dark to make out the face of the figure standing before her. All she could tell was that he was large, with broad shoulders, and a decidedly aggressive stance. He moved slowly toward her, and her gasp filled the air as recognition finally struck.

"Armand!"

"You shouldn't be here, Genevieve."

"Armand, what have you done—"

"There's no time for explanations now." He moved forward quickly, taking her firmly by the arm. "You must leave the ball at once. It's far too dangerous—"

"No time for explanations?" she repeated in stunned amazement. "That's it? That's all you have to say?" She jerked out of his grasp, anger and disbelief written clearly on her face. "I *trusted* you, Armand. My father loved you as his own son. And this is how you repay us? With lies and betrayal?"

"Genevieve, you should have stayed in Paris. I made special arrangements for you—"

"I don't need your 'special arrangements,'" she spat out, true loathing in her eyes. "I'll never forgive you, Armand. You killed my father, just as surely as if you'd run a knife through him."

Even in the dim light, she could see his face pale at her words. "You can't believe that, Genevieve."

"What else am I to believe?" she choked out, her voice thick with pain. "You were after the treasure all along. You

wanted it so badly you let my father hang for stealing it."
She took a deep breath, then looked him bravely in the eye.
"But we both know it hasn't been found, don't we?"

She heard Armand's quick intake of breath as his hands
locked around her upper arms. "If you know anything,
Genevieve, tell me now. Tell me where to find the treasure."

"Why should I? Will you kill me, too?"

Anger darkened his face as he tightened his grip on her
arms. "You told me in Paris that your father sent you letters.
His last letter, Genevieve, think hard, what did it say?"

She lifted her chin, gazing at him in defiant silence.

He met her silent, angry stare, and they both stood
motionless until a sudden noise from outside captured his
attention. He jerked his head around, peering into the
darkness, then turned back to Genevieve. "Go back," he told
her shortly. "Go back to Captain Morgan. You don't belong
here."

"Jonathon! But how do you know—" she started, but he
was gone too quickly for her to finish. She raced to the
window, watching as he lowered himself by the thick
branches of an adjacent tree down to the street. "Armand!"
she yelled, but he didn't slow down. She hesitated for the
briefest second, then leaned out the window, grabbed a
sturdy branch, and set out after him.

Jonathon waited impatiently for Genevieve to return, his
keen eyes scanning every face that moved before him as
he silently cursed himself for letting her go. She had been
gone too long, far too long, to mend a simple tear in her
gown. He pushed through the thick crowd, moving in the
direction she'd gone, when his gaze lit upon the woman who
had pulled her away. "Where is she?" he demanded roughly,
jerking her to him.

The woman recoiled, shrinking back from the dark rage
she saw in Jonathon's eyes. "Who?" she cried weakly.

Jonathon's grip tightened painfully on her arm. "I'll give
you one more chance to answer my question," he growled.

"The woman whose gown you ripped—where did you take her?"

The woman's face paled with fear. "There," she answered, lifting a shaking arm to point to the thick door through which she'd pushed Genevieve. "The man gave me a coin to bring her there."

"What man?"

"I don't know. I swear I don't," she interjected quickly as she watched Jonathon's jaw clench in silent fury. "A Frenchman, that's all I know, I swear," she stammered.

Berthot. Jonathon shoved the woman aside, his long strides carrying him swiftly to the heavy door. He threw it open, expecting to find Genevieve locked in a lover's embrace, and fully prepared to tear the other man limb from limb, but stopped in mid-stride as he realized the chamber was empty.

She was gone.

The door swung open wider behind him, illuminating Ty's figure as he stood in the doorway. "Jonathon—"

"Genevieve's gone. She left with Berthot," he stated flatly, cutting him off.

Ty nodded, his face tense. "I've found Phelps, but he's leaving, too. He just called for his carriage."

"Follow him. They've obviously made all the arrangements they needed to make tonight. They're going after the treasure now."

"What about Genevieve and Berthot?"

Jonathon turned toward his brother, his eyes dark, hard, and absolutely pitiless. "I'll find them," he stated with chilling finality.

Genevieve ran blindly through the dark, narrow streets, searching frantically for Armand, but he seemed to have vanished among the dense crowds of revelers. She stopped to catch her breath, her eyes widened as she took in the wild, uncensored activity churning around her. The steady, rhythmic beating of drums that she'd heard earlier had escalated to savage, ceaseless pounding, the sound of it stirring the blood of every man and woman on the street. Sweaty, writhing bodies twisted around her in a frenzied, macabre dance. The eyes of the dancers were fevered and glazed as their clutching fingers reached out to grab her.

Assembled in the center of the street was a grotesque wedding party, in which an enormous bride, complete with horns, tail, and cloven hooves, was exchanging vows with a nearly naked dwarf. Genevieve turned away, wanting to run, but felt as if she were trapped in a nightmare, too terrified to move. Nameless faces swarmed before her, then swooped away, while lights from glowing torches flickered in the warm breeze, throwing wild, distorted shadows everywhere.

A shrill cry suddenly tore through the air, giving her frozen limbs the impetus to move. Stifling a cry of her own, she lifted her skirts and ran, desperate to find rufuge from the madness which surrounded her.

She realized too late that she was being stalked.

A pair of strong hands reached out from behind her, spinning her around as she gazed up at the tall, faceless being who held her so tightly. He was dressed entirely in black, his face covered with a coarse, dark hood, secured at his throat with a heavy rope. Rough holes had been gouged out for his eyes and mouth.

Genevieve cried out and struggled against him, pulling away briefly, but he caught her at once, his rough hands tearing at her gown as he pulled her up sharply. He clamped his arm tightly around her waist, locking her arms against her sides as he stuffed a thick cloth into her mouth, effectively silencing her cries of protest.

He shoved her into a dark alleyway, his tall frame silhouetted in the dim light from the street as he placed himself between her and her only route of escape. Genevieve was backing up, tugging the gag from her mouth as she searched in vain for a weapon or means to defend herself, when her back came up against a thick, solid wall.

"There's nowhere for you to run, no one who's going to

help you," he confirmed, seeing the stark terror in her eyes, his voice thick and muffled from beneath his hood. Moving with slow, careful precision, he reached to his belt and withdrew a long, jagged knife.

"Please—" Genevieve began, her voice a hoarse whisper.

"I want the treasure, Genevieve. Tell me where it is."

Whoever he was, he not only knew her name, he knew about the treasure, she thought wildly, her heart hammering with fear. "I don't know," she stammered, "I don't know what you're talking about."

A heavy silence filled the space between them as her captor studied her face. He raised his arm, the razor-sharp steel of his blade glittering like liquid silver in the flickering torchlight. He took a step forward. "Tell me where it is."

Genevieve shook her head numbly, stark fear choking off her voice as she lifted her hand in a vain attempt to defend herself. But just as he stepped forward, bringing the hot steel of his knife to rest against her throat, a loud, boisterous group burst in upon them. "Carnival, Carnival," they chanted in drunken merriment. The revelers surged around them in good cheer, heedless of the scene into which they'd stumbled. They left as quickly and noisily as they'd come, their shouts echoing off the thick alley walls as Genevieve whirled around in stunned amazement.

The man with the knife was gone.

It was all she could do to keep her legs from buckling beneath her in overpowering relief. She moved in mindless terror, fleeing the dark alley, her trembling limbs carrying her back to the crowded streets. She fought her way through the drunken masses, nearly sobbing as she finally secured a carriage and driver to take her back to Jonathon's home.

Incredibly, fate seemed to be on her side, for she spotted his carriage in the drive and knew that he, too, must have returned from the ball. She burst through the entry, his name falling from her lips, then stopped short as she saw him standing at the bottom of the landing, silently staring at her. "Jonathon!" she cried, relief pouring through her as she flung herself into his arms. "Jonathon, thank God I've found you," she sobbed.

Her pride forgotten, she clung to him, the harrowing experience she'd just endured still fresh in her mind. "A man grabbed me in the street," she finally managed to choke out. "He had a knife, he was going to hurt me, I was so afraid. I couldn't see his face—"

"Why did you come back here?"

The coldness of his tone struck her like a physical blow. She stepped back and looked up at him, her deep blue eyes wet with tears. "What?"

"I asked you why you came back." He pushed her away, his gaze sweeping over her with undisguised contempt. "But you don't have to answer that. I can see by the looks of your gown that your reunion with Berthot left much to be desired."

Genevieve glanced down at herself, automatically clutching the ripped bodice of her gown and pulling it back together. "I told you," she stammered, shaking her head wildly, "a man grabbed me in the street. He had a knife—"

Jonathon's eyes darkened as a stormy rage took over his rugged features. "Do not," he commanded harshly, using every ounce of his will to control his rage, "ever lie to me again, Genevieve, or I swear to God I won't be responsible for what happens."

"Lie? I never lied—"

She jumped as Jonathon's fist slammed onto the small table beside him, sending the vase which sat atop it crashing to the floor. The sound of shattering crystal rang in her ears as his deep voice thundered out, "It's been nothing but lies from the day we met! You've been in league with Berthot from the start."

"No! No, Jonathon, that isn't true."

Hearing her say his name, hearing her soft voice deny everything, stirred his anger even more. "Did you think I wouldn't find out about him? Your father's first officer, your fiancé, the one whose name you claimed you couldn't remember?"

Genevieve swallowed hard, bravely lifting her sapphire eyes to meet his heated glare. "You've a right to be angry about that, but—"

"I don't need your permission to be angry!" he roared.

"Listen to me," she pleaded. "I didn't tell you about Armand because I wanted to give him a chance to defend himself. I didn't believe he could have done anything to hurt me or my father." She paused to take a deep breath, the pain in her voice heartbreakingly clear. "But I was wrong. He's here, I saw him tonight. He wants the treasure so desperately he'll stop at nothing to get it." She bit her lower lip to keep it from trembling, then continued, "He must have been the one who grabbed me, who had the knife."

Jonathon stared at her for a moment, his face impassive, then coolly shrugged. "Your plan failed, so now you're turning on Berthot," he stated flatly. "I've always heard there's no honor among thieves; I suppose this proves it." Anger flashed in his golden eyes as he watched her expression change. "You can drop the shocked, innocent look now, the game's over."

Genevieve felt her stomach tighten at the deliberate cruelty in his tone. "You think I'm a thief? That I've been lying to you?"

"No, I don't think that, Genevieve," he answered calmly. "I know it." He reached into the top drawer of the table beside him and withdrew a sheaf of papers, then turned back to her. Casually propping one hip up on the table, he stretched out his long legs before him. "Now why don't I tell you what I did tonight. That is, after you left me to go meet Berthot."

"It didn't happen like that! The woman tore my sleeve and—"

"After you left with Berthot," Jonathon continued as if he hadn't heard her, "I attempted to follow you. But, as doubtless you'd planned, the thick crowds made that impossible. So I joined forces with Tyler instead, and went after Colonel Phelps. He's been arrested, along with several other prominent Southerners who took part in this conspiracy."

Genevieve just stared at him in wild disbelief, a mixture of fear and dread keeping her firmly rooted where she stood, like a small animal caught in a snare.

"Phelps confessed everything," he went on ruthlessly, "the fact that he and his conspirators had made arrangements to purchase the arms, as well as the fact that it was to be financed by your father and Berthot, using the stolen treasure."

"No," Genevieve choked out in a dull, frightened whisper. "Phelps is lying. He's lying. My father never would have agreed to that."

Jonathon's golden eyes were hard and flat. "I told you, Genevieve, it's too late for that now. We've all the proof we need to insure that each of you remains locked up for a very long time."

"Proof? What proof can you possibly have? This is insane. It isn't true, it can't be true."

"Really?" he jeered. "Then perhaps you'd like to take a look at this. Though I suppose you'll have a lie ready to explain it away as well." He coldly thrust the sheaf of papers at her.

Genevieve stared into the icy rage of his eyes, then, with a trembling hand, slowly took the papers. It took a moment for her to properly focus on the thick documents, for the words she was reading to truly sink in. Finally, however, they did. The color drained from her face as she caught her breath and felt the world spin beneath her, but Jonathon's cold voice brought her immediately back.

"That's quite a convincing reaction, my dear. I'd almost believe you were truly shocked."

She raised her eyes to him in stunned horror, but no words would come as he took the papers from her hand and tucked them neatly inside his coat pocket. "I only returned here this evening to retrieve these documents. I've been assured they'll be quite useful when the case comes to trial. Now I must return to my men, they're out looking for you and Berthot as we speak."

"Out looking for me? Why?"

Jonathon stood up, his expression rigid. "To arrest you, of course," he answered, ignoring her sharp gasp of dismay. "Let me advise you, Genevieve, of how futile it would be for you to try and run. Martinique is a small island, you'll only make it worse for yourself. There's no place to hide, no ship that will leave without being thoroughly searched. And that includes tearing apart each and every crate aboard it," he finished darkly.

Genevieve shook her head, fighting to hold back the tears that filled her eyes, her voice choked off behind the thick lump in her throat. It was useless to try to defend herself, she realized. He didn't believe a word she was saying. He'd had those documents all along and never told her about them, watching and waiting instead to use them against her. All those times he'd held her in his arms and made love to her had meant nothing to him. Nothing. No wonder he'd refused to give up his mistress.

Jonathon watched her, his jaw clenched in helpless fury. For a moment, the pain in her eyes had looked so real to him it was almost unbearable, the intensity of it slamming into his gut like a sail cut loose in a gale storm. "There is one thing I still don't understand," he said, his amber eyes locked on her. "Why did you come back here tonight?" He waited, but when it became clear she wasn't going to speak, he turned away from her and left the room.

Genevieve heard the door slam behind him, then the sound of horse's hooves as he galloped away into the night. But still she didn't move, standing motionless in the center of the now silent hall. She was conscious of nothing but an icy stillness and the tight, piercing pain in her chest as her heart splintered into a thousand small, brittle fragments.

CHAPTER TWENTY-ONE

"Why doesn't it stop?" Genevieve asked. "Mardi Gras ended last night." Her forehead rested numbly on the glass of her bedroom window as she watched the spectacle beneath her. Servants and field hands gathered in the courtyard, all dressed in black and white, with ash dotted liberally on their faces, and all carrying hand-carved skeletons. They danced and shouted and drank as they prepared to return to town, their mood only slightly subdued from the night before.

"Mardi Gras, yes," Marie answered. "This is the Celebration of Death."

The Celebration of Death, how appropriate, Genevieve thought grimly as she pulled away from the window.

"Today we mourn King Carnival, who is to die in a few hours," Marie explained softly. "He will be carried through the streets in effigy, then burned at dusk at the waterfront park."

"I see," Genevieve answered tonelessly as she crossed the room to sit at the foot of her bed. "Marie," she began hesitantly, "has . . . anybody returned yet?"

"If you mean M'sieur Jon, no, he has not."

Genevieve cleared her throat and looked away. "I see," she repeated.

"Mam'selle, I must speak to you."

Genevieve looked up in surprise at the urgency in her tone and stern expression, then sighed resignedly. "Marie, I know you don't believe me either, but I swear I didn't know—"

"Shhh, *chérie*," Marie soothed, her hand coming to rest softly on Genevieve's shoulder. "You do not have to tell me. I know what you are saying is true."

"You do? But Jonathon, he—"

"M'sieur Jon is a good man, but he has let his pride blind him. Once his anger fades, then he, too, will see the truth."

Genevieve shook her head miserably, Marie's words even more painful to her because she wanted them so desperately to be true, and knew with heartbroken certainty that they never would be. "You're wrong, Marie. It's too late now."

"No, *chérie*," Marie corrected her softly, "it's never too late. It's never too late to love and be loved, to forgive and find forgiveness." She straightened, her rich voice once again strong and confident. "But now, you must listen to me. I visited our *quimboisseur* last night, and I bring you a message."

"A message? For me?"

Marie nodded, her lovely dark features full of wisdom and mystery. "I am to warn you that you are in grave danger and must be careful. There is a man around you, a tall man you thought was a friend. You must not trust him, or go near him. He will hurt you."

Armand. Genevieve sighed, taking Marie's hand. "Thank you for the message, and for believing me, but your *quimboisseur* is too late. Surely the message was meant for last night, not today."

"No, mam'selle, today. The message is for today."

"You don't understand, Marie. It's all over. Colonel Phelps has been arrested, and they're out looking for Armand now. The danger is past."

Marie stubbornly shook her head. "You have been on this island only a short time, and do not yet understand the ways of my people. You do not believe in the power of the *quimboisseur*, I know. Today, however, you must believe." She paused, drawing herself up to her full, regal height. "My sister is the *quimboisseur*," she reminded Genevieve proudly. "She sees all that happens on this island and beyond. And it was our grandmother who told Josephine she would one day leave Martinique to marry Napoleon, and that together they would rule all of France."

"And you told your sister about me?"

Marie smiled softly as she rose and went to the door. "No, *chérie*."

"No? Then how did she—"

"I did not need to," Marie explained simply. "She already knew." She turned to leave, then hesitated, her face once again serious. "Remember, the warning is for today."

Genevieve watched the door close softly behind her, leaving her alone once again. With a heavy sigh she went back to the window, her thoughts as bleak as her future appeared to be. She glanced at the two pieces of paper which sat on her bedside table, tormenting reminders of her foolish trust and naivete. The first was the map she'd sketched long ago, complete with neat boundaries marked off as she and Jonathon had surveyed the area in their search for the treasure. The other was the last letter she'd received from her father. She picked this up slowly, her heart tightening in her chest as she looked at the familiar, beloved handwriting. Although the words had long since been committed to memory, she read it again.

My dear daughter,

I write these lines in great sorrow, for I fear I may never return, may never see your shining face again.

Know that I love you, and will always keep you with me in my heart.

Follow in my footsteps, my daughter. Wait for true love to cross your path, then marry well, for true love can build an empire.

May God bless you and keep you,
Your loving father

Genevieve stared at the letter she had always cherished. It had brought her such strength and resolve, but now brought nothing but pain. She let it slip through her hands and fall to the floor as she shifted her gaze to the turquoise sea which surrounded the island. The servants had all left for town, leaving nothing behind but a quiet, haunting stillness.

She was not going to try to run. Not because of Jonathon's warning that she wouldn't get away, but simply because she had no place to run to. No place that could give her back all she'd lost, no place that could take away the past and make her believe once again in tomorrow.

She was staring blindly out, her thoughts drifting blankly, when Marie's words suddenly began to echo through her head. "It was my grandmother who told Josephine she would marry Napoleon and rule all of France." Rule all of France. Build an empire. Marry well. Genevieve stiffened and turned from the window, reaching down to grab her father's letter. It was right there. She'd had the answer all along but had never seen it.

"Follow in my footsteps . . ." He was *telling* her where to find the treasure.

LeClerk, Napoleon's brother-in-law, had buried the treasure in the church where Josephine's parents had been married! She was certain of it. Her father hadn't stolen the treasure, but left it where LeClerk had buried it over fifty years ago.

She left her room, racing down the back stairs and out to the stables, her mind whirling in a thousand different directions as relief and confusion flooded through her mind. Why had her father signed that paper? If he'd known the location of the treasure, why hadn't he simply proven his innocence by turning it over to his commanding officer at his trial? And what was Armand's part in all this?

She had no answers to any of those questions, but knew where to find them. This had all begun with the treasure, and that was where it would all end.

*   *   *

Jonathon raised his arm to signal his men, watching through the thick morning fog as they silently spread out, positioning themselves. It had taken them all night to track Berthot, his trail finally leading to a small, seedy tavern on the docks of Fort-de-France. "Wait here, Tyler," he ordered curtly. "Watch the windows and back door, and stop anyone who tries to leave. I'm going in after Berthot."

"Not alone you're not."

Jonathon drew himself up, glaring at his brother. "That was not a request."

"I didn't think it was," Ty replied smoothly, matching him stride for stride as he headed for the tavern.

"Then get back to the men. I can take care of Berthot by myself."

"My point exactly," Ty said, nodding toward Jonathon's clenched fists. "We're here to arrest Berthot, not murder him. I just want to make sure there's enough left of the man to bring to trial."

Jonathon stopped. "I don't need you to remind me why we're here," he answered, a coldness to his voice that Tyler had never heard before.

With a look of silent understanding they stepped inside, taking a moment to adjust their eyes to the darkness of the interior. Jonathon quickly scanned the room, dismissing the table where four men sat slumped into their cups, his eyes narrowing on the lone figure who sat silently watching him from across the room. He moved forward, his rage tightly controlled as he stopped inches from his table. "Berthot?" he growled.

The other man slowly rose. He was dressed neatly, his officer's uniform a perfect complement to his tall build, his smooth good looks. His gaze flicked over Jonathon briefly, then he extended his hand. "Captain Morgan, I presume."

Jonathon glanced contemptuously at the offered hand. "This isn't a social call, Berthot."

Armand shrugged, lowering his hand to his side. "Very

well, why don't you tell me what this is about? As you've obviously gone to considerable trouble to find me here, I would imagine it's rather important." He frowned, his face suddenly tense. "Gennie's all right, isn't she?"

Jonathon stared at the tall, arrogant Frenchman, barely able to keep his anger under control as he heard him speak Genevieve's name. Not even Genevieve, but Gennie. His Gennie. A pet name. A lover's name. "If you want to live long enough to see tomorrow," he ground out between clenched teeth, "you won't let me hear you say her name again. Ever."

Armand stiffened. "Where is she? What have you done?"

"Don't worry, you'll see her soon enough. You may even find yourself in adjoining cells."

"Adjoining cells? What—"

"Save it, Berthot. I didn't come here to listen to your lies. My men have the place surrounded. You're under arrest."

Armand's eyes widened as a hint of a smile played about his mouth. "Ah, so that's it. You've come to arrest me." he said, thoughtfully surveying Jonathon. "It must have been your men who took the papers off Phelps's courier. I'd wondered about that—why they never resurfaced."

"Then you admit to signing them?"

"Of course. It was foolish of Phelps to send for them, but he needed something to blackmail me with, in case I had second thoughts about turning over the treasure, you see."

Jonathon's eyes narrowed. "You seem rather calm about all this, Berthot," he said, rubbing his fist against the palm of his hand. "Surely you're not foolish enough to believe you're actually going to get away with it."

"Surely you're not foolish enough to believe you're actually going to arrest me."

"Try and stop me."

Armand's smile grew. "I do believe that was a challenge." He leaned forward, his smile vanishing as his deep blue eyes turned to ice. "What a shame I shall have to wait for a more appropriate place and time to answer it."

Jonathon slowly shook his head as he drew himself up. "Right here, Berthot," he growled. "Right now."

Armand tensed, meeting his cold stare, a thick silence falling over the room. It was finally broken by the sound of a chair scraping over the rough wooden floor. "M. Berthot's right, Captain Morgan. This isn't the time," stated a firm voice from near the door. The four men who had been slumped over their cups only moments ago all stood, moving with remarkable sobriety and purpose.

"I hadn't intended to be seen here," the governor of Martinique continued, speaking with characteristic briskness, "but I can't let you arrest M. Berthot. Not when he's been working with me."

Jonathon's and Tyler's heads moved almost in unison, their gazes shifting from Armand to the governor, then back again to Armand. "What the hell is this?" Jonathon demanded.

"I hate to be the one to tell you this, Morgan," Armand answered dryly, "but you and I happen to be on the same side."

"Like hell we are."

"He's right," the governor interjected. He was a short, balding man with a protruding belly, but he carried himself with the air of a longtime dignitary, his speech authoritative and sharp. "Though your timing did make things rather difficult for us, Captain, getting Phelps arrested when you did."

Jonathon's eyes turned to narrow slits of amber. "Things are going to get even more difficult for you, Governor, if you don't tell me what's going on here."

The governor frowned. "I dislike threats, Captain Morgan."

"Unless, of course, you happen to be the one making them," Ty remarked.

The governor pivoted, his dark eyes raking over Tyler. "Precisely," he concurred, then turned to Armand. "We're losing too much time here. Perhaps you ought to supply the good captain and his brother with a few of the facts they seem to be missing."

Armand nodded, meeting Jonathon's cold stare. "Phelps approached General DuPres over a year ago. Not only did he know of the existence of the treasure, he knew details of LeClerk's voyage, details that could only have been known to the highest-ranking officers. He wanted to make a deal."

"Right," Jonathon interrupted impatiently. "We know, we have the papers. The treasure for the arms; and in return you and DuPres become part of a select group of men who will rule the new Confederate nation."

Armand shrugged. "Crudely put, but basically correct."

"Let him finish, Captain," the governor put in smoothly.

"The general decided to play along with Phelps. The threat was enormous, after all. Whoever he was working with was not only highly placed enough to know specifics about the treasure, he was also able to smuggle a ship carrying over a million dollars in French arms out of the country without being detected."

"That's quite a story, Berthot," Jonathon replied coldly. "I suppose you expect us to simply take your word for it."

"You could ask the general's commanding officer, everything was reported to him." He paused, his deep blue eyes clouded with anger. "Though I doubt General D'Abbaye will be very cooperative."

"General D'Abbaye," the governor explained simply, "is our arms supplier."

"General DuPres wanted nothing to do with Phelps's scheme," Armand continued. "He immediately reported everything to D'Abbaye, who ordered him to take whatever steps necessary to uncover who he was working with. The very next time he met with Phelps he was asked to sign a paper—the one you found, Captain—to solidify their pact. They were to meet again a week hence, at which time the general would meet the man supplying the arms."

"That meeting never took place," the governor interjected. "General DuPres was arrested and brought to trial two days later—on D'Abbaye's orders—the documents he'd signed being the chief evidence against him. D'Abbaye flatly denied the general's assertions that he had been working under his orders and gave him one final choice: prove his innocence by turning over the treasure to him, or hang for treason."

"So the general chose death rather than betray his country," Jonathon concluded, then turned to the governor, "If you've known all this, why hasn't D'Abbaye been arrested?"

"We needed proof," he answered simply. "I've had my suspicions about D'Abbaye for some time, suspicions that were further confirmed when M. Berthot came to me with his allegations of what had transpired at the trial. But suspicions aren't enough to convict someone of D'Abbaye's rank and power."

"Now you have Phelps's confession that he was working with D'Abbaye," Ty asserted.

"Unfortunately, we don't," the governor replied. "D'Abbaye's too careful to get his hands dirty himself. He's been working through intermediaries, refusing to make himself known until the actual treasure was delivered. I don't think Phelps has any idea who he was actually dealing with."

"Which made it very easy for me to convince him that I would carry out General DuPres's plan," Armand continued. "I'd a meeting arranged last night with Phelps and D'Abbaye to turn over the location of the treasure in return for the location of the ship carrying the arms—a meeting that was to be witnessed by a dozen of my men, followed by the immediate seizure of the arms and the arrest of both men."

Jonathon looked from Armand to the governor, then broke the thick silence which suddenly filled the room. "And I arrested Phelps before that meeting could take place," he stated flatly.

"You did," the governor agreed succinctly. "But there still may be time to remedy that. D'Abbaye has no reason to doubt M. Berthot or his devotion to the Southern cause, for it was you and your men who arrested Phelps."

"D'Abbaye is interested in only one thing," Armand interrupted contemptuously, "and that's getting his hands on the treasure. He's too greedy to leave without giving it one last try." He pulled a watch from his pocket, glanced at it, then continued. "I've a meeting with him in exactly four hours. He's given me that long to get the treasure and conclude our deal." He paused, determination filling his eyes. "That means his ship is moored somewhere off the coast of this island. My men are out looking for her now. They're going to find her."

A cold chill ran down Jonathon's spine as the full realization of what they were saying suddenly became clear to him. "Last night," he said urgently, "you were with the governor, waiting to meet with Phelps and D'Abbaye?"

"Yes," Armand answered.

"You didn't see Genevieve?"

"Briefly, yes, at the ball, but I sent her back to stay with you. Why—"

But Jonathon had already turned away from him to issue short, terse commands to his brother. "Tyler, take Berthot and the governor aboard the *Liberty*. You know these waters as well as any man alive, there's not a shallow bay or rocky cove small enough to hide D'Abbaye if you and the crew want to find him."

"Where are you going?"

"Home," Jonathon shouted over his shoulder, not breaking his stride as he raced for the door, the magnitude of his mistake now painfully clear. His heart slammed against his chest as an image of Genevieve flashed through his mind: stumbling through the door last night, her gown torn and her face pale with fear.

There was one question that Genevieve had never answered, one question that had haunted him throughout the night. Why had she come back? He finally had his answer. She'd come back because she was innocent, because she was terrified, clinging to him for protection because some-one had pulled a knife on her, dragged her into a dark alley, and tried to kill her.

And what had he done in return? Called her a liar and a thief, condemned her father as a traitor, then left her alone to face God knew what. Terror and self-loathing swept through him in equal measure as he leaped for his stallion, spurring him at a breakneck pace toward his home.

There was someone else after the treasure. Someone they'd all missed. Someone who was now after Genevieve.

Chapter Twenty-two

❧

Genevieve lifted her arm and brushed her hair off her damp forehead. In her haste to leave she'd forgotten her hat, and the heat and humidity of the day bore down heavily upon her. She squeezed her eyes shut, then opened them again in a useless attempt to clear her blurred vision. Her gown clung limply to her as she pressed her thighs against the flanks of her horse, its flesh as slick and sweaty as her own.

The gentle mare responded to her silent command, straining forward, taking them up and over the final crest in the road. Genevieve caught her breath. There, glistening like a white jewel against the shimmering blue-green sea, sat the village of Les Trois Islets. She'd made it. She swung her mount around to the left, galloping past the outskirts of the quiet village and directly toward Empress Josephine's former home.

She dismounted at the church and stumbled inside, taking a moment to adjust her eyes to the pitch-black stillness of the interior. A tall, narrow window behind her let in a piercing ray of sunlight, which traveled across the dark room, illuminating the wooden cross above the altar. A shiver ran down her spine as she moved slowly toward the altar, her eyes fixed on the wooden cross, which seemed to glow in the darkness like a living, breathing thing, beckoning her forward. Her father's voice whispered in her ear, "Wait for true love to cross your path. . . . *Cross* your path."

The treasure was buried beneath the cross. She fell to her knees and began clawing away at the rough earthen floor. When the soil became too hard for her to break through with her fingers, she grabbed a sharp stick and dug with that. She drove the stick deeper and deeper, not stopping to rest, her back and arms aching, her hands cut and bleeding from the splinters and sharp stones in the dirt. She kept on, pausing only when she heard a resounding thud and the stick would go no further. Using her hands once again, she frantically brushed the dirt away from the cold, hard surface she'd struck. She took a deep breath to calm her racing heart, then peered into the dim hole.

There, lying deep within the dirt, was a sturdy seaman's chest, engraved with Black Bart's infamous insignia.

She'd found the treasure.

She rocked back on her heels for a moment and stared at it in stunned disbelief, then, shaking herself free from her stupor, grabbed the stick and loosened the earth surrounding it. Though the chest wasn't very large, it was extremely heavy, and she needed all her strength to lift it. She ran her hands down the sides of the chest, wishing she could open it. But a thick metal lock clamped it securely shut. Taking the rusty lock into her bare hands, she tugged at it with all her might.

"If you'll allow me, mademoiselle, I believe I can assist you in removing that lock."

Genevieve gasped and whirled around. Harry and Constance stood together in the doorway, watching her, serene smiles on both their faces. She lurched to her feet, clutching the folds of her gown. "What are you doing here?" she demanded, attempting to hide the chest beneath her long skirt.

"We followed you," Harry answered calmly as he walked toward her. He stopped in front of her, his smile vanishing as he raised his pistol and pointed it directly at her. "Move away from the treasure, Genevieve," he ordered coldly.

Genevieve swallowed hard, then lifted her chin. "This

chest belongs to the people of France," she answered firmly.

A brief smile flickered once again over Harry's face. "Now it belongs to me," he replied coolly. He released the safety of his pistol, then cocked the trigger. "Move away."

"You won't get away with this," Genevieve warned in a low voice, her fists clenched tightly at her sides as she bravely stood her ground.

Harry merely shrugged his shoulders. "It seems a shame to spill blood all over that pretty gown of yours." He raised his gun. "But I will if I have to."

Genevieve hesitated, then reluctantly edged away from the treasure. Harry's cool gray eyes gleamed victory as he watched her move slowly away, revealing the sturdy seaman's chest. With a quick thrust of his pistol he motioned her back, then stepped forward and lifted the chest onto the altar. He gazed at it reverently for a moment, running his hands lovingly over the dark wood, then blew the heavy lock off with a single shot from his pistol. He passed the gun to Constance, then slowly raised the lid.

A thick silence fell over the room. Harry hesitated, then dug his hands into the chest. When he lifted them, his fingers dripped with heavy strands of pearls, thick gold coins, and sapphires, rubies, emeralds, and diamonds of such startling magnificence it was almost impossible to believe they were actually real. He dug deeper into the chest and lifted a pair of solid silver goblets, intricately carved, and the hilt of a sword so ornate and richly bejeweled there could be no doubt it had once been the possession of a mighty medieval king.

Genevieve knew that each piece within the chest was worth a fortune by itself—amassed together, the value was inestimable; wealth and riches beyond any fantasy. "It's incredible," Harry whispered, giving voice to her thoughts, "more than I ever dared imagine. And it has been here all along. I was so close, so very close." He tore his gaze from the treasure and turned to Genevieve, his eyes burning with fanatic intensity. "There's enough here to build more than just an army. There's enough here to build an entire nation. The Confederate nation."

"It's such a shame you won't be around to see it," Constance added, smiling maliciously at Genevieve. "Especially since you've been so helpful. Why, if it wasn't for you, we might never have found the treasure."

"You brought me here weeks ago," Genevieve said, looking at Harry. "You must have known all along that the treasure was buried here."

He smiled as he shook his head. "If I had, I would have killed you that very day, rather than lurking in alleyways last night."

Genevieve's eyes grew round as she took an involuntary step backward, away from Harry. "That was you under the black hood," she said in a strangled whisper.

Harry nodded. "I only feigned drunkenness at the ball to divert attention away from myself. I didn't want any questions asked when I went upstairs and 'passed out' from too much drink. It was simple to slip out unnoticed and follow you. You see, my dear," he continued ruthlessly, "it was just too great a risk to let you live any longer. You might have eventually stumbled upon the treasure—without my being there to claim it."

"Without *our* being there to claim it," Constance put in, stepping forward. "It's your fault I've lost Jonathon," she said, her dark eyes raking over Genevieve. "It's your fault that he's turned away from me, that he hasn't once come to call since you've been on this island."

Genevieve felt a sudden, absurd sense of elation as she stared into the dark anger of Constance's eyes. Jonathon had not been with Constance. That realization filled her with hope and a reborn sense of strength and courage. "The treasure won't do either of you any good now," she announced bravely. "Colonel Phelps was arrested last night, along with the other rebels who took part in this scheme. It's all over now. You've failed."

"Failed?" Harry repeated with a smile as he dug his fist

into the chest, lifting a handful of precious jewels. "Not when I have this." The rare stones dripped from his fingers. "You're the one who failed, Genevieve. Just as your father failed."

"My father? What—"

"General DuPres never intended to turn the treasure over to the South. I knew it all along, but my father refused to listen. Now, because of you and Morgan, he'll spend the rest of his life in prison." He paused, then lifted his shoulders philosophically. "Such a pity, really. The old man could have been quite useful."

"You can't still believe you're going to get away with this."

Harry looked at her in genuine surprise. "Of course I am. Don't you understand? This is my fate, my destiny. I now have everything I need to lead my people to freedom. The South will never again bow to Northern rule. The great Confederate nation shall rise at last, and I shall be the one to lead her."

"Then you will be leading your people to needless slaughter," Genevieve answered quietly. "For no matter how great the treasure is, a nation built upon the enslavement and suffering of others will always be impoverished. You cannot build a nation upon your people's backs. Your country will fall, Harry," she finished simply.

Harry stiffened, his cool gray eyes taking her in appraisingly. "You remind me of your father, Genevieve. He, too, refused to see the glory of the Southern cause, and thought he could stop us. He failed, of course, just as you have. I wonder if you will accept your death as bravely as he accepted his." His gaze flicked to Constance, and the pistol she held in her hand. "Shoot her," he ordered curtly.

Genevieve gasped, her heart jumping to her throat as Constance's hand came up. She braced herself for the impact of the lead, forcing herself not to cry out. She lifted her eyes to meet the other woman's and saw, to her amazement, that they were as wide and frightened as her own.

"Harry, this isn't the way we planned it," Constance cried, her hand shaking visibly. "You told me we would send her back to France! You told me we were just going to get her out of the way. That's all I wanted!"

A vein bulged in Harry's neck as he stared at his cousin. "I give the orders now, Constance! You will do as I tell you," he raged. "Shoot her!" Constance's hand began to shake even more. "Shoot her!" Harry roared. "Go on, you stupid bitch! Shoot her!"

The pistol shot rang through the small church.

Chapter Twenty-three

Genevieve jumped, her hands wrapping automatically around herself, but to her astonishment, she felt no searing pain. It took her a moment before she realized it was Harry who'd fallen to his knees, clutching his shoulder, and an even longer moment before she recognized Jonathon's tall, muscular form silhouetted in the doorway. A thin stream of smoke blew from the barrel of his gun. "Make one move, Phelps," he growled, "and I'll kill you." It was not a threat. It was a plain, simple, statement of fact.

Harry shook his head wildly. "I'm unarmed! I'm unarmed!"

Jonathon moved slowly forward, his pistol raised. "Genevieve, are you all right?" There was no mistaking the emotion in his voice, the raw fear.

Genevieve nodded mutely. "Yes," she finally choked out. "Yes."

"Throw down the gun, Constance," Jonathon instructed, his eyes never leaving Harry. Constance, who stood as if frozen until now, finally moved, her entire body shaking as she slowly brought down her arm.

Genevieve's knees nearly gave way in relief when a sudden motion caught her eye. "No!" she cried, but she was too late. Harry lunged sideways, knocking the pistol from Constance's grasp as Jonathon dove forward, both men firing at once. The bullets ricocheted off the thick white walls as Harry twisted toward Genevieve, pulling her down beneath him.

"Drop your gun, Morgan!" he screamed. "Do you hear me? Drop your gun!" Harry lifted himself slowly up onto one knee, holding Genevieve in front of him, the cold steel of his gun pressed against her cheek. The blood streaming from the wound in his shoulder filled her nostrils with a dark, heavy odor.

Jonathon came instantly to his feet. "Let her go, Phelps."

"I said drop your gun."

"Jonathon! No! Don't—" Genevieve began, but Harry silenced her with a quick, sharp jab to her ribs.

Jonathon's eyes flashed fire. His muscles tensed, yearning to leap forward, to wrap his hands around Harry's throat, but he held himself back, clenching his jaw in silent fury as Harry tightened his grip on Genevieve. Jonathon held his arms out in front of him, the gun loose in his right hand, then slowly released it. "Now let her go."

Harry's deep laughter filled the room. He staggered to his feet, pulling Genevieve up with him. "You're very good at giving orders, Morgan. But you seem to forget who's holding the gun." He cocked the trigger, sliding the barrel along Genevieve's smooth temple, a satisfied smile on his face as he watched Jonathon's skin turn ashen. "I give the orders now."

Jonathon nodded slowly, his heart pounding in his chest, knowing one wrong word or move from him would cost Genevieve her life. "The treasure's yours, Phelps. Take it. I won't try to stop you. Just let her go."

Harry listened, savoring the moment. It was the first time he'd ever heard fear in Jonathon's voice, and the sound of it affected him like a heady drug, fueling his feeling of omnipotence. "You're right, Morgan," he agreed, "on both counts. The treasure's mine now, and you won't stop me." He lowered his arm, pointing his gun directly at Jonathon.

Genevieve didn't have time to think. She reacted instinctively, shoving Harry off-balance as she drove her fist directly into his wound. Harry's groan of pain was swallowed by the blast of his gun as they both toppled over backward. Jonathon leapt forward at the same instant. The bullet tore through his upper arm but it didn't slow him down as he pulled Harry from Genevieve, his fists flying in a blind, merciless rage. After a few minutes, Harry's limp form sank back to the floor.

Genevieve staggered unsteadily to her feet, her head spinning as she surveyed the interior of the tiny church. Constance had shrunk back into a corner, her arms wrapped around herself, her dark eyes wide with fear. Harry lay motionless on the ground, his shirt soaked with blood. The rough wooden pews had been upended and thrown at wild angles, the altar smashed and the chest knocked over, scattering precious gold and jewels over the floor. Two guns rested in the dirt.

The only thing that hadn't changed was the tall wooden cross, which hung serenely unaltered, a glowing white presence above them all.

Jonathon stepped in front of her, searching her pale, frightened face. "Genevieve? Darling?"

Genevieve gasped, her eyes fixed on the blood that seeped from his wound. "Your arm—"

"It's nothing," he said quickly, cutting her off. He stood motionless, then slowly reached for her, unable to control the shaking of his hands but desperate to touch her, desperate to allay the fear that gripped his soul, that still wouldn't release him. With a soft, trembling touch he placed a gentle finger under her chin, lifting her face so that her eyes met his. "Are you all right?"

Genevieve couldn't find her voice. Death and violence and greed lay strewn all about her, but when she looked up into Jonathon's face, all the horror disappeared. His golden eyes bored into her, burning with the light of love, lifting her and caressing her, bonding her to him in the searing, glorious silence. "Yes," she finally managed to choke out, stunned by the raw intensity of her emotion. "Yes. It's all right now. Everything's going to be all right."

Tears streamed down her cheeks as Jonathon pulled her

into his arms, locking her in a shattering embrace. "Genny," he whispered hoarsely, rocking her against his chest, his powerful arms trembling with relief. "Genny, I thought I'd lost you. I thought I'd lost you."

Genevieve shook her head mutely against his chest. "Never, Jonathon," she whispered softly. "Never."

Night fell in its usual island splendor as Genevieve stood silently in the gardens of Jonathon's home and watched the sun sink slowly into the sea, turning the sky from a soft, rosy pink to deep, starry lavender. A gentle breeze carried the scent of wild orchids. It stirred the night air, tossing her thick golden curls loosely about her face and lifting her long skirts. A strange and wonderful tension suddenly filled her stomach as a warm glow spread through her limbs. She smiled, recognizing her body's reaction: Jonathon was near.

She turned slowly around, finding him immediately despite the silence of his approach. Twilight shadows hid his face and threw his large, powerful form into stark relief, reminding her of the first time they'd met. Her eyes lovingly took in his form, and she smiled at the man she'd come to know so well. "It's all over now, isn't it?" she asked softly.

To her surprise, Jonathon stiffened at her question. He nodded tightly in response, as if he no longer trusted his voice to speak.

Genevieve's delicate brows drew together, puzzled by his reaction. "Is something wrong?"

"No."

But something was wrong. It was obvious Jonathon was holding himself back, tightly under control, as if pained. "Your arm!" she cried in sudden understanding as she rushed toward him.

He stepped away the moment she reached for him. "There's nothing wrong with it. It's just a scratch."

His voice stopped her cold. He didn't want her to touch him. She'd thought, she'd hoped, that once he saw her again he'd sweep her up into the same fierce, loving embrace they'd shared at the church. Her hands dropped to her sides as she stared at him, suddenly lost, needing desperately to know if the love she'd seen burning in his eyes had been real or if she'd only imagined it.

Luc had arrived only minutes after the last shot had been fired, bringing with him a small army of men, many still in costume from the day's celebration. One look at the grim scene inside the church and he'd followed Jonathon's orders immediately, whisking Genevieve out and onto the back of her gentle mare before she could protest, seeing her safely back to Jonathon's home.

As the reason for Jonathon's strange mood slowly dawned on her she lowered her eyes, thoroughly ashamed for having been thinking only of herself. "Jonathon," she began, "I'm sorry about Constance. I know you cared for her—"

"No," he interrupted. "I know this will only worsen your opinion of me, Genevieve, but you deserve to know the truth. I never felt anything for Constance, even when she was my mistress. I never even knew feelings like that were possible until I met . . . I never knew," he finished abruptly.

"She saved my life. She didn't shoot."

An expression she couldn't identify passed over Jonathon's face. "I think I felt more for her in that single second, simply because she didn't listen to Harry, than I'd ever felt for her before."

Genevieve watched him, unsure of what to say. A servant moved in the library, lighting the hurricane lamps which stood on a desk by the window. The light reflected through the glass, softly illuminating the area in which they stood. The gentle glow encircled them, pulling them together, but a deep, silent chasm separated them. "How did you know to find me at the church?" she asked at last.

"Your father's letter," he answered simply as his eyes drank her in. He forced himself to memorize every detail, from the deep sapphire of her eyes to the ruby warmth of her lips, the gentle timbre of her voice, every smooth curve of her body, and the velvety softness of her skin. Once she'd left, the memory would be all he'd have. He took a deep breath, forcing himself to get on with it, to say the words he knew would send her away.

"The treasure's been returned, Genevieve. All of it. General D'Abbaye, the man responsible for your father's death, has been arrested and his ship confiscated. Your father died a hero. Your lands and properties will all be restored to you when you go back . . ."

When you go back . . . Genevieve's head snapped up, the rest of his words lost as that phrase echoed through her head. "Back to France?"

Jonathon stopped, his amber eyes searching her face. "That was what you wanted, wasn't it?" he asked carefully.

"Yes," she slowly agreed. That *was* what she wanted. How important it had seemed to restore her father's good name, to regain her home and possessions, to take her rightful place among the French elite. Now none of that really mattered anymore. Nothing had been the same since she slipped and slid through a pile of fish guts and landed at the feet of Captain Jonathon Morgan. But she didn't get a chance to explain any of that before he continued.

"Right," he said tightly. Although she couldn't see his face, the strain was clear in his voice. "I saw Berthot a few hours ago when we returned the treasure. He's leaving for France tomorrow morning. He wants to take you back with him."

"Tomorrow," she repeated in stunned disbelief.

Jonathon stared at her, his jaw clenched tightly as he stiffly nodded. "He's a good man, then, Berthot?" he asked hoarsely. "He'll make you happy?" The words came out a dull whisper. He swallowed hard, his eyes burning into hers as he continued. "I don't expect you to ever forgive me, Genevieve, but I want you to know how sorry I am—"

"Jonathon, you don't—" Genevieve choked out, her throat thick with unshed tears.

"Please, Genevieve, let me finish," he insisted, determined to finish what he had to say, then get out of her life forever. "When we returned from Mount Pelée, I was shown the documents your father and Berthot had signed, and I learned that Berthot was your fiancé. I thought you two were working together, and that's why you hadn't told me about him. I couldn't see anything else. I couldn't see how wrong I was." How horribly, foolishly wrong he'd been. So wrong it had nearly cost her her life. It had cost him almost as much: He was losing her forever.

"Before you go—" he started, then tried again. "Before you go," he said, but broke off as the words stuck in his throat. He turned away from her, a dark, awful laugh coming from deep within him, his muscles rigid with tension as he raked his hand through his hair. "I'm trying to say good-bye," he admitted hoarsely, shaking his head in utter defeat. "God, Genny, I just don't know how to do it. There are so many things I imagined saying to you, so many words I wanted to say, but I just can't find the ones to tell you good-bye."

"Good," Genevieve answered in a rough, aching whisper. "Because I don't want to hear them. Don't say it, Jonathon. Promise me you'll never say good-bye."

Jonathon's head jerked up. He stared at her, his heart hammering against his chest, afraid he hadn't heard her correctly. "You're not leaving?" His heart doubled its tempo as she wordlessly shook her head, her beautiful smile shining through her tears. With a low moan he pulled her into his arms, his lips crushing down on hers in a deep, burning kiss that spoke his love and desire. "What about Berthot?" he asked as he finally lifted his lips from hers.

He felt Genevieve's gentle sigh against his chest. She knew she had to find Armand and talk to him, but right now that would have to wait. "I love Armand, but as a brother, nothing more. I think we both agreed to the engagement more out of love for my father than for any other reason," she answered honestly, smiling as Jonathon's arms tightened around her.

She gazed up at him, her face bathed in the moonlight,

her sapphire eyes glowing with love. "Promise me, Jona-thon," she whispered solemnly. "Promise me you'll never say good-bye."

"Never," Jonathon swore. "Not when there are so many other words I want to say to you . . ."

"What words?" she asked achingly.

Jonathon stared at her, his heart glowing in his eyes. "Words like, I love you, Genevieve," he replied fervently. "I love you," he whispered against her thick golden hair. Tears of joy streamed from her eyes as he lifted her into his arms and carried her back inside. "I love you," he repeated, his smile as wide and quivering as her own.

The words echoed through the empty garden, falling on the wild orchids until they were lifted and carried by the warm breeze, over the island and out to sea.

EPILOGUE

Martinique, 1863

Jonathon stood alone on the smooth, white beach and watched the turquoise waves lapping gently against the shore. The sound of shouts and excited laughter interrupted his thoughts, and he turned to look back over his shoulder.

"Daddy, Daddy, look!" His son raced toward him, his cheeks flushed with excitement. He came to a stumbling stop, bouncing off Jonathon's leg as he thrust a thick, coarse piece of paper at him. "Look, Daddy, a pirate map!"

Jonathon smiled, bending down on one knee as he drew his son close to examine the paper. "Where'd you find this, James?" he asked, looking over the boy's small, dark head at Genevieve, who'd walked up quietly behind him. She set down their golden-haired daughter, who waddled over to join in the excitement.

"I dug it up in the garden," he explained breathlessly. "I found it myself. Mama says it's real."

"I'm sure it is," Jonathon agreed, though he had no trouble recognizing his wife's smooth writing where she'd marked off the clues. He returned the map to his son, then stood, wrapping his arm around Genevieve's waist as he pulled her to his side.

They watched as their son turned to his little sister. His stern expression was an exact replica of Jonathon's, which was hilarious on his small, childlike face. "This is important, Missy. We're hunting for pirate treasure now, so you're gonna have to listen to me. Don't do anything unless I tell you to, okay?"

Tiny Melissa nodded, her deep blue eyes brimming over with adoration for her older brother, then turned and headed for the spot under the tall palms where she'd seen her mother digging earlier that morning.

James stared after her, his expression changing from stern authority to pure male frustration. "Missy, wait for me!" he yelled as he took off after her.

Genevieve and Jonathon laughed together, but Genevieve noted it wasn't long before her husband's eyes sobered once again. She took his hand, nodding at the letter he held. "Any news from Ty?" she asked softly.

Jonathon shrugged. "No, nothing new, really." Tyler had been gone for over two years now, taking the *Liberty* north to engage in blockade duty at the Southern ports. But it was more than just Ty's safety that concerned him. The laughing, easygoing brother he'd always known had slowly disappeared, the tone of his letters becoming increasingly harsh as the war drew on, so much so that Jonathon barely recognized Tyler in the letters he sent.

"It didn't do any good, did it?" Genevieve asked. "I thought we could stop the war by stopping the sale of arms, but it came anyway."

"We might just as well have tried to stop the wind or the tide," Jonathon answered, wrapping his arm lovingly around her shoulder. "But what we did helped, Genny, I'm certain of it. The South now has that many fewer guns to fire, that many fewer cannons to send into battle."

"Which means that Ty will be back that much sooner, darling."

"You're right," Jonathon agreed as they walked slowly along the beach, the warm Caribbean sea rolling softly at their feet.

"Daddy, Daddy, come see!" James shouted impatiently, waving at his parents while Melissa jumped gleefully beside him. "We found the treasure!"

Jonathon smiled, his gaze shifting from his children to his beautiful wife. "So did I," he answered softly. "So did I."

FREE

Romance
(a $4.50 value)

Send in the Coupon Below

To get your FREE historical romance and start saving, fill out the coupon below and mail it today. As soon as we receive it we'll send you your FREE Book along with your first month's selections.

- -

Mail To: **True Value Home Subscription Services, Inc. P.O. Box 5235**
        120 Brighton Road, Clifton, New Jersey 07015-5235

YES! I want to start previewing the very best historical romances being published today. Send me my FREE book along with the first month's selections. I understand that I may look them over FREE for 10 days. If I'm not absolutely delighted I may return them and owe nothing. Otherwise I will pay the low price of just $4.00 each: a total $16.00 (at *least* an $18.00 value) and save at least $2.00. Then each month I will receive four brand new novels to preview as soon as they are published for the same low price. I can always return a shipment and I may cancel this subscription at any time with no obligation to buy even a single book. In any event the FREE book is mine to keep regardless.

Name _____

Street Address _____ Apt. No. _____

City _____ State _____ Zip Code _____

Telephone _____

Signature _____
(if under 18 parent or guardian must sign)

Terms and prices subject to change. Orders subject to acceptance by True Value Home Subscription Services, Inc.

11750-1